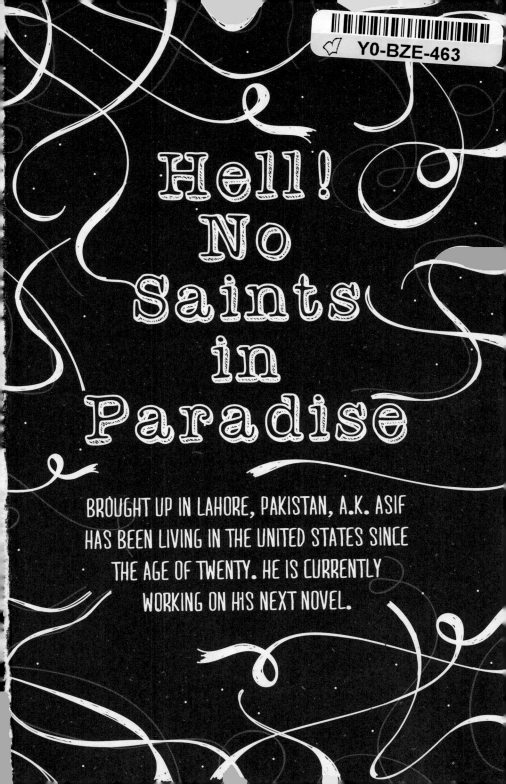

Hell! No Saints in Paradise

BROUGHT UP IN LAHORE, PAKISTAN, A.K. ASIF
HAS BEEN LIVING IN THE UNITED STATES SINCE
THE AGE OF TWENTY. HE IS CURRENTLY
WORKING ON HIS NEXT NOVEL.

Hell!
No
Saints
in
Paradise

A.K. Asif

HarperCollins *Publishers* India

First published in India in 2017 by
HarperCollins *Publishers* India

Copyright © A.K. Asif 2017

P-ISBN: 978-93-5277-055-7
E-ISBN: 978-93-5277-056-4

2 4 6 8 10 9 7 5 3 1

A.K. Asif asserts the moral right
to be identified as the author of this work.

HarperCollins *Publishers*
A-75, Sector 57, Noida, Uttar Pradesh 201301, India
1 London Bridge Street, London, SE1 9GF, United Kingdom
2 Bloor Street East, Toronto, Ontario M4W 1A8, Canada
Lvl 13, 201 Elizabeth Street (PO Box A565, NSW, 1235), Sydney
NSW 2000, Australia
195 Broadway, New York, NY 10007, USA

Typeset in 11/14.3 Sabon LT Std
By Saanvi Graphics Noida

Printed and bound at
Thomson Press (India) Ltd.

If I survive this life without dying, I'll be surprised.

—MULLA NASRUDDIN

1

❦

I MET PETRA ON a Friday night in late October 2050. I met her in Grasshopper, a candlelit cannabis cafe in the West Village. The cafe was one of a handful of businesses which had managed to thrive in the aftermath of Isis, a Category 4 hurricane that had pounded Lower Manhattan with a twenty-foot storm surge eight days earlier. Modelled after a warren of subterranean caves, the cafe attracted the usual sorts, including insomniacs working on advanced degrees in the arts and humanities; insomniacs much like myself. Like all hipster enclaves everywhere, Grasshopper was also a great place to meet interesting girls who were more than willing to help you brainstorm your academic thesis. And more.

The night I met her, the cafe had been packed as usual for a Friday night. With my cup of spiked latte in one hand and my tablet in the other, I drifted to the back looking for a quiet corner to hunker down for a couple of hours and plunge undistracted into my thesis.

Petra was sitting alone. How could I not notice this olive-skinned bespectacled girl with long black hair that was tucked into a red headband stretched over her luminous forehead? I approached this bohemian beauty with a closed-lip grin.

Striking up conversations with girls had never posed much of an obstacle in my social life. I was thirty years old and gymfit. With my perpetual five-day stubble and tousled black hair, I had always been well-received. And I had to admit I was a handsome bastard.

I quickly discovered that Petra was a psychoanalyst in-the-making, and that she specialized in psychedelic-assisted psychotherapy. Having completed her masters in clinical psychology, she had been gathering ideas for her doctoral proposal.

Once I got the hint that she was lesbian, the conversation stayed pretty much focused on our respective academic endeavors. She thought my thesis was ambitious and seemed to delight in telling me that. I responded by saying hers was intriguing so our conversation continued to flow. As the night progressed, fuelled by a few more spiked lattes, the conversation turned into a highly invasive psychotherapy session—my psychotherapy session.

'You seem more like a poet to me,' she said, studying me over the top of her glasses. 'Or a writer with the moral compass of a player! The department of religion is the last place I would expect to see you hanging out in,' she added, pushing her square-framed glasses back over her upturned nose. Her eyes sparkled with excitement and I was the perfect captive audience.

'Appearances can be deceptive,' I said as my lips curled in a smile. 'Perhaps the department of religion is where my demons reside.'

'Now we're getting somewhere!' she said, folding her arms under her breasts. 'Demons! My specialty.'

I just shook my head and stole a glance at her exposed cleavage, which had become accentuated by the push from below. All I could do, however, was focus on her next query.

'Let's see. What made you choose the topic of your thesis, Paradise and Hell?'

'It's complicated!' I replied and we both laughed.

'Okay, so un-complicate it for me.' Resting her elbows on the table, she leaned toward me.

I drained my almost empty cup, rubbed my forehead, and thought of how best to answer her.

'Well, I've chosen this particular topic because it's a matter of identity; my identity apart from my dad's. Really though, it had been the only option that would give me the power to stand up to my father on his own turf: religion.'

'Very insightful,' she said with a smile, encouraging me to elaborate. 'Tell me more about your dad.'

Where was I to start? I had to give this a lot of thought.

'Well, my dad's life has been about some future life-to-be, lived in the next world. This world doesn't mean much to him.'

'Your father must be a true ascetic.'

'Not when it comes to women. The women of this world and the next—and he likes money.'

'How interesting!'

'And he won't settle for anything other than the highest level of Paradise when he dies. When he wasn't thinking or talking of Paradise, he was projecting all the gory scenes of Hell on the screen of my impressionable young mind. He delighted in pummelling me with stories of the horrible punishments awaiting those who strayed from *siraat e mustaqeem*, the so-called straight path. He saw me as a sinner who was ruining his chances of entering Paradise. That's all he talked about: *Jannah* and *Jahannum*. Paradise and Hell ...' I paused and took a deep breath. She was listening to me with rapt attention. 'I can't tell you how much he enjoyed describing the torture in the grave at the hands of Munkar and Nakir—the two fearful angels,' I said. 'Those were my bedtime stories.'

Petra's brows furrowed and her eyes seemed genuinely concerned and troubled. 'What a traumatic childhood!'

'Now you understand why I chose this particular topic for my dissertation.'

'Yeah, understandable. It's therapeutic and highly personal,' she said, nodding. After a moment's pause, she continued. 'But what I don't understand is what makes you so convinced that Paradise and Hell aren't real?'

'Because they just aren't,' I snorted, thinking we were back to square one.

'See, deep inside, you're a man of conviction. But you try so hard to project to the world the image of a man of logic, a man of the intellect,' she spoke slowly, enunciating each word as if rendering a final verdict. 'If you're so convinced that your father's so-called next world isn't real, then what exactly is the difference between you and him? Like him, you're just believing as well.'

'You're being pretty judgmental,' I said, now feeling annoyed at her audacity.

'Goes with the territory. Self-discovery can be a bitch,' she added, and I sighed in reluctant agreement.

'Things would be much simpler if I could afford a shrink,' I said. 'Midlife crisis can be a bitch too.'

'You don't need a shrink and you're too young for a midlife crisis. You haven't earned one! Besides, you can do it yourself.'

'How?'

'Ayahuasca, the psychedelic brew from the Amazon. That's all the rage—'

'I don't do drugs and I've got no experience with psychedelics.'

'For your information, *yagé* isn't really a drug. It's more like a medicine, which the shamans have been using for centuries for healing. And if I were you, I'd totally experience the spirit world before I presumed to write a paper about it,' she said.

'I think we're getting confused here. The spirit world you're talking about is different from the kind I grew up with,' I said. 'My spirit world is either Jannah, a Muslim Paradise, that's filled with voluptuous virgins, streams of milk and honey, fruit-laden trees and non-alcoholic beverages. Or Jahannum, Hell, where a blaze awaits those who've strayed from the straight path, where sinners quaff bottomless goblets of boiling pus and get marinated in huge vats of their own piss. You know, stuff like that. Between Jannah and Jahannum, there's no intermediate world. No middle ground for someone like me.'

'That's all the more reason to seek the truth,' she said. 'But remember, the spirit world can terrorize you if you aren't properly prepared. A bad trip on Ayahuasca could certainly be seen as a journey through Hell.'

'Exactly! It's nothing more than what you make of it. Paradise and Hell don't have any tangible existence of their own. This is what my dissertation is all about,' I said.

She was clearly in a combative mood. I sensed she was used to winning most arguments and expected to bag this one too.

I poked my forehead with the tip of my index finger.

'It's all in here,' I said slowly through clenched teeth, trying to make her understand. 'Nowhere else. The human mind on a trip; that's it. Either with the aid of hallucinogens or just numbed and damaged by indoctrination. We see what we've been trained to see since childhood. It's the mind, stupid!' I rolled my eyes and shook my head.

'You may think I'm crazy, but I see a halo around you right now. It's a little spooky,' she said, her eyes looking dreamy all of a sudden.

'What? A halo? Where did that come from?'

'I'm very sensitive to the vibrations around people,' she said. 'There's a very special kind of energy about you.'

'Oh really. What else do you see?'

'Big holes. Your vital energy is leaking away constantly. Like from a wound.'

'Jesus Christ!' I roared, and a few people looked in our direction. This girl was weirder than I had thought.

'It's the childhood trauma which has left holes in your being.'

'I think it's the system we live under which saps our energy,' I said, meaning every word of it. 'The modern life.'

For the last six months, I had been working twelve hours a day in the university library with three triple espresso breaks per shift. On weekend nights I was driving a yellow cab and squeezing in a break here and there. The harsh reality of doing a self-funded PhD had only begun to dawn on me lately.

'You're stuck in the system—your present—because of your past.' She was becoming more and more relentless.

'When are you going to start seeing patients?' I needed another stiff cup of coffee.

'You're too muddled. You're fighting the tide and you need clarity. And—'

'And the quickest and surest way is Ayahuasca,' I quipped.

'I recommend YYC—the Yage Yoga Center. It's near Columbus Circle. A bit pricey, but you get what you pay for,' she said, shoving a five-dollar bill under her coffee cup. She exuded the air of been-there-done-that, and I just stared at her, not knowing what to say.

'Good luck, Ismael. It was nice talking to you.' She got up and left without looking back, leaving me scratching my head.

I ordered another latte and brooded over her words and what I really wanted from life. I leaned back, closed my eyes and let my mind drift.

I felt like an empty canister bobbing along a sewage pipe toward a recycling plant. My future struck me like a candle, slowly and unpleasantly dwindling into non-existence. I became more and more uncertain of my next steps; these were thoughts that had crossed my mind before but which I put off, mainly because of my irredeemable financial troubles.

Before I got recycled in the modern machine, I needed to travel, bike across continents, write a travelogue, perhaps one day visit my country—the one I had once loved because of its natural beauty. I wanted to hike and camp out in its magnificent north. Most of all, I needed to attempt to patch things up with my father, regardless of our differences. He still lived in Lahore, in Faisal Town, the place where I was born. Abba was my only known living blood relation.

Last year, after having completed my masters with the department of religion at Columbia, I had gotten my first US passport. I even had it stamped for a multiple-visit entry from the Caliphate of Al-Bakistan. But at the last minute I dropped the whole plan. It was turning out to be too expensive a trip to even contemplate. Besides, I wasn't sure I was really ready to see my father after all these years.

That night, before I left Grasshopper, I successfully enrolled myself for an Ayahuasca ceremony at the Yage Yoga Center in three weeks. I needed at least two weeks to detox myself to avoid a bad experience—and afterwards several more to pay off the bill.

2

T HE A-TRAIN ARRIVED FIFTEEN minutes late at Columbus
Circle, forcing me to make a run for it as soon as I got
out of the station and hit the street. Breathless when I arrived
at Yage Yoga Center—a sprawling new-age complex off the
Westside Highway—I was just in time for the ceremony. A tall,
dark-complexioned girl at the reception desk welcomed me with
a bright toothy grin.

'I'm registered for the 9 o'clock ceremony,' I said, trying to
catch my breath.

'Name?' she asked, gazing at the hologram that sprang up
from the glass countertop.

'Ismael—'

'Please read and sign the disclaimer,' she said, pointing to an
iPad near my hand.

I stared at the letters as they zoomed out of the screen and
floated in front of my face. Big, bold and red, they declared:

I VOLUNTARILY ASSUME FULL RESPONSIBILITY FOR ANY RISK
OF LOSS, PROPERTY DAMAGE, PERSONAL INJURY OR DEATH.

I swallowed hard and scribbled my name on the indicated
dotted line.

'The ceremony hall is on the seventh floor,' the girl continued,
fluttering her eyes and using that soft, oh-so concerned voice

all new agers seemed to be blessed with. 'From the elevator turn right; the entrance to the hall is at the very end. Locker rooms are on your right. Yours is 786. You've got five minutes before they close the doors,' the girl added, having already moved on to the next person in line.

Thanking her, I dashed towards the elevator and punched number 7.

If the lofty claims made about Ayahuasca were true, tonight could be a night of discovery for a skeptic like myself; someone who had written their doctoral dissertation to refute the existence of any spirit worlds albeit in my own case, of the Islamic variety: Al-Jannah and Al-Jahannum. I had titled my thesis *Paradise and Hell: Metaphors in the Making of the Muslim Mind*. In the paper I argued that these binary worlds were mere metaphors, a theoretical construction, and a work of creative imagination of the human mind, and that these worlds and their infamous inhabitants had no external existence of their own.

In the locker room, I hurriedly changed into my white ankle-length cotton tunic with long sleeves, the traditional Arabian robe or *thawb*, my loose-fitting dress for the occasion. I hadn't worn the thing in over a decade but it was still loose on me. Clutching my yoga mat, I pushed open the ten-foot tall mahogany door and entered the large circular candlelit hall. The space was designed to look like the inside of a jungle hut and was large enough to hold a hundred people.

The walls and conical roof were covered with thatched straw that had been stuffed behind wooden planks. The place smelled of pine and the air was distinctly pleasant to breathe, thanks to the high concentration of oxygen that was supposed to enhance a deeper experience. This process had been thoroughly explained in the two-page email YYC sent me at the time of enrollment.

Thirty or so people, mostly in their twenties and thirties and dressed in white clothes, sat on their yoga mats meditating with their backs against the walls. In the center of the room, perched on a long wooden bench, was a man draped in black robes. The man's long flowing black hair fell to his shoulders and was held in place by a black headband. Beside him, on a large stone block, stood three pitchers and a number of clay cups.

A tall black girl, dressed in a burgundy-coloured robe tapped my shoulder and smiled as she handed me an orange-coloured purge-bucket lined with a sealable vomit bag. Then she led me to the far end of the room and showed me my designated spot amidst a sea of whispering attractive young bodies.

To be honest, more than wanting a glimpse of the supernatural world of the shamans, which I believed to be the work of a brain on hallucinogens, I had been drawn to Ayahuasca because of the purge: the legendary cleaning up of subconscious trash clogging the mind, body and soul. I was prepared to puke my guts out as long I could rid myself of my past demons, inherited and acquired.

'Tonight we're really lucky to have Don Miguel here to conduct the ceremony,' she whispered. 'His trips are the best.'

'Nice!' I said, staking out a spot against the wall. Positioning my bucket at arm's reach, I unrolled my yoga mat. A red-headed girl sitting about ten feet to my right gave me a conciliatory nod as I sat down, as if to acknowledge some shared secret.

Don Miguel spoke for a few minutes in heavily accented English. He was giving last minute instructions: breathe deeply; keep a straight back, keep your eyes closed, stay focused on the intention. The clearer the intention, the deeper the experience; and don't hesitate to raise your hand if you think you need more than one cup. Let your mind ride the *icaros*, the shaman chants, the cantos for travel into the spirit world.

When Don Miguel stopped speaking, five of his cohorts, three men and two women clad in black robes, joined him in the centre of the room. As soon as they sat down on the floor in front of him, there came the sound of rain; each drop landing with a distinct plop as if falling on a tarp overhead. One of the women started to hum softly.

After a few minutes, Don Miguel began pouring a thick, dark liquid into little cups which were carried on trays to the participants by two male assistant shamans.

The drink stank of putrid earth. I closed my eyes, held my breath and knocked back the pernicious brew in one gulp. The bitter aftertaste had a long, lingering finish of rotten leaves with just a hint of ground insects. As soon as the concoction hit my stomach I dry-heaved and my torso began to spasm violently. I gripped my bucket in my lap, but thankfully the nausea subsided after a few seconds. I closed my eyes and my mind started to drift on the hypnotic chant as it faded into the rhythmic patter of gentle rain.

3

I HAD NO IDEA HOW LONG I had been sitting there, zoning out and tripping on the *icaros,* the chants. The patter of rain had transformed into an undulating wave of crimson dots, while a vocal ribbon of colours coiled upwards in helical formation like the strands of DNA. My stomach gurgled; it dawned on me that I could see the inside of my stomach where an orange-ish liquid formed pools in its folds like prehistoric shale in a network of antediluvian canyons. This orange liquid was now seeping through every hidden cave of my body, saturating my flesh like a spring thaw permeating the earth, like what people described when they talked of LSD.

Suddenly alarmed by this vision, I opened my eyes. Don Miguel's head seemed to have become elongated and was pushing backward at an unnatural angle. I then turned and stared at my neighbour. Her fingers were impossibly long, and they pointed and moved with a creepy fluidity, each with a life of its own. The walls of the hall were swollen and they pulsed as though we were cradled in the womb of a living thing. At that point, another wave of nausea threw my stomach into spasms. I squeezed my eyes shut and reached for my bucket. The red-head next to me was retching loudly between tormented sobs. The purge had begun.

My ears began to buzz with a crescendo of vibration and my heart pounded along with a distant drumbeat. It sounded just like a *dhol*, the barrel-sized drum beaten at the Sufi shrines of Punjab on Thursday nights. My father had always forbidden me to visit these shrines. Sufis, the mystics, were heretics according to him and he had no tolerance for their antics. For him, they represented the adulteration of the true teachings of Islam as contained in the Quran and *Hadith*, the latter being the saying of the Prophet, a corpus four times thicker than the Quran if combined with *Sirah*, the deeds of the Prophet.

I began to breathe deeply, thinking about my intention. I wanted to know if Paradise and Hell were real. I wanted to purge my demons. As soon as I thought of this intention, it sprang visibly before my eyes like a rope of shimmering colours that stretched to infinity. This rope coiled itself around me and began pulling me out of my body. In a panic I opened my eyes and looked at myself. My white robe seemed to have lost its fullness now. Then a realization hit me: I wasn't in my robe. I screamed but no sound came out of my mouth. In the next moment, I was engulfed by a dark stillness.

I had no name, no body and no feelings. I was just a presence, a floating awareness in a dark, cozy womb. I had no idea how long I remained suspended there; and then slowly, drop by drop, I began to take form again.

I was back inside my body, walking up a steep green slope. The air was luminescent and exquisitely fresh, and the sky was a radiant purple but there was no sun. My legs had a mind of their own as they carried me along, pushing me higher and higher toward the top. I knew with a strange certainty that someone was waiting for me up there.

I was breathless when I reached the tabletop summit; my ears filled with the ringing of an old-fashioned bicycle bell. About a hundred or so feet away, a wiry little man stood next to a black-framed bicycle that was leaning on its kickstand. It looked like a made-in-Pakistan Sohrab roadster and was fitted with a rear carrier. He was waving at me. Filled with curiosity, I marched toward him. I was about ten feet away when he called my name.

'Babu Ismael!'

How the hell did this strange-looking fellow know my name? And where did this 'babu' thing come from? Babu was the word used by the villagers of Punjab for an educated city dweller.

Garbed in the traditional dress of rural Punjab, a white kurta over a white dhoti—an unstitched cloth wrapped around the waist and legs and knotted at the waist, resembling a long skirt—the fellow was barely five feet tall and wore a huge white turban. His eyes were extraordinarily bright and his skin was wrinkled like the parchment of an ancient scroll. The old face had a fine, white stubble.

'Hope is the engine that drives the universe forward,' he said in a lilting, fluid and unaccented English.

Tongue-tied, I merely nodded. The intensity of his gaze made my legs tremble, but I wasn't afraid of him exactly.

'Right person, right time, right place makes what we call action; everything else is merely a reaction.' I remained quiet, still wondering who he was and how he knew my name.

'Babu, your intention and mine has met across many worlds and made this moment possible,' he said. 'I am Khidr,' he declared as he stepped forward and extended his right hand. 'Chacha Khidr.'

He had only one tooth in his mouth and it stuck out from his lower lip like a shark's fin. Curiously, his speech had no hint of impairment one might expect from a toothless man. The skin of his hand was as smooth as silk.

'I'm so honored to meet you Chacha Khidr,' I said, not sure if I could believe my ears. Was this the vision of al-Khidr out of legend? He was known as the mysterious prophet, the eternal wanderer and the hidden initiator of those who walked the mystical path. He was known to have coached even Moses in divine mysteries.

'Just call me "Chacha",' he said. His crisp voice, like his brilliant eyes, was in sharp contrast with his ancient tottering appearance. Al-Khidr was known as the Green One, always wearing a green robe. But there was certainly nothing green about him. This man's appearance was clearly Punjabi, as opposed to the Hebrew Prophets.

'Yes, Chacha.' I nodded as I clasped the tight-gripped smooth hand. Since the word Chacha meant uncle in Urdu, the old man had to be from Pakistan or India.

'Babu, you're going to help us clean up a big mess,' he said.

'I am?'

'You'll be leaving for Pakistan.' His tone was straightforward.

'Pakistan!' I shook my head in disbelief. 'I don't have the money for that kind of travel.'

'Once you land in Lahore, we'll contact you,' he said, ignoring my protest.

'Fine,' I was fully aware that I was in the grip of an Ayahuasca vision which would evaporate as soon as the chemical burnt itself out in the circuitry of my brain.

'Fate has chosen you for a huge task. Looking at you, I can see that fate has chosen wisely.'

'Chosen me for what?'

The old man climbed onto his bicycle, his feet barely touching the ground. I saw he was wearing a pair of golden *khusa* with upturned toes.

'It's a mysterious world we live in, Babu,' he said. 'Start preparing for the trip.'

Before I could fire off any more questions, he started pedalling away. He quickly picked up speed and in a few seconds he turned into a vertical streak of brilliant light against the purple sky. Then he was gone.

I was left with an overwhelming sense of loneliness in this oppressive vastness, broken only by soft rolling mounds of green. Overpowered by convulsions in my stomach, I collapsed on the grass and began retching.

In the next moment everything vanished. It was pitch dark around me. And then, I nearly screamed when I felt a hand grabbing my shoulder. I sat bolt upright in panic.

'Open your eyes,' I heard a voice nearby say. Somebody else was strumming a guitar in the background.

When I opened my eyes, I was staring into the face of Don Miguel. The black headband across his forehead was soaking with sweat, and every muscle on his face was alive with movement in the flickering light of the candles. I was sitting with my back against the wall, my breathing now calm and slow.

The head shaman squatted next to me; the vomit bucket in his hand was pressed against my chest. It had collected most of my purge. The rest made my robe feel sticky and wet against my skin and I smelled horrible.

'Are you feeling okay?' one of the Don's female assistants asked gently.

'He's fine,' said Don Miguel. His face pulsed with so many emotions it was hard to guess what he was feeling or thinking.

The truth is I was feeling fine and was determined to tell them that; it was one hell of a trip. But I couldn't put these words together into a sentence.

'You've just met with your destiny, Ismael,' Don Miguel said but I noticed he never moved his lips.

It was the most astonishing thing; he had somehow transferred his words directly into my mind without actually speaking. I wanted to say something, but once again I was lost for words. It was shocking to hear his voice speaking in my head, saying my name. How the hell did he know it? I doubted he would bother remembering the names of every participant present. How could he possibly know what my vision had been? Perhaps it was just one of his stock phrases to keep the crowd mesmerized by their respective trips.

'Hold on to your breath. You're not done yet,' Don Miguel said to me as he and his assistant got up and moved on to attend to another participant who was slumped on his knees and elbows. The guy's head was completely inside a bucket.

I closed my eyes and let my mind take me wherever it wanted to go. The guitar was incredibly soothing and gradually faded to complete silence.

I was at peace. After a while I was given another cup to drink, which went down effortlessly this time. The second cup didn't lift me off, literally speaking, to the other world like the first one had. Nor did it facilitate a meeting with any strange beings. But it did take me into my past and gave me new perspectives and insights on secrets long buried there. Most of these visions were gloomy and involved tense interactions with my father. I had just a fleeting glimpse of my deceased mother lying beside me in bed, paralyzed. I was a year old when she died of polio.

As Abba's sole heir, I had been a complete disappointment. His presence hovered over my childhood like a storm cloud, unpredictable and full of thunder and lightning. My defiance and resolve had only earned me shame and guilt. For the first time in my life, thanks to a little earthen cup of Ayahuasca, I saw my rebellious stance as a sign of having a healthy soul that refused to submit to Abba's twisted worldviews.

The sacred vine of the Amazon was truly helping me transform my pain and guilt into self-awareness, and I began to understand my father's limitations. There had never been anything personal in his actions and thoughts. He had just been regurgitating what had been fed to him: a narrative manufactured and perfected over centuries and never questioned or critically analyzed. I felt sorry for him really. He was a prisoner, a victim of indoctrination. I wanted to forgive him and I wanted to see him.

The rest of the night blazed past. As sunlight streaked into the hall from a window facing east, it was hard to believe I had been sitting in this place for the last ten hours. People were stretching, yawning and beginning to stagger to their feet. They approached Don Miguel one by one for a farewell handshake and he hugged each of them before they left the hall.

My neighbour, the red-headed girl, got to her feet and threw herself into my arms, giving me a good three-minute-long hug. I patted her head without saying anything. There was nothing for me to say.

I approached the shaman feeling a little unsteady.

'Thank you, Don Miguel,' I said. 'It wasn't as bad as I was expecting.'

'A great task has been given to you, Ismael. Make yourself available to it no matter how strange it may appear.'

'How do you know, if I may ask, what kind of task I've been given?' I asked.

He tapped the headband across his temple and looked me in the eye.

'The people of the spirit world have their own special method of communication,' he said.

'What do you recommend I do?' I asked, recalling my encounter with a strange-looking man who had ordered me to start preparing for a trip to Pakistan.

'Learn to shut-off your analytical mind from time to time. All wisdom is in learning how to go with the proverbial flow,' he said, giving me a warm smile.

'Provided you know what the flow looks like,' I said.

'You'll know,' he assured me. 'You'll learn to recognize it.'

I nodded and headed toward the exit. I couldn't wait to take off my robe, which reeked of putrefied soil. I longed for a shower with the special kind of urgency I previously reserved for getting laid.

The locker room was buzzing with activity. The night's

excursion had left people dazed, dishevelled, and keeping to themselves. After taking the most invigorating shower of my entire life, I put on my clean clothes: a pair of red chinos and a gray fleece top. By the time I stepped out on the street, it was 7.30 in the morning.

The sky was blue and the air balmy; traffic was light since it was a Sunday. I began walking toward Columbus Circle to catch the northbound A-train. My body was stiff and disoriented and I felt like I was re-entering the real world after a long absence. My mind was still not fully obeying the practical commands of my brain, as though it sought to drag me deeper into the past.

After getting off the A-train at 110th Street, I stepped into a bagel shop on Cathedral Parkway. My toasted bagel with cream cheese and a black coffee tasted heavenly as I listened to the Beatles' '*Yesterday*' floating toward me from somewhere in the kitchen. In order to prepare myself for last night's trip, I had abstained from the staples of modern life for two weeks. No coffee, cannabis, tea, beer or alcohol, meat of any kind, salt, spices or dairy. I had forgone the Internet, TV and social media. To complete my transformation into an ascetic zombie, I had also forced myself to stop hankering after women as I hung around the coffee houses near campus.

Savouring my breakfast, my mind quickly latched on to my encounter with the bright-eyed, ancient-looking man clad in his dhoti. The sound of the bicycle bell, the conversation we had, the task he had talked about and the manner in which he had turned into a streak of light before being swallowed by a vast green emptiness—it all remained vividly fresh in my mind, and I realized I was smiling at the memory.

The more I puzzled over the experience, the more convinced I became that my so-called task had something to do with reuniting with my father. I thought of my financial constraints that prohibited even contemplating such a trip. Perhaps Abba would help me out. After all, he was a rich man.

'Something fundamental had changed within me during the Ayahuasca trip; something extraordinary that was beyond the pale of any rational analysis. To be able to think of my father in a compassionate way was absolutely new to me. But it was proof of a major shake-up in my psyche. Suddenly, I wanted to have a cup of tea with my Abba in the front lawn of my childhood house while we soaked up the warm late afternoon sun.

Ayahuasca had not only heightened my curiosity about the spirit world, it had also made me think about Paradise and Hell in a new way. Petra had told me that by insisting Paradise and Hell were nothing more than the work of my imagination, I had been acting out my personal convictions, all the while secretly believing otherwise. Maybe she was right. Perhaps I was unable to break free from the internal fight I had been having with my father all these years. It seemed as if I had lived my entire life as a reaction, while regarding myself as a man of action.

4

YESTERDAY WAS STUCK IN MY MIND and I had been whistling the haunting tune throughout my leisurely walk home. I halted as I stood at the front door of the one-room apartment I occupied, courtesy of the university apartment housing of Columbia. The door was ajar. Someone had broken in. I entered slowly and looked around. Finding no sign of activity, I tiptoed further inside, tensed, ready for either fight or flight.

The place smelled of cinnamon and tobacco, though not my cinnamon and tobacco. Instead of stealing anything, the intruder had left a Styrofoam cooler on my kitchen counter. It was the kind used to ship medicines on icepacks.

A large brown manila envelope with my name scrawled across it in a heavy black marker lay beside the cooler. Inside the insulated container, wedged between two icepacks, was a finger-sized plastic vial filled with a pinkish fluid. Its label read 'Single Dose OPV'. The brown envelope contained a business-class ticket on Khalifa Air's Flight 786. The flight departed at 9.00 p.m. from JFK on Monday, the following night. My eyes narrowed as I read the destination: Lahore, Pakistan, arriving 6.00 p.m. on Tuesday night. It was a one-way ticket. In the envelope was also a bundle of worn Dirham bills, ninety-nine of them; about a thousand dollars' worth. There was a handwritten two-page note in a beautiful flourished script too.

Dear Ismael,

Knowledge, like a rare metal, is a precious commodity and the price to gain the direct knowledge of Paradise and Hell is way too steep to be afforded if you are a mere mortal. However, there are methods known only to a select few— called the guides—who alone can unravel such mysteries. They exist to help those who seek with sincerity and unwavering intention. The time has come for you to prepare yourself for the most important journey of your life. You will be contacted once you arrive in Lahore.

Your father is a well-connected man and a highly regarded entrepreneur in the Caliphate. Obviously, his business is now a household name. We know that the two of you are estranged. Please understand that regaining your father's trust is the path to the success of our mission, a mission whose details will only be revealed to you when you are prepared to take action—at the right time, at the right place.

You are to call your father tonight at midnight. It will be 9.00 a.m. where he is. Let him know that you will be flying to Lahore to see him and that you have missed him very much. The two of you have a lot to discuss.

There are some basic reminders: your greatest enemy will be fear, and your greatest distraction will be desire or lust. Doubt causes paralysis and resentments shackle one with chains. Anger burns what is vital and impatience slows things down. Curiosity can have you killed. To succeed, you must learn to conquer these conditions that afflict other people. You will be tested at every step of the way.

If you have understood the above and still wish to continue on the Path to High Knowledge and undertake such a demanding journey, you must take the polio drops after reading this note. Your immune system needs to be optimal by the time you land.

Do not attempt to overthink or make sense of matters from here on for it may prevent you from choosing the right course of action at a crucial point in time. We will be monitoring your progress closely once you land. Failure is not an option and obedience thwarts many a catastrophe. Your success will ensure your entry into the most ancient circles of the Elite.

Pir Pul Siraat

P.S.: Arrangements have been made to make you completely debt-free, hence financial issues should be the last of your worries.

At the bottom of the note was Abba's mobile's number next to his name: Hajji Ibrahim. He hadn't changed his number in all these years. Maybe that was a good omen.

Bloody hell! I let out the breath I had been holding for the last few seconds and continued to stare at the note, numb with shock. This couldn't be happening. It seemed like some kind of over-the-top spy movie.

I read the note several times, my confusion mounting each time. Pir Pul Siraat. What a weird name! Pir meant guide and Pul Siraat that mythical tightrope. I had always imagined it to be a steel cable that hung high above the fire pit of Hell which, after death, every believer had to traverse barefoot. Most would fall off, except the true believers and those who died in the way of Allah: the martyrs. I had imagined seeing lush rolling mounds of green as far as the eye could see on the other side, and beyond that would be the real Paradise.

The more I tried to make sense of this baffling missive, the more restless I became. I paced back and forth in my tiny apartment as my mind raced over the possibilities in play. Then a thought occurred: I was doing exactly what I wasn't supposed to be doing—trying to make sense of things, things I supposedly couldn't understand anyway. How about: let's see what happens?

Morning gave way to noon and by then I had read the note so many times that I memorized it. The writing radiated a power that made me feel small and greatly agitated. Unable to sustain a state of hyper-arousal, my wakefulness progressed to the point of collapse. As soon as I hit the bed, I was taken by a deep, dreamless sleep.

When I woke up, the room was dark. Feeling disoriented, I glanced at my watch. It was 10.30 p.m. I bolted upright, thinking that the note and its accompanying items left on my kitchen counter by the intruder must have been part of an ongoing vision from last night's trip, the lingering effects of the sacred vine.

But the cooler was still sitting there on the counter and lying next to it was the opened manila envelope. A feeling of enormity and inevitability began to envelope me.

I got up and read the note once again, hoping new revelations would hit. Nothing. Everything was happening so fast. It was all so freakish and totally bizarre. Who really were these people and what did they want with me? It was clear that my encounter with Chacha Khidr wasn't merely my mind conjuring under the influence. The note had blown me away. It had made a hole so big in my conception of reality that I felt bodily transparent.

Did they even pick the right person? Was I just being given a crash course in conquering my weaknesses, fears and doubts? Now I was impatient and curious as hell. Obedient I was not and Abba could testify to that. Free from lust, most definitely not, since I had gotten it genetically.

One thing was for sure: my long-repressed sense of adventure was out of the barn and kicking up its hooves. Pushing the envelope had never been something I was afraid of—even though it often ended in regret. The bottom-line was this: I was intrigued; hell, I was hooked!

There was something big happening here and I wanted a seat

for the whole ride. Not to mention the debt-free deal which was, of course, way too sweet to pass up. More importantly, I wanted to find out what the hell my father had been up to these days. What topped the list was that he was the key to the success of my mission. Whatever that mission might be. It was time to take the polio drops.

I snapped open the end of the vaccine vial, took a deep breath, and emptied the contents into my mouth. A faint bitterness spread across my tongue. I opened the fridge and pulled out an icy bottle of Heineken and let the beer kill that unpleasant aftertaste. The next two took the edge off the growing sense of unease gripping me as I watched the hand of the clock edging slowly toward the fateful midnight hour and my phone call to my father.

I plopped down on my ragged loveseat in a horizontal position and stared at the ceiling, my head resting against the armrest. A spider lay motionless in its tiny hexagonal hammock, waiting for its wayward victim, a moth that circled overhead. The filaments of the web were radiant and I gazed in amazement.

The wind rose suddenly, howling and rattling the windows. I shivered, suddenly noticing the temperature in the room had dropped. Stepping over to the window I peeked through the blinds. There was something unsettling in the air. It was snowing and the sidewalks and parked cars that lined the street below were covered.

I returned to my loveseat and began watching the moth. It was banging against the walls every few seconds, but it managed to stay clear of the spider's deadly trap. A part of me felt like that moth, about to be engulfed in the gossamer threads of an unseen world. But the other part of me was the spider, having been duly sent the nourishment I needed from the beyond. I emptied my mind and waited for midnight.

The moth was still fluttering around the room when my watch showed five minutes to midnight. It was unbelievable that I had been staring at the ceiling for the last hour and a half. It was time to call Abba. I felt rested, energetic and ready to take on my assignment. I took a deep breath and, studying the note, dialed Abba's number.

'Hello!' he answered in the old, familiar, intense tone of his.

'Abba? It's—it's Ismael.'

After a long pause I heard his breath becoming irregular.

'I don't know if I should believe my ears,' he muttered. He didn't sound particularly happy to hear my voice. 'I thought I'd never see you again,' he added, sounding anxious and distant.

'I'm sorry, Abba. I've thought of calling you many times, but ...'

'But what?' he barked.

'Abba, I miss you,' I said, drawing a deep breath and cringing.

'Where are you calling me from?' he demanded, sounding genuinely puzzled now.

'New York City, Abba. I'll be in Lahore soon.'

'What? You're coming to Lahore?'

'Yes, Tuesday night. My plane lands at 6.00 p.m.'

'Which Tuesday?' he sputtered, his voice clipped and tense. 'You never fail to surprise me!' I now recalled that my father had never been particularly fond of surprises.

'This coming Tuesday, Abba—in two days.'

'Is everything all right?'

'Yes. I just miss Lahore and I miss being with you,' I said, gritting my teeth as I spoke. I didn't remember having ever said this to him before, and it didn't sound very believable even now.

'Are you well, Ismael?'

'100 per cent,' I assured him.

'It's a very different place here, from what it used to be,' he said. 'I hope you know the requirements for the entry. They are very strict on immigration these days.'

'I think I'll be fine,' I said, rubbing my cheek and feeling my week-old stubble. To get through immigration, the length of my beard had to be the size of a grain of rice. That much I knew, having read it in the news somewhere a while ago. 'I'll make it.'

'I'll send my driver to the airport. His name is Wali.'

'I'll just take a taxi, Abba.'

'This isn't the same place anymore.'

'Oh? Is it really that bad?' I was a little taken aback by the obvious alarm in his voice.

'It's bad all right, but it's not terrible. Most of what you hear about our country is all western propaganda,' he said. 'The Jews!'

'I know, I know,' I said. 'The Zionists.'

'Zionists or Jews, they're all the same. They're the killers of our Prophet—disliked by the Almighty the same.'

Horrified by his reply, I remained silent.

'Why are you coming?' Now his tone was calm but deliberately so.

'We'll talk about it, Abba, when we meet.'

'I won't be in Lahore until Thursday. So you'll have a couple of days to yourself to get settled in and recover from the jetlag. Wali and Ghulam Rasool will be in the house to look after you.'

I was happy to hear that Ghulam Rasool, the cook, was still around. His kind face, warm smile and the delicious food preparations flashed through my mind. I had never met Wali before.

'Thank you, Abba—it's very kind of you.'

'It's fine. It's fine. Wali will pick you up from the airport. But please, and this is very, very important. You must remember: do not discuss religion with him, at all. Avoid the subject completely. In fact, do not talk to anyone at the airport. Understood?'

'Yes, I'll keep that in mind.' A knot was forming in my stomach.

'You can't help it at times,' he added more to himself than me.

I remained quiet.

'Good, then, *Inshallah*, we'll meet on Thursday evening,' he said curtly. Then he was gone.

I guess it was really happening. I stared at the phone, thinking there was no way on earth that I could ever hope to gain my father's trust, and certainly not on his terms. But his trust was deemed a critical key to this nebulous success I was tasked to so ardently seek. The thought of visiting my native country, now the Caliphate, filled me with a mixture of terror and excitement. Shouldn't be a problem adjusting to the current norms, I consoled myself. After all, I did spend eighteen years of my life there—albeit as a rather poor example of a Muslim. I had never once set foot in a mosque in America. And if I still considered myself a Muslim, it was as a culturally self-hating Muslim.

I craved a cigarette. Though I quit a couple of months ago, I was really feeling it tonight. I got up and started to pace again, fighting the urge to go out and score a pack of smokes at the 7-11 down the block. Maybe I should get my laundry done. I needed a clean *thawb* for the trip. I discarded the idea because I knew if I went out I would be buying cigarettes. And then I remembered I had another similar robe somewhere in the back of my closet. I kept it as a souvenir since I had been wearing it when I left home: a faded blue denim jellaba splattered with a patchwork of red, green and yellow squares. Abba hated it.

'Only a heretic would wear this kind of robe,' he told me more than once, thus providing me with a good reason to wear it even more often.

I tried it on in front of the mirror. It used to hang loosely on me but now fit perfectly. With my stubble it made me look like a dervish. I could get a new one once I got to Lahore, but since I needed to change my attire before we landed in the Caliphate, I would have to carry it with me on the plane. Change the clothes, change the man, or woman. So went the prevailing mindset. I had heard stories of women flocking to the bathrooms during a flight to change their identities from chic urban dweller to pious Muslimah before landing on their grandparents' home soil.

Since I had no idea how long I would be gone, I threw whatever I thought I would need for a week or two into my suitcase. By the time I finished packing I was exhausted. As soon as my body hit the bed I passed out.

I stood in a vast courtyard lined with white marble tiles. It was dusk and I was staring at a massive white tent in front of me. Four pencil-shaped pillars stood at the tent's four corners. The place looked familiar, but I couldn't tell what it was or where I had seen it before.

In my hand I held a weightless ball of white light. An intense glow emanating from the sphere filled the whole area with dazzling brightness. A man wearing a black cloak and black turban, his face concealed by a veil, approached me. He stopped twenty feet from me.

Against the light his shadow stretched from his feet to the top of the tent like a dark band. Suddenly, the sphere burst into brilliant streaks of white light—like laser beams they shot across the night as far as the eyes could see—and then with a grunt the man vanished like darkness at daybreak. I opened my eyes. I was perspiring profusely and my shirt was drenched with sweat. It was 1.00 p.m. Being a light sleeper, it was unusual for me to have slept for such a long time without waking up even once. Something extraordinary was in play here. Something inexplicable yet palpable.

For one, I was disoriented as to time, and second, I had this vision of the present moment like a portal into a timeless dimension, where a limitless worlds churned about, each being a distinct entity, each staying clear of the other, and I existing in all worlds simultaneously. I shook my head in an attempt to dispel this strange vision.

It must have been the after-effects of Ayahuasca. Sitting on the bed as I wiped sweat off my forehead and tried to clear my thoughts, the dream came back to me. It was still so vivid. It had all seemed so real! I could still see the huge courtyard, the white tent, the cold marble beneath my bare feet and the intense white glow of the sphere's light upon my skin.

My curiosity to know the realities of Paradise and Hell had hit a new high. I wanted to know what mission Pir had been talking about, but worried whether I really was prepared for the weirdest of journeys one could possibly imagine. But I also had a certainty that by having the polio vaccine I had already accepted fate and taken the plunge.

5

To get to the airport I had taken the Air-train from Manhattan to JFK. Throughout the ride I couldn't help but marvel at the newfound clarity of my vision, the vividness of colors, this certain sharpness about the world around me, which I had never appreciated before. The weather was perfect and I was dazzled by the luminous edges of the clouds under the shocking blue of the sky, the radiant city skyline receding from my view, the untold stories etched on the human faces, the gestures betraying people's inner thoughts and the stark three dimensionality of space which I had ordinarily taken for granted, wrapping everything in its fold.

Feeling giddy from my heightened senses, I arrived at the airport two hours before takeoff. The flight was completely booked. A burqa clad airhostess stood at the doorway of the wide-bodied Airbus A500. Peeking through the narrow slit in her veil, her big black kohl-lined eyes looked resplendent. I froze, hypnotized by the beauty of those luminous orbs, wondering if the original purpose of the burqa had been to enhance the power of a woman's gaze. A nudge on my back made me step forward. What was the old saying about eyes? Souls? They sure had that right.

The woman looked at my boarding pass and pointed me towards the business class section with nothing more than a sweep of her eyes. Reluctantly, I headed toward my seat but couldn't help turning back a few times, hoping to catch another glimpse of her.

The piercing loveliness of those eyes had looked right into me. I was overcome as if by some strange potion. Unfortunately, she had moved on to the next passenger who hadn't even glanced at her veiled face.

There were about twenty or so comfortable, dimly lit private cabins on the aircraft, each stocked with the predictable amenities. The air smelled of fresh roses, with a hint of cinnamon. I slipped into my own cabin and took off my backpack. Inside, I detected a waft of jasmine. Either my olfactory senses had been heightened like everything else in my perceptual field or the atmosphere was exactly the way Khalifa Air had intended it to be. I wasn't quite sure.

I turned around and froze. A full-lipped girl in glossy red lipstick, wearing a red airline cap stood smiling at me. She was probably in her early twenties with long silky straw-coloured hair trailing down her back to her waist. She wore a tight maroon-coloured suit, but no blouse under her jacket. By the time she spoke, the eyes of a certain airhostess in the economy class were nothing more than a distant memory.

'Good evening, sir. My name is Alina. I'm at your service for the duration of the flight,' she said, reaching around behind me, touching the middle of my spine with her fingers.

'What's going on here?' I stammered, realizing I was holding my breath for several moments. I felt ashamed for uttering such a dumb response to her greeting.

'I understand your confusion, sir. You're flying with us for the first time. Is that correct?'

'Right.'

'Sir, this is the business class. Burqa-wearing hostesses are for the economy class only.'

'But aren't we all flying to the same country?' I asked, as I eased into my seat. Again, I vaguely detected the stupidity of my question.

'Sir, I'm from Latvia and am with a company hired by Khalifa Air to serve the business class. We aren't required to cover up, sir, because we aren't Muslims.' Her lips almost touched my ear lobe. My heart fluttered imagining the scope of the 'amenities' that were to unfold once we took off. The whole thing was so far out.

'What would you like to drink? No alcohol, of course,' she said softly. I scratched my chin and looked into her eyes, thinking my journey had perhaps kick-started on a wrong note. I wished lust had been the last thing to focus on, or at least until I landed in Lahore.

'I'm fine for now,' I said, looking around to see whether our conversation was being overheard.

'Are you by any chance a Shia, sir?' she said, lowering her voice further.

'Why do you ask?' I was struck by the oddity of her question; and a little apprehensive.

'Well, if you are, and would like to enjoy our complimentary full-service spa, you can register for the *Mut'ah* contract for the duration of this flight. Fourteen hours to be exact. I can bring you the register if you like. It's kept in the cockpit.'

'I'm neither,' I mumbled. I couldn't believe what she just said. Mut'ah or temporary marriage had been allowed in the Shia sect of Islam where the duration of such contract had to be specified and agreed upon in advance.

'What do you mean, sir?'

'I'm neither a Shia, nor a Sunni.' I tried to figure out the practical ramification of this obscene perk reserved for the business class passengers.

'Well, sir, for this flight, you're required to be one or the other.'

She had to be kidding me. Was this a test of some kind? Suddenly America seemed located in another time, a place where I once used to live a long time ago.

'Would you help me decide?' The girl had surely charmed me so I surrendered to the game. I was curious to see how far this would go.

'I personally don't like the paperwork, sir, if my humble wishes are to be considered,' she said with a playful toss of her golden hair and a smile that was anything but submissive.

'Well then, let's fly Sunni!' I said, replying to her smile with a grin.

'An excellent choice, sir! Once we take off you're invited upstairs for some relaxation and a massage.'

'I'll keep that in mind,' I said, smiling and admiring the view as she turned and slipped out of the cabin.

The entire flight was resplendent with the wonders and unexpected amenities of exceptional quality. I didn't even want to guess how much all cost whoever was footing the bill. But one thing was certain: I had failed my first test when it came to conquering my lust. Though I successfully refrained from having the 'full-service massage,' I succumbed to the happy ending part of it. For the rest of the flight I had a nagging feeling that I shouldn't have done that. After all, I was on the Path to High Knowledge, and indiscretions had no place in such endeavors.

I had slept through most of the latter half of the flight and was awoken before landing by my lovely Latvian hostess, Alina.

'Sir, you may now change into your mandatory attire.' She helped me to sit up. 'We'll be landing soon. I hope you enjoyed your flight. Thanks for choosing Khalifa Air.' She slid my cabin door open to leave.

As she left the cabin I slid into my blue denim jellaba and prepared for touchdown into the land of my birth. The side-pocket of my robe, the only pocket, was large enough to accommodate my fat wallet and cell phone. I carried my ticket and passport in a neck pouch that dangled in front of my navel. I was planning to tuck the pouch under my robe once I was through Immigration and Customs. As the plane began its descent, I was flooded with the memories I had avoided recollecting ever since I left home.

I was eighteen when I left. That was twelve years ago, the summer of 2038 to be exact. My father, a mid-level bureaucrat-turned-entrepreneur with his hand in every pie, was fifty-two at the time and had just married Sophie, his seventh wife. She was a beautiful, willowy, fifteen-year-old girl from the Kalash tribe, which occupied the picturesque valley of Kafiristan in the shadow of the Hindu Kush range in the former Republic of Pakistan. Sophie was also my first love. It was a love that blossomed long before Abba ever laid eyes on her.

My father was always careful not to exceed the four-wife limit in order to remain within the good graces of the Sharia Court. My mother, Jannat was Abba's first wife. Like so many, she had fallen victim to a perfectly preventable disease. Abba regarded the polio vaccination programmes provided by various global humanitarian agencies as part of a western conspiracy. A scientifically engineered genocide, he would call it.

I had met Sophie while Abba and I were spending the summer in Kafiristan the year before I left home. It was Abba's third trip to the region and he had fallen in love with the idea of converting the whole Kalash tribe, the kafirs, or the unbelievers, to Islam. These hardy mountain folk were thought to be the descendants of the armies of Alexander the Great as he marched through the northwestern Indian Subcontinent toward the fertile plains of Punjab. His quest for immortality. The truth of this could be gleaned from the light-skinned faces, pale brown hair and blue eyes so frequently seen in the far-flung and isolated valleys of the North.

Under the inspired and persistent leadership of Abba, Kafiristan became Nuristan, the Abode of Light. This whole Kafiristan affair boosted Abba's prestige in a land that was destined to become the Caliphate of Al-Bakistan. Most of the ancient tribe of Kalash had become extinct overnight. Those who resisted were killed. Many fled, taking refuge in the mountains. Women and children were captured and distributed as slaves among the affluent. Abba took Sophie for himself even though she never accepted Islam.

A month into her wedding, Sophie ran away in the middle of a dust storm that enveloped Lahore in an opaque crimson haze, bringing the city to a standstill for three days on end. She was never found despite Abba's best efforts. She may have been gone but never from my mind, for in every woman I had since, I would look for her trace, her reflection, her taste.

She had the courage to bolt for freedom and she inspired me to do the same. It took me a month to muster up the courage before I, too, said farewell to Abba and his world. I had left without saying goodbye. He was somewhere in the north at the time. But I left him a courtesy note, letting him know he wouldn't be seeing me for a very long time and not to waste his time looking for me. I said I would come back when fate chose and not a day before.

At the time I left home, Abba was living with his two wives: Safa and Marwa, his fifth and sixth wife. They were in their twenties and quite attractive. Up until Safa and Marwa, I had been an only child, the sole heir to Abba's expanding fortune. Since I turned out to be a complete disappointment, Abba had desperately wanted another son in whom he could see himself. This son would be just like him—somebody who carried the mantle and furthered his mission to help spread the light of his faith, and in the process ensure him a suitable palace and a prime piece of real estate in Paradise. I had no idea if he had another child since my departure.

After saying goodbye to Pakistan, it took me two gruelling years across five countries and two continents before I arrived in the United States. I was twenty years old. As luck would have it, I won the Green Card lottery and became a legal resident the following year.

I spent most of the next decade in libraries doing a series of odd jobs to support myself through college. I dived deep into

the study of religion in order to understand its science and the
mysterious power it held over people like Abba and countless
others throughout the centuries.

Abba saw me as a rebel without a cause; a pitiful excuse for
a son who was sure to ruin his chances in the Next World. He
often publicly voiced his regret at having invested so much time
and energy in someone who turned out to be all but a complete
failure.

When I was ten, my father had seen to it that I committed
the whole Quran to memory and became a *hafiz*. For that he
procured the best tutors money could buy and tolerated nothing
short of perfection from me. By the time I became a certified
hafiz, something great happened: my father's growing political
connections and popularity got him sidetracked.

Abba was seen less in Lahore, where he owned a chemical
factory, and became far more visible in Islamabad. Freed from
his watchful gaze, within a year or two I had all but forgotten
most of the holy text.

He eventually found out about my lapses and had taken
this neglect of mine rather too personally. To my father, and
all men like him, this was an unpardonable sin of the highest
magnitude and an affront to all things decent. From that point
our relationship had slid downhill until it hit rock bottom,
broken. It had never recovered.

6

A T THE IMMIGRATION COUNTER, the officer holding a handheld scanner passed it over my face before speaking a word to me.

'Unfortunately, you can't enter the country,' the immigration officer intoned grimly, his heavy lidded eyes staring at me with contempt. 'You'll have to be quarantined for at least three days,' he continued, as though the injunction amounted to some sort of personal triumph. 'Until your *beard* satisfies the proper criteria for entry.'

He eyed me with tight-lipped disapproval while fingering his own twenty-plus pious inches of wooly growth. Except for his eyes and forehead, the man's face was covered with jet-black hair. The tip of his beard trailed across my passport where it lay on the counter. Clearly I was in a land where size definitely mattered.

'Unless, of course, you wish to pay the fine,' he added, his lips curled in contempt.

'I'll pay the fine, sir. How much?' I asked, not taking my eyes off from his. It secretly pleased me when he was the first to look away.

'Three thousand dirhams,' he stated in a voice clipped and bristling with pride. 'For each day your beard must grow to meet the legal requirement so ...' He paused, inspected my face, his eyes narrowed. 'For you, it will be ten thousand in total; nine for three days, plus one thousand for handling-charges.'

'Thank you, sir,' I said, peeling ten one-thousand-Dirham notes apart, roughly equivalent to a hundred dollars, and offering the bills to him.

I exited the immigration area and headed straight for the baggage carousel. I had definitely landed in a foreign country. All signs were in Arabic, now the official language of the Caliphate. In the good old days, they at least had the courtesy to put the Urdu translation beside the Arabic. Such courtesies and others, as I was soon to discover, were long gone.

A recitation of the Quran poured from the intercom system and drowned everything in an aura of otherworldliness. At the customs window, a fiery looking officer with a bulging belly and jet-black dyed beard looked me over from head to toe. A matchbox-sized copy of the Quran dangled from his neck on a gold chain.

'Carrying anything we should know about?' His mouth widened in a mischievous smile.

'No, sir. Please feel free to check anything you'd like.'

He made me open my suitcase. Fumbling through my clothes, he extracted my shaving kit. Unzipping the bag, he pulled out my razor and held it in front of my face.

'What, exactly, is this doing here?' he inquired as if discovering the most heinous piece of contraband. 'Did you keep this shamelessly petite little beard just to get into the Caliphate?' he demanded. His nostrils flared but he never took his eyes off me as he plunged his hand deeper into my shaving kit like a diver searching for sunken treasure. This time he pulled out a half empty tube of Colgate toothpaste.

'This brand is haram, forbidden in the Caliphate!' he hissed.

'It's just toothpaste—for God's sake.' I hissed back.

'It contains alcohol and pig's fat,' he said, shaking his head like he just couldn't fathom what he was seeing and what on earth it was doing in my bag. He looked infuriated. My tone probably had something to do with that.

'Please feel free to throw these things away. I apologize.' I said, sensing trouble.

'Recite the fifth *kalima*, then the third, then the first and then the sixth. In that order,' he demanded. He reared up and folded his arms across his broad chest, swaying back and forth in front of me like a cobra. With his deep set eyes boring into me, he studied me with a predator's attention. Suddenly, I felt embarrassed—for having once been a hafiz, the person who was supposed to recite the entire Quran solely from memory. The memorization of these six kalimas, the standard Arabic phrases mostly taken from *Hadith*, the saying of Prophet, had long been part of the syllabus of grade three education in Pakistan. Now all I could remember was the first kalima, called *Shahadaa*, the shortest but the most important one, the one whose utterance was all one needed to be a Muslim instantly.

'I could recite the first,' I suggested, breathing out a sigh.

'Three thousand dirhams for each kalima that you've forgotten. Eighteen thousand Dirhams in total,' he said, extending a huge open palm toward me and rubbing his fingers together.

'Wait a minute,' I said. 'What's the total number of kalimas we're talking about here?' I reached into my pocket for the cash. I knew there was an ancient controversy if there were six kalimas or five.

'Ten thousand Dirhams in addition to the eighteen. The additional fine is for not knowing how many kalimas there are in total,' he said, narrowing his eyes. 'Now you owe me twenty-eight thousand dirhams.'

'That's kind of steep.'

'I'll let you go for twenty-five.'

By the time I left the customs window my wallet had lost one-third of its bulk. The customs officers at Lahore airport had been known for their heavy-handedness, but they were now operating on a whole new level.

I walked out of the luggage area and rolled my suitcase toward the exit and the pick-up and delivery area. My eyes scanned a thick knot of noisy jostling bodies of bearded men. Many were drivers with the names of travellers written on cards dangling from their chest.

No sign so far of Wali, my dad's most trusted right-hand man who was supposed to drive me home. In the hallway, a ten-foot long water bottle hung from the ceiling by chains. It was labelled 'Paradise Water: Your only reliable source of clean water, Khalifa Inc'.

A large crowd had gathered to my right beneath a flashing red neon sign that read Judgment Day Bar. What the hell was this all about? With mounting curiosity, I inched my way toward the entrance. About a hundred or so men crowded the doorway under the flashing lights.

'What's going on here?' I asked a young man in his twenties who stood next to me.

'Today we're having both a stoning and a beheading at the same time,' he said, giving me a nudge in the ribs.

'Really?'

'Usually, it's just one or the other,' he said, shoving himself deeper into the crowd, presumably to get a better look at the show.

'Good Lord! Why at the airport?'

'Can you think of a better public place than an airport?' he asked, looking at me suspiciously. 'Did you just say, Good Lord?'

'No! Mashallah Alhamdolillah. Jazakallah.' I sputtered. 'I'd better get going.'

'Wait! What kind of Muslim are you?' he stammered. 'You're not going to watch the beheading? It's how we kill the infidels in Islam; it's the preferred way! Stay, brother. It will make your faith strong!' he cried out with excitement. But I was already rushing for the door.

'I'm in a hurry, some other time!' I shouted over my shoulder. 'My father's waiting for me outside,' I said. The guy emerged from the crowd again and stood by my side, staring at me. 'Actually, if I remember correctly we have front row seats for next Friday's hand-chopping ceremony at Charing Cross.' I had no idea how I came up with this excuse.

'Actually on Friday they do hangings after the Jumma prayers,' he said smugly, as though he had a box seat for all the hot events on the Sharia calendar. 'Where have you been living?' He stroked his properly bearded chin and looked me over from head to toe as if considering what to do with me next.

'Yeah, well, I've been away for a while. On business. It'll take a few days to get used to the system again.' Rolling my suitcase out of the door, I continued scanning the crowd for a placard with my name on it. The light was diminishing, the sky turning purple at the horizon. I almost lost my balance when my eyes caught sight of a whole bunch of camels hobbled in the taxi stand. I gaped at a passerby.

'Do you see what I see over there?' I said, pointing towards the camels.

'Yes. The taxi stand,' he said, giving me a curious glance as if it was obvious.

'That's not what I meant. I mean, do you see what's inside the taxi stand?' I asked.

'Taxis,' he said. He looked at me like I was from another planet and then, shaking his head, he walked away.

It was only when I moved closer to the camels that I realized they really were taxicabs. Yellow cabs of Lahore! Each cab was fitted with the replica of a legless camel on its top.

As I tried to figure out the practical use of this contraption, I was surrounded by about a dozen people of various ages, each trying to snatch my suitcase. One kid had his hands on my backpack, aggressively yanking on the strap to dislodge it from my shoulder. Tightening my grip on the handlebar of my suitcase, I shouted. 'Hey, hey! Get away! All of you,' I yelled, realizing they were all either cab drivers or worked for one. 'I don't need a damn taxi. I've got my own driver!'

'What's going on here?' I heard a loud voice bark over my shoulder. A tall lanky man wearing a Kalashnikov over his shoulder approached. The guys jostling for my suitcase melted into the crowd and I held my breath.

Before I could say anything, the armed man hoisted my suitcase and dislodged my backpack. The suitcase hung in his hand like a child's toy. The backpack was slung over his shoulder, the shoulder that wasn't sporting a high-powered military grade weapon.

'Are you Wali?'

'I'm Sher Khan. You're coming with me.'

'But I'm waiting for Wali,' I insisted, growing increasingly uncomfortable by the minute.

As if he hadn't heard me, the fellow started to walk away, taking my luggage with him.

'Jesus Christ!' All I could do was follow. 'There must be some mistake, Sher Khan,' I insisted without effect.

Someone shouted behind me. 'He's a Christian.'

Shit! I quickened my pace, berating myself for having uttered something out of habit.

Not looking back, Sher Khan entered the taxi stand. Keeping about a distance of five feet from him, I followed. He approached a taxicab and pulled a latch located on the camel's belly. The camel's hump swung skyward, revealing a luggage compartment. He threw my suitcase into the camel's belly, brought the hump down, and secured it with a sharp click.

'Amreeki babu,' he said, opening the door of his cab for me like a spider inviting a fat fly into its web.

'Alhamdolillah, someone is picking me up. You should have told me.'

His face loosened upon hearing the magical Arabic words.

'Babu, only Sher Khan can guarantee full security of his passengers. I swear by Allah, I'll kill the bastard who dares mess with you.' He rubbed his hand down the length of his Kalashnikov like it was a favourite hunting dog.

'Jazakallah! I'm very, very grateful for your kindness, Sher Khan. I would love to have you as my driver one day. Inshallah! But tonight, someone else is supposed to be picking me up. Can I have my suitcase back, please?'

'Once the suitcase has been loaded, it doesn't come out until we reach the destination,' the man said, gazing toward the sky.

'Look, I'll give you some money for the hard work you've already done carrying my stuff to your taxi—Inshallah! Once again, please take my suitcase out of the trunk and give it back.' My patience was getting shorter by the minute.

'Have you got dollars?' he chirped, his eyes lighting up. I suddenly realized how much taller he was than I.

'I'll give you one thousand dirhams,' I said, realizing that I didn't really know the value of the currency here. But I did know that I had been stripped of thirty-five thousand dirhams out of the ninety-nine I had in my possession at the time of landing.

'Babu, you've come from Amreeka, but you behave as if you're from Afghanistan.'

'How much do you want?' I stammered, glancing around.

'How much you're carrying?' He took a step toward me. I looked for help. I didn't want to lose my entire cash. To my amazement, a sizable crowd had gathered around the taxicab-stand—at least twenty or thirty people were standing twenty feet from us. They had all been keenly watching my exchange with Sher Khan. I waved at them.

Inside I felt ashamed for being too quick to offer him money for my kidnapped luggage. That was nothing short of an admission of weakness. Weakness, I knew, didn't play well in these parts; not back in my day and sure as hell not now.

Sher Khan was now standing next to me, rubbing his palms. Feeling helpless I slid my hand in my pocket and looked toward the crowd. And there he was! Holding the placard with my name on it. Wali had just joined the crowd. Ignoring Sher Khan, I broke into a sprint towards Wali.

'Wali! Wali!' I shouted.

The man clearly stood out from the crowd. Wearing an orange-coloured jellaba that almost glowed in the dim light of dusk, he raised his arm and waved in my direction.

'Sir Ismaelji, what are you doing here in the taxi stand?' he asked. He was in his late fifties, his back a little hunched, his bony shoulders drooping. He also sounded annoyed.

'I'll explain. First thing: that man took my suitcase,' I said, pointing towards Sher Khan's taxicab.

'And you let him? Sirji!' He threw the placard on the ground and approached Sher Khan, his shimmering robe flowing gracefully around his lean frame.

I was sure that robe was meant to glow in the dark. Wali stood next to Sher Khan, his right arm on Sher Khan's shoulder. From where I stood, it looked like they were negotiating some sort of deal. Sher Khan looked down at the ground, rubbing his temple from time to time. And suddenly it was over.

Sher Khan nodded once, then went to his cab, pulled my suitcase out of the metallic camel's hump and angrily slammed it shut. He ambled over to where I was standing and dumped my suitcase on the ground in front of me. Then he disappeared into the knot of bystanders.

Wali hauled my suitcase to his car, a shabby light green Corolla, which was parked not too far from the taxi stand. It was hard to believe that Abba, who always loved cars, would be driving this piece of junk.

Wali placed my suitcase in the camel's hump and opened the rear door for me.

'Welcome to Lahore, sirji.'

'Thank you, Wali. It feels so nice to be back here.' It wasn't entirely an inaccurate statement. I had run away from Abba, not from Lahore, the city I loved for its energy, food and parks.

The first thing I noticed as we pulled out of the airport were all the billboards plastered with pictures of men who had wild unkempt beards.

'Sirji, when was the last time you have been to Pakistan?' Wali asked, lighting up his *beeri*, a dried rolled up leaf filled with tobacco flakes, the poor man's cigarette. We were on the airport road heading towards Fortress Stadium.

'Twelve years,' I said, looking at the billboard where a handsome looking elderly man with a long salt-and-pepper beard stood tall, his arms folded across his chest. He was surrounded by four burqa-clad women, all with remarkably beautiful eyes. 'So many women available to one man!'

'It's not that there are so many women, it's because the men are in short supply.'

'Why are men in short supply?'

'You'll find out,' he said, cutting sharply to the right to avoid a big crater on the road.

7

❦

WE STOPPED AT THE traffic light. Wali turned on the stereo and the euphoric strain of a Bollywood musical filled the car. It had a pair of powerful woofers in the back which rattled with the deep bass waves.

'Wali,' I yelled so he could hear me. 'I thought music wasn't allowed in Pakistan anymore. Especially Indian music,' I added, bringing my face closer to his ear so I wouldn't have to scream over the singer.

'Sirji, pay attention to the lyrics. It's not what you think it is; it's a *na'at*.'

'What did you just say?' I asked.

'It's a na'at,' he repeated, turning the volume down.

He was right. It was indeed.

'Oh, so music is allowed as long as it's in praise of Muhammad,' I said.

As soon as I uttered the name, Wali kissed the tips of his fingers and started mumbling a prayer, his face unreadable and his eyes shut. Then his face turned red and flecks of foam appeared on his lips. I stared in alarm, not sure what I could to do.

The traffic light turned green but oblivious to his surroundings, Wali kept his eyes shut as his lips trembled. Cars behind us started honking. Without any warning, he threw open the door and leapt out onto the street. He left the door wide open and the other cars swerved to miss slamming into it.

Ignoring the cacophony of cars honking, Wali knelt on the ground and then lowered himself further into *sajdah,* his forehead and nose on the dusty asphalt, the Muslim prostration. I looked back through the rear window, my heart pounding. Cars behind us had started reversing. The traffic was moving again, leaving our standing vehicle behind. By the time Wali got up from the ground and sat back in his seat beside me, the light had turned red again.

'What was all that about?'

Without saying a word, he opened the glove box and took out a round, palm-sized object. It was a clasped knife. He pressed one end and an evil looking blade sprung out. I could tell it was razor sharp and must have been as long as my forearm. I jerked back in my seat, eyes wide open.

Wali turned toward me and grabbed a hold of my collar. His eyes bulged; two angry pools of black fire. Without a word he pressed the sharp cold steel against my throat as I tried hard not to swallow.

'Wali, what's wrong?' I sputtered. 'What's happened to you? Take it easy buddy, relax,' I pleaded. This was all too strange and had happened so fast I barely had time to register the shock.

'You have uttered the name of You Know Who without the salutations; and that is a terrible crime punishable by death,' he groaned, pressing the blade harder against my throat.

'Wali, come back to your senses man!' I barked. 'What's wrong with you? Come on, let's get going, look, the light's green. Let's go, please. We can talk about this over a cup of tea in the Fortress Stadium. I can explain.' I hoped to have sounded convincing and unfazed by his sudden outburst but I knew I was tasting my first dose of real fear since I landed.

Sweat poured down my forehead as I recalled my father's words: 'You'll be safe with Wali. He's the only one I trust to deliver you safely to my house.' I also recalled him warning me not to speak with Wali about religion under any circumstances.

'I've beheaded four idiots like you,' he bellowed. 'I did it right here where you sit on your stupid butt. And you will be my fifth,' he said. The traffic light had turned red again.

'Aren't you done then? I mean, four's a pretty decent number. Come on, Wali, let's not do anything rash,' I said, hoping this nightmare would end soon. 'My father's not going to like it if you kill me.'

'Mufti Sahib says that if I can personally behead seven kafirs in total, my place will be assured in the highest level of Jannah,' he said, as his eyes glazed and his face flushed with exultation. He wasn't the same Wali who had picked me up a few minutes ago at the airport. He started looking crazier by the minute.

'It's been getting more and more difficult to encounter enemies of faith like you,' he continued, not even looking at me in the eye. 'As far as your father is concerned, he'd be glad to see you killed after what you've done. He wouldn't even attend your funeral.'

'Wali, please! Have mercy. Remember that old hag?' I asked, suddenly recalling something that might break his concentration. 'That old woman who used to throw trash on You Know Who's head every time he'd pass by her house.'

Without a word Wali withdrew his knife from my neck and laid it on his lap, though he continued to hold his face close to mine and looked into my eyes. The terrifying fury that seconds before distorted his face melted away like ice.

'So you know?' he asked, his voice now normal and composed. 'Then you damn well know that the story of the hag cost me the seventh Heaven!' he then roared with renewed fury.

'Fifth Heaven, Wali, fifth,' I corrected him.

'You gotta get to fifth before getting to the seventh.' Wali picked up the knife and I stiffened for a new assault was coming my way, but he just shook his head, snapped the blade shut and tossed the thing into the glove box.

'On what level do you start getting the virgins?' I inquired, trying to move the conversation in another, hopefully less inflammatory, direction. I was actually genuinely interested. After all, it was a matter that concerned Paradise as well as my hard-to-control lust.

'I've got to ask Mufti Sahib about this,' he said, lost in thought. 'But I suspect you start getting them right after you drink the sweet water of *Hauz-e-Kauser* directly from the hand of You Know Who,' he replied, nodding with satisfaction.

Ever since I was a child I wanted to see Hauz-e-Kauser—a pond filled with sweet water at the gates of Paradise—just to see what it looked like. It was even mentioned in the Quran.

'I heard Mufti Sahib say that the virgins come flying towards you when you have drunk enough water and your thirst is quenched,' he explained, as though sharing a treasured memory.

'Can we start driving now, please?' I asked, fixing my collar, feeling satisfied by my performance. I had successfully managed to overcome my fear. Pir Pul Siraat should be pleased with me. For some odd reason Faisal Town seemed worlds away. 'Do you remember where we're heading—in this world I mean?'

'Fortress Stadium, of course. Sirji, you'll have to fulfill your promise. A true believer never breaks his promise even if it's about a thing as small as a cup of tea. In fact, I was thinking of stopping by the stadium myself and having a cup of tea.'

The signal turned green. It seemed we had been standing for all eternity. Something was still terribly wrong with my perception of time. Good thing I had a watch.

'Maybe you can help me buy a nice present for Abba,' I suggested. 'I left in such a hurry that I didn't have the time to bring him anything from the U.S. Now I feel terrible. I'm seeing him after such a long time; I must give him something special.'

The night descended around us faster than I expected. The air was still pleasantly warm. I noticed with amusement that nearly every car had been fitted with fake camel bodies on the top. It was an odd sight but it had its use: an extra trunk.

'Wali, please don't be offended, but what made you do sajdah after I mentioned You Know Who?'

'Sirji,' he began, shaking his head. 'Your knowledge of Islam is so terribly poor that a true Muslim will have no remorse or hesitation killing you on the spot after hearing such a stupid question.'

I refrained from asking Wali for further clarification. The last thing I needed was another scary confrontation with someone like him, the kind that would probably prove fatal for one of us. And at the moment, in this car I was the only likely candidate facing extinction.

I couldn't believe my father would actually send a man like Wali to pick me up from the airport. Did he want me dead? Ever since I had boarded Khalifa Air almost nothing that had transpired made any sense whatsoever. And here I was, doing it again: trying to make rational sense of things.

By the time Wali pulled into the Fortress Stadium parking lot it was already dark. The shops, embedded into the circular wall of the stadium were lit by gas lamps. Wali parked the car not too far from the main entrance. I remembered the place well; it used to be a popular hangout with the college crowd and for families to dine out and shop at some of the nicest boutiques in Lahore.

'Sirji, remember this; it may save your life,' Wali began. 'If anyone utters the name of You Know Who, you should immediately close your eyes and send a blessing. You should know what I'm talking about: I'm talking about *drood*, the blessing sent to all the prophets of the line of Hazrat Ibrahim *alaihis-salaam*.'

'Yeah, I know that part,' I said.

'But what you obviously don't know,' Wali continued, lowering his voice and gripping my arm firmly, 'is that right after saying your drood, you do the sajdah and recite the first Kalima thirty-three times. Why?' he asked, pausing to study my face. When I didn't answer he continued. 'Because it's the law. If you ever get caught ignoring this law, you will be killed on the spot. And remember: most people around here have only gotten to the third or fourth Heaven. They're stuck there, searching for ways to break into the higher Heavens. And since their fate for all eternity depends upon it, people won't hesitate for a second to behead you—that's how it goes here nowadays. You just remember that.'

'Understood! Wali, you are a true friend,' I said, patting him on the back and wondering what else people did around here. Besides trying to ascend to the higher Heaven.

'Sirji, I don't know why, but I like you,' Wali said, shaking his head as though I was a mystery beyond all comprehension. 'What could possibly be better than constantly thinking about the Next World—the real world? It's like being in a state of permanent worship.'

'Excellent point, Wali,' I said, nodding as though I completely understood what he was saying. I didn't.

'I mean, do you really believe for one minute that this world of ours is worth living for?' he asked. 'Do you think that this world will hold any attraction for a believer? Our present life is a trap, sirji. A trap!'

After several moments of awkward silence we finally got out of the car. An eerie sort of calm permeated the air, the kind that descends right before a monster storm breaks. The stadium was lit by floodlights mounted on poles which bathed the whole area in a weird sickly glow. I saw hordes of robed men with hairy faces walking in through its massive gates.

A stray dog that looked like a beagle ran past me. It was being chased by a huge cat the size of a panther. The cat leapt in the air and landed on the dog, pinning it to the pavement. Then it proceeded to maul the poor thing in a flurry of claws. The dog howled as the cat sunk its teeth into its throat. The cat's powerful jaws gripped its victim, shaking it once, twice, until it was dead. The victor dragged the corpse of the dog away and was gone.

'A clear sign the Day of Judgment is upon us!' Wali exclaimed in triumph. He seemed to really enjoy watching me witness this spectacular aspect of nature.

I had landed in a very strange place. Something incomprehensible, something very bad, had happened to this country and its people. The whole place seemed to shimmer like a phantom in some parallel universe.

By now the crowds streaming into the stadium had swollen considerably.

'Night cricket, I guess?' I asked.

'Oh, much more thrilling than night cricket,' Wali said, as we walked toward the entrance. 'Let's grab a cup of tea and go inside. I promise you'll have fun.'

'Don't you think we should go to the house?' I asked, feeling some bad vibes. Very bad vibes. 'I had a long flight and I'm pretty beat.'

'No one is waiting for us at home. Your Abbaji is in Islamabad at the moment. He's not going to be in Lahore until Thursday.'

'But I—' I tried to protest but he chopped the air with his hand and cut me off.

'Your Abbaji has instructed me to show you around, to get you fully oriented with this place in his absence,' he declared in a voice that warned me he would tolerate no further breaches of protocol.

I had no interest in watching a night game or spending any more time with Wali for that matter. Right now all I wanted was to get home as soon as possible, lounge in my bed and think about what the hell I had been sent here for.

'Can we first buy some gift for Abba?' I suggested, hoping to distract Wali from whatever festivities were underway.

I knew there was no gift in the world that was going to send my father and I running back into each other's arms, but I was hoping to at least begin the thaw. According to the note, I was to be contacted shortly after I arrived, though I had no idea what form that contact would take.

'Your wish is my command, sirji,' Wali said, touching my arm and pointing toward the shops.

We passed a line of stores and headed toward the tea stall. I stopped to look at a sign on the sidewalk: 'SALE!' it read in bright red letters. The items on sale in the store were listed in proud detail:

'Top of the line Martyr Vests! All sizes! We proudly sell only Mujahid brand. Accept no imitations! Remote Control Detonation 4-packs also on sale. Martyr Vests for Children. Graduation Gifts! Exploding Toys! And much more! Come inside and see!'

Another sign by the store's entrance read: 'Pellets for quick stoning. Stones with special grips. No Refunds after use.'

Every sign I read seemed more bizarre than the first and I had a sinking feeling that entering the shop would be the start of just as bizarre an adventure.

'This is a good place to find some nice gift for your Abbaji,' Wali said, his voice dripping with excitement.

He had been watching me closely as I read the list of merchandise while standing utterly speechless at the entrance of the shop. Wali slipped inside and made a beeline for the men's martyr vests. I saw him pick up one of the grotesque garments. He glanced back and forth from me to the vest, then held the thing up in my direction. What the hell? This must be a dream! Closing my eyes I shook my head from side to side, wondering exactly what sort of gift Wali wanted me to present to my father.

8

I STOOD ROOTED TO THE SIDEWALK, unable to go inside. Who wouldn't be a little jittery around that kind of merchandise? Wali had disappeared from my view.

The area was now quite crowded and outside the shop bearded men strolled along the sidewalk in flowing Arab-style robes with a *keffiyeh* and *agal* on their heads. Trailing a few steps behind them were their women, completely concealed beneath black burqas. The women outnumbered the men by ten to one. Some burqas didn't even have a slit for their eyes, only small fabric screens.

I made a mental note of the surreal, or rather drastic, changes in the culture I had become immersed in since landing just a couple of hours ago. This was a brave new world of Islam, about which I hadn't the slightest clue and which seemed ready to blow itself up any minute. I wondered what exactly this brand of Islam was, the ones being practiced in this godforsaken place. Where did it come from and how?

Wali appeared at the shop's entrance and gestured for me to come inside. Before I could put one foot inside, I was knocked aside by a man, his wife and their three teenaged beardless sons. They streamed into the shop—the parents first, followed by the three boys about a year or two apart in age. I fell into step behind the last boy and entered the shop.

Lit by gas lamps, the shop was tiny and crammed, the items in each of the aisles stacked up to the ceiling. Martyr vests of all sizes and colours covered one wall and also hung from the ceiling on hangers.

The shelves overflowed with curious goods: stones, wicked-looking scythes, swords with Arabic inscriptions, curved daggers which had handles studded with jewels, tangled heaps of cheap-looking plastic *tasbih* rosaries, delicately carved glass perfume bottles, ammunition belts, plastic tubes, books on Islam, incense, bolts, nails, nuts and copper hooks all lying around in no visible order. It looked like the prop department of a very bad movie.

The owner was a large man of about seventy with tiny silver wire-frame glasses perched on the end of his nose. He sat on a three-feet-high wooden ledge, the size of a queen-size bed, amidst a pile of vests. Stacks of colourful prayer mats and rugs decked the periphery of the ledge. His face was scrunched in concentration as he absent-mindedly combed his fingers through his henna-dyed beard that trailed into his lap. He looked like a wild mountain warlord sitting in a teashop. I had to force my eyes away from this colourful spectacle before he noticed me staring at him.

The man was sewing what looked like finger-length red-coloured explosive tubes into the lining of one of the vests. Next to him sat a long glass counter with an old-fashioned cash register. Behind the counter stood a boy of ten or twelve who was sorting boxes of ammunition and eyeing all the new customers.

Between me, Wali, the family of five, the proprietor and his shop boy, the place felt uncomfortably crammed with people. Wali had made a place for himself at the far end of the counter by shoving a pile of vests out of his way. I squeezed past him and the tallest boy of the family that came in.

Wali pointed toward something behind the shop boy's head. It looked like some sort of rock—flat at the bottom, roundish on top, dark rust in colour. It had sharp spikes on top and looked like a cross between a porcupine and a soccer ball. The shop boy took it down from the shelf, using both hands, and his face strained as if in pain.

Keeping the rock held aloft, the boy leaned over the counter as Wali took it from him and weighed it in his hand. Without any warning he shoved the rock into my hands. I gasped and almost dropped it on my foot. It must have weighed at least twenty pounds.

'A perfect gift for your Abbaji,' Wali announced proudly.

'What's this supposed to be?' I asked, staring at him.

'Sirji, it's from *Maidan-e-Arafat*, the place where every soul will rise one day. It's an imported item. The finest quality!'

'So?'

'Sirji, I think this is a most excellent present for your father. Tell me if I'm wrong, but what better present can there be than this rock for doing your *wudu* every day? It must have been around for thousands of years.'

The wudu or ablution with water before each of the five daily ritual prayers, or *namaaz*, was an integral part of one's faith. But when water wasn't available, a stone could be employed instead. In that instance one would touch the stone and follow through the same motions as if doing ablution with water. 'This precious stone was touched by the blessed air of Maidan-e-Arafat. It's from the place chosen by the Almighty, the very place where He will raise the dead when the horn is blown on the Day of Judgment,' Wali explained.

'Oh, I understand!' I assured him. The last thing I wanted to do was to offend Wali again or, for that matter, anyone else in this shop.

The smell of danger floated in the air like incense; the unmistakable odour of ammonium nitrate that is used in explosive devices, mixed with the stench of my own fear-laced sweat.

'But aren't rocks and stuff used only when there's no water available to do wudu? What's that called? *Tayummum*, right?'

It felt good displaying what little knowledge I had. I moved the rock around, shifting its prodigious weight in my hands. The spikes bit into my palms and hurt like hell, but I somehow managed to keep a cheerful mask of curiosity on my face.

Everyone turned around and stared as if I had said something wildly inappropriate. Had I? I simply couldn't tell in this place. I felt glaring eyes sweeping over me, judging my all-but-naked face with its pitiful little illegal beard.

'Sirji has just landed from America,' Wali announced, casting his eyes over the crowd. Sure, it was only eight people but it felt like an angry mob. 'He is looking to buy a special present for his Abbaji,' he continued as though a satisfactory explanation might determine if I were getting out of this place in one piece or not. 'He forgot to buy something before he left America; so happy he was at the very thought of seeing his Abbiji after a long separation. Mashallah!' he concluded.

I wasn't sure if Wali was mocking me or just trying to be helpful. One of the teenage boys, standing right next to me, had slipped on one of the Mujahid vests. He had chosen a slick black number with crisscrossed red stripes and green tubes tucked neatly into loops sown into the webbed lining. I wondered if they were filled with some homemade explosives.

The shop boy placed a mirror on top of the counter and adjusted it so the boy could admire himself. The boy tried to turn around so he could look at himself from all sides, but he couldn't budge an inch. He was pressed up against me tightly. I stood next to Wali and Wali was still pinioned against the wooden ledge next to the counter. The boy's father nodded approvingly.

'Cool design,' the boy said, nodding and all grins. Was this kid real?

Wali distracted me as he whispered, 'Sirji, no one uses water here for wudu anymore—not in Lahore. Not anywhere.'

'What?' I said. 'Why?' I whispered.

'Because there is no clean water available. The water out of the tap is all mixed up with the sewer. It stinks.'

'So how do people get by without clean water?' I asked. 'I mean, what do they use for drinking and cooking?'

'We use Paradise Water for that purpose,' he replied. 'And in the tap water we put pinky.'

'Pinky?'

'Gentian Violet, sirji. It kills the germs and most of the smell, but still doesn't make it drinkable.'

My head reeled with the implications. I then remembered the huge bottle filled with clear water hanging from the ceiling at the airport labelled 'Paradise Water: Your only reliable source of clean water, Khalifa Inc.' Then I noticed something else in the air, something different from the smell of ammonium nitrate wafting off the Mujahid vests and permeating the shop; something ominous. I was brought back to my senses by a female voice.

'Let's try another size,' the boy's mother said to the henna-haired proprietor. 'Show us some nice ones. This one is a bit tight around the chest—and look at the fabric, it feels so cheap. Surely you can do better,' she said as though she had just suffered an unforgivable insult.

'And I want a better price. This is too much for such shoddy workmanship.'

The old man grabbed a cane that was fitted with a copper hook at one end. Without bothering to stand up, he raised the cane over his head and started sorting through dozens of vests which dangled from the ceiling. His hook grabbed a hanger with the one of the vests.

He then released the hook and carefully eased the vest down the length of the cane a few inches at a time. It was quite an elaborate procedure, one obviously developed with great care over many years. I didn't dare breathe until the vest was safely cradled in his lap.

'Bajiji, we also make videos, for a nominal fee of course, in the next shop. You get a discount if you buy a vest from us. Just imagine your son opening his eyes by the exalted pond, Hauz-e-Kauser, filled with sweet water of Jannah. How blessed he is to be given water by the seal of the prophethood, Muhammad, peace be upon him, himself.'

All movement came to a sudden halt. Only the white, hot flame of the gas-lamp hissed on, unaware of the ominous silence. The rock I held in my hand slid a notch down along my belly while everyone closed their eyes and started moving their lips with ferocious speed.

I closed my eyes, but kept one eye slightly open to see what was happening. The shop boy was the first to go into sajdah and disappeared behind the counter. I was shoved back by Wali who was trying to make room for himself to do his prostration. The henna-bearded proprietor bent all the way down while still sitting on the ledge. He had his forehead rested on the tubes of explosives he was sewing into the vest.

The couple, both heavyset, somehow managed to maneuver themselves into a kneeling position. The two younger boys had already hit the floor, one piling on top of the other as their foreheads struggled to touch the cement floor. The whole thing looked almost choreographed.

The boy wearing the vest remained standing with his too small vest still zipped up and strapped in place. He shoved me out of his way as he scrambled toward the ground. The shove was very hard and I barely managed to avoid tumbling over and crashing on top of Wali's spine—thanks to the weight of the rock pressed against my stomach. I looked around, desperate to find a way to get rid of the rock.

The countertop had no space; besides, it was glass and would never hold the weight of the rock without shattering. The holy rock from Maidan-e-Arafat suddenly grew heavier manifold and

I had to bend backward to counter it. And I froze with panic when I looked down.

To my horror, the detonation loop on the boy's vest had got caught on one of spikes of the sacred rock in my hands. The boy, in his desperation to find a place to rest his forehead and without the slightest idea of what he was doing, kept tugging on the loop.

Clearly I was holding him back from doing his sajdah. I thought of dropping the rock, but it would have landed on the boy's back, fracturing his spine. Smoke rose from the vest and a pungent odour filled the shop. I shut my eyes and prepared for annihilation. My mind sank into an image of space, a black, vast, cosmic wilderness.

But the blast and the cosmic wilderness didn't arrive. I opened my eyes and everyone was still down on their knees. A thin ribbon of blue smoke rose from the vest close to the boy's armpit. The ninety-nine seconds, provided each recitation of the first kalima took three seconds, seemed to have lasted an eternity.

My fingers, white-knuckled and locked onto the heavy stone with a death grip, cramped violently. Then everyone jumped up, patted their clothes and coughed as the acrid smoke clogged their throats.

Before I got a chance to put the rock away, vest-boy's father slammed my head down on the counter next to the mirror. He dragged a monstrous dagger from somewhere inside his black robe and pressed it hard against my throat. This was getting old fast.

Following their father's cue, the three boys drew out their own knives and pressed them to my throat. In the mirror I could see four furious sets of eyes and teeth glowering at me.

From under a pile of vests, the shop owner pulled out his own blade that was about the size of a bayonet and pointed it to my face, while the shop boy fumbled with a Swiss Army knife. I longed to let go of the rock but it would have smashed my toes; so I held onto it.

'This kind of auspicious opportunity doesn't arise every day,' the father growled, locking his eyes with mine, his nose flaring. I almost thought he was about to start hyperventilating. 'As soon as I knew he had come from America,' he continued, grinning with twisted rage-filled delight, 'I knew he'd have no respect for our religion. I think I'll let Saad, my youngest son, enjoy the honour of killing you,' he said, dragging his dagger away from my neck and nicking the flesh. I didn't know what these people would do if they actually smelled fresh blood. I was terrified.

There was a sudden flurry of activity behind the father. The woman, his wife, had unveiled her eyes and shoved her sons out of the way. In her hand she clutched a huge butcher knife, the *toka*. Pushing past her husband as well, she advanced towards me.

Suddenly I realized the immense benefit of death by explosives. Maybe it was pretty painless. In a matter of seconds, you would cross over to the other side. I regretted not having a Mujahid vest of my own under my robe. I would have gladly taken every asshole slathered in this shop with me straight to Heaven, or even Hell for that matter, as long as they were going with me. It was such a stupid waste for my life to end here and now getting slaughtered by people I had always thought of as nothing more than angry villagers.

'Now everyone, hold your horses, take a deep breath and listen to me,' Wali shouted from behind. 'It's a fine thing to desire Paradise above all else, but you are just too eager to get there. You have all failed to notice that sirji, Ismael, couldn't even find a place to do his sajdah. He kept looking for space for himself.'

'Yes! Alhamdolillah! Wali is absolutely right. I was looking for a clear space,' I said. 'Also, what's that weird smell and where's all that smoke coming from?'

'This smell is common in places where explosives are stored,' the henna-bearded man replied with an impatient flick of his hand. At least he took his knife away from my throat and laid the wicked-looking blade down on the counter.

'No, it's more than just that,' I said, trying to muster a little courage from somewhere. 'Look what happened,' I hissed, raising the sacred-rock with great effort and holding it under the medley of knives still rammed against my throat. The loop of the small-sized Martyr vest was still hooked onto the spike. They all stared at the rock, with their eyes wide and mouths gaping.

'Corruption has eaten like a worm into the very bones of this nation,' Wali moaned. He seemed genuinely disappointed. 'They can't even sell a properly working vest. Mujahid brand, my foot!' The knives were lifted off of my neck and then they disappeared. Only the woman gripped her blade tightly and lunged like a tigress towards the shop owner to slide her huge knife across his throat. The man glared at the woman but didn't flinch. I had the uncanny feeling that the owner could have taken this woman down any time he wanted.

'So you sell second-rate merchandize in this store? Mujahid brand I doubt it. It's good we found out before we laid down our hard-earned money. We're going to report you,' she roared in indignation. 'All these vests are fake Mujahid brand. I could already tell that from the quality of fabric,' she growled, pulling the vest off her son and shoving it into henna-beard's hands. 'Thieves!' she continued with a shriek. 'May Allah roast you in Hell's fire! My son would have been humiliated with a misfire like this. What's your name?' she screamed, pressing the toka deeper into the man's neck.

'Bibiji, I'm sorry. I think maybe the vest got left out in the rain and was ruined by the water.'

'I'm asking you your name,' she roared through clenched teeth.

'Muhammad Sadiq.'

As soon as I heard the name Muhammad, I immediately lowered the rock onto the floor, closed my eyes and plunged towards the ground. I was not going to miss my turn on the floor this time around. I said my kalima thirty-three times, as required by the law of the Caliphate. I counted them slowly and deliberately on my fingers.

When I stood up, I realized that no one had joined me on the floor. No one had attempted to prostrate. They all just stared at me. Without another word, the patriarch of the party shook his head in disgust and the family headed toward the door as they looked at me with palpable contempt. Then they all disappeared from sight.

'How much for this beautiful sacred rock?' I asked, trying to dissipate a cloud of embarrassment. I had done something incredibly stupid, that much I knew, but I couldn't figure out exactly where I went wrong and how.

'Twenty-five thousand Dirhams,' the shop boy said. 'You want me to wrap it up for you, sir?'

'No, no, don't trouble yourself,' I said, peeling apart a stack of bills and realizing I was quickly running out of cash.

Once out of the shop, we took turns carrying the sacred rock to the car.

'Oh, Wali. What a narrow escape!'

'Death comes at the appointed time, sirji—no point wasting time thinking about it.' He opened the camel's hump and pushed my suitcase to one side. He then gently placed the rock into the boot like it was a sleeping infant and clicked the hump shut. 'Sirji, you paid too much money for the gift—way too much.'

'I had no choice after what happened?'

'Sirji, you don't go in sajdah when you hear the name of a regular person whose name just happens to be Muhammad,' Wali explained in a serene voice.

'What about now?' I asked. 'Right now you mentioned that name. What should one do in this case?'

'That's a very good question, sirji. I'll have to ask Mufti Sahib. Let's grab a cup of tea and watch a little bit of the game.'

'Wali, I think we should push on,' I whined. 'I'm telling you I'm utterly exhausted.'

'Sirji, if we watch the game inside the stadium, you'll catch up on many important things going on in this country. What you must learn and understand very quickly. Otherwise you'll remain confused as well as in danger for the rest of your trip. I'm under orders from your father to get you oriented and keep you safe.'

'Wali, I need to think. I need to sit alone for just ten minutes and think in peace,' I pleaded.

'Thinking will get you killed here very fast. This is a place of doing; a place of action, sirji. Life is all about action. Thinking kills action,' Wali explained, his voice now that of a stern but kind father or elder brother.

Wali's words sounded shockingly familiar: '*Do not attempt to overthink or make sense of matters from here on, for it may prevent you from choosing the right course of action at a crucial point in time. We will be monitoring your progress closely once you land.*' How the hell were Pir and company supposed to be monitoring my progress in this bizarre place, where I was darn lucky to still be alive—thanks to the kid's counterfeit martyr vest that didn't fit properly.

'Tea is much better for you right now than thinking.'

I really needed to sit down and gather myself. I needed to figure out what the hell was going on and how to navigate through it all without getting my throat slit like an Eid goat. Why was all this happening to me? I knew at least part of the answer to that question: my father. He was the man to unlock this whole damn mystery for me.

I opened my wallet and took out a thousand-Dirham note.

'I don't have change.' I figured it was time to count my remaining money. Having to pay twenty-five thousand Dirhams for a piece of rock that almost got me killed was nothing but a huge rip-off. No wonder I was seething.

Wali strolled away, presumably in search of his precious tea, while I looked around for a bench to sit down. But there weren't any. I supposed that must be haram too. The area had no electricity and there was no sound of generators either. The glow of gas lamps imbued the air with a stillness but it was far from peaceful and relaxing.

The stadium's interior, on the other, hand was aglow with floodlights mounted on huge poles. I sat down at the edge of the sidewalk, grateful for a place where I could rest my feet and think without the company of those who delighted in judging my right to continued existence at every turn.

Closing my eyes, I looked inward and tried assessing my bearings. They seemed to have gotten stuck in a maze with no outlets, a moth in a spider's web. I skimmed over the entire text of the Pir Pul Siraat's note from my memory and realized I was far from conquering anything that had been pointed out to me in that note. Never before had I experienced fear like now and I was overwhelmed with doubt. The ineffable mission I had been tasked with seemed like a cruel joke. How was I even suitable for it? I was resentful and angry at myself for not thinking this whole thing through before I snapped the vial of polio vaccine. But for some odd reason I remained curious—a trait that could get me killed—as to what Pir and Chacha Khidr were doing. Were they really even monitoring me in this mess. And how? Suddenly a thought occurred to me: I was thinking too much, thus preventing myself from choosing the right course of action.

9

I SAT ALONG THE EDGE of the sidewalk waiting for Wali to return with our tea, feeling drained despite the adequate rest and sensuous massage I had in the business class section of Khalifa Air. It was the jet lag and I was dog tired, so I closed my eyes and rested my head on my knees. Memories I had fought long and hard to banish from my mind streamed to the surface and I was too exhausted to resist.

Again I remembered Sophie—technically now my mother because of a marriage that lasted no more than a couple of days. She was strolling through a field of mauve flowers which bloomed each spring on the grassy slopes of the mountain not far from her home. Her long black skirt and red shawl with a knotted fringe fluttered in the wind as she walked.

In her delicate hands she carried a large bundle of tiny purple blossoms and a sprig of something green was tangled in the loose strands of her dark golden hair that fell into her eyes. From where I sat on the slope, the guesthouse—where Abba, I and his fourth wife Salma were staying—seemed tiny where it lay nestled in the distant valley. With its red tin roof, it looked like toy house waiting for a child.

For the last ten days, I had been hiking up here each morning to see my beautiful Sophie. It was an elevation of over a thousand feet above the guesthouse. Wind rustled through the tall, sweet-smelling grasses. Sophie was bathed in a warm yellow light, her golden-brown braids touching her pale cheeks. I remembered her full red lips, the taste of fresh apricots on her tongue. I cringed when I thought of her sleeping with my father and wondered if anyone had heard from her again or if she was even alive.

Since those idyllic days of windswept fields filled with flowers and tall grasses, Kafiristan had been invaded by the Caliphate and those beautiful slopes had turned red with blood. The place was now called Nuristan and the irony of this ravaged area being called the Land of Light in these sad times was infuriating.

'Here is your tea, sirji, and your change,' Wali said, jolting me from my reverie. He was already sitting next to me holding two steaming cups.

I shook my head to clear my thoughts and took one of the cups in my hands.

'This is exactly what I needed,' I said, taking a sip even though it was too sweet and creamy for my taste. 'You can keep the change.'

'Never, sirji. It's your money. And you're our guest.' He shoved several 100-Dirham notes in my hand. I tucked them into my wallet without any further argument.

'Time for the game, sirji,' Wali said with a grin as he tapped my arm. 'We don't want to miss the opening.'

Reluctantly I got up, stretched my legs and yawned. The massive walls of the stadium loomed over the crowd as they streamed through one of its many gates. Holding our tea cups, we fell in line with the procession.

'How long are we going to stay?' I asked, trying to keep pace with Wali.

I knew that a typical cricket match could easily go on for hours and I was becoming more irritable by the minute. I knew what was coming. For me, irritability quickly passed into a dangerous territory known as belligerence. I didn't want any of that while I was under Wali's questionable protection. Oh, how I longed for the comfort of my cabin aboard Khalifa Air.

'We'll stay only for one over,' he assured me. 'It's a semi-final, sirji—we must watch!'

'So what time do you think we'll get home to Faisal Town?' I asked, recalling that an over comprised only six throws and wouldn't take more than fifteen minutes.

'Faisal Town?'

'Yes, Faisal Town,' I replied, wondering if he was hard of hearing.

'There's no guarantee of anything in life. It may take an hour, it may take a day, it may take a week,' Wali said. 'Keep this in mind: we may never reach Faisal Town at all. Nothing ever happens without Allah's will.' With his long strides and quick gait, Wali quickly moved ahead of me and I struggled to keep up.

'Don't we have to buy tickets?' I asked, wondering how much more damage this game was going to do to my wallet before I finally escaped from this damned stadium.

'We will buy them on our way out,' Wali said, holding his cup above his head and throwing himself into the crowd of people.

I followed closely, not wanting to lose sight of him in the middle of this chaos. Trying to decode what he had just said was nothing more than a waste of time, so I remained as clueless as ever.

Once through the gate, we slowly pushed our way to the top of the stands. There were plenty of empty seats and loudspeakers blasted Arabic over the crowds. Almost everyone in our section wore a headdress: a black turban or a black skullcap along with a long white robe. Curiously though, some spectators wore helmets while others watched the field through their binoculars.

As far as I could remember, the Fortress Stadium had never been used for sporting events. Its grounds had been the home of the annual national horse and cattle show, the industrial exhibition of small industries, and the Defence Day parades.

Wali hurried toward a row of empty seats and scrambled over the laps of a few angry spectators. All I could do was mumble a string of sorry's as we pushed through the crowd. The teams were already out on the field and there were a lot more players than for any regular cricket match I had ever seen. There must have been at least twenty or twenty-five of them. I took my seat beside Wali, looking at the two batsmen standing at the crease, both with their bats resting on their shoulders.

Wali tapped my arm to get my attention. He was holding a six-inch long tube, the diameter of a flute, in his hand.

'What the hell is this?' I blurted. The tube was metallic and weighed about half a kilo.

'*Doorbeen*, sirji,' Wali said. 'Military-grade telescope.'

'What are the names of the teams and which side are we on?' Shutting one eye, slowly adjusting its focus, I pointed the high-quality spyglass at the field. The sight made me jump. Resemblance to any normal game of cricket pretty much ended right there. My skin crawled as I focused on the bizarre scene where each of the fielders was brandishing a long curved sword in one hand and a heavy, metal-banded shield in the other. The light from the overhead lamps bounced off the swords and threw the players into a 'Danse Macabre' within an absolutely surreal scene.

'The semi-final is between the Karbala Cats and the Wahab Squad,' Wali shouted in my ear. 'The winner will play the Badr Brigade.'

For a moment everything felt like a dream. I looked at my hands, opening and closing them as I tried to push the fingers of one hand through the palm of the other. Nothing. There was no pain to wake me up. This was no dream.

'Wahab Squad!' Wali boomed, punching the air with his fist. 'Don't even think about supporting the kafirs of the Karbala Cats when you're in a Wahab stand!'

I scanned our section and spotted at least six men wearing Martyr vests within a twenty-metre radius of where we sat.

'What's this game called, Wali?' I asked, feeling my heartbeat quickening as I handed his spyglass back to him.

'Cricket!' Wali exclaimed, his face beaming with pride.

'This can't be cricket!'

'Modified on the orders of Khalifa to reflect the principles our Khilafat is based on.'

Unbelievable!

'Sirji, our Khalifaji has connections, you know, top floor,' he said, winking and pointing his index finger toward the sky. What could Allah have to do with cricket?

Khalifa, or the caliph, had been the absolute ruler of the country for the past eight years. He was a mysterious figure—never seen in public—and his spectacular rise to power could be attributed to his occult powers as much as to his campaign of terror, which he had unleashed from his remote hideout in the Hindu Kush mountains in the north of Pakistan. He built his power on the model of Hassan-i Sabbah, the legendary terror master of eleventh-century Persia, dispatching his highly trained assassins, *fedayeen*, to take out the country's key political and military figures. Rumour had it that he could talk to animals and was known for his fondness for cats.

'The legend is that one night Khalifaji had a dream,' Wali continued. 'He was shown what the game of cricket should look like if it were according to the principles of Sharia. The next day everything changed. Khalifaji corrected the rules and here we are,' he explained with a broad sweep of his hand toward the field.

A handsome boy in his mid-teens squeezed through the crowd and approached us. Hanging from his neck on two cords was a tray stacked with *papads,* the spicy paper-thin crunchy tortillas. He was also wearing the ubiquitous Martyr vest. The thing was torn in several places, loose threads dangled from the seams, greasy food stains covered the front and a few of the explosive tubes were missing. He was lean, a little over five feet tall and

stood right in front of me, one hand resting on the triggering-
loop of his vest. Pulling on the loop from time to time, which
made my hair stand on end, he just stared at me with his big
bright eyes.

'No, thank you,' I muttered, keeping my eyes glued to his hand
while my heart continued to pound.

'Get lost!' Wali said, shooing him away. 'Go sell your bhang
papads somewhere else.' As the boy wandered off, he glanced
back at me several times before being swallowed by the crowd.
Bhang-laced papads had always been a hot-selling item during a
cricket match in the good old Pakistan. I was glad to know that
at least one tradition had persisted in the Caliphate.

'When one is at play, one must also be at worship. Do you
understand, sirji?' Wali continued, his eyes narrowing as they
bore into mine.

'That's brilliant,' I said, not knowing what the hell else to say,
but knowing by now that it damn well better be in agreement.
'And why are there so many fielders on the field and what are
those swords for in their hands?'

'The fielding is now done by the players of both teams at the
same time, and—'

'That's impossible. How could both teams field at the same
time?'

'Unlike the original western-style game, suited only for sissies,'
he continued, 'now the fielders of both teams engage in battle,
real combat, as they compete for the ball. As they fight one
another with their swords, the batsmen keep running between
the wickets to earn *swaab*. Yes, sirji, that's the major change
Khalifaji brought to the game,' Wali said, beaming with pride at
the accomplishment of his revered leader. 'He replaced the system
of runs with the system of earning swaab! Is that not brilliant?'

Swaab or blessings were the points a believer earned by
following the dicta of his faith. 'What the hell does any of that
have to do with cricket?' I asked.

Ignoring my question Wali pointed and I followed his finger with my eyes. There it was. The swaab board stood tall over the stands, the former scoreboard.

'How can players not get hurt when they battle for control over the ball?'

'Hurt, sirji? Hurt?' he roared, mocking me with a roll of his dark eyes. 'It's an honour to die in the field, sirji.'

It took me a moment to realize the game I was watching was a creative mixture of cricket and a gladiator arena of ancient Rome. The thought made me queasy.

'So they're real swords?' I asked.

'Sirji, yes, ultimately, it's all just practice for the Final Battle, for the final victory.'

'A Muslim killing a Muslim. That doesn't make a whole lot of sense to me.'

'Sirji, Khalifaji says: whosoever dies in the practice battle will be given the exact same place in Paradise as those who die fighting real Jihad against the kafirs.'

Taking a deep breath I asked, 'How many players are on each side? At the start of the game, I mean?'

'Eleven at all times on each side. There are always about twenty replacements standing at the sidelines, ready and eager to jump in if one from their team is martyred.'

'And how many die by the time the game ends? On average?'

'Three, four, sometimes as many as eight. I've even seen games with only one survivor. The others? Gone to Paradise!' Wali exclaimed, his eyes wide, his voice like that of an old storyteller recounting the early days of the community at Medina.

'How many overs are there in a game?' My stomach had begun to churn. I shifted in my seat and looked around. Two young men in their early twenties had just taken their seats next to me. By now, I wasn't surprised to see them wearing the Martyr vests. Suddenly I was hit by a strong desire to eat bhang papads.

'Three overs each—six overs in total,' Wali replied.

'Only three? The game must be over in a short time, then?'

'Sirji, even in one over a team can sometimes earn as much as a hundred swaabs.'

'Wali, can we go and sit somewhere else?' I asked, eyeing the young men sitting next to me out of the corner of my eye.

'What happened, sirji?'

'Nothing!' I snapped nervously.

Sensing my anxiety, Wali chuckled.

'Don't pay too much attention to those vests boys wear around here. It's just a fashion statement to them. It makes them feel important.'

'How do you know they're not real vests?' I asked, still not at all comfortable with their proximity.

'Actually, you can't know.' Wali pressed my arm. 'Sirji, just relax. Let's watch the game.'

The wind had started to blow. For a fall evening in Lahore it was a bit chilly, but still pleasant. A bright sickle moon hung over the stadium in the dark sea of night and a star twinkled like a distant beacon guiding somebody somewhere. The sky brought me a feeling of sanity. The spectacle was way too far out to be comprehended by someone who had just landed in what was undoubtedly the most bizarre place in the whole universe.

The Karbala Cats' fast bowler started his run up and our side of the stadium roared in excitement. Halfway down his run, the man's robe filled with air and fluttered around his body like a parachute. The batsman, who wore no protective pads, missed the ball and it whizzed toward the wicketkeeper's hands like a bullet.

Wali stood up, blew a whistle and then sat down again.

'Why do we buy tickets on the way out and not when we enter the stadium?' The question had been nagging me ever since Wali mentioned it.

'Sirji, why would anybody buy tickets going into a place when he doesn't even know for sure if he'll ever get back out again?'

Wali replied without turning to look at me. His eyes were locked on the game and he didn't bother to elaborate.

I thought it best to keep my mouth shut as I tried to digest yet another new and harrowing piece of information.

'The vests you're seeing everywhere,' Wali said, finally turning toward me, 'they're good for cultivating courage. Khalifaji says that courage is what we'll need in the end times—when everything blows up.'

'How much do the tickets cost, Wali?' I asked. My hand unconsciously went into my pocket and searched for my wallet.

'One hundred Dirhams each,' Wali said.

'Wali! I can't find my wallet!' I gasped in alarm. It took me less than a second to realize that my cell phone was gone too.

'Not a leaf moves without His command,' Wali said. 'Him in whose hand is your life which will also be taken from you one day.'

'But this is serious! You've got to help me to find my wallet and cell phone,' I cried, thinking of my passport. I checked to make sure the pouch was still on me under my robe and was relieved to find it remained hanging from its cord. 'How the hell are we going to buy tickets on our way out?'

'Relax, sirji. We may not have to. Perhaps it was a sign,' Wali said.

'A sign of what?' I demanded. Of death? I was more than a little irritated with this nonchalant attitude of his.

He said nothing but just sat staring at me. Then his face broke into a warm smile and he shook his head. I felt like punching him on his nose.

The boy selling papads wended his way back through the crowd and halted in front of the vest-wearing boys sitting next to me, a pleading look in his eyes. After some haggling, he succeeded in selling them some of his wares. The boy next to me, who had thick matted hair like a bird's nest, bought at least a dozen or so. He gobbled down most of them in a matter of minutes. I wished I had my wallet with me. I certainly didn't want to ask Wali for money for bhang papads. In all honesty, I really craved a spiked latte from Grasshopper.

The ball had been driven deep into the offside. The fielding pair ran along with the ball, the tips of their swords pointing toward the sky and their shields clutched tightly to their chests.

With a sudden surge of action, the two fielders locked swords and rammed into each other with their shields as they scrambled after the ball. The batsmen ran between the wickets while the rest of the players on the field started shouting *Allah Hu Akbar*. The swaab board had started to roll.

A roar spread through the stadium and the ball had come to a stop. The two fielders were locked in a ferocious battle, swords clashing and shields banging against each other as the melee continued. Both batsmen were dashing between the wickets while the two umpires stood erect and studied the fight through their binoculars.

There was no question in my mind that this sword fight wasn't going to end well and I wanted to get the hell out of the stadium as soon as possible.

The kid next to me unfolded a piece of white cloth, kissed it and then wrapped it carefully like a headband around his Afro-like hairdo. The cloth was inscribed with shahadaa, the first Kalima, in black ink. The papad boy had disappeared once again somewhere in the crowd. The whole thing was surreal, almost drug-like as time seemed to slow to an imperceptible crawl.

'Sirji, we've earned twenty-five swaabs!' Wali screamed. Tears ran down his face. He was clearly swept away in some collective ecstatic euphoria. But my anger at him was growing.

'You're not paying attention, sirji,' he growled, his voice suddenly filled with rage. He was waving his arms in the air. His bright orange robe must have been visible for miles.

The Afro-kid with the white headband jumped up, straightened his vest and tightened its straps, then sat down again. One of his companions pulled out a cell phone and started shooting a video of him munching his papad. I pulled away to avoid getting caught in the video and yanked on Wali's sleeve to get his attention.

'Sirji, you're missing all the action. Come on, stand up here with me' he shouted down at me.

I did as instructed because it seemed the only way to escape being in that video.

'Wali, look! What are they doing?' I asked, jerking my thumb at the boys and their camera.

'He's having his friend make his farewell video. Let the kids play.'

'What?' I yelled in disbelief.

'Sirji, forget about them. Watch the fight; they're getting tired now—the real fun is about to begin,' he shouted.

The papad boy materialized again from of the crowd. He stood next to Wali's chair, his tray now empty and his eyes glued to the boys shooting the video.

Ignoring Wali I looked at the Afro-kid who was mumbling something in Arabic. The red light of the cell phone camera started blinking. But then something happened on the field and everybody gasped. The fighting pair had fallen to the ground, their robes splattered with blood. A hush fell over the stadium as the Wahab's fielder slowly raised himself off the ground, his sword held high in the air. The batsmen had stopped running. I looked at Wali. He stood motionless, his hands dangling at his sides. He stopped yelling his excited commentary at me.

As soon as I looked back at the field I felt sick to my stomach. To my horror, the Wahab Squad's player had cut off the head of his opponent in one clean sweep of his sword. As he lifted the severed head above his own, his fist clenching the victim's hair, the stand erupted in a roar.

'Sirji, one down, ten more to go!' Wali shouted at me amidst a deafening noise. 'Not a single leaf moves without His command.'

Then the Afro-kid next to me erupted in a hysterical fit of giggles. I jerked away and almost fell on the ground.

The boy's friend, the one who had taken the video, threw himself on the ground in front of me, also wracked by spasms of hysterical laughter. Soon they were both rolling around on the ground in a fit. The papad boy had drawn closer and was laughing uncontrollably too. I stood up to leave without Wali, but sat back down remembering I had no money to pay for my ticket at the exit gate.

As soon as the noise subsided, someone shouted 'Allah Hu Akbar!'

The shout came from nearby, flooding my mind with the no-nonsense words of the pilot of Khalifa Air: 'Duck without any shame or reservation when you hear, in a crowded place, a loud Allah Hu Akbar.'

I hit the ground next to the Afro-kid, my mind reeling with the bloody images of the carnage I had just witnessed.

The Afro-kid stopped laughing like someone had flipped a switch; then he got up and jumped onto his seat.

'I've seen many like you!' the boy yelled facing the back rows. 'I dare you! Let's see who goes first.'

'Sir, I can tell you're not from here, but don't be afraid,' a friendly voice whispered in my ear. 'Why worry yourself when you know that death comes only at the appointed hour?'

Trembling with fear, I looked up and saw the cheerful face of the papad boy, his eyes peering at me with amusement. He was kneeling beside me with his hand on my back. I was embarrassed that I was getting a pep talk like this from a kid. Composing myself and wiping the sweat away from my forehead, I staggered to my feet just as four black-robed men of the Karbala Cats were whisking the headless corpse of the fielder away on a handheld stretcher. They were followed by two white-robed men supporting the injured combatant by his shoulders as he limped off the field, the severed head swinging by his side.

The Afro-kid was still hurling insults at somebody in the back. The game resumed and the stadium swelled once more with cheers, curses and prayers as they were shouted from the four corners of the field. I closed my eyes and wished I could just beam myself out of this hellhole. My trip so far had been nothing but an interminable nightmare of the highest order.

'Sir, the man shouting "Allah Hu Akbar" in the back is a big bluff. He's just trying to scare people. He does it all the time, at every game,' the papad boy informed me.

'You sell bhang papads in a mad-house like this?' I stared at him.

'My papads save lives, sir. They make people happy; bhang calms people down and makes them forget.'

'What's your name?' I asked, admiring his cool attitude.

'Tarzan.'

'That's an interesting name.'

'Sir, there's going to be an explosion twenty feet from here in about ten minutes. Just so you know,' he whispered in my ear.

'What? How the hell do you that?' I was terrified.

'Because I was the one who planted it.' He explained without a trace of guilt or worry on his young face.

'You just said you were here to save lives and make people happy,' I gasped, stealing a look at Wali, I asked, 'Wali, can we get out of here?' I pleaded. Even in this open-air stadium I was feeling suffocated.

I looked at Tarzan, searching his face for answers and the admission that he was bluffing and just having some fun at my expense.

'Tarzan, my friend,' I began nervously. 'Where exactly is this bomb we're talking about, the one that's going off in ten minutes?'

'Eight,' Tarzan said. 'It's eight minutes now.'

'Wali,' I said, turning to my companion and shaking his arm. 'You have to listen to me. We're getting out of here

now!' I insisted. 'Did you hear what I just said, Wali? Now!'
I screamed.

'Sir, don't be afraid. It's just a shoe bomb,' Tarzan said.

'A shoe bomb? What the hell is a shoe bomb?'

'A bomb made of old shoes stuffed in a burlap sack.'

'What?!'

'When it goes off, shoes come pouring down from the sky
like rain.'

'But it can physically hurt you, right?'

'It all depends on where the shoe hits you and what speed it's
travelling at.'

'Great!' I said, wondering what exactly the purpose of a bomb
like that was. 'But why a shoe-bomb?' I sounded ridiculous.

'Sir, for a man there's nothing more insulting than having a
shoe land on your head,' he explained as though I was a two-
year-old.

'So you're a secret fan of Karbala Cats, eh?' I asked, looking
into Tarzan's eyes. 'Planting shoe bombs for them in a Wahabi
stand.'

'I plant my shoe bombs on both sides, sir,' Tarzan said,
pointing at the stand across from us. 'I do this everywhere,' he
explained, his dark eyes glistening with mirth. 'After I blow this
one, I'll go to the other side to finish off the day's work.'

'Do you get paid for this?'

'Of course. From both sides. Sir, you can't eat two meals a day
with one job. Everything here is so damned expensive.'

10

I LOOKED UP AT WALI. Oblivious to his surroundings, he was standing on his seat, absorbed in the game again. Afro-kid was jumping up and down on his chair along with everybody else. His head was flailing back and forth like a head-banger lost in the music. The shouts of 'Allah Hu Akbar' had now been replaced with a deafening wail of whistling and yelling.

I was convinced that surviving this blasted insane asylum of a game would be a matter of pure luck. Grudgingly, I took my seat. I grabbed the hem of Afro-kid's robe and gave it a couple of tugs.

'Sit down,' I said, patting his seat. 'Come on brother, sit down.'

'Are you from America?' he asked, looking down at me with a big grin.

'If you sit down, I'll be happy to tell you where I'm from.'

He dropped into his seat and offered me his hand. He was dark-skinned, around twenty years old and skinny as a twig. His hair was sticking out of his white headband like Medusa's snakes and he looked more than a little crazed.

'Pleasure to meet you!' I grabbed his hand and gave it a single shake.

'Yo, ma maan!' he cried, trying to sound like some urban homeboy and almost succeeding.

He just sat there grinning at me and rocking from side-to-side. I looked around for Tarzan, but he had disappeared.

Then it happened; my worst fear materialized. About twenty rows below us a huge fireball rose in the air and was followed by a deafening sound. A gust of hot wind hit my face and I ducked forward without thinking, tucking my head between my knees.

I heard screams all around me. When I finally looked up, I saw Afro-kid stretched out on the ground face down in front of me. There was a pool of blood around his head on the concrete beneath my feet. Yet the game carried on.

Below us, the site of the explosion was in chaos with people swarming over each other like ants as they scrambled toward the aisles. The screaming became unbearable; overhead the loudspeakers blared and the air reeked of gunpowder.

I reached over and grabbed Afro-kid's wrist in my trembling hand. He had a pulse and was bleeding from an ugly gash over his right brow, but he was alive. His friend was nowhere to be found. I peeled off the kid's white headband and reapplied it over his laceration as tightly as I could. Next I got the accursed vest off him and shoved it out of the way. I had no way of knowing if it was real or just a 'fashion statement' as Wali described.

'Wali,' I shouted, 'enough of this damn game. I'll see you at the car.'

Hoisting Afro-kid's limp body over my right shoulder, I made my way down the stands and hurried toward the gate. Before I could reach the exit, a blast ripped through the air behind me. I kept moving without looking back. A smoking shoe hit the pavement about four feet in front of me. It was a military boot, its sole filled with holes.

'Sirji, wait.' Wali's voice bellowed from behind. 'The game was just beginning to heat up.'

I turned around and stared at him. He was out of breath from chasing me through the stands and I was intensely relieved to hear his voice.

'Wali, I hope you have money to buy the tickets. I'll pay you back the whole amount. If we ever get to Faisal Town that is.'

'I've got some money, but it might not be enough for all three of us.'

As we stepped up to the ticket booth, another explosion rocked the stadium.

'Looks like the VIP stand, sirji. Look over there.' He pointed toward the far pavilion. A bluish gray cloud of smoke hung over the crowd.

'How many?' a man demanded from inside a ticket booth.

'Two,' Wali said.

'And the one on his shoulder?' the man asked, shooting me a curious look.

'This one has crossed over,' Wali said. 'Alhamdolillah!' he added, sliding his hand across his throat.

'Yes. He's dead.' I was pleased with Wali's quick thinking. I was never any good at lying.

The ticket agent gave me a piercing look. Then he shot up from his seat and marched out of his booth. Standing beside me he put his hand on the side of Afro-boy's neck. Shaking his head he went back into his booth.

'Two hundred and fifty Dirhams,' he said, holding out his hand.

Without a word, Wali counted the money and we made it out of the stadium without any further mishaps.

'Sirji, if you had kept quiet, we wouldn't have had to pay the extra fifty.'

'Why fifty for him? And not one hundred?'

'The injured pay half the price.'

'Great! So they don't charge for the dead.'

'He got suspicious when you chimed in,' Wali said.

This game had shattered all my previous understanding of this land I once called home. It was a terrifying place, to put it mildly. But what mystified me the most was the palpable, absolute fearlessness that pervaded the air. People had developed a complete disconnect with the fear of dying, not just in the stadium but everywhere in Pakistan. They had embraced death as a way of life 'Wali, we have to take this guy to the nearest hospital.' It seemed like the only course of action to take. Where the hell was Pir Pul Siraat? When was he going to show up, if ever, and pull me out of this nightmare?

Wali didn't say a word as we walked to the car. My shoulder ached under the weight of Afro-kid and I needed to set him down soon.

'Sirji, we should have left him behind in the hands of Allah,' Wali said.

'Shut the fuck up!' I screamed at him. I was sick of all this shit: that freaky game of cricket, lunatics wearing Martyr vests like they were the latest fashion trend from Paris and most of all, I was sick of this asshole Wali. I was furious with myself to be in this impossibly insane place. Was I really on some Path to High Knowledge? Or was I just plain high?

Spreading its tentacles, a deep doubt entangled my brain. Whatever happened to my mysterious mission, details of which were supposed to be revealed to me at the proper time? So far I had been a rousing example of failure. And now I would have to deal with this complete loser until we got home.

'You're taking me to the nearest hospital. You got that?' I roared, slapping Wali's back with my hand.

'Sirji, who told you to pick him up in the first place?'

'Allah!'

'That tells me that you really don't trust Him, sirji.'

'Are you crazy?' I was gritting my teeth. 'How can you say that?' It was impossible to explain anything to him.

'Because you didn't trust Him enough to take care of this boy without any interference from you,' Wali said, taking long, hurried strides toward the car.

'He needs stitches and a CT scan of his head,' I stopped next to the car. My throat was parched and felt like sandpaper; I was horribly dehydrated.

'Wali, can you just get me some water?' I asked, feeling the weight of Afro-boy on my shoulder. I couldn't wait to put him down.

'Water's hard to get these days, sirji, as I've explained already.' He opened the rear door of the car.

I laid Afro-boy on the rear seat and shut the door.

'You mean you can't even get bottled water?' I asked.

'Oh, the Paradise Water is in short supply as well because the demand is so high, sirji,' Wali said.

'What about some sodas, cola, whatever. Right now almost anything will do.'

'Sirji, we've only got one kind of cola, Hoor Afza. It's nothing like the Rooh Afza we used to get in the old days, but it does have its own unique flavour and effect.'

'Would you please get me one? And keep a tab on the money you're spending. I'll ask Abba to pay you back once we get home.' Having to ask for money from this asshole must be a test of some kind. I was seething inside.

'Sirji, money is just a piece of paper. Don't worry about it,' Wali said, shaking his head. 'Although I wouldn't waste my money on a bottle of Hoor Afza. I always carry water with me in the car,' Wali said. 'You can have some from my bottle.'

He opened the rear trunk, revealing a pair of gas cylinders lying side-by-side. They took up most of the trunk except for a foot of space in the middle. They had begun to rust and looked really old. One of the tanks had 'Allah' painted along its side in red and the other had the word 'Akbar' in yellow. Wali stuck his hand between the tanks and pulled out a bottle half filled with water. The label read 'Paradise Water, Khalifa Inc.'

'Big tanks you've got in there, Wali?' I asked, taking a swig from the bottle. At the sight of these massive tanks my anger dissipated like mist at sunrise. The water had a strange metallic taste and smelled of diesel.

'Yes, you're looking at a pair of custom-made martyr tanks, sirji,' Wali said, beaming with pride. 'Those silly vests are for kids who just wear them to show off.'

'Martyr tanks?' The feeling of alarm returned as I took another swig from the bottle.

'Relax sirji. They're just CNG tanks,' he said, staring at me amusingly.

'Oh, compressed natural gas,' I said, exhaling a sigh of relief. CNG had been used as a kind of car fuel for ages in this part of the world.

'Sirji, there's a two-month waiting period to have your car fitted with these rockets to heaven.'

'Rockets to heaven?' I asked. Clearly I had missed something.

'I'll show you. Come,' he said excitedly as he opened the driver's door and pointed.

'See these two buttons?' he asked, touching two red ones located next to the headlight knob. One was inscribed with 'Allah' and the other with 'Akbar'. 'Press these two together at the same time and you're gone, sirji.' He snapped his fingers. 'Vapourized! The West may be advanced in technology—but we know the secret of a direct flight to man's eternal dream: Paradise.'

'A two-month waiting period!' In a flash I realized the logic of having an additional trunk on each car's roof. They needed the trunk for the CNG tanks and a two-month waiting period meant that most of them were fitted with martyr tanks.

'Sirji, the man who designed these special modifications is a superb mechanic,' Wali explained with great admiration.

'You can be one hundred per cent sure that if you hit a pothole or bump into another car, or even get into a serious accident, the device won't blow,' he assured me. 'You must press both buttons together for five seconds to get the desired effect and begin your journey to Al-Jannah.'

'Great security feature, for sure but you can explain the rest while we drive? We have to move. This guy's going to die if we don't get him to the hospital soon.'

I took my seat in the rear next to Afro-boy who was mumbling something, his head pressed against the window and his knees rammed up against the back of the front seat. Wali started the engine.

'Don't worry, we're taking you to the hospital,' I said, placing my hand on his shoulder.

Wali gave me a glaring look and I had no choice but to stare back. Obviously he wasn't pleased at the prospect of having to take a detour just to help a stranger. As he put the car into gear, I spotted Tarzan sprinting out of the stadium's gate, a burlap sack bouncing up and down on his shoulder. He halted for a second and looked around, as if deciding which direction to take off in.

'Tarzan!' I yelled, getting out of the car and waving at him. I wasn't sure if he had seen us.

As soon as he spotted me, he started running toward the car. Two other men in white robes were chasing him. Tarzan darted across the tarmac like a gazelle. Transfixed, I stepped away from the open car door. He tossed the sack into the back seat then jumped into the front seat next to Wali. I climbed back in next to Afro-boy and pulled the door shut.

'Wali, let's go.' I shouted. 'Come on. Go, go, go!'

Wali grabbed his head with his hands for a moment and then we were speeding down the road out of the stadium. I looked out of the rear window and saw the white-robed guys piling into a blue pickup truck.

'Sirji, if you keep picking up whoever crosses your path, we'll never get to Faisal Town.'

'How far is the nearest hospital?'

'Sir, the nearest one is KUH.' Tarzan answered as Wali turned onto the main road. There was a bridge about half-a-mile up ahead.

'Khidamat-e-Ummah Hospital, sirji,' Wali said.

'It used be Services Hospital, sir,' Tarzan jumped in.

'Why are we going that far?' I asked. 'What about all the private hospitals around Fortress Stadium?'

'Sirji, they've all been shut down,' Wali replied.

'Why?'

'Because there were no doctors to run them. They've all left,' Tarzan replied.

'Where'd they go?'

'Some ran away to foreign countries,' Tarzan said bitterly. 'And some—'

'Went to next world,' Wali interjected.

'Sir, you can drop me once we're out of here' Tarzan said. He was trying to look relaxed, but his eyes kept darting back and forth between the mumbling Afro-boy and the rearview mirror.

11

THERE WASN'T MUCH TRAFFIC ON THE ROAD when we
left the stadium. But like a bad case of acne, the road
was pocked with craters of all sizes and shapes. Wali drove
expertly, cutting a sharp turn every few seconds to avoid the
potholes from ripping the undercarriage of the car. It was hard
to sit still. I was thrown around in the back seat as my head
slammed against the door every time Wali jerked the wheel. As
seen from the Mian Mir Bridge, the city of Lahore was steeped
in a murky darkness.

We passed a rickshaw with a CNG tank the size of an oil
barrel bolted to its back bumper. I noticed Wali veered to the
right, giving the rickshaw a wide berth. We were heading down
the bridge when he glanced in the rear-view mirror and cursed
under his breath.

'We're being followed,' Wali muttered.

I looked behind us and saw a pair of headlights tailgating us.
By the time we crossed the bridge, the blue Mazda pickup was
right next to us on Wali's side of the car. The guy in the passenger
seat rolled his window down and started thrashing his arm up
and down, yelling at us to pull over.

'Tarzan, who are these guys?' I demanded, my heartbeat
speeding up. 'What do they want?'

Before Tarzan could speak, Wali started yelling as he bore down on the wheel and floored the engine. The car kept ahead of the pickup truck.

'I told you sirji,' he bellowed, his face red with anger. 'You don't just pick up people you don't know!'

'Everything happens because Allah wills it to, remember?' I said, bristling with pride when I saw him glaring at me in the rear-view mirror. He opened his mouth to let me have it but then decided not to. I was quickly picking up on the lingo and how to counter Wali's infuriating flood of religious mantras. I wasn't sure if I had won this round, or if he would just rip me a new one once we got home, or worse, report the whole incident to his master, my father.

Tarzan's eyes darted back at the pickup while he dug through in his burlap sack. I grudgingly admired Wali's driving skills. He masterfully avoided most of the holes and bumps without slowing down and we left the blue pickup a good hundred metres or so behind.

'What's going on, Tarzan?' I asked.

Afro-boy began to moan. The dark swelling over his eye looked like it was about to burst.

'Sir, all I can say is that if you stop the car, we're all in very deep shit,' Tarzan replied, taking what looked like a can of soda out of his sack.

'Sirji, you've been away too long,' Wali growled over his shoulder. 'This country is a powder keg. You touch anything here and it blows up.'

'Sir, please tell him not to stop,' Tarzan pleaded, gripping my arm so hard I cried out. 'That pickup is fitted with a portable hand-chopper,' he continued. 'They won't only chop my hand off, but all of yours as well. Right here on the spot.'

'Wali, is he telling the truth?' I gasped, feeling like I needed a breath of fresh air.

'Sirji, yes,' Wali explained as he swerved sharp to avoid the pickup. They had overtaken us again and the driver was trying to run us off the road.

'Sir, many of my friends are missing one of their hands or feet,' Tarzan explained, dousing all hope that maybe, just this once, the bizarre reference was simply a harmless trope.

I looked away and shut my eyes, thinking I was going to vomit. The kid had talked about a hand being chopped off like it was no big deal. Just like getting your ear pierced.

'And what do they do with the hands and feet they've chopped off?' I asked, regaining my composure but still feeling nauseous. 'What about the pain later, what about any infections?'

The pickup had fallen behind now but was gaining on us again.

'Sirji, they take the parts as proof,' Wali said, looking in his rear-view mirror 'The more chopping you do, the greater the commission you make.'

'Before they drive off and leave you standing wherever they found you, they hand you a roll of dressing, a bottle of Panadol Extra and a bunch of penicillin capsules,' Tarzan said.

'Khalifaji says, "Show kindness even to the criminals, once the punishment prescribed by Allah has been administered",' Wali said. 'Islam, sirji, is all about kindness and caring for one another.'

Just then the pickup pulled alongside us again and Wali let out a string of curse words through his gritted teeth.

'Wali, what are we going to do?' I yelled. 'Should we stop? They're going to run us off the road if we don't.' Just as I completed the sentence, the pickup rammed us against the median.

'Let me think for a minute, sirji,' Wali replied, slowing down the car. 'Remember, we haven't stolen anything, so we don't deserve a hand-chopping.'

'Well, that's a relief.'

Sensing Wali's intention, Tarzan lowered his window. The cool air hit my face and it was exactly what I needed, except that it stank like hell; somewhere between an abandoned chemical dump and an *abattoir* on a really hot day.

The pickup, now only a few inches from the car, was ready to ram us again. All its windows were down and I could see the barrel of a revolver next to a chubby-cheeked and bearded face staring at me, bug-eyed from the back seat. It seemed like Wali had no choice but to pull over.

But then something happened that nobody saw coming. Tarzan twisted the top on the canister he had pulled out of his sack and lobbed it into the open window of the pickup. The thing blew up just as it fell through the pickup's window. Smoke filled its cabin instantly and the car swerved out of control and away from us, its tires screeching. The truck hit the median and its front wheels slammed into a huge pothole with a loud bang as the impact popped one of the tires. The force knocked the truck off the median and it rolled end-over-end, landing on its roof in the middle of the road.

Wali slammed his foot on the gas pedal and I was thrown into the side door.

'What the hell was that?' I screamed. 'Tarzan! Are you out of your fucking mind?' I was starting to hyperventilate as I stared at Wali in panic. 'Wali, what the hell are we going to do?'

'I really don't know, sirji,' he said, now perfectly calm and tooling along like we were on our way to a picnic. 'I guess we'll do what Allah wants us to.'

'Well, in that case, we all know that Allah has already commanded me to take this injured man to the hospital,' I said, as wind from the open window whipped through my hair. I glared at Tarzan.

'What was that for?' I asked, looking into his eyes. 'Who were those guys? And dude, from now on, no more surprises that go boom. Deal?'

'Those men were Commaqaadis,' Tarzan said. 'They're the only ones who drive those blue Mazda pickups.'

'Commaqaadis?' I said. 'You mean the cops?'

'Sort of, sirji,' Wali chimed in. 'A commaqaadi is half-commando and half-qaadi. Swift action. Swift justice. Right on the spot.'

'Tarzan, why were they chasing you?' I finally asked, giving him a piercing glare.

'Because they think I've got something they want,' he answered with a sly smile.

'What do they think you've got, and why do they think it?' I inquired, wondering if I would get a straight answer or just some hustle, religious or otherwise.

'I have a whole bunch of things.' Tarzan said, flashing me a smile that was anything but innocent. 'It's hard to say which one they're after.'

'What's in the sack besides explosives?'

'Items of loot, what else?' Wali answered, swinging left onto Canal Road.

The moon perched low in the sky above the Green Tomb Mosque. Lit by concealed floodlights, the luminous green dome looked like it was floating in midair. Suddenly I was hit by the stench of rotten flesh.

'Would you roll the window up?' Again I felt like I was going to puke.

Tarzan did as I asked, but still hadn't answered a single one of my questions.

'The smell is from the water in the canal,' Wali said.

'Tarzan, I asked you a question.' The kid just stared out the window. 'Hey! I'm talking to you, Tarzan.'

'Raw material,' he replied, turning to look at me with a puzzled look on his face like he had no idea why I was making such a big deal out of it.

'What raw material?'

'Shoes,' he replied.

'And where'd you get all these shoes?'

This joker wasn't telling me the whole truth and I was regretting bringing him on board miles ago. When I was exhausted and irritable, like now, I could be a real son of a bitch if I felt like I was being played, and right now I did.

'Wherever I can find them,' he muttered. 'You can collect a lot of shoes at a scene right after a blast.'

Afro-boy was now awake. Keeping his palm over his swollen eye, he moaned incessantly.

I was beginning to understand the nature of Tarzan's profession. He was a scavenger. I could see him in my mind's eye sprinting through the area of a blast with his burlap sack over his shoulder, pilfering bodies of the dead and injured for their valuables. It was hard to believe that somebody like him would limit themselves to stealing shoes only.

'So what else did you collect tonight besides the shoes?'

'Nothing in particular, you know, the usual items,' Tarzan said absently, glancing at Afro-kid. 'What's the story with this guy? How did he end up in your car?'

Before I could open my mouth to reply, Wali interrupted. 'Sirji is from America. He believes it's his duty to solve everybody's problems.'

'Oh Wali, shut up,' I snapped. 'Keep your eyes on the road and drive.'

I knew I was being rude to him but I no longer cared. He had crossed the line with me so many times already that I had lost count.

The image of a smoke-filled pickup doing a somersault through the air kept flashing through my mind as we sped down Canal Road towards Jail Road. I wanted to ask Wali to stop the car and leave Tarzan and his burlap sack along the roadside. But I let it go. Maybe I was scared of him. Maybe I had begun to secretly admire him. What he did to the pickup truck with his smoke bomb had in fact been quite impressive. We turned right onto Jail Road and headed toward the former Services Hospital. I had seen more traffic in this area, but now at 10.30 p.m. the place looked like a ghost town. Plunged into the dark, the buildings with their indistinct outlines looked like abandoned ruins. Our heads banged against the roof again as Wali hit a pothole.

'Wali, what happened to all the traffic and the people? This place used to be buzzing with life, even late at night.' I asked, chilled to the bone with the bizarre changes that had come over this place since the last time I was here—some twelve years ago. I supposed it was a rhetorical question because I already knew the answer. I had seen it all on the news as the chaos here in Pakistan replayed itself over and over again. And my few hours here confirmed it all in gory detail.

A decade ago the country was not yet as isolated from the rest of the world as it was destined to become. The process was gradual, but irreversible. Lahore had seen a succession of bloody riots that cost hundreds of thousands their lives. It had all started out as Jihad against the corrupt elite and the speed at which the riots engulfed the city had taken everyone by surprise.

From Lahore they spread to the rest of the country like wildfire. Horrific scenes of carnage were seen everywhere; whole neighbourhoods had been massacred by mobs armed with everything from Kalashnikovs to farm tools and kitchen knives. Homes, state buildings and marketplaces were torched and looted. The people had wanted Islam. They wanted Sharia and they were duly obliged when the terror master of Hindu Kush, the Khalifa, descended from his mountain perch and took over the country without facing any resistance.

The poor, the destitute and the disenfranchised—they became the new powerful elite as the Sunni revolution spread and eventually devoured the whole country. Armed gangs of bearded young men wearing Arab-style robes invaded the affluent neighbourhoods of Lahore.

A mass grave, dug for the Defense Housing Society—the rich and educated were seen as slaves of America—was said to contain more than five thousand heads. The beheading ceremony took place on the sprawling golf course of the Lahore Gymkhana club. The headless corpses were burnt at the site but the heads were staked on spears and paraded to DHS as a spectacle for the adoring masses who cheered along the roadside while impromptu stalls sprang up selling food and souvenirs.

There were similar mass graves in many areas of Lahore and other cities. The wealthy, and anyone who had the means and a place to go, left the country. The masses swarmed into upscale neighbourhoods and made in abandoned houses and storefronts their homes. Others set up permanent camps where they torched the spoils of looted museums in great bonfires which burnt for weeks. In the subsequent months and years that followed the riots, there had been a complete reordering of society.

'Sirji, people just went mad. The lava burning deep in their souls finally found its way to the surface,' Wali said with a sigh.

Something monstrous had happened here; something far worse than anything televised on the daily news around the globe. Like some unearthly tsunami, it had washed through Pakistan until everything in its path had been obliterated, leaving only devastation in its wake.

'What happened to the water, Wali?' I asked. 'I had no idea the situation was so dire.'

'Some believe it was the water that made people behave like rabid dogs,' Wali said, his voice strange and hollow. 'If it weren't for Islam and our Khalifaji, everyone would've died. Only Khalifaji could guarantee peace and security, sirji.'

I remained quiet. Wali slowed the car down and pulled into the emergency room parking lot of Khidamat-e-Ummah Hospital. I held Afro-kid by his shoulder and helped him out of the car and up the stairs to the emergency room. Tarzan followed me, his sack still slung over his shoulder while Wali stayed with the car.

'What's your name?' I asked the injured kid.

'Omar Sharif.' He stared at me with his good eye, and then

began sobbing. He was wobbly on his feet and we had to help him walk.

The power was out in the hospital and its vicinity and only a few gas lamps and battery torches lit the way. As we climbed the steps, my eyes fell on a glowing sign painted on the glass entrance door: *Death Visits at its Appointed Hour*. I pushed the door open and staggered in with Afro-kid leaning against me as Tarzan followed us.

'Tarzan, you probably should have waited with Wali.' I said as we stepped into the entrance hall.

'I need to use the toilet,' he said, adjusting his sack over his shoulder.

'Well, if I don't see you again, good luck.' I was hoping he would get the hint and just disappear after he was done with his business.

'Same here, sir,' he said. 'If you ever need my help in any matter, you can count on me.'

'Appreciated, thanks,' I said, not fathoming what this guy could possibly do to help me short of landing me in jail awaiting execution. But as they say, it is the thought that counts. All I wanted to do was finish with the hospital and get on with my life, whose purpose had been all but shattered by the events of the last few hours. I wanted nothing more than to crash in a bed and sleep until this nightmarish journey of mine was over.

Tarzan walked toward the rear of the building and disappeared down a dark hallway.

Afro-kid tried to walk normally but I had to steer him in the right direction. I wanted him to be registered as a patient, hand him over to the staff on duty and get the hell out of there.

We entered the waiting area, my arm still around the kid's shoulder. The place was lit by half-a-dozen candles and smelled of sweat and wax. A group of fully veiled women sat in a corner, indistinguishable from their shadows on the walls. After easing the kid into a chair, I went to the reception desk.

A pair of large candles were placed on either side of a bulky old-fashioned computer monitor, and I stifled a smile. A hand-written note was stuck to the side of the monitor and said everyone was on break for namaaz of *ishaa*, the last and the longest of the five daily prayers.

I heard a soft rustle of skirts as a figure in black materialized out of the darkness and glided toward the desk.

'We've got a possible concussion here,' I told her, pointing to my slumped companion. 'He's got a black-eye, a gash on his right brow the size of my finger and it'll definitely need stitches.' Then I blurted, 'It's urgent!'

'Can't be more urgent than preparing for the next world,' the figure replied in a soft, sweet voice. Through a two-inch wide slit in her veil, her big, black eyes, expertly outlined with kohl, shone like lamps in the darkness. Suddenly the room felt stiflingly hot and I was hit by a powerful déjà vu. It was as if I had known those eyes all my life.

'Please! This guy needs a doctor to be see him right away,' I pleaded, trying to think why she looked so familiar.

'Haste is from the Devil, brother.' I imagined her smile behind that veil, picturing her teeth, her lips. I had no doubt in my mind that she was beautiful.

'How long before you start seeing patients again?' I asked, trying to keep my temper in check.

'Whenever the doctor returns. He's saying his ishaa prayer.'

'Oh good, it shouldn't take that long then?' I said, thinking it was getting rather late for the prayer of ishaa—even if one said all seventeen *rakaat*.

'Doctor sahib will be free after he completes his lecture,' she said.

'Lecture on what?' And for whom I wondered, having seen no one here besides this solitary enigmatic woman and the three silent figures huddled in the corner.

'Doctor Tariq is a great scholar,' she said, raising her hand as though she were introducing him at a podium. 'He is writing a very important book on the principles and practice of Islamic medicine for the Ummah, the Muslim world.'

'Sister, my name is Ismael,' I said slowly through clenched teeth and locking her eyes with my own. 'I'm here with a patient. He's a boy of about twenty and needs medical attention,' I continued, dragging it out so she would see that I was neither playing, nor impressed with that holier than thou veil of hers.

'His cut needs stitches,' I repeated, while she just stared unblinkingly at me. 'Now, sister, can I entrust him to your care or not?' I allowed my irritation and sarcasm to flow unfiltered into the conversation. 'I mean after getting him registered and all?' I added. 'Would you be so kind as to ask the doctor to see him whenever he's available for the affairs of this world?'

'Where's the patient?' she asked, her eyes sweeping the room.

'The one with the white headband,' I answered, pointing to him out. 'You know, the only male in the room besides me?'

'Do you live abroad?' she demanded.

'Landed this evening, yes,' I said. 'Why?'

'America?'

'New York.'

'Same thing,' she said. She was in a mood to tease me but I was in no mood to take it.

'Actually, it's not,' I countered and wondered why I was adding to this ridiculous chatter.

'Why not?' she asked, blinking a few times as if I had startled her with some miraculous revelation.

'Because New York isn't the America you seem to have in mind.'

She started at me unblinkingly and at last said, 'Bring the patient over. I'll register him. Meanwhile, you go and buy these items from across the road.'

She handed me a photocopy of an invoice from some Shafaa Medical Store. I took the piece of paper from her and looked at it. The price of each item to be purchased was blacked out, as was the total billed amount. Staring at the list, I felt an imminent meltdown coming on. I was completely baffled and she obviously read that on my face.

'Without these items we won't be able to treat him,' she explained quite seriously, all sense of teasing vanishing from her voice. 'The hospital doesn't carry any of these things and all patients have to buy their own supplies.'

'All right, I'll be back soon,' I said. Leaving Afro-kid sitting on the chair, I left the emergency room and made my way back to the car where I found Wali smoking a beeri. The broad smile on his face when he didn't see Afro-kid vanished when I handed him the invoice.

'Not again!' he said, shaking his head. 'Sirji, the deal was to get him to the hospital.'

'Wali, I need to borrow some more money. Expect a large tip when we get home.'

'Credit is the scissor that cuts the thread of friendship,' Wali warned gravely.

I remained quiet. My mind was a jumbled mess of thoughts and images, none of which would make any sense in the world I belonged to, but which seemed perfectly normal in this nut-house of a country.

'Okay sir, how much do you need?' I heard Tarzan's voice over my shoulder. I jumped, startled to find him standing behind me.

It cost 15,000 Dirhams for every item on the list. Tarzan accompanied me to Shafaa Medical Store and paid for everything without batting an eye. The way he laid down the cash, you would have thought it was just pocket change.

The haul of medical supplies included a couple of packs of sterilized non-absorbable silk, syringes, a 50-ml vial of Novocain, a 4-oz bottle of antiseptic solution, a roll of cotton, a box of

2x2 gauze pads, one roll of 4-inch dressing gauze, a tube of an antibiotic cream and a vial of something for tetanus. In addition, I even grabbed a couple of bottles of Hoor Afza.

'Good luck with that,' Tarzan said with a snort and his eyes glued to the bottles of Hoor Afza.

'I shouldn't have bought them?' I asked, feeling confused.

'Sir, I think you can handle it,' he said with a wink, heightening the mystery surrounding the innocuous-seeming beverage.

Outside the store, Tarzan stuck his hand in his pocket. He pulled out several 1000-Dirham notes and shoved them in my hand.

'Sir, keep this,' he said with a smile and a reassuring nod. 'You'll need it.'

'I'm not taking your money, Tarzan,' I replied, trying to stuff the bills back into his pocket.

'No, really sir, it's okay.'

'But I'm not sure if or when I can pay you back.'

'Consider it a gift from a friend,' he said, clasping my shoulder and giving it a friendly shake.

'No, Tarzan, it's okay, really,' I protested, feeling awkward and embarrassed by my predicament. 'I very much appreciate your kindness.'

'Sir, take it as a loan if you must,' he insisted, shoving the notes back into my hand.

'Well, I will pay you back, Tarzan. You can be sure of that,' I said, reluctantly taking the cash from him. 'Thank you.' My stomach felt queasy at the thought of this unexpected financial entanglement with a person who'd just causally blown up a police truck.

As I returned to the emergency room with the brown paper bag filled with supplies, the power came back on. A white fluorescent light painted everything with a sterile glow that burnt my eyes. Afro-kid was no longer slumped in the waiting area and the trio of nondescript women was gone as well.

So was the mystery that had permeated the place: the swaying shadows on the walls, the murky darkness where anything could have been lurking, even the hypnotic eyes of the receptionist. The glaring light had transformed her into just another professional woman seated at her post doing her very mundane job.

At that moment she was trying to reboot her computer while talking to an elderly woman seated on a stool next to her desk. When she saw me enter the room, bag in hand, she gestured for me to take a seat.

She struggled with her computer for a good five minutes, and then another ten, while the elderly patient sat waiting to register. I had no recourse but to sit uncomplainingly and wait for her to call me.

When it was my turn, I walked up and put the bag of supplies on her desk. Then I dropped a couple of 1000-Dirham notes into the bag, making sure she saw me do it.

'Please make sure he's well cared for,' I told her, forcing a smile. More and more, my jet-lagged body longed for a place to sleep.

'I certainly will.'

'What's your name?' As I said these words, I was struck by the idea that it might be a grievous offence these days to ask a strange woman her name.

'Laila.'

'You know what that means?'

'Darkness,' she replied.

'Night,' I corrected her with a smile.

'Same thing.'

'No, not at all,' I shook my head, puzzled by her apparent obliviousness to the poetic beauty surrounding her name.

'Why not?'

'Night is not darkness.' I longed to see her face.

'Do you want to see my face?' she asked softly, as if reading my mind.

The question sent an icy wave up my spine. She locked her magnificent eyes on mine for several seconds before lowering them. Something warm and energetic filled my whole body.

'Maybe one day,' I said, trying to compose myself, not knowing what else to say, what else was permissible.

'Or maybe one dark night,' she said, again looking straight into my eyes and releasing a tinkle of soft, intoxicating laughter.

'We'll see,' I said, turning on my heel and hurrying out of the room without looking back, my whole being aflame with desire.

12

THE POWER WENT OUT AGAIN as I raced down the steps of the emergency room, savouring the thought of having the entire backseat of the car to myself. Once outside the hospital gate, I looked for the car but there was no sign of it or Wali. I just stood there, shaking my head, staring at the empty spot where the car had been.

What now? I wondered aloud.

Jail Road was deserted except for a pair of flashing red lights in the distance which moved closer as I stood there. Then I heard Tarzan's voice, filled with panic.

'Sir, over here!' he shouted from the darkness.

As soon as I saw him, he sprinted up the steps of the emergency room.

'Come on!' he screamed. 'Follow me!'

'Tarzan, where's Wali?' I demanded, running to catch up with him. The sense of impending doom had returned and was forcing its way through the fatigue. 'What the hell's going on now?'

We took the steps three at a time and Tarzan flung open the door for the hospital. Once inside, Tarzan stopped to catch his breath. He peeked out the glass doors as if he was hiding from someone.

Two blue pickups, red lights flashing and sirens rupturing the silence, zoomed through the gate and screeched to halt in front of the stairs. Their headlights swept the steps we had just vacated and I saw the doors flying open.

'Come on,' Tarzan panted. He started running again and there was nothing to do but follow him.

'Tarzan, wait! Please! You've got to tell me what's going on,' I begged, scrambling down the empty hall, like we were tethered by a leash. 'Where the fuck is Wali?'

'You've just got to trust me right now. There's no time to explain,' he yelled over his shoulder as he ran toward the rear of the building.

'Do I have a choice?' I screamed, my fear and anger rising to a new high.

'Not if you want to see the sunrise in one piece,' he snapped.

We barrelled down dark deserted hallways, made a couple of turns and then reached what looked like a dead end. Tarzan turned on his flashlight and I saw that the dead end was really a huge pile of junked hospital furniture stacked from the floor to the ceiling. Tarzan scrambled over rusted metal cabinets and disappeared into what looked like a closet while I was left standing in complete darkness.

'Would you talk to me for heaven's sake?' I demanded, leaping onto the pile and feeling it rock precariously beneath my greater weight. Staring into the closet I could now see Tarzan standing on the other side of the heap, his flashlight illuminating the passage.

'Where are we going?' I asked slowly, dragging out each word so the kid knew I was serious.

'Faisal Town,' he said from the other side. 'Don't stop, just keep going. You've got to crawl a few feet at the end.'

I inched along on my hands and knees through what seemed like a tunnel. It was like some twisted rabbit hole and I was definitely following a Mad Hatter.

By the time I emerged, I was completely covered in a fine dust that I half expected to have magical properties.

We stood next to a door. Tarzan had his sack with him again and I couldn't imagine where he had stowed it until now.

'Tarzan, how did you find this place?' I marvelled at this wild hideout he seemed to have discovered. He had obviously scoped this place out before.

'I smelled it,' he said, pushing the door open.

That sounded really weird, but I decided to drop it because he clearly wasn't in a talkative mood.

We stepped into what looked like a large public restroom that had been out of commission for months. The place stunk of pot, like somebody had been smoking a joint just a minute before. Tarzan threw his sack on the floor and pulled out an old brown leather briefcase.

'Tarzan, if you're not going to tell me what the hell's going on, I'm leaving,' I said, sounding lame even to myself. 'Please, just tell me where Wali is. I'm tired, man!'

He didn't answer. Instead, he handed me his LED penlight.

'I need some light here,' he instructed. He took out a roll of red adhesive tape and a cigar-sized green tube from the sack. He positioned the tube over the number lock of the briefcase, taped it down, and then pulled a lighter out of his pocket.

'I hate these number locks,' he muttered, bringing the flame to a shoelace dangling from one end of the tube. 'Go!' he suddenly shouted, shoving me hard toward the door.

I leapt through and Tarzan followed, slamming it behind us. He started counting. When he reached seven, a muffled blast shook the door. Tarzan pushed it open and we stepped back into the bathroom. The place was filled with billowing acrid smoke. As Tarzan took the penlight from me, I almost fell over when he pointed the beam of light at the floor. Bundles of 1000-Dirham notes were scattered all over the filthy broken tiles. The briefcase, minimally damaged though, still contained the bulk of money stacked in neat rows. No more than a handful of bills appeared to have been burnt.

I stood speechless as Tarzan gathered up the money from the floor and carefully tucked it back into the briefcase. I sighed in frustration, wishing this whole thing to be just some jet lag-induced hallucination that would soon be over.

Reaching down to give him a hand, I saw a palm-sized black leather-bound book lying under the sink. I picked it up and brought it closer to the light. Flipping through its pages I saw they were all blank and looked like some sort of graph paper for high-school maths with a dozen boxes to a page. The book consisted of thirty numbered pages.

'Keep this,' Tarzan said, tossing me a wad of Dirhams and tucking a couple of bundles into his robe.

'I'm not taking any of that,' I tossed the money back into the briefcase. I had no intention of risking life and limb for petty theft.

'What's in your hand?' he asked, clicking the briefcase shut. Except for its blown handle, it was undamaged. My admiration for Tarzan's expertise climbed a notch and I wondered where he had gotten his education in these matters.

'Just a book of blank pages, looks like some kind of graph paper,' I answered.

'Do you think it was in the briefcase?' he asked, stuffing the briefcase back into his sack.

'I don't know, maybe,' I said, smelling the book for gunpowder. 'It was just lying over there under the sink.'

'It's not safe to pick up stuff that's lying around,' he said. 'Let's get out of here now. Wali's waiting for us.'

Tarzan put his sack on the floor and climbed onto the seat of a toilet, holding his penlight between his teeth. Sliding his hands up the wall, he grasped the sill of a large black window overhead. He released the latch and pale moonlight flooded through the open window. Sticking the penlight back in his pocket, he grabbed the sill, hoisted himself up and swung a leg through the window. He sat there straddling the opening and stared down at me.

'Sir, would you please hand me my bag?' he asked.

'Okay, but where's Wali waiting for us?' I demanded. 'Just tell me what the fuck is going on.'

'You'll get your answers as soon as we're out of here,' he replied.

'How the hell am I supposed to climb up?' I said, hoisting his sack over my head and shoving it into his hands.

'You can do it, sir—it's not that hard,' he replied and then disappeared. My heart simply sank. I couldn't cope with the thought of getting trapped in some abandoned restroom-slash-drug den.

I had to admit though, I was curious about that book. Its blank pages had to mean something. It clearly didn't look like an ordinary diary or notebook. Whatever it was, I wanted it and decided to keep it. If I survived this long strange night, I would figure out something to do with it.

Holding the book in one hand, I climbed onto the seat of the toilet and looked up. It would take both hands to pull myself up. I decided I would lay the book on top of the water tank up on the wall, and once I climbed up the windowsill I could lower myself a bit and retrieve the book without any problem. What I didn't see, however, was that the lid of the tank was missing and the book fell right in with a soft thud.

Shit! It must have been ruined.

Standing on my toes, I put my hand into the tank and sighed with relief. There was no water in there and the book was safely resting at its dry bottom.

I made it to the windowsill on my third try. With considerable effort I was able to drag myself through the opening and straddle the sill the way Tarzan had done. I reached down and tried to grab the book, but the tank was out of reach and I couldn't risk losing my balance. I had no choice but to let the book go.

I jumped down—we were about five or six feet from the ground—and landed on a soft patch of grass.

'Nice going, sir! See, it wasn't so hard,' Tarzan teased, slapping me on the back. 'Now, let's get out of here.'

We walked over to the hospital's boundary wall with Tarzan leading the way as we crawled through a crack in the crumbling masonry. Outside the wall, we turned onto a road lined with gated houses on both sides.

'We're right in the rear of Shadmaan Market,' Tarzan said. 'Wali's parked at the end of the street.'

'How did you get him to move his car over there?' I asked, thinking of Wali's Teflon-like character, his imperviousness to any earthly persuasion.

'He's a tough nut to crack, that's for sure!' said Tarzan.

'What did you say to him then?'

'Nothing—I just had to take over his mind.'

His answer made me stop in my tracks.

'How do you take over someone's mind?' I asked.

'We'll talk about it some other time, sir,' he replied as he stopped walking and turned to face me. His eyes looked unusually bright in the darkness.

'Where the hell did you learn all this stuff?'

'Jinns,' he answered casually.

Now he was pulling my leg. It was impossible to get a straight answer out of him—that much I knew. I gave up and resumed walking.

'You're a rich man now,' I said, as we walked toward the Shadmaan Road. 'You don't have to sell papads anymore, or plant explosives in the stadium. Take a vacation or something.'

'It's not my money! I have to deliver it to my boss.'

'Oh, I thought you were self-employed,' I said. 'What about the bundles you stashed inside your own pocket? Won't he find out?'

'That's my commission,' Tarzan said with a toss of his head and a chuckle. 'Pir Pul Siraat doesn't care too much about money matters.'

The name, Pir Pul Siraat, stuck me like a bolt of lightning. Whatever was left of my sanity had now blown into pieces. Bending forward I rested my palms against my knees lest I passed out.

'Sir, are you okay?'

It took me a while before I regained my bearings.

'What? What did you just say?' I stammered, feeling as if I were waking from a dream.

Tarzan looked at me all puzzled.

'Pir Pul Siraat is your boss?' I stood back up. 'This is fucking crazy!'

'Yes, he is the Man, the head of the Resistance Movement, and he's waiting for us,' he said, turning my budding understanding of him on its head.

'Waiting where?' I asked. So this is how I was supposed to be contacted once I landed. *You'll be contacted once you arrive in Lahore.* The whole thing was impossible to accept, way beyond what my analytical mind could grasp.

'Shah Jamal,' he said, his face lit with pride.

'And what's this resistance movement all about? Resistance against whom?' I asked, feeling the return of the alarm that had dogged my Path to High Knowledge ever since landing here an eternity ago and fearing his answer.

'Against the Khalifa.'

Holy crap! This new revelation left me speechless; I realized I was a pawn in the hands of players I knew nothing about. I had so many questions that I didn't even know where to begin.

So if Pir had been the head of the resistance movement against the Khalifa, then Abba had to be connected to the latter in some important way. *Please know that regaining your father's trust is the path to success of our mission, a mission whose details will*

only be revealed to you when you are prepared to take action.
Suddenly, Abba, whom I had genuinely wanted to patch up with
after my Ayahuasca experience, seemed more ominous than my
childhood memories of him, which were all but terrifying. I
remembered the brutal campaign he had led against the hapless
Kalash tribe of Kafiristan for not only gaining popularity and
fame but also the choicest berth in Paradise.

Indeed, the price to gain direct knowledge of Paradise and Hell
was turning out to be way too steep for a mere mortal like me.
Shivering with a mixture of terror and excitement, I braced for
more disasters on the Path to High Knowledge I was supposedly
treading at the moment.

The excitement and curiosity of meeting with Pir Pul Siraat
had taken the edge off my fatigue, but now I was thirsty as hell.
My throat stung as if it was lined with sandpaper. Remembering
the two bottles of Hoor Afza lying on the backseat of the car, I
quickened my pace, my mind desperately trying to make sense of
things. All I was certain of was the fact that I had failed miserably
in each of the tests on every step of the way.

The power was still out in the area. Submerged in darkness,
the houses looked like they had been abandoned for years. The
howls of numerous cats pierced through the silence, growing
louder as they were joined by more of their clowder to go about
their nocturnal rounds. An eerie glow from a crescent moon
overhead bathed the area in milky light, and huge shadows
crawled over every surface.

Among other things, my perception of time had suffered a
blow as well. It was good I had my watch on. It was quarter
to one in the morning and my flight had arrived at 6.00 p.m.,
around seven hours ago. My journey so far felt like some never-
ending dream, barrelling along out of control and tumbling

toward a dark abyss. It could not be reality, I knew that. Yet I knew this was only the beginning.

The landscape itself was surreal, irrational, and the oddity so pervasive that people had stopped noticing it. This certainly wasn't how they behaved when I had lived here.

'Tarzan, I need to use your phone,' I said, thinking that perhaps I should give my father a call, although I wasn't sure if it was a good idea to do so at this hour.

'The phone's dead right now. I took the sim card out.'

'Why?'

'Orders from the boss. I think you should stay with us tonight at Shah Jamal. It's not safe moving around after dark.'

'As long as Wali is willing to drive, I think I'll leave right after meeting your boss.'

'Sir, you don't get to meet a person like Pir Pul Siraat every day.'

'Oh really?'

'Pir has *powers*.'

'Powers? What kind?'

'We're not allowed to talk about those things,' Tarzan replied solemnly.

Up ahead I could see the faint outline of a car and I silently prayed it was Wali's.

'What if I don't want to come along with you?' I had come to realize that asking Tarzan indirect questions was the best way to draw out information.

'But I can't show up at Shah Jamal without you. You don't have a choice here, sir.'

The look on his face told me that if he needed to drag my dead body to Shah Jamal, he would. 'Orders from the boss' meant pretty much the same thing here as it did everywhere in the world and in all languages.'

'Okay, fine. I'll go with you—but just for a few minutes.'

'That's great, sir,' Tarzan said. 'Pir will be happy to see you.'

Wali was waiting for us at the end of the road, just as Tarzan had promised. He was lounging on the hood of the car with his head resting on the windshield, smoking a beeri and gazing up at the moon. Seeing us he jumped off the car and gave us a hug like we were his long-lost relatives.

'Sirji, I'm really glad to see you,' he said, opening the rear door of the car for me.

I was about to slide into the backseat when I caught sight of some movement out of the corner of my eye. Crouching a few feet above my head on a tree branch was a huge black cat. Its long tail whipped back and forth as the creature studied me with fluorescent yellow eyes.

I froze. Before I could take a breath, the cat lunged through the air and landed on the roof of the car, snarling and baring its long curved fangs. The creature was so close that I could have reached out and touched it. I stumbled backward and Wali started banging on the bonnet with his fist. Startled by the noise, the animal jumped down and darted into the shadows.

'Damn! That was one huge cat!' I exclaimed. It was the size of a young leopard.

'We're seeing them more and more, sirji,' Wali said. 'They've even started attacking people.'

'Where do they come from?' I asked, scouring the darkness, my body tense in case the thing reappeared. 'I've never seen anything like that before in my life.'

'There used to be fewer of them, but their population suddenly increased when the dogs disappeared,' Wali said.

'What do you mean "the dogs disappeared"?' I asked.

'They were all killed. Slowly all were exterminated. Now, Alhamdolillah, you hardly ever see a dog in this country.'

'How could you possibly kill all the dogs in a country this big?'

'It was the order from the Khalifaji.'

'But why?'

'Sirji, don't you know that dogs block the flow of Allah's blessings when they are present in an area; whether it's a small house or a whole country? There is a hadith which says that the angels of mercy won't come to you if there's a dog nearby.'

'And people agreed to kill their own pets? That's horrible! And kind of hard to believe.'

'Well, if you're getting one free bottle of Hoor Afza for each dog you kill, that's pretty much all the incentive most people here need. Hoor Afza had just come on the market when the dog killings started.' Wali explained this mass extermination of millions of animals, many of whom must have been beloved family pets, like it was a nothing more than a new recycling policy.

'What's so special about Hoor Afza?' Now I was really curious about the drink, which only doubled my thirst.

'There's no point talking about it, sirji. Why don't you try yourself and see what happens? You've got two bottles in the car.'

It seemed like the perfect time to try it—quench my thirst and my curiosity at the same time. I got in the car, grabbed one of the bottles lying on the seat and drank the whole thing in one go. It was a mango-flavored, sugary soda drink with a peculiar, mildly sour but pleasant aftertaste. Wali and Tarzan exchanged glances when they saw me opening the second bottle.

'Anyone interested in Hoor Afza?' I asked, holding the bottle up. They both shook their heads and I gulped more than half of the second bottle in one go.

'Wali, we're not far from Shah Jamal, right?' I asked.

'Sirji, it all depends on the road conditions,' he said.

'Road conditions? We're not travelling on Karakoram Highway to China for God's sake! I could probably walk there in twenty minutes.'

'Things around here have changed, sirji. Have you ever seen Lahore this quiet before?' He was right. Shadmaan market was empty and as silent as a graveyard. There was absolutely nobody out on the street.

'Okay, let's get going, Wali. It's already one o'clock,' I said, feeling a pleasurable tingling sensation through my body. 'Tarzan can lead the way. We'll spend a few minutes at the shrine of Baba Shah Jamal and then go on to Faisal Town.'

'Your wish is my command, sirji,' Wali said.

For the first time in a long, long while I felt at peace. The prospect of meeting Pir had lifted my otherwise ravaged spirits. I was happy to just be relaxing in the back seat of the car. I leaned back and surrendered myself to the peace and quiet. The tension and foreboding that had gripped me since I first stepped off the plane had been replaced by a delicious indifference to all but the pleasures of lounging here in the back of the car. I watched Tarzan climb into the seat next to Wali and smiled. They looked like a pair of old buddies.

I was beginning to understand Wali's attitude toward life. There was no guarantee of anything in this world—especially at one o'clock in the morning in Lahore where my father's old car, equipped with a pair of martyr tanks and a handy safety switch, could be the safest bet in town.

The road was terrible and the car bounced along as if the ground beneath us had been carpet-bombed. Gravel hitting the undercarriage of the car sounded like firecrackers going off under my feet. My arms and legs lay heavily as if made of out lead and a warm cloud of euphoria lulled me like the siren song. I drained the last few drops of the second bottle of Hoor Afza and tossed it on the floor. I took a deep breath, held it, and then sighed.

I felt lightheaded, so I closed my eyes as another delicious wave of warmth washed away my body, the car and my companions. A flurry of images raced through my mind. The vivid clarity of these scenes made me open my eyes in alarm. It was like watching a movie.

In the front seat, two heads bobbed up, down and sideways. I giggled. They looked so hilarious, like a pair of bobble-headed clowns. I recalled from somewhere that these heads were named

Wali and Tarzan. I felt remarkably still, as if anesthetized, as the head belonging to Tarzan swivelled around and gazed at me through huge dark eyes.

'Is everything okay, sir?' a gentle, hollow voice coming from the head asked.

'Yeah, I'm good,' I said, laughing softly. I shut my eyes again and the images resumed their silent parade across the inside of my closed eyelids. Clearer, sharper images now crowded my inner vision—the faces of my ex-girlfriends. I couldn't even remember the names of many of them. Everything seemed so real. But something wasn't right. With supreme effort I opened my eyes again.

'Guys, what exactly is in this Hoor Afza?' I said. 'It's making me see things.'

'Sirji, with two whole bottles of that stuff in you, we're sitting here betting on how soon you'll spot a *hoori* sitting next to you back there,' Wali said. 'That's why it's called Hoor Afza.'

'Spot a what? A hoori? You mean the virgin of Paradise?' I said. 'Are you kidding me?'

Suddenly I felt elated. My aches had completely gone and my thoughts soared, except they were all about women. I was completely detached from my body; in it but unfettered, like a morning breeze drifting through a grove of sandalwood, like a butterfly looking for nectar.

'Sir, this is why the boss forbids us to drink Hoor Afza,' Tarzan remarked. 'He says it's crap—number-two stuff.'

'What the hell are you guys talking about? This is crazy!' I wondered what the number-one stuff would be like.

'Sirji, don't waste time talking. Just relax, close your eyes and dream,' Wali advised. 'Enjoy it as long as it lasts.'

My body tingled and started to flush. I felt as if I was held in a soft embrace of a warm, viscous liquid. All my blood seemed to be rushing towards my loins. Just go with the flow, I thought, closing my eyes.

I saw myself sitting beside four girls whom I had dated while doing my masters: Christen, Judith, Aisha and Kim. They all wore bikinis and lay on towels spread over lush grass. I could do anything I wanted to with them. They were there just for me.

'Holy shit!' I said loudly, grabbing my head.

'Sirji, is she sexy?' Wali asked. 'When you relax, they look better and better by the minute.'

'There are four of them, Wali,' I said.

'It's good practice for the seventy-two you'll get up there,' he said, winking and jabbing his thumb toward the ceiling of the car.

'Sir, the drink brings out one's fantasies,' Tarzan chimed in. 'You see what you've been wanting to see deep in your heart.'

'Don't tell me this shit is available to the public.' My loins throbbed and threatened to carry me over the edge. I struggled with the decision to either proceed with my Hoor Afza-induced mental imagery and gratify myself with these four ravishing beauties simultaneously or stop immediately by opening my eyes.

'Sirji, now you know what I was talking about?' Wali said. He seemed to be having quite a lot of fun at my expense. The car hit a deep pothole and my head banged against the roof. My eyes shot open and I stared at Wali.

'Sorry, sirji, I didn't mean to spoil your fun.'

'Sir, two bottles of this stuff can drive anyone crazy,' Tarzan said.

'How long does this shit usually last?' I asked, covering the obvious bulge under my robe with my hand.

'Long enough to cum once; maybe twice if you get lucky,' Tarzan snickered, turning around and ogling me. 'It all depends on how fast you can get it up again after the first time.'

Wali looked at Tarzan and they both roared like a couple of teenagers.

'Don't talk like that in front of sirji, Tarzan!' Wali scolded, his tone mocking and ready to erupt with laughter again. 'Show some respect!'

'What if I keep my eyes open?' I asked, ignoring their fit of giggles.

'Sirji, then what's the point of drinking Hoor Afza?' Wali asked. 'Shut your eyes and go back to playing with yourself. We won't look. This time,' he added, stifling another round of laughter.

'What happens to women when they drink this stuff?' I asked, shoving the bulge down between my legs.

'They're forbidden to even touch Hoor Afza, sirji. No one in their right mind would sell that stuff to women. They put you in jail for things like that,' Wali said. His voice sounded like it was bubbling up from the bottom of a deep well.

Drifting off again, I wondered if I could control my trip vision and direct it to go wherever I wanted it to. I closed my eyes and conjured up the face of my beautiful Sophie. She was standing exactly where I had first kissed her, by the waterfall. A rainbow formed over the curtain of mist as water crashed over the boulders and gushed down toward the valley below.

She stepped forward and brushed my neck with her soft fingers. Her lips parted and my mouth touched hers. She tasted like apricots. Suddenly overwhelmed with guilt, I opened my eyes. Somehow it didn't feel right to be thinking about her. Not like that. I felt angry at my father. Why in the hell did he decide to marry my girlfriend, of all the women in the world?

I closed my eyes. This time I would just look at her possibly from far away. A lush green hillside opened up before me: living, breathing, three-dimensional. I could even smell the little purple flowers and the tall grass.

Once again, I could see Sophie standing in the distance as if through a pair of powerful binoculars. There was a bunch of wild purple flowers in her hands. She wore her favourite long, black skirt and the red-fringed shawl wrapped loosely around her shoulders trailed down her back, getting entangled in her hair. She was gathering flowers as she waded through a field of mauve blossoms that spread over the green slope. Wind brushed through the golden grass like a great unseen hand. All I could think of was her hair, bathed in the crimson rays of the setting sun.

About fifty feet from where she stood, a dark shadow emerged from the tall grass. I gasped when I realized that the shadow was of a heavyset, dark-skinned man wearing a black shawl. He crouched like a tiger, slowly creeping closer toward Sophie as I watched helplessly from my self-imposed distance. Oblivious to her stalker, she knelt down to pluck a bunch of wildflowers. That was when the man sprang forward and dashed toward her. Before she could flee or even cry for help, he was on top of her.

Terrified, she screamed and beat his chest with her fists. But he was too big and powerful to have felt her blows. He grabbed her by the waist, lifted her off the ground and then threw her over his shoulder. She kicked the air desperately but to no avail. The hideous intruder darted across the meadow, carrying Sophie over his shoulder like a sheep for the slaughter.

The man came to a halt at the edge of a hole in the ground. Just then I opened my eyes. I was sweating, completely shaken. I knew beyond all shadow of a doubt that the man had jumped into that dark round pit. My Sophie had been taken into the underworld.

I struggled to keep my eyes open until we reached Shah Jamal. It was a bone-rattling ride over a cratered road littered with rocks and debris. Though shaken by a vision so real I could still smell the flowers and see that hideous, gaping hole, I was gripped by the crisis between my legs at that moment which had become almost unbearably painful.

I glanced at the front seat and saw Wali and Tarzan chatting. As promised, nobody was looking. I pulled my robe all the way up to my waist. I reached down and wedged my right hand between my legs and rocked against the seat, making sure my cum stayed within my underwear. After a couple of minutes, my body shook with delight and I felt the warm wetness over my groins.

A few minutes later Wali stopped the car in front of the shrine of Baba Shah Jamal. By the time Tarzan opened his door, about a dozen men dressed in black surrounded the car. Their faces were masked with veils, rendering them almost invisible in the darkness that engulfed the shrine.

'Everybody out!' one of the men barked.

'Tarzan, this wasn't part of the deal! Now what?' I managed to whisper into his ear.

'Be calm, sir,' Tarzan said. 'They're just doing their job.'

We all got out and stood by the car. The air was filled with the sounds of howling cats. They were somewhere up in the trees and their wailing filled the night like a song of death.

Entering the shrine's grounds I saw many people seated in groups around fires. A dense cloud of smoke hung over their heads and the pungent aroma of cannabis saturated the air. The cats had become silent as they watched from the trees.

Escorted by half a dozen armed men, Tarzan and I walked past the fires. The men were all smoking hashish from rough carved pipes that were being passed around the circles. No one bothered to even look up as we passed. They were lost in another world.

'Where's Wali?' I whispered.

'He's staying with the car.' Tarzan said, his burlap sack hanging from his shoulder. 'Sir, don't be afraid, they're going to blindfold you now.'

Before I could speak, someone threw a piece of cloth over my head and tied it behind my neck, covering my eyes and my face. Then someone else grasped me firmly by the arm and walked me around in circles. We walked like this for a good five minutes before descending a steep, narrow stairway.

My shoulders rubbed against rough stone walls as we made our way downward. I counted nineteen steps before my feet hit a flat surface. We walked again for a minute or two before halting;

then my blindfold was removed. I was standing next to Tarzan on what looked like a rocky ledge. We were overlooking a huge courtyard filled with about thirty people; mostly boys in their teens. The men who accompanied us had disappeared.

Lit by a dozen or so gas lamps hanging around the periphery, the courtyard looked like it was floating in the air. Three tightropes were stretched across the courtyard, each tied to the apex of a pyramidal assortment of four metal poles set in a concrete base on either side.

All three tightropes had boys edging their way across the open space of the courtyard some twenty feet below, their arms spread out and their faces strained with concentration. The rest stood below, watching the action with rapt attention.

A man wearing a white-striped black tracksuit walked around beneath the tightropes, monitoring the progress the boys were making and barking instructions from time to time. He wore a red headband across his forehead and his long white hair hung limp down his back. He must have been six feet tall and was well built. I figured this had to be Pir Pul Siraat.

We were gathered inside some massive building or subterranean cavern. There was no moon visible overhead, nor could I see any ceiling above. The man with the red headband turned and walked toward us, looking straight ahead. Two large black cats dashed across the courtyard and he stopped to scratch their ears and stroke their sleek fur. They flanked him as he walked, their tails raised in the air and their sides brushing his legs. They looked like two young black jaguars.

'Tarzan, where the hell are we?' I managed to whisper.

'We're inside the world of Pir Pul Siraat.'

13

PIR PUL SIRAAT AND HIS TWO CATS disappeared beneath the ledge where Tarzan and I stood watching below. Down in the court, the tight-rope exercises continued. Somebody hoisted a bicycle up to one of the boys on the tight-rope. The kid put the bicycle on the rope, and with one foot on the pedal he rode for a few feet, then crossed his other leg over and pedalled with both feet.

'Where did Pir go?' I asked Tarzan.

'He's gone to change.' he replied, tossing his burlap sack to the ground.

My underwear had begun to dry out, but not without leaving me with a sense of gnawing guilt. This Hoor Afza fiasco had turned out to be a fitting tribute to my utter failure to overcome my weaknesses, the ones I had been warned about at the outset of my journey. The Path to High Knowledge had me entirely exposed.

'Well, well! If I may have the attention of the gentleman from the Big Apple.' A deep musical voice reverberated through the air. I looked out into the darkness to locate Pir, but didn't see a thing. I turned around. He wasn't standing behind me either.

Feeling unsettled, I turned around again and there he was, standing just a few feet from us, dressed in a luminescent green robe. Two boys, twins from the look of it, flanked him on either side. Their eyes danced in the flames of huge torches which they held aloft to light the way for their master.

Pir's face, glowing in the golden light of the fire, looked like some sort of ritual mask, yet it was strikingly handsome. His lean frame, chiseled features and fine high cheekbones made it impossible to guess his age. He could have been anywhere from forty to sixty years old. His trimmed beard with streaks of white gave him a dignified, almost academic air. But it was his eyes—two white-hot searing probes—which surveyed me from head to toe in one blazing sweep. I stood still, mesmerized by the shimmer of his robe. It was impossible to continue looking into those almost non-human eyes that bore into me and left me feeling more naked and exposed than when I had had my robe hoisted up around my waist in the car.

The red headband across Pir's forehead bore the Nike logo and kept his long white hair out of his face. He wore a pair of earphones with two fine white cords disappearing into the side-pocket of his robe. I stepped forward clumsily, as if drawn toward him by a magnetic force. I was pretty sure he was seeing through me and nothing could possibly be kept from him.

'I'm honoured to be here, sir,' I said, gingerly extending my left hand, not wanting to touch him with my right which had dealt with the urgent needs of my swollen manhood.

He took the offered hand and gave it a brisk shake with no sign of awkwardness. Before I realized, it slid out of my grip like an eel.

'This is an amazing place! Your boys are doing great on the ropes.'

'It's not a difficult skill to learn,' Pir said with a smile.

'Nothing's difficult when you're young, I suppose.'

'Age doesn't matter. It's all in here,' he replied and motioned, tapping his temple with his index finger. 'Everything!'

'I know what you mean. Surely nothing is out of reach of man, for he is the greatest of all creations.'

'Greatest of all creations?' he boomed. 'I sincerely hope you don't believe any of that bullshit.'

I remained quiet, having absolutely no idea what to say. Was he mocking me, having known my real inner condition?

'Man's highest achievement is to elevate himself to the moral status of the animal kingdom. He must learn the nobility that's natural to all animals except man,' he said, staring into the flames.

'I've never heard of a noble monkey. Or a noble cat. Or even a dog.'

'Just because you haven't heard of it doesn't make it any less true,' he looked at me without blinking. 'One pack of wolves doesn't punish, persecute or kill another pack of wolves because they eat a different kind of meat.' His voice was firm, yet calm. 'Or have a different colour of fur.'

Feeling at a loss for words, I glanced at Tarzan who had a mischievous look on his face and seemed to be immensely enjoying Pir's interrogation of me.

'All of man's so-called higher intelligence,' Pir continued after a pause during which he just stared at me until I began to squirm, 'is wasted searching for newer and better ways to destroy everything that exists. No animal is capable of the level of moral depravity that is the trademark of humanity.'

Sweat poured down my forehead, my mind grappling with the shock of meeting with Pir Pul Siraat. Thankfully, he turned toward Tarzan before I could come up with a response.

'Let's see what you've got.' Pir said, stretching his open hand toward Tarzan. Without saying a word, the boy pulled the briefcase out of his sack and placed it in his master's hands.

Pir turned the briefcase over and examined it from all sides. The strange twins moved closer to him to provide more light from their torches.

Pir then turned the briefcase upside down and the bundles of banknotes fell out at his feet. I then noticed he was wearing black military boots. He tapped the empty briefcase with his knuckles and examined it closely.

'What happened to the lock?' he demanded, scouring Tarzan's face with a fiery glance and sniffing the briefcase.

'I don't know. Probably got damaged by the blast,' Tarzan replied, glancing at me for a second. I kept a straight face and refused to meet his eyes.

'Probably got damaged by the blast?' Pir cried, looking around. 'So there was nothing else in it besides the money?' He let the empty briefcase fall onto the pile of money lying at his feet. Clearly he knew the boy had tinkered with the lock.

Tarzan plunged his hand into the sack again and brought out a faded brown leather pouch with straps, like the kind travellers wear around their necks for carrying travel documents. I felt my own pouch, which I had tucked under my robe. It was there; my US passport was still on me.

'This may be what you're looking for,' Tarzan said.

Pir's nostrils flared briefly as his eyes fell on the pouch Tarzan pressed into his large hand. One of the twin boys whispered something in Pir's ear and the old man smiled and looped the string of the pouch around his neck.

'You're sure there wasn't anything else in here?' Pir glanced at me this time but I just shrugged. Could he possibly be looking for the book, the one I had left back at the hospital? I had suspected it to have been blown out of the briefcase along with the banknotes. I decided to keep that bit of information to myself for the moment.

Just then someone called Tarzan's name from the courtyard below and broke the heavy silence around us.

'Go. Your friends are waiting for you,' Pir said. 'Just remember: I want you to spend that money you've got tucked under your robe wisely. That's your whole year's salary.'

'What money?' Tarzan asked. His voice was calm and his face showed not even the slightest trace of guilt. Damn, the guy was good.

'Get lost!' Pir yelled and Tarzan took off like a horse bolting from the starting line.

'Sir, Pir will take good care of you!' Tarzan yelled to me over his shoulder with a smile. Then he was gone, swallowed by a knot of noisy young men.

Pir smiled, looking me in the eyes. 'My lieutenant!'

'I'm not sure I'd promote him any time soon, though,' I exclaimed.

'I don't do promotions,' he said firmly.

'He's a smart kid.'

'Indeed. He found you much faster than I'd anticipated,' Pir said as we started walking. 'Let's talk in my room.'

'What do you mean he "found" me?' I sensed there was a hell of a lot more going on here than was obvious. Anything seemed not only possible, but guaranteed in this strangest of all imaginably strange places.

As we walked side by side, the torch-bearing boys walking along with us held us within a golden halo of dancing light. The heat from the flames brushed my body with pleasurable warmth, and I was lulled into a sense of delicious peace.

Pir pulled the pouch out from under his robe and opened it.

'Here, I believe this is yours,' he said, slapping my wallet into my hand.

I stopped in my tracks, shaking my head.

'That lieutenant of yours appears to be adept in quite a number of fields,' I said, taking my wallet from Pir's hand. 'Do you by any chance have my cell phone in there too?'

'I'm afraid not,' he said, shaking his head in mock pity. 'But then, had my lieutenant not picked the pocket of the pickpocket who picked your pocket, you wouldn't have your wallet either.'

'If I may ask, sir, why exactly am I here?' I was now sure that Tarzan must have been tracking me since I left the airport. But how did he manage it, given the fact that he had no transport?

'You mean, why are you here right this minute?' Pir asked, bringing me back from my ruminations.

'Yes, at this very minute,' I said.

'You're here because of me.'

'And what exactly are you here for?'

'I'm here because of you,' he replied, a shadow of mischief appearing and quickly vanishing from his face.

'Okay, then,' I continued, intrigued yet rapidly tiring of our little word game. 'Why are both of us here at this moment?'

'Now that, my dear Ismael, is a most excellent question,' he said, stabbing the air in front of my face with his fingertip. 'We are both here because of Khalifa.'

'That I'd already figured out,' I said. 'It's not what—'

'I know you've got a lot of questions, Ismael. But you won't be able to understand the answers if they're given to you at the wrong time. For now, you have to trust that you're among friends.'

The words of that strange, ancient-looking man with the bright eyes whom I had met in my Ayahuasca vision rang in my mind like the tinkle of his bicycle bell: *Babu, you're going to help us clean up a big mess.*

'Were you with Tarzan when he blew up the handle on the briefcase?' Pir asked.

'Yes, I was.'

'Was there anything else in the briefcase besides the money?'

'I'm not sure. It was dark,' I said, knowing he didn't believe me. By now I was convinced that Pir was after the black book.

'What exactly are you looking for?' I asked anyway.

'It's the thing upon which Khalifa's power rests,' Pir replied. He led me through an arched doorway into what looked like a large rough-hewn cave strewn with tribal rugs across the dirt floor. Lit by dozens of candles set into small niches within the walls, the place was steeped in an otherworldly tranquility.

Pir gestured for me to sit down on one of the four chairs placed around a square wooden table in the centre of the room. As I sat down, my eyes fell on a red rose lying in front of me. Next to it lay a white porcelain ashtray.

There was a rustle over my shoulder which startled me and I glanced up. My breath caught in my throat as I looked into the eyes of one of the boys who was holding a torch over my shoulder. His eyes had vertical slits, just like the eyes of a cat. The boy averted his glance, looked straight ahead and walked over to Pir.

'These are jinns,' Pir said to me. He placed a hand on the shoulders of his twin boys and beamed like a proud father.

'Jinns? For real?'

'Yes.'

'So all the big cats you see roaming around Lahore attacking people are jinns?' I asked.

'Very few of them. Most of those big cats owe their existence to Khalifa. He had them specially bred in the mountains up north.'

'This is crazy!' I said, recoiling in my seat, trying to fathom the logic behind this mass-scale production of giant cats. 'Is he trying to compensate for the loss of all the dogs he had killed?'

'Relax, lean back,' Pir instructed. 'You'll feel a lot better after having a cup of hot tea; it should be here any minute now.' He dug out a pack of Gold Leaf cigarettes from his pocket and offered one to me. 'Would you like to smoke?'

'No, thanks,' I said, resisting a powerful urge to take one. 'All I want is to know why I'm here. That's all.'

The boy holding the torch behind Pir's shoulder brought the flame closer to his master's face and lit his cigarette.

'You're here to see your father, remember?' Pir said, removing his earphones. He took a puff of his cigarette and nodded at the boy.

Both boys padded out of the room, leaving the two of us sitting face to face in the dim light of the candles. Pir tapped the ash of his cigarette into the ashtray and leaned back, eyeing me closely.

'Ismael, you're here for a very important reason. If you don't successfully complete the task we're about to give you, we won't be able to complete ours.'

I remained quiet and tried to keep calm, but my breathing was shallow and fast.

'Do you understand what I am trying to tell you?'

'Yes, I think so,' I said, feeling my heart pounding in my chest, my guilt lifting off of me like mist in the morning sun. Despite all my shortcomings I was still a candidate for *the most ancient of the circles of the Elite.*

'Hajji Ibrahim, your father, is one of the Khalifa's closest confidants,' Pir's eyes still locked on mine.

'Not surprising,' I said. 'He was a businessman whose political ambitions were legendary and far-reaching. When I left home, some twelve years ago, he owned a chemical factory. But I suppose you know all this already.'

'Of course. He's still a businessman. But he's branched out a bit in your absence and no longer confines his activities to the typical chemical industry,' Pir said.

'Not surprising. He was always an entrepreneur.'

'These days your father's real money and power is in manufacturing martyr vests. And as incredible as it may sound, it is currently the most lucrative business in the Caliphate.' Pir broke out into a smile.

'What?!' I bolted up from my chair and stood glaring at him.

'His company manufactures the most popular brand of these nasty little things, the Mujahid vests,' Pir explained. 'They're in very great demand all across the country.'

'You're telling me...' I stammered, and then stopped to shake the dizziness from my head. 'You're telling me that my father is the one who owns Mujahid vests, the suicide vests?' My body convulsed inwardly with disgust. 'I think I'll take one of those smokes now, if you don't mind.'

'Please sit down,' Pir opened the pack of cigarettes, slid one out halfway and extended his arm toward me. My fingers shook as I pulled it out of the pack. He held up his lighter, flicked it once and I drew in a deep drag.

'I can't believe it!' I said, coughing out the smoke.

'He produces the best martyr vests ever made,' Pir said, his brows raised. 'Please, I insist, sit down.'

Ignoring his request, I took another long drag from the cigarette. The smoke burnt my throat like acid and I went into a violent coughing fit.

'Have some water,' Pir was holding a glass up to me. I didn't remember seeing any water on the table when I first walked in. I took a few sips and set it down.

'I don't think I want to see my father after all,' I coughed, choking a little as I struggled to control my breath.

'Ismael, you're not only going to see your father, but you're going to convince him you're now a true believer,' Pir said. 'A devout and pious Muslim son he can be proud of.'

'Hah!' I snorted in disbelief. 'That mission is doomed from the get-go. It would never happen in a million years,' I said in a hoarse voice.

'Oh yes, it'll happen all right,' he countered. 'And it'll happen long before a million years has elapsed. We're here to assist you and make damn sure it happens.'

'So I've come all the way from New York to Lahore for this—to turn myself into a true believer?' I asked. 'What for?'

'To gain his trust,' Pir replied.

'What makes you think I even want his trust? What if I refuse to accept this assignment? And what if I take the next flight out of this madhouse and return to New York?'

'I'm not going to ask you again, please sit down, please,' Pir said in a voice that would brook no refusal.

Shaking my head, I sank back into my chair, fuming from hearing of my father's business.

'You have to remember two things: first, as I said, your father is one of the most important men in the Khalifa's inner circle. Second, he's vulnerable when it comes to matters of faith.

Nothing will please Hajji Ibrahim more than to discover his only son and heir has finally rediscovered his faith.'

'But that'd be a lie!' I cried, helping myself to another cigarette. 'A great big fucking transparent lie. My father's a lot of things. But stupid isn't on that list.'

'Remember Ismael, in love and war,' he said with a curious twinkle in his eye. 'How does the saying go? Nothing is true, everything is permitted?'

'But I'm terrible at lying.'

'You're a hafiz, right?'

'I was,' I admitted, recalling those torturous years when I would get up before dawn and head down to the cold dank madrassa for Quranic lessons in a language I didn't understand.

'For you, the Holy Book is the quickest and most direct route to the heart of your mission: your father's forgiveness and loving embrace. And by *that* I mean that you once again become an authentic and verifiable hafiz,' he explained. The look on Pir's face assured me he understood the irony of his words.

'But that's impossible! I'm meeting him on Thursday, in two days.'

'You'll be amazed by how quickly you can recall the whole book.'

'I don't think so,' I said, blowing smoke over my shoulder. 'I've forgotten even my basic kalimas—except the first.'

'What would you say, Ismael, if I told you that by the time you get to your father's house, you will once again be an impeccable hafiz?' he asked.

Suddenly curiosity took hold of me, but with the realization that it could have me killed, or at the very least, have me do embarrassing things the way Hoor Afza did.

'I wouldn't mind having my memory improved,' I said, feeling a surge of excitement. I was eager to experience the man's powers firsthand.

Suddenly, the flames flickered and the tinkling sound of a bicycle bell filled the air. A movement caught my eye and as I turned I saw a man gliding across the room on a bicycle. I froze, feeling as if I was going to pass out. I was now looking at Chacha Khidr.

He was dressed in exactly the same clothes he was wearing when we first met in that empty green wilderness under the purple sky on my Ayahuasca journey.

He stopped a few feet from the table, jumped off the bike and kicked down the stand. He then approached me with an extended left hand and a wicked grin on his wrinkled face. The incredible brightness of his eyes was at such odds with his decrepit look.

'Chacha Khidr!' Pir cried out with delight. 'We've been waiting for our tea for a long time now. I hope it's still hot.'

I wanted to get up, but my legs were powerless, nearly buckling underneath me. I blinked, my mouth gaping open and my breath caught in my chest.

'Babu Ismael, very glad to meet with you again,' Chacha said in a crisp voice that could only have come out of the mouth of a very young man.

'Same here, Chacha,' I managed to say, taking his hand.

He then turned toward Pir. 'It's windy out there,' he said, exchanging glances with Pir. 'I almost got blown away by the winds,' he added, taking a stainless steel thermos out of a wicker basket that hung from the bike's handlebars. As he put the thermos on the table, he stared at me for at least five seconds, his mouth still stretched in a wide grin. His only incisor in his otherwise toothless oral cavity protruded from inside his lower lip like a shark fin. Definitely someone impossible to forget.

'Welcome to Shah Jamal!' he said. There was such warmth in his voice that I couldn't help but smile and mouth my silent thank you.

He returned to his bike and pulled out two white china cups from the basket. I noticed a burlap sack, just like Tarzan's, tied to the rear basket of his bicycle.

'Chacha,' Pir said in a scolding voice, 'how many times have I told you to get a headlight for that bike of yours? I don't understand how you can ride around in the dark.'

'Headlight? What for? I can see perfectly in the dark,' Chacha protested, standing his ground.

'I know your eyes are good, Chacha, but get a headlight anyway. Not so much for you, but for everybody else; they'll see you coming!' Pir said, teasing the old man as he poured tea into our cups. The room was filled with the sweet fragrance of cardamom and a few other spices I couldn't place.

'How come you didn't bring any biscuits for our guest from America?' Pir asked.

'How could I forget those?' Chacha said, putting his hand inside the basket again and retrieving a pack of cookies. 'I knew you'd ask me about biscuits. I brought your favorite brand: Barakat Biscuits.'

Chacha watched Pir peel back the wrapper on the biscuits and lay them on the table next to my cup.

I picked one up and took a bite. It tasted of coconut and melted in my mouth, leaving an indescribable taste on my tongue. I took another bite and then another. Pakistan, in the good old days, had been known for producing the best tea biscuits in the world. But this brand was like nothing I had ever had before.

'Chacha, these biscuits are the most delicious thing I've ever tasted,' I said, wondering if he was some thousand-year-old jinn. He certainly didn't look like he was from this planet. I had my suspicions about Pir Pul Siraat as well.

While we were enjoying our tea, Chacha Khidr walked to his bicycle to untie the burlap sack and dragged it over to the table. Holding it upside down, he let the contents tumble out onto the floor. I spewed out tea and biscuit from my mouth in a wide arc when I saw the pile of objects lying at Chacha's feet.

They were the disassembled parts of a man's body. A leg severed at the thigh, a shoulder attached to a piece of chest complete with jagged white ribs, a forearm with an attached hand whose middle finger still wore a ring with a large turquoise stone, a head with long curly hair and a hairy face severed at the neck and many other pieces that only a surgeon could hope to identify. The blood of the victim formed a dark crust over the torn edges of flesh.

I squeezed my eyes shut as my stomach heaved; I almost vomited. I missed Wali, his benign company and predictable ways. At least, relatively speaking, things made some kind of sense when I was with him.

'Chacha, please be a little more sensitive in front of our guest,' Pir's voice was saying from somewhere far way and he sounded upset.

Do not attempt to overthink and make sense of matters from here on, for it may prevent you from choosing the right course of action, I chanted to myself silently, remembering the instructions from the note and hoping it would keep the meager remains of my lunch inside of me.

'At my age, one doesn't have time for such trivial pleasantries,' Chacha's voice grumbled from near his bike. 'Our guest is a grown man. He can handle it. After all, he's the one who will help fix it all.'

I opened my eyes, feeling an acute sensory overload and the short-circuiting of my mental circuitry.

'There's such a thing as being delicate and subtle,' Pir insisted. 'Ismael has just arrived in our country.'

'Delicate and subtle! I am fed up with being delicate and subtle. It's time for action. Military action.' Chacha Khidr roared as he squatted on the floor and stuffed the pieces of carcass back into his sack. My mind, frozen with shock, had indeed lost its ability to think straight.

I watched in a daze as Chacha grabbed the severed head by its hair like it was a dead rat and flung it back into his sack. I doubled over, the bile threatening to pour out onto my lap.

'Ismael, please drink your tea before it gets cold—and don't mind Chacha Khidr,' Pir said.

I obediently followed Pir's command, hoping the tea would calm my stomach and wash away the taste from my mouth. But the memory of that hairy head wasn't going anywhere.

'Chacha, you may go now,' Pir said, looking at the old man. 'And please throw that mess of yours in the ditch.'

'Not in the ditch—that would be a waste! I've got a much better place to dispose him,' he said. The old man looked at me and smiled, baring his shark fin tooth over his lower jaw. 'Call me if Babu Ismael feels like doing a little sightseeing.'

I had no idea what the hell these two disturbingly odd men were talking about. I just sat there, slowly sipping my tea and munching on more biscuits. When I put my empty cup down on the table, Pir refilled it immediately.

The tea and biscuits were the only decent thing that had happened to me since I arrived in Lahore. I felt a pleasant warmth spreading from my stomach through the rest of my body. It washed away my exhaustion, the anxiety and nausea as well as all my unanswered questions.

Chacha Khidr tied the burlap sack back onto the rear of his bicycle and mercifully rode away. After drinking my third cup of tea, I leaned back in my chair, finally feeling completely relaxed. I had gobbled up half a dozen biscuits already and wanted more.

'I've never tasted anything like that before,' I said.

'That's because this tea and these biscuits are not made in this world,' Pir said casually.

'Then where are they made?' I said, keeping my tone polite.

'The Other Side.'

'What's the proof?'

'You don't need proof if you see and experience it first-hand.'

'And how is that done?'

'By learning how to tread the Pul Siraat,' he said.

'Oh, the metaphorical tightrope. And you're the guide—Pir of Pul Siraat.'

'There's nothing metaphorical about Pul Siraat,' he said, giving me a piercing look, his mouth stretched in a grin.

It was hard to digest what he was saying. Then a realization hit me: I was here primarily because of my intention, my own personal quest to know the realities of Paradise and Hell. I understood in a flash the words of Chacha Khidr when I met him for the first time: *Your intention and ours have met across time and space and made this moment possible.* I had begun to get a vague sense of the scope of my mission.

'Unless you have direct experience, you can't and won't understand,' Pir was saying.

Had I been utterly wrong all my life thinking Paradise and Hell as mere metaphors, figments of the human imagination? Was he training the boys down in the courtyard to tightrope across the fabled wire? It was a far out thought, but nothing seemed far out anymore in this strange land where talk of the next world was on everyone's lips. Everybody was either dying to get there or helping others to. I longed for another cup of tea then.

'There's more in the thermos,' Pir said, clearly having read my mind. As I helped myself to another cup, he continued to study me. Reaching into his pocket he brought out a palm-sized piece of perforated paper, similar to a sheet of postage stamps. He pulled apart one of the small squares and laid it on the table next to my cup.

'This is your key to remembering the Quran, becoming a

certified hafiz again,' he said, tapping the tiny paper with the tip of his index finger.

'What am I supposed to do with it?' I asked, picking it up off the table.

'Put it on your tongue. It may taste a little bitter at first.'

'I don't do LSD,' I said with resolve.

'It's not LSD—it's DSL. Think of it as a high-speed connection to your brain that will allow you to download the lost data very quickly,' he said, smiling.

'Pir, I'm not exactly looking forward to recovering any data from my past,' I said, shaking my head.

'We're talking about restoring a particular kind of data, not your entire past,' Pir said.

'What if I develop a reaction to this stuff?' I said, thinking of Wali. The poor old chap had been left with the car outside the shrine's walls beneath a tree swarming with jinns. He had probably fallen asleep in the car by now. At least, I hoped he had.

'I thought you'd welcome the opportunity,' Pir said.

'I'm not sure, Pir.'

'You've forgotten your intention.'

'But what does this have to do with my intention? I remember my intention.'

'I thought you understood your purpose of being here,' Pir said firmly.

'Not completely.' I marvelled at his ability to read my mind with such precision.

'You wanted to know if Heaven and Hell existed. And you also know there's a price for it.'

'What if I can't afford it?'

'Obedience is all you need to afford it. You'll do what I tell you to do; it's the only way your intention and our task can move forward. You'll have to trust me.'

I felt extremely alert, without a hint of fatigue or exhaustion. I steeled myself and looked at the tiny square of paper.

'Thinking is the enemy of action,' Pir reminded me.

He was right; ever since I landed I came to realize thinking was a pretty useless activity. If anything, mulling over each and everything that crossed my mind had only made matters worse and done nothing to alleviate my confusion and uncertainty.

I opened my mouth, pressed the stamp over my tongue and took the plunge of faith. After a minute or so the paper dissolved, leaving a mild bitterness in my mouth.

I sipped my tea and thought about my future as a hafiz. It was a dreadful one in which I would have to pose as a pious man of faith in order to gain the trust of my father, a man I never even wanted to see again. I was being forced to do something against which I had rebelled for as long as I could remember.

My part of the mission, it seemed, was becoming more despicable and offensive by the minute. I wondered what other terrifying commands and revelations were in store for me. There was no doubt in my mind that this strange and powerful man, Pir Pul Siraat, meant business.

14

T HE TEA SUCCEEDED IN FLUSHING out the bitterness from
my mouth. From which fantastical world had Chacha Khidr
procured this peculiar tea at such a tender hour? I was now
totally psyched about the big data recall, the one Pir had called
a high-speed connection for my brain.

How would it feel to remember the long-forgotten text whose
every word had once been a jealously guarded treasure in the
innermost recesses of my mind?

Pir leaned forward, putting his elbows on the table, holding
a cigarette between his fingers. His dark eyes probed mine,
searching for what I could not guess.

'Chacha Khidr is the real master of Pul Siraat,' Pir said,
blowing smoke in the air. 'He's been travelling back and forth
across the abyss his entire life—that's all he does.'

'Then who are you?'

'I'm his deputy,' he replied without further elaboration.

I felt like he was pulling my leg.

'Is Chacha a jinn?' I asked.

'No one knows what he is, except that he's skillful and the
best guide there is.'

'Is he the real Khidr?'

'Maybe you should ask him that question,' Pir said, shaking
his head and smiling.

'And Tarzan?'

'Oh, he's all too human of course. He was just a baby when a jinn found him lying on Mall Road in front of the Governor's House. For one so small, he was crying and throwing his legs in the air, raising one hell of a fuss. He's human all right, but he was raised by jinns. He's got their fingerprints all over him,' he said, grinning.

'Ah, like the Tarzan raised by a family of baboons?' I asked.

'Exactly.'

'Are you a jinn too?' I asked pointedly.

'I'm a hybrid,' Pir laughed, looking at me with an amused expression.

'What the hell's that supposed to mean?' I asked, trying to remember if I had ever heard of jinns impregnating humans, or vice versa.

'You won't understand even if I explained it—not until you've got the necessary experience under your belt,' Pir said.

'Necessary experience?' I asked, feeling strangely relaxed, lucid even. I had to admit that I hadn't felt this good in a long time. All I knew was that, whatever this 'necessary experience' was, I wanted in.

'Necessary experience is only attained through what we call Direct Perception,' he explained.

'And Direct Perception is?' I prodded.

'If you take a ride across the abyss yourself, your experience of Pul Siraat will be direct, immediate and unmistakable. And it'll save us both from a lot of the basic questions.'

'Ride? I always imagined Pul Siraat to be some kind of wire that a believer walked on with his bare feet,' I said. 'How do you ride it?'

'On a bicycle. How else?'

'That's insane!'

'It was Chacha's idea. For my part, I was perfectly happy teaching traditional tightrope to the select few,' Pir said.

'How wide is the abyss?' I asked eagerly. My curiosity was racing and I could barely keep up with my own thoughts. 'I mean, how long is Pul Siraat? It's a physical thing and not just your imagination?'

'Now listen,' Pir said, impatiently. 'The Abyss, and the way over it, changes according to the intention and capacity of the believer.'

I realized he hadn't blinked in several minutes. His eyes looked like two bright mirrors suspended in the dark in front of my face. Was Pir trying to hypnotize me? If so, should I resist or surrender to the power of his gaze?

'What if you're not a believer?' I asked, finding it hard to break eye contact.

'Belief is the crutch for the blind,' he said. 'I think you should avail yourself of the opportunity and go see with your own eyes. Go for the ride.' He looked dead serious which made me very uneasy.

'Maybe another time. Wali, my driver, is waiting for me in the car. He must be wondering where the hell I am.'

'That's what drivers are for, Ismael. They wait.'

I felt lightheaded thinking about crossing over some mythical abyss, traversing the fabled wire stretched over a pit of fire, on a bicycle!

'But don't you have to be dead to experience everything we're talking about?' I asked.

'Yes, typically. But there are shortcuts for everything, my dear Ismael,' he said, straightening his back. 'And certain people know all of them.'

'Certain people like Chacha?' I ventured, sensing some understanding of things in the belly of my mind.

'Fear has remained your greatest enemy, Ismael—a trip to Hell will be really helpful in your case,' he said, slipping a hand into his pocket and drawing out three glass vials the length of my little finger.

He raised them to the light and I could see each vial was filled with a transparent liquid—one red, one yellow and the third one green. He laid them on the table.

'What are those for?' I asked, eyeing the delicate little receptacles.

'This is the shortcut,' he said.

'The shortcut?'

'Crossing the abyss is an extremely dangerous affair,' he explained. 'It requires years of discipline and training before you can even think of putting the first foot on the wire. The elixir in these vials contains a formula designed to reduce that time to a matter of minutes.'

Pir seemed almost ruthless in pushing his concoctions on me so quickly. After all, he had only met me less than an hour ago. In comparison to the shamans running sacred ceremonies in the yoga centres of New York City, Pir seemed to be operating on a whole new dimension. The man was clearly a master, but of what though I wasn't quite sure.

I touched the vials with my fingertips, rolling them on the table in front of me. After all the marvels I had already witnessed and consumed in this place, I could only wonder about the secret chemistry contained in these three vials.

'You must choose one,' Pir said.

I picked them up and held them to the light of the candle, shaking them gently. They reminded me of a traffic light. Was I standing at the crossroads of life and death? Or on some threshold far more crucial to my existence than even that?

'What are the chances that I won't make it back?' I asked, searching Pir's large fiery eyes for reassurance but finding none.

'There's no guarantee of anything in life.'

'I meant probability. High? Medium?' I said trying to steady my voice. Pir just sat there.

'Low?' I whispered. He just shrugged.

'Low to medium, maybe,' he admitted, stroking his beard, his large bright eyes staring at me like those of a sphinx.

The vials were of pharmaceutical grade with tapered necks for easy snapping. I stared at them, massaging my lip with my finger. Red could be too hot to handle while green could be too weak for someone like me. I smiled inwardly, like some psychedelic Alice in Wonderland.

'Since I've got to choose one, I'll take yellow.'

'Good choice,' Pir said.

Keeping the yellow vial in my hand, I put the other two back on the table. As I rolled the vial around between my fingers, stalling as much as possible, I heard a faint drumbeat in the distance. It grew louder as if some spectral drummer marched through the unseen toward us.

'In life, Ismael, timing is everything,' Pir said, standing up and walking over to the entrance of the room. He stood there for a moment and motioned for someone to enter. The drummer picked up his tempo as he entered the room. His drum was the size of an oil barrel and hung from his neck by an old leather belt, its weight resting against his thighs. Pir came and sat back down at the table.

'For the elixir to work, the crusted matter that's deposited on one's soul must first be polished until clean.'

Before I could open my mouth to ask another question, the cadenced drumming rose to a deafening volume that reverberated deep in my chest. For a moment I thought I had heard this drumming before. But where?

The drummer had long black and henna-stained dreadlocks which hung to his waist. He reminded me of a chunkier Bob Marley. Trailing behind him were the jinn boys holding their torches. The room swam with dancing red and gold light and the walls came alive with shadows moving in time with the drum's rhythms.

The drummer marched over to us, beating his *dhol* with such ferocity that his drumsticks blurred and all but disappeared. I grabbed the edge of the table to steady myself against the cacophonous vibrations which shook my eardrums. Pir raised his hand in the air and the man stopped immediately. In the absolute silence that descended upon us, I could actually hear the crackling of the boys' torches.

'Ismael, it's time to break the vial,' Pir said, sliding back into his chair. 'And give me your watch.'

'Why do you want my watch?' I asked, reluctantly sliding it off my wrist and handing it over. I noticed it was half past one. We had started from Shadmaan around one. It had taken about twenty to twenty-five minutes to get to Shah Jamal. Was it possible that I had spent only a few minutes in Pir's company?

'Time will only complicate things for you,' Pir said, dropping my watch into his pocket, reading my mind once again.

I took a deep breath and tried to empty my mind of the doubts that had plagued me since Pir showed me the vials. I hoped I had made the right choice.

But one thing was certain: there was no point in trying to figure out where this whole thing was headed. I just had to trust him. So I held the little vial in my fingers, feeling the cool smooth surface. Then I snapped the neck and poured the yellow liquid onto my tongue. I had expected an unpleasant taste—like that of Ayahuasca—but the elixir was completely tasteless. It evaporated from my tongue, leaving a peculiar but not unpleasant dryness.

And that was it. The shamans had a long way to go in improving the taste of their jungle concoction. The contents of Pir's vial were smooth and delicate.

Then I glanced up and saw the drummer beginning to move his body, whirling slowly at first and then gaining speed. His dreadlocks whipped back and forth like a dense black cloud as he began to pound the drum again. My body rocked involuntarily as the rhythm of the drummer washed over us. I resisted the urge to get up and whirl around with the drummer like he was my dance partner from Hell. The man was a gaping vortex of pure, raw energy. I closed my eyes and allowed the wave of sound to sweep me over the edge.

Just twenty-four hours ago I was in Manhattan, a place that might as well have existed in another time, another dimension, for all I cared. I almost couldn't remember the man named Ismael who had lived there once.

A long time passed. I couldn't even say how long, but it was enough for me to have forgotten all about time and to become utterly absorbed in the moment. The man ceased his drumming. He stood motionless, his sticks resting on the drum. Sweat poured down his face and he was heaving as he struggled to catch his breath. Pir raised his hand again and the man bowed and slowly walked out of the room, followed by the jinn boys and their bobbing torches.

I heard someone moving around behind me and turned to see Chacha Khidr again, standing next to his bicycle, his arms folded across his chest. His eyes were as bright as ever and like before, they were locked onto mine with a disquieting twinkle. He seemed to have materialized out of thin air. I had no idea how he had even entered the room.

'Ah!' Pir said, waving at the old man like he had been gone for centuries instead of just a few minutes. 'It looks like your ride's here, Ismael. You may now request Chacha to escort you across the abyss.'

Before I could reply, Chacha said, 'I hope Babu Ismael won't mind holding my sack as we cross over.'

Clutching a burlap sack stuffed with human body parts and sitting on the back of a cycle behind this crazy old man who probably wasn't even a man was not my idea of the best way to cross any abyss. Fortunately, my unbridled passion for adventure wiped out all trace of disgust, misgivings and bewilderment still lurking in me. 'Not a problem!' I said with unbridled enthusiasm.

'Excellent!' Chacha said. 'There's no turning back now anyway, Babu.'

'Chacha, don't worry about me. I'm not turning back; not now, not ever,' I assured him.

I got up from my chair feeling a delicious tingling vibration coursing through my body. It felt like somebody had struck me like a tuning fork. I was as light as a balloon, filled with helium and ready to float away had there not been some unseen hand holding me back by a string. Chacha picked up the burlap sack and without a warning, lobbed it at me from a good ten feet away. I threw my arms out and caught the sack. It was so light it could have been filled with feathers. I fought the urge to think of what the sack really contained.

'Let's go, Babu Ismael,' Chacha said, wheeling his bike toward the entrance.

Pir stood up from his chair and we all left the room together. The jinn boys were outside waiting for us, their torches illuminating the darkness. We returned to the ledge overlooking the courtyard, still illuminated by the many lamps.

The boys on the wires were still practicing and I spotted Tarzan riding a bicycle across the middle wire. I wondered if he had ever ventured to the other side or if he was still a novice learning the high art handed down by Chacha Khidr.

Chacha straddled his bicycle, his feet barely reaching the ground. 'Ready when you are!' he shouted.

I looked at Pir. His earphones were back in his ears and his lips moved without making any sound. He gripped my shoulder and gave it a shake.

'No matter what happens, don't panic.'

Was he kidding? Then he slapped me on the back and headed back toward his room without another word, the jinn boys close on his heels.

Without a word or warning, somebody killed the lights in the courtyard, plunging the place in complete darkness. I saw a pair of eyes in the dark about five feet from me. It was Chacha. Under any other occasion the sight of him would have scared the hell out of me, but tonight it was strangely comforting.

I hopped sidesaddle on the back of Chacha's bike and his pedalling was immediately fast and furious. Sitting like this was the only position that allowed me to maintain my grip on the bag that teetered precariously in my lap.

There was nothing to see or hear besides the rustling of Chacha's robe as he pedalled deeper into the sightless void. The sheer audacity, style and scope of this adventure had punctured a gaping hole through my logical self. My right foot found the footrest just in time as Chacha bore down on the handlebars of his cycle and we picked up even more speed.

'Hold on!' Chacha shouted, glancing back at me.

In the next moment, we were rocketing down a steep slope in a free fall. I let out a scream—the kind you hear from people strapped to a rickety seat on an evil roller coaster ride, half terror, half ecstasy. The bike plunged several hundred feet before finally levelling off. We must have been barrelling along at a good hundred miles an hour.

The air had become stifling hot and dry as we hovered weightlessly. The darkness was less intense here and the skies shimmered with a warm glow of that mystical hour just before dawn. Soon we were enveloped in a gray mist which morphed into a shimmering glow of crimson rather quickly. I looked down and the scene below jolted every nerve in my body. My first thought was that only a miracle would get us out of here alive.

Like a bird in a nosedive, we plunged into a vast chasm that opened up beneath us. I was numb with shock when I noticed the steel cable, as thick as my wrist, on which our bicycle sped through open space. The bottom loomed a good mile below and swelled with a scintillating river of boiling blood-red magma. It was a monster of a canyon with its distant rims shrouded in darkness. My cheeks burnt and my throat contracted as a sulfurous heat washed over us from the floor of the abyss.

'Are you enjoying the view, Babu Ismael?' Chacha asked.

'Was—was this the route you took to bring us the tea?' I stammered.

'I cross over every day, Babu. Often several times a day,' he said.

'So this is what Pul Siraat looks like,' I said, still numb with fright.

Instead of answering my question, Chacha began singing a song—an old pre-Partition Indian one about princesses and unrequited love. Black smoke rose from the bubbling river of liquid fire and the air smelled of sulfur. My fear began to fade with the retreating darkness and I resigned myself to whatever was to assail my senses next.

Steep canyon walls emerged through the mist revealing tall spires of twisted black rock rising toward the sky like minarets. Some of them reached as high as the cable, while others disappeared above our heads.

'Chacha, was this the route you took to bring us the tea?' I repeated my question.

'No Babu, that is the long way. There are many other routes, in fact. The cable chosen for your journey is shorter than that,' Chacha explained as I struggled to hear him over the noise. 'I thought Babu Ismael could use a little adventure! You're not in any big hurry, are you?' he asked, as another mighty gust of blistering wind shot up from below and almost swept us off the bike and into the chasm. I began to shiver uncontrollably.

Looking into the distance I saw a black bird the size of a small plane rip through the air and plunge downwards. Chacha leaned closer into the handlebars and I hugged him from behind.

'We better stop—the winds are getting worse and we could get blown off the wire.'

'Stop? Where? Is that even possible?' I screamed, watching in amazement as the gigantic bird surged back up from the bottom of the abyss, its enormous red-tipped black wings kept flapping despite the brutal blasts of heated air.

'There's a rest area just up ahead,' Chacha said, pedalling faster. 'Don't panic.'

Don't panic? DON'T PANIC?!

'How far?' I asked, still watching the massive bird ride the currents up the canyon. 'Do they serve tea there?'

The bird shifted its angle of flight and turned right into our path. It came up alongside us and hovered about twenty feet to our left. Up close I would say it had the face of an owl, but its long pointed beak was that of an egret. Fresh blood dripped down its beak and talons. I thought at its prey and shivered again. The bird regarded us closely with black, jewel-like glittering eyes.

'Chacha, are you seeing this?'

'Here we are!' He announced as if he hadn't heard me. The bike stopped moving. Seeing the ground beneath my feet, I jumped off the bike and so did Chacha.

The ground was solid volcanic rock, black and as jagged as broken glass. We were on the flat top of a rocky column no more than a hundred feet in diameter. The bird was now circling us. Chacha started walking toward the edge of what looked like a broad mesa, keeping an eye on this winged thing from hell; I followed, my legs wobbly.

The bird emitted a shrill cry, folded its wings against its body and plunged back into the abyss. I laid the sack down and walked over to the edge where Chacha stood staring after it. Together we watched the bird's descent. It sped down in a spiral arc, crossed the burning river of fire and landed on a rocky ledge a couple of hundred feet above the floor of the canyon. Black smoke continued to rise from the pit and obscured both the ledge and the monstrous raptor that perched there.

'Babu, this is called the Lookout Point,' Chacha said.

I realized we were standing next to a rusted pipe fixed to a pole. Touching the pipe. I noticed it was quite warm, but not infernally hot like everything else in this place.

'Chacha, what the hell is this thing?'

'A telescope!' he said, pulling it toward himself and bringing it up to his eye. 'What's the point of touring Hell if you can't have a Lookout Point complete with a telescope?'

'Hell!? I'd always thought—'

'Yes, that's right. At this very moment you're looking at one of the tributaries of Hell.'

The Lookout Point was the tallest rocky spur that rose from the floor of the grand canyon of Hell. It was no more than a needle in that boundless space but it afforded a staggering panoramic view of the pit of horrors and despair below us.

'God Almighty!' I gasped. 'Who built a telescope in a place like this?' Was Chacha going to point out the roasting bodies of the sinners with the help of this metal tube engraved with the word 'Galileo' next to the viewfinder?

'It's been here ever since Hell came into being,' Chacha said, peering into the canyon.

'Chacha, telescopes were invented only a few centuries ago,' I said. 'And Hell is supposed to be older than humanity.'

'Time is important only because things need to happen one after the other, Babu Ismael,' Chacha replied. 'Or at least, it has to look like they do,' he added with another of those infuriating winks of his.

Focusing on the bottom of the canyon, I looked through the lens of the telescope and adjusted the glass until everything came into sharp focus. I gasped and jumped back, bumping into Chacha. The old man just cackled and held his sides.

'Looks close enough to reach out and grab it!' he cried.

That was actually an understatement. The surface of the river of fire was so clear that I could see bubbles and geysers forming on the surface and then exploding to emit puffs of gas and plumes of debris.

If Hell was real, Paradise had to be real too. At that moment I knew with certainty that I was done with my doctoral thesis trying to prove otherwise. I wondered if I would be given a glimpse of the latter at some point.

I slowly moved the telescope over the distant wall of the canyon, searching for the basalt ledge where the raptor had perched.

Finding the spot, I scanned the area looking for the creature but what I saw instead stunned me. Where the bird had been, there was now a man just standing there. He was tall and muscular, his body chiseled like a statue. His copper-coloured skin glistened with sweat and his face was as red as the flames that licked the earth at his feet.

I shuddered with alarm when I saw the guy wasn't standing there at all; he was bound to a pole. His hands were chained high over his head and his ankles were crossed one over the other by a heavy manacle. A dark liquid oozed from a deep gash at his side.

Some movement on the other side of the ledge caught my attention. The bird waddled out from a cave in the wall of rock. The man's head slumped on his chest at a sickening angle. Making its way over to his captive, the bird thrust its enormous beak into the gaping wound on the man's ribcage. The raptor shook and twisted its beak with such terrible ferocity it would only be a matter of minutes before it ripped the poor fellow apart.

The man looked up, his face a mask of unspeakable pain. For a moment, our eyes met and I stopped breathing. He opened his mouth and screamed in agony as the bird ripped deeper into his tortured flesh. Sweat poured from my body and I gagged. I tried to tear my eyes from the horrific spectacle below, but it was impossible.

At last the monster pulled its beak out from the man's side. It swallowed whatever hideous trophies it had extracted from its victim and then lifted its massive body and took flight. Beating its enormous wings against the volcanic currents, the creature disappeared into the smoke rising from below. I turned and looked for Chacha, but he was no longer by my side.

Panicking at the thought of being alone in a place like this, I almost cried out with relief when I saw him standing next to his bike, gripping the ghastly burlap sack. The bird reappeared and soared upward across the canyon toward us.

'Chacha, what's going on down there?' I demanded, trying, with little success, to stifle the terror in my voice.

'Time to feed the birds,' Chacha replied, flashing me his toothless grin once again.

I heard a rustling noise and looked up. I held my breath as the raptor from Hell descended above our heads. Chacha rushed to the far end of the mesa and dumped the rotting contents of the sack onto the ground. He then turned and rushed back to where I stood.

We watched in fascination as the bird landed its enormous bulky body next to the carrion, with its wings still held aloft. The sword-like beak contained hundreds of dagger-sharp teeth which still dripped blood from its recent feasting on the captive below. 'Let's go!' Chacha gave my arm a tug.

A gust of wind lifted what looked like a scrap of paper from the remains of the corpse and dropped it next to us. I collected it off the ground and looked at it. It was a certificate of *shahadaat* or martyrdom. The bottom of the paper was scorched but I could still read most of it. It said: 'Fida Muhammad, resident of Faridkot, embraced martyrdom for Allah and entered Paradise on...' The date and place of his death had burnt away. I tossed the paper into the scalding wind.

Chacha was perched on his bike and ready to go. I jumped on behind him as before, my eyes still glued to the bird. The creature clasped the severed head by the beard and swung it back and forth like a pendulum in its enormous beak. It gained momentum with each swing and the skull cracked like a gourd. With ravenous eyes the bird pecked on the emulsified brain, its long black tongue scouring the inside of the skull.

'The bird loves brain,' Chacha said solemnly.

Fighting sensory overload and the urge to vomit, I closed my eyes. Soon I wound up suspended between sleep and wakefulness. I had no idea how long we rode or what surrounded us, but I awoke with a start, clutching Chacha's waist.

'It's time for tea,' his voice chimed within my dreamless reverie.

Opening my eyes, I saw a tent large enough to fit a dozen people set up in a large grassy field. The tent's faded green cloth was patched in many places and reminded me of a dervish's robe.

Chacha parked the bike and we made our way over to the tent. The grassy area looked over on a lush beautiful valley on one side and the broad sweeping canyon of Hell on the other. Not far from the tent, a wooden table and a set of benches were set on a patch of grass, so we sat down.

The place smelled of roses and the occasional whiff of sulfur; the air danced with golden beams of light filled with sparkling dust. Rolling green meadows stretched out below us and a grassy slope drenched in mauve was ringed with waterfalls. Birds of all kinds soared over the valley. At the far end, a dark band stretched across the horizon. It took me a moment to realize that I was looking at a massive wall that, given its immeasurable distance from us, must be a hundred times taller than the Himalayas.

'Wow! Is that really a wall?' I asked Chacha. 'What's behind it?'

'Paradise,' Chacha replied, retrieving a pack of cigarettes from his pocket. He looked old and weary now, and I wondered again about his true age.

Before I could learn anything more about the place, a man holding a tray emerged from the tent. His face was radiant and his eyes were as bright as two moons.

'Welcome to the Bihishti Tea Corner, sir. My name is Ibrahim.'

15

❦

IBRAHIM SET A PAIR OF TEACUPS and a plate of biscuits down on the table in front of us. The tea was the same delicious tincture that Chacha had served at Pir's compound. But this time it didn't rejuvenate me the way it did before.

Ibrahim sat down on the bench next to me and pulled out a flute. As I sipped my tea, he lifted the slender reed to his lips and began to play. It was such a hauntingly beautiful and sad melody that I was soon overcome with inexplicable grief.

Time seemed to have stopped around us. When Ibrahim finished his tune and set the flute down, I was absolutely heartbroken. I could've spent the rest of my life sitting there listening to the sad cries of Ibrahim's flute and staring into the verdant meadow that lay below us like an exquisite silk carpet.

'How far is Paradise from here?' I asked Ibrahim, certain his flute had carried me half the distance already.

'It depends on how fast you ride your stallion and what challenges you meet on the way,' he replied.

'Where do you get stallions around here?'

'From the country down below,' he pointed to the rolling green slopes.

'Let's say you've got the speediest horse and there are no obstacles to slow you down, how long would it then take to get to Paradise?'

'Seventy years, if you go by human time.'

'Seventy years?' I cried out in shock. I would be almost a hundred years old if I set out for Paradise right this minute.

Suddenly, out of nowhere, a rush of shrieking cries filled the air. The light was fading, my head felt hot and beaten like an anvil; it was becoming harder to keep my eyes open. I heard Chacha's voice behind me.

'Look up, Ismael!' Chacha shouted, pointing to the sky in joyful agitation. 'The ababeels! A black cloud of birds stretched across the sky. The massive flock undulated sensuously as it turned into one unit and darted back and forth across the heavens.

'They were last used fifteen hundred years ago on earth,' Ibrahim shouted over the din, which was so loud I could barely hear what he was saying.

'They're used only in the direst of emergencies,' Chacha chimed in. 'And here they are!'

I wanted to be part of the conversation but felt too drained and overwhelmed to speak. I knew they were talking about the incident that had occurred a decade or two before the birth of Prophet Muhammad. It was even mentioned in the Quran. According to the legend, a flock of ababeels, carrying stones of baked clay in their beaks and talons, descended on the mighty army of Abrah Al-Ashram—the king of Abyssinia who had attacked Mecca in order to destroy Kaaba—and discharged their payload, turning everything to husk.

'I think he couldn't hold out any longer.' I heard Chacha say from somewhere.

Overpowered by exhaustion and sleep at last, I let my chin drop to my chest and slept.

'Wake up, Ismael, we're back in Lahore.' A familiar excited voice broke through the thick silence. I opened my eyes and noticed I was still seated behind Chacha on his bike, my hands gripping the fabric of his robe. It was dark and we had come to a halt.

I jumped off and rubbed my eyes, feeling strangely refreshed and rested. We were back in the exact same spot where we had begun our ride—the ledge overlooking the courtyard in Pir Pul Siraat's compound. Tarzan was still on the wire pedalling his bike. It looked like we had never even left.

'Chacha, what time is it?' I asked.

'Time is always *now*!' he declared, pushing his bicycle toward Pir's sanctuary.

I walked by his side, recalling the night's journey. It was still so vivid and fresh. The shamans of Lahore were clearly operating on a completely different level of reality. Whoever they were, they were worthy of far more respect than I had given anyone before.

Entering Pir's candlelit room, we saw him sitting at the table, one leg over the other with a cigarette in his mouth and a black leather book in his hand. Two of the jinn-cats lounged on the carpeted floor at his feet. Pir jumped up when he saw us and threw his arms in the air, clutching the black book in his hand. He gave me a firm hug, slapped me on the back and smiled.

'So the prodigal son returns. Welcome! So, are you a believer now?'

I had no idea how to respond to his question. The crazy ride on Chacha's bike had shredded my concept of reality to bits. There were so many questions, many more than I had at the beginning of my trip to Hell. I looked back on the moment I first arrived at this compound as the good old days of innocent simplicity. I realized I had done nothing but waste all that precious time writing my dissertation on a topic I had no freaking clue about.

'Would you like some more tea?' Pir asked.

'No, thank you,' I said, even though I craved its rejuvenating effects and otherworldly taste. I had no desire to send Chacha back across Hell's abyss just to get me one cup of it.

'I think you need to get some sleep.'

It was time for me to leave and I was being, at least for the moment, dismissed. I wondered when the potion that was meant to make me remember the Quran would take effect.

'The recall of Allah's word is tricky business,' Pir explained. 'Each word, each dash, every dot must be checked and rechecked before it's restored to its original place within the mind of the hafiz.'

I looked at Chacha. He stood by his bike and nodded in agreement.

'Babu, with smallest error your brain could be permanently damaged. Try not to force any recall tonight,' Chacha said placing a warm hand on my shoulder.

'It'll happen on its own when the time is right,' Pir added.

I felt naked in Pir's presence. The man read me as easily as the most elementary volume in his library. He tapped my chest with the black leather diary he held in his hand.

'This is a very special Quran, Ismael. Always keep it on your person. As they say in America: "Never leave home without it",' Pir said.

I took the Quran from his hand. Its pages were burgundy parchment with fine hand-lettered text penned in lustrous gold. The text stood out from its dark background and almost hovered over the page. This was clearly the work of a master calligrapher. It radiated an ineffable but palpable energy that pressed upon me like an unseen hand.

'This is the most beautiful Quran I've ever seen,' I said finally, staring at the golden text as it glittered in the soft candlelight. It was unbelievable that I once used to recite the whole book from memory, sometimes in one sitting, but not knowing what it really was—a miracle in its own right.

'It's yours now,' Pir said.

I opened the Quran to a random page and silently read the first line. Then I closed my eyes and tried to recall the next line. But it eluded me like a shy mistress avoiding my gaze.

'I told you not to force it!' Pir barked. 'You've been warned. You'll lose your mind if you aren't careful, if you don't follow my instructions to the letter,' he said.

'Patience is the fastest way to achieve one's goal, Babu,' Chacha said.

'I understand.' I apologized, though feeling annoyed and embarrassed.

'This Quran is the key to our mission's success,' Pir continued. 'The secret will reveal itself when the time is right,' he said, taking his red headband off and handing it to me. 'Wear this.'

I took the headband from him and slipped it over my forehead, wishing he would stop being so cryptic and tell me all the facts and the truth.

'I'm not the only one who can read your mind,' Pir said, glaring at me. 'Some of Khalifa's people are trained to do that as well. They're damned good at it, too. That's part of Khalifa's impenetrable security system. It's the most sophisticated one ever developed. For now, the less you know, the safer we'll all be.'

'How can someone read minds?' I asked. I was a little creeped out, yet intrigued by the idea.

'It's easy. All you need is a medium,' Pir said, bending down and stroking one of the cats. It responded by standing up and rubbing the side of its head against his leg. There was no doubt in my mind that these two cats and the torch-bearing boys were one and the same.

'All animals are telepathic—not just the jinns. It's in their nature. The big cats bred by Khalifa are used for this very purpose,' he said. 'They are the most perfect telepathic medium known to man. There's no information so private, so guarded and protected, so deep that they can't easily lift from your skull.'

'That's wild!' I said, thinking how every goddamn thing about this place was weird as hell!

'The animals are innocent in all this, of course,' Pir continued. 'They aren't conscious of their mind-reading ability, nor are they aware of leaking such information to those who know how to interpret it.' 'It's unbelievable!' I said. 'Very sophisticated indeed.'

Pir smiled and looked at me without saying any more. I was startled to hear his voice in my mind.

'One day this Quran may have to be ripped apart to activate its power.' His voice sifted through the folds of my mind like a warm breath.

'I don't want to die so young,' I replied, just thinking it to see if he heard me. The idea of ripping up a Quran in a place like the Caliphate of Al-Bakistan stopped the blood in my veins.

Pir threw back his head and laughed out loud. Chacha joined him from behind me where he had been standing as a silent witness to our discussion.

'The tele-band worked!' Pir said aloud with a smile. 'It passed the test.'

'I don't like it when people laugh at me,' I thought angrily, squeezing my brows, but that only made them laugh harder. I wasn't sure what Pir meant by the tele-band. Did he mean the headband I wore was meant for telepathic communication?

'I'm afraid you'll still have to be blindfolded on your way out,' Pir said out loud. 'It's better that way—for you and for us. This place is under constant surveillance and we are under the threat of our cover being blown by Khalifa.'

I turned around and looked at Chacha. There was a worried look on his face, but he just shrugged when our eyes met. The cats snarled once, flicking their tails and baring their teeth. I heard footsteps and knew my escort had arrived.

'Babu, whenever you encounter a suspicious cat, empty your mind of all thoughts,' Chacha said. 'It doesn't work all the time, but it may give you some protection.'

'Put the headband over your eyes,' Pir said. 'Keep it with you all the time along with this Quran; put it on when you find yourself in trouble.'

'Thank you, Pir,' I said, also nodding at Chacha.

'You've been wanting to ask me something. Just ask it,' Pir said.

'Since you've been more than kind to allow me a visit to Hell, would it be possible to arrange a visit to Paradise?' I asked. 'With Chacha, I mean.'

'Life arranges things according to one's intention, capacity and performance,' Pir said. 'We're here only to help you accomplish the task we'll soon set before you.'

I had an uneasy feeling that I might never see any of these unusual people ever again. It was a thought that saddened me intensely, strangely enough.

'Your request will be considered depending on how you perform this time around,' Pir smiled. 'Desire alone will not take you there. There has to be a need for such a visit to take place.'

I looked at Chacha. He was scratching his temple as if considering my request.

'Chacha, I'll never forget the ride over Pul Siraat,' I said, sliding the headband over my eyes. 'Thank you.'

'Let Tarzan know where the book is. I need to have it in my possession as soon as possible,' Pir's voice resounded in my ears. Startled, I uncovered my eyes and looked at him. He was a brilliant mind reader.

'The book with the blank pages,' I said. 'Don't worry, it's safe.'

'If it's not with me, it's not safe,' Pir barked. 'Nobody is safe.'

'What could be so important about a book with blank pages?' I asked.

'Its pages aren't exactly blank,' Pir said. 'That book is loaded with enough power to take a whole village to ...' He paused for a second and then continued. 'We don't have time, Ismael. I must have the book in my possession as soon as possible.'

'Take a whole village to where?' I insisted he finish his sentence.

'Paradise,' he replied.

'How is that possible?'

'It's only a matter of time before Khalifa finds it.' He had ignored my query.

'He'll never find the book,' I said casually, and immediately realizing the idiocy of my statement.

'Don't be a fool!' Pir said, exploding from his chair. 'We can never underestimate Khalifa's power.'

'All right, I'm sorry,' I said, all my smugness deflating in the face of Pir's anger. 'I'll tell Tarzan where the book is; he'll know exactly how to get there. But it's in a place that would be impossible to stumble upon and I really don't think—'

'No, you really don't think! You *really* don't think that trained psychics who you know nothing about could possibly find that book?' Pir said, glowering at me like I was a child who had just ruined his day. 'Oh, all right,' Pir said, his voice suddenly softening and his warm smile returning gradually to his face. 'But you tell Tarzan I want that book. NOW. And Ismael, don't ever hold information back from me again or we're finished.'

'I understand. Mind reading aside,' I said, having fully recovered from Pir's outburst, with a closed-lip smile on my face. 'I need to know more, a lot more, about my mission.'

'There's no harm in giving a basic brief to Babu Ismael,' Chacha said. 'It's a fair request.'

Pir and Chacha exchanged glances for a moment.

'All right.' Pir took a deep breath, looked me in the eyes and continued. 'What you need to know is that over the years Khalifa has been systematically contaminating the water supply of the entire country. City by city, town by town, he is making all the water in the country inconsumable. He now produces his own brand of water, the only clean and drinkable water available. It has become his private monopoly. Then there's the Hoor Afza, his very lucrative side-business.

'The water he sells under the brand name "Paradise Water" is laced with a tasteless, odourless chemical that, when consumed in sufficient quantities over time, starts to work its sinister magic. It puts people into a trance-like state that allows them to go about their daily lives while becoming obsessed with the thoughts of Paradise and how to get there as quickly as possible. It makes them volatile. Emotionally unstable.' He paused, watching me intently. 'Do you follow?'

All I could do was nod at this troubling revelation. I now understood a lot about this place. The people's obsession with Paradise had turned them all into a nation of bloodthirsty zombies. They had disconnected from reality. I began to remember: people like Wali, his mood swings; that family of five oblivious to their obvious brush with death in that accursed martyr-vest shop; the hordes cheering the bloody sport called Cricket and being blown to bits; beheadings and stonings; car trunks fitted with martyr tanks; and of course, my father's business which had become a household name.

'And now, Khalifa has something very special planned; a real spectacle,' Pir said, cracking his knuckles. 'If he's not stopped as soon as possible, this world and the next will need a major cleanup that will stretch into the not-so-foreseeable future. Without that book, he won't be able to bring his plans to completion. Your job, Ismael, is to help us stop this man. And that's all you need to know for now.'

'So if you get the book, it's all over for him, is that it?' I asked, feeling dazed by the scope of the mission at hand.

'No. But it gives us an opportunity to strategically insert you into the scheme of things,' Pir said, giving me a mischievous smile. 'He'll get another book like this soon—the backup copy. He's relentless in his pursuit of Paradise.'

Pir's words left me speechless and gripped by more questions than ever. There was still so much unexplained.

'So am I being strategically placed for you to get to Khalifa using my father as a bridge?'

'Don't think too much into it,' he said. 'Just do it.'

'Is that the price I've got to pay to walk the Path to High Knowledge?'

'Certainly.' Pir's eyes brightened and his mouth stretched into a grin. 'Remember: the basic reminders I jotted down for you, once upon a time? They still apply, especially the lust part. You're expected to perform better this time around.'

'I'll try my best.' I knew that he was referring to the *basic reminders* he had written down for me in the note.

It was now time to leave. I couldn't wait to get back to the car to sort myself out. I needed to make sense of my mission. Most of all, I needed to recover from everything that had happened in the last however many hours, weeks or centuries that had elapsed since I had landed on this godforsaken continent of wonders and horrors, of Heaven and Hell.

I covered my eyes with the tele-band. His large hand firmly grasping my shoulder, Pir walked me to the door and handed me to somebody who led me back into the real world of ordinary heroes and monsters. The world that I knew.

It was Tarzan who pulled the headband off my eyes. We were back in the courtyard and the buzz of dozens of hushed conversations filled the air. Men were still hunched around their fires under thick clouds of smoke and the yard was thick with the pungent fragrance of cannabis. Nothing had changed. As we walked back to Wali's car, I told Tarzan about the black book and the exact location where he could find it. He laughed when I told him how urgently Pir wanted the book.

'It might be tricky getting back in there again tonight. But I'll try. Pir can be *persuasive*. Don't you worry, sir,' Tarzan said.

Half a dozen armed men dressed in black followed us, all but invisible in the murky shadows. Outside the walls of Pir's compound I spotted the car parked under the giant banyan tree. The cats, roused from their slumber by our approach, resumed their haunting symphony overhead. I saw a cluster of glowing yellow eyes moving among the huge tree branches.

The entire thing was alive with cats. They crawled along the thick branches, their howls piercing the air like the voices of the sirens. I wondered if they were all jinn-cats, or the specially bred psychic variety, or a mixture of the two. I figured they were probably the former guarding the shrine of Shah Jamal from the latter. Everyone in Pir's entourage seemed to have his task, his mission and sacred duty.

Wali, completely indifferent to the cats by now, lounged as before on the hood of the car, smoking his beeri, his eyes glued to the bright crescent moon that hung low in the sky. An empty teacup sat beside him. He gave me a surprised look and slid off the car.

'We took care of Wali while you were gone,' Tarzan whispered in my ear as one of the guards picked up the empty teacup from the hood.

I wondered what he meant by that. Had they spiked Wali's tea? And if so, why? Without saying a word, Wali opened the rear door of the car for me. Tarzan and I shook hands and then I slid into the back seat.

Tarzan waved goodbye and flashed me a warm smile, his teeth white as ivory. Two armed men stood a few feet behind him, but their faces obscured by shadows. Wali turned the headlights on, momentarily flooding the two guards' faces with light. One of them looked vaguely familiar, but I couldn't place where I had seen him.

We had only driven a few feet when Tarzan suddenly dashed toward the car and slammed his hand on the window. Wali braked.

'What's up, Tarzan?' I asked, rolling down the window.

'Your watch!' he said, grinning and dangling the watch in my face. 'And here's the phone number of one of my associates,' he added in a whisper as he pressed a small folded piece of paper in my hand. 'If you need to reach me.' As I slid my phone into my pocket, I noticed it was 1.38 a.m.

'Thanks!' I said, tucking the paper into my wallet. 'We'll be in touch.'

Wali increased the speed of the car as I rolled up the window.

'Wali, what's the time?'

'Sirji, my watch always runs ten or fifteen minutes late,' he said, turning on the overhead light and bringing his wrist to his face. 'It's half past one.'

'And what's the time on the car's clock?' I said.

'The car's clock stopped working five years ago, sirji.'

'How long was I gone then?' I asked, feeling completely disoriented.

'Gone where, sirji?' Wali sounded alarmed. 'You never left the car since I picked you up from the airport.'

'Wali, we stopped at the fortress stadium for shopping, watched a game of cricket, then we were at the hospital, remember? And...' I said, baffled by his answer.

'Sirji, I think you need some rest. You had a long trip and I know this place can drive anybody mad,' he said.

What he said just then was like a slap in the face. I understood exactly what Tarzan meant when he said they had taken care of Wali.

They had wiped his memory of the night's bizarre collection of curious and inexplicable events. He was now oblivious to the fact that he had picked me up from the airport hours ago. He was also oblivious to the fact that we were still barely halfway home, and on a route far afield of our expected one.

16

❧

WALI DROVE SILENTLY AS WE NAVIGATED our way over the guttered remains of Canal Road. But that was just fine by me. Clutching the Quran Pir gave me like it was my only hope for survival, I scrambled to calm my jagged nerves by forcing myself to stay focused on my mission. Other than tossing a couple of vague and disturbing hints around, Pir had done nothing to give me a foothold to speculate on. His message was clear. All I needed to know was that the less I knew the better it was for all of us. I just had to live with that; at least for now.

A hundred questions ran amuck in my head. How could a goddamn book, one that at the moment was resting peacefully at the bottom of a dried-out water tank, transport a whole village to Paradise? Assuming Pir got the book by tonight, and I was pretty sure he would, what was up with this *backup* copy? What did he mean by having me 'strategically' inserted into the scheme of things before Khalifa got his hands on this backup copy? What sort of spectacle was Khalifa planning? How would his plan, if executed successfully, require a major cleanup not only in this world but also the next?

The more I tried to fathom the mystery surrounding my mission, the more I was baffled. My personal quest to understand the realities of Paradise and Hell, which had apparently kick-started all this craziness, felt insignificant in comparison to what

Pir and Chacha were up to. If it weren't for my father, one of the most important men in Khalifa's inner circle, I wouldn't be here. I wondered how I would feel when I finally laid eyes on Abba for the first time in so long. What would his reaction be? Would I be able to convince him, of all people, that I was now a true believer? And I simply couldn't wrap my head around the fact that my father was the owner, the mastermind, behind Mujahid Vests Inc.

My rumination came to a sudden halt when Wali slammed the brakes at the roundabout of Kalima Chowk. Several armed men carrying high-powered flashlights and ubiquitous Kalashnikovs surrounded the car. Hammering their fists on the hood, the men gestured for us to roll down the windows.

'Sirji, we're in big trouble. These guys are the *shikaree*, the hunters. They travel around at night in packs,' Wali said. 'I hope you still remember a little bit of your *deen*.'

'Hunt for what?' I asked, covering my eyes with the Quran to hide my panic.

'They hunt for infidels. Every kafir they kill will bring them one step closer to Paradise,' Wali said.

I recalled the sharp cold edge of Wali's knife pressed against my throat. He too was a shikaree deep down. Fortunately, thanks to Tarzan's concoction, Wali had no recollection of that particular event.

'But isn't everyone around here trying to advance to the next rung of Paradise—by killing those they consider infidels?' I asked. The men were now beating on the windows with their knuckles and the car was rocking back and forth.

'Yes, sirji, it's the duty of every believer to aim for the highest heaven. But most people, like me, have to work all the time just to make ends meet. The shikaree don't do anything but this. They've given up all other purposes of living in this world,' he explained, rolling down his window. 'Just keep calm and let me do the talking.'

'Where are you heading?' one of them barked at Wali through the open window, his face hidden behind the glare of flashlights.

'Faisal Town,' Wali replied.

'Who's that in the backseat?' the man demanded, having spotted me. Several flashlight beams hit my face, blinding me.

'Sirji Ismael,' Wali announced.

'Wali, don't give them any more information about me,' I whispered harshly, hoping he had heard me but the others hadn't.

'Tell your sirji to get out of the car. Now!' the man bellowed in rage.

'Wali, let me handle this,' I said, pushing the door open and stepping out of the car, the Quran pressed to my forehead to protect my eyes from the blinding glare.

'Hands up!' one of them shouted at me. From his voice I could tell he was probably very young, maybe twenty years old.

I raised my arms above my head.

'What's in your hand?' the same voice shouted.

'The Quran, Alhamdolillah,' I tried to sound confident and relaxed.

'Never heard of a brother who could read the Holy Book in the dark,' the man said, his voice lilting with sarcasm. 'We've seen many like you before. Out of fear you try to deceive us by merely pretending to be a believer.'

'I'm a hafiz,' I said, immediately regretting it. What if they decided to test me?

'Which sect?'

For a moment I didn't know what to say. My father had always been a hard-line Sunni of the Salafist faction. I considered declaring my sect, but what if these guys turned out to be part of a Shia gang? Very few Shia remained in Pakistan after the revolution, but those who did were known to be active, striking Sunnis wherever they could. Statistically, telling them I was a Sunni was a safer bet.

'Alhamdolillah, I'm a Sunni,' I said. 'Who are you people and what do you want?' I asked, hoping I seemed both indignant and calmly respectful.

'Who *we* are is none of your business. What you need to know is that if we find a non-Muslim reciting the holy text of the Quran, his blasphemous crime is punishable by death. Now, you will tell us which sect of the Sunnis you belong to.'

'Alhamdolillah, brother, I watch the beheadings on the Omar Media. My hero is Dandy Chowdry of the UK.' This guy was probably tricking me into choosing a sect, but that was all I could think of at the moment.

'Oh, you mean Hazrat Dandy Chowdry. The man who's helping spread Islam in the West!'

'Yes, exactly,' I said with excitement.

The beams of light retreated from my face. I took a deep breath and stared at the patch of darkness that descended over my eyes like a veil.

'Tonight, I'm in a mood to listen to *surah* Al-Bakrah from a hafiz such as yourself,' a raspy older voice I hadn't heard so far demanded.

Damn! Al-Bakrah was the longest surah of the Quran. Even if recited at a breakneck pace, it would take a good part of the night to complete. I remembered this surah was the most difficult one to memorize, even in the heydays of my hafizhood. I berated myself for opening my big mouth and foolishly declaring myself a hafiz.

'I would love to say this most beautiful part of the Quran, but I'm so very tired at the moment and I've got work to do early in the morning,' I knew it sounded lame and I feared it wouldn't work, but things had already spun out of control. If Pir's DSL didn't kick in soon, I would soon be a dead man walking. Then I remembered Pir's headband. I had been instructed to wear it whenever I was in trouble.

Without warning, the ominous cadre of figures parted and a man of medium height elbowed his way toward me. I took this as an opportunity to reach into my pocket and grab my headband.

Standing at an arm's length, the new person scrutinized me from head to toe, aided by a flashlight in someone's hand. The headband was out of my pocket and in my hand, like some magical cloak of invisibility. I needed to somehow get that thing onto my forehead.

'What kind of work you do, sirji, bedsides being a hafiz who makes pitiful excuses when asked to recite the holy words?' he demanded with an arrogant toss of his head. Clad in a black robe, he was barely distinguishable from the darkness that surrounded him. I could hear a few muffled chuckles ripple through the group. The man cleared his throat and dislodged a huge wad of phlegm onto the ground at my feet.

It would be suicidal to let him suspect that I found him disgusting or that I had just arrived from the US. I wondered if I invoke my father's name. As the maker of the hottest selling brand of martyr vests, my Abba must be like a household deity to this crowd.

'Are you really a hafiz?' he asked, running his hand through the huge beard that sprouted from his face like a thicket of bramble.

'It's not advisable to recite the holy text under stress,' I said, quickly putting the headband on my forehead.

'What are you doing?' he bellowed, thrown off by my sudden move. A few more of the flashlights illuminated my face.

'It's just a headband. I sweat when I'm exhausted and under stress,' I touched the cloth and adjusted the Nike logo over my brow as Pir had done.

'Al-Bakrah!' the man roared. 'Now!'

'I need some light here,' I said, fumbling with the Quran in my hand.

'Recite!' The menacing figure moved closer to me, coughed,

and let out another ball of phlegm that landed about an inch from my shoe.

Feeling like a cornered animal, I closed my eyes and almost gasped with surprise. Something warm poured into the top of my head and my brain swam in a circling wheel of sparkling light. Radiating outward, points of golden luminescence breathed like living creatures and then morphed into the shimmering words of the Quran.

Shocked, I started reciting the text. My eyes closed and I was afraid to open them. What if I lost sight of the words as they danced behind my eyelids? Line after line spun like gold from the swirling circle of lights as if from Rumpelstiltskin's enchanted spinning wheel.

What poured out of my lips was clear and powerful; each word recited with perfect enunciation and musical grace. I relaxed and was momentarily startled as my hands rose till my chest, palms up, in the gesture of ritual supplication.

My volume increased as the words tumbled from my lips like the waters of blessed Zamzam. As my voice soared through the darkness, a hushed stillness descended around the men who held me at gunpoint, Wali and I. The more I recited, the more confident I became. The desert melody tore my heart. Time itself paused as if listening with rapt wonder to the Word as the tears flowed down from my eyes.

I had no idea how long I went on like this, but I must have recited at least five pages. When I opened my eyes, the shikaree had vanished. They had slipped away into the night, though I hadn't heard them move away. Wali sat beside my feet, his head bowed and body swaying from side to side. I placed my hand on the top of his head. He jumped up and hugged me so hard that I almost couldn't breathe.

'Sirji, I beg for your forgiveness,' he said, his palms pressed together in front of me.

'Forgiveness? What for?' I asked, touched by his sudden change.

'For not giving you the respect you deserve,' he said, wiping his eyes with the back of his hand. 'I assumed you'd forgotten your religion while living in America.'

'Let's go Wali. It's getting late,' I said, not exactly sure what had just happened.

The rest of the drive to my father's house was uneventful. As we entered Faisal Town, I was struck by the startling transformation of the houses. There was now a dome on top of every house as though it were a mosque. Not a single flattop or pitched roof remained. Every gate and entrance was now flanked by minaret-shaped pillars.

I thought about the run-in we had had with the shikaree. It was absolutely mind-blowing to have been able to recall any surah of the Quran at will, with or without the headband. I still marvelled at the sight of the luminescent text forming with perfect clarity in my mind's eye. By the time Wali turned into the street where my father lived, I was able to see the text even with my eyes wide open and was able to close the vision at will. This was way more than the usual recitation of a hafiz. I wondered how long the effects of Pir's prescription would last, or if this would be a permanent feature of my new skill set.

Wali pulled up in front of a multi-domed building where had once stood the house of my childhood. The place was lit by gas lamps which lined its periphery. The house had been constructed from the ground up to look like a mini replica of the Blue Mosque of Istanbul.

'Wow!' was the only word I could think of, startled by the transformation of the house I had been born in. 'When did Abba build this house?'

'It was completed last year—took three years to build,' Wali said, looking at me through the rearview mirror, his eyes glistening with reverence. 'Allah has blessed Hajji sahib with a noble son and an exalted business. He is indeed a winner in this world and will be in the next too.'

I glanced at my watch and saw it was 2.40 a.m. I was glad my father wasn't home, since I would need every minute of the next two days to be by myself, to repair what was left of my sanity before he returned.

Wali honked and someone opened the gate from inside. The car rolled into the grounds toward a broad wrap-around veranda lined with columns. Ghulam Rasool—my father's cook for as long as I could remember—pulled the door open on my side.

He had aged considerably since I had seen him last. Under the harsh white light of the gas lamp at the entrance of the house, his wrinkled face looked emaciated and pale. He welcomed me with a warm smile as he held my arm and helped me out of the car. I hugged him and all I felt was skin and bones. Wali stood by his side and whispered something in his ear.

The two men stared at me, wide-eyed, their hands clasped over their navels. Ghulam Rasool dragged my suitcase down from the camel's hump and carried it to the front entrance while Wali gently shouldered my backpack as if it belonged to a beloved saint.

At the front door, panelled in exquisite woodcarving, Wali handed Ghulam the seemingly precious backpack and said goodbye to us. Then he took off toward the servant quarters while Ghulam pushed the front door open and stepped aside.

'After you, *saab*,' he said.

'Thank you,' I said, as I entered the mansion. The palatial residence looked like it belonged to a Turkish sultan of a bygone era. Gone were my expectations of some big emotional turmoil as I entered my childhood home. This place bore absolutely no resemblance to the place I grew up in. All I really felt was a sense of sad detachment. It was only the warm presence of Ghulam Rasool that reminded me I was indeed home.

The house smelled of stale smoke, old rugs and tribal leather. It looked like there was no one home but us.

'Has Abba got any more children?' I asked.

'No, saab. You're his only son,' said Ghulam, as he led me under a massive crystal chandelier, with dozens of real candles, that hung above the foyer. 'I thought you'd never come back.'

'Whatever happened to Sophie?' It was the question I was most afraid to ask.

'She was never found. We believe she died long ago,' he said, shaking his head sadly.

'Where are Abba's wives?'

'They all live in Islamabad.'

'Then who lives here?'

'Nobody. Wali and I take care of it. Hajji sahib stays here whenever he comes to Lahore for business.' Ghulam then led me into a large living area. 'He's given us the car Wali drives for the upkeep of the house.'

A monumental landscape painting dominated the entire wall above the fireplace. The work depicted a crimson mushroom-shaped cloud over a miniaturized Indian subcontinent on one side and the Middle East bordered by the Mediterranean on the other. The sky was suffused with billowing clouds of smoke rising from the lower half of the painting. In the upper right corner, a monstrous black bird with bloody eyes and wings of fire spiralled toward earth.

And if the mural's message weren't clear enough, a gleaming crescent and a sword dripping with blood hovered over the scene like some Masonic all-seeing eye. Despite the horrific vision, I could not deny the exquisite workmanship that was evident in this masterpiece. It was not the work of some heavy-handed zealot. The calm, reasoned execution and masterful brushstrokes made the painting all the more chilling and impossible to turn away from.

The other walls were decorated with equally beautiful paintings too, either of mosques or Arabic calligraphy. Ghulam Rasool led me over a seemingly endless succession of fabulous Persian rugs which had not adorned the floors of my boyhood home. I was in absolute awe of a collection that was easily worth as much as the house that displayed them.

It seemed the martyr business was truly heaven-sent for Abba. He had never been a poor man, but I remembered our lifestyle was rather simple.

I wondered whether the carpets represented a newfound aesthetic passion or a pragmatic desire to keep money-on-the-hoof on hand in case of unexpected emergencies. I also wondered if my father had a cache of blood diamonds hidden somewhere behind a secret panel in the wall. Or they could be under the portrait of Armageddon over the fireplace.

'How are Uncle Umer and his sons, Tariq and Khalid?' I asked, remembering my father's younger brother and my cousins who lived in Defense Housing Society. Uncle Umer exported handmade rugs to Europe and was known for his not-so-secret liberal views. Abba had always detested him for that.

'The mob burnt down their house while they were still inside, saab' Ghulam said, as he led me into my room.

This news upset me greatly and all I could do was say a silent prayer for them.

After making sure I was comfortable, Ghulam Rasool said goodnight and returned to the servant's quarters. My room matched the grandeur of the rest of the house, but the only rug in sight was a threadbare prayer one at the foot of the bed; it was my prayer rug from when I was a kid. Message noted.

The room was lit by a brass lantern on a mahogany nightstand next to the king-size bed. On a table near the window sat a jug of water and a glass.

I stretched out on the bed and put the Quran and the headband Pir gave me under my pillow. The cheery flame of the lantern danced feebly and eased me into a delicious drowsiness. I was overcome with sleep about sixty seconds after my head hit the pillow.

My dreams were a disjointed mess; too fragmented and hazy to piece together or remember. I woke up around noon, my throat feeling like sandpaper. I drank a lot of water and then fell asleep again.

The room was submerged in total darkness when I opened my eyes. I bolted upright, not sure where I was when I felt Ghulam Rasool's hand on my shoulder nudging me awake. I got up and he turned the lights on, pointed at the tray of tea and hot snacks he had made for me. I looked down at my watch. It was 9.00 p.m. The day was Wednesday and the year 2050; that would be 12.00 noon in New York. I had slept for seventeen hours straight. I felt as if my circadian rhythm had been permanently damaged due to the surreal events of the past day.

'Saab, just to let you know, the electricity will go off in twenty minutes,' he said, setting the tray down on my bed.

'Oh, great!' I said sarcastically. 'They used to have generators. What happened?'

'They have been banned, saab, for both residential and commercial use. Only mosques are allowed to have them now. For one thing, the noise—you could hardly hear the call to prayer when they were running. And they prevented people from practicing their *deen*, their religion in the true spirit according to the natural times of day decreed by Allah.'

I understood the first reason well enough. But I had my doubts about that second one, though it seemed awkward to ask for an explanation.

'Your father called—he told me to wake you. Saab, you've been sleeping all day without any food or drink in your stomach. It's not good for your health,' he said, putting the morning paper, *The Daily Khalifaa e Waqt,* in front of me beside the tray. 'This country has been inviting the wrath of Allah for a long time—I'm glad you left,' he added, smiling to himself. 'I'm really happy to see you, saab, but you should have stayed abroad, if I may say so.'

I rubbed my eyes, looked at the headline, and almost fell off the bed. '*Blast at Shah Jamal.*'

With a surge of panic, I picked up the paper, my hands shaking, and scanned through the details quickly. Someone had martyred himself at the shrine of Shah Jamal, killing seventeen people. The explosion had taken place around 2.00 a.m., according to eyewitnesses.

My lips trembled as I stared at the picture under the headline; the severed head of the suicide bomber nestled within a wreath of red roses. I had seen that face before, but where?

And then it came to me like a flash flood racing down a mountain gorge. I knew that face! It was of the man who had been standing behind Tarzan outside the shrine, one of the two armed guards who had escorted us to Wali's car. And in another flash, I realized it was also the same bloody face I had seen being thrashed against the rock by Hell's winged minion; it was the face of Fida Muhammad.

But how could that be? How on earth was it possible to see the bomber's carrion, which Chacha Khidr had fed to the bird, before the man actually killed himself?

I broke out into a cold sweat and the bile rose in my throat as I recalled Chacha Khidr's words: '*The bird loves brain.*'

Clutching the newspaper in my hands, I held back my tears. Had Tarzan been killed?

I remembered his handsome, smiling face as he handed me my watch along with the phone number of one of his associates. He might have survived, if he had gone to retrieve the book right after I left.

'Saab, you look ill,' Ghulam Rasool said, looking alarmed.

'Ghulam Rasool, I need to make a phone call.' I said, remembering the words of Pir: '*We can never underestimate Khalifa's power.*'

'You wait here; I'll get the phone. It's in the kitchen,' he said, hurrying toward the door.

He brought me a cordless phone and I dialed the number Tarzan had given to me, but there was no answer. I gave up after a few more tries.

The blast was obviously directed against the head of the resistance movement, Pir Pul Siraat. Did he and Chacha Khidr survive the attack? As I recalled, Pir's abode wasn't located at the shrine, where the blast had taken place. I remembered walking blindfolded for a good five minutes, and then going down nineteen steps to reach his quarters. I dropped the newspaper on the bed.

'Ghulam Rasool, please arrange for the car. I need to go see someone.'

'Saab, are you all right?' he asked. 'Wali will take you anywhere you want to go,' he assured me as he refilled my cup.

'I can drive myself—I don't need Wali.'

'Saab, but I made a club sandwich for you, still your favourite, I hope. You'll enjoy having it with your tea. Let Wali go with you, it's not safe to drive alone at night in Lahore these days.'

'Please go and arrange for the car. I promise I'll eat,' I said, regaining my composure. 'I know how to take care of myself.'

Ghulam Rasool left the room looking puzzled and shaking his head, probably worried about what my father would say if I was not well cared for and coddled.

My perception of reality had taken another huge hit. I was left with no appetite. Sipping tea, I took a few bites of my favourite sandwich just to fill my stomach. My mind coiled around the shocking tragedy. Stop, I told myself. Nothing could be solved by me sitting here on my ass, becoming paralyzed with anxiety.

Slowly my thoughts were replaced by blind rage. I loathed my father and everything he stood for with all my heart. I could envision all the martyrs out there, high on Paradise Water, using his brilliant invention to beam themselves to the next world. How about I blew myself up by wearing his vest when he gave me the obligatory hug?

The phone rang. I knew it was him, my father. Gritting my teeth, I picked up the phone from beside the bed.

'Hello.'

'Assalamualaikum, Ismael. I hope you had a good rest?' my father asked. 'I was busy last night and could not call you.'

'I'm good,' I said. 'My phone was stolen anyway.'

'It happens all the time. Wali will take you in the morning to the market. I'll call the store in advance. You may go and pick whichever one you like. Do you use an Android or Apple?'

I did not say anything, but he never noticed and went on talking.

'I'll be back in Lahore tomorrow evening. Until then you have a driver and a cook at your disposal. This place is not as bad as it may seem on the surface. Did you like the house?'

'I love what you did to it.'

'Allah has never been so gracious and kind. When I see you, we'll talk, Inshallah!'

'Okay—until then Allah Hafiz.' I tried to sound bright and friendly.

'Allah Hafiz,' he said, and the line went dead.

I was glad he was in no more of a mood to chat than I was. If my father was such a big honcho in the Khalifa circle, his phone was probably being tapped by Khalifa's security. And I was possibly already a known entity somewhere high up in the Caliphate.

I felt frustrated by the absurdity of a mission that required me to gain the trust and affection of a person like my father. The whole thing would have been a lot easier were he a complete stranger. If I didn't pull this mission off, the fact that I was the man's son would do nothing to help me and would probably hasten my spectacular demise. Pir and his crew had taken extraordinary measures to make a seemingly unthinkable task seem thinkable. But all this was for what?

I had never been a man of faith as far as its ritualized version was concerned. I had taken the religious text to be a manufactured narrative that had been propagated over centuries without having to face any serious examination, but in all honesty, I had never given a serious thought to God. I considered myself an agnostic, I wasn't sure what it was I had to deny or believe in. But now I couldn't deny that I had been shown Hell, and I had also seen the luminescent golden light that bathed the lush countryside studded with waterfalls and across from it the walls of Paradise, some seventy years away on the back of a horse. I had sipped tea with Chacha at the Bihishti Tea Corner and listened to the haunting melody from the flute of Ibrahim. And I had seen ababeels. Was there some mysterious divine intervention at play here, and I a part of it?

Ghulam Rasool barged back into my room carrying a milkshake.

'Another favourite of yours, saab!' he said with obvious delight.

Not wanting to disappoint the old man who was taking great pains to please me and make me comfortable, I took the glass and tasted his confection.

'Delicious as ever,' I said, giving him a smile. 'Is my car ready?'

'Saab, Wali will take you anywhere you want to go,' he insisted once again.

'Tell him to get the car ready, I'll be out in fifteen minutes,' I said, heading to the bathroom but suddenly remembering the water situation.

'Is it okay to take a shower?'

'No good, saab. There's a bucket in there I just filled with warm water for you. I've put in an extra dose of Gentian Violet. But it may still smell though.'

'Thanks! So very thoughtful of you. Everyone around here uses the bottled Paradise Water for cooking and drinking?'

'Of course, saab. What else would we use?'

I stood in front of the bathroom mirror surveying my facial piety when the lights went out.

At 9.40 p.m. I was back on the road, thankfully alone, with just the Quran and Pir's headband tucked in my pocket. It was a pleasant night, chilly but not unseasonably cold. Wali, of course, had insisted that he come along. Except that he had no choice but to obey my orders and stay behind.

I instructed the two of them that I would probably return around midnight, but no matter how late I was out, they were not to panic and start calling my father. They both urged me to take their cell phones along, their faces reflecting grave concern for my safety, but I refused. I didn't want to be tracked.

The streets were a disaster, filled with potholes, having suffered everything from prolonged neglect to roadside bombings. The upside was that traffic was light and confined to emergency travel and dire necessity. I got to Shah Jamal without any incidents and parked the car in the same spot Wali had the night before.

As soon as I got out of the car, I was welcomed by the piercing howls of the cats as they moved about in their massive Bunyan tree. There seemed to be more of them gathered now than the previous night. I looked around for emergency barricades, the kind you would expect at the scene of a violent crime, but there was no sign of any police activity.

The place was deserted and dark, but it wasn't difficult to guess why. These ferocious animals, in such numbers, could terrorize a whole town if they wanted to. Oddly enough I felt relaxed and quite alert. The trip to Hell seemed to have done wonders for my fears. I slipped Pir's headband over my brows and started toward the entrance.

I was a few feet away from the arched gate when I heard a soft thud behind my back. I froze in my tracks. Then I heard another thud. I turned around and saw two cats standing about ten feet from me. I held my ground as they padded silently toward me. Their steps were slow, deliberate and non-threatening. I recognized them; they were Pir's jinn cats.

They stood at my side, regarding me with those mesmerizing yellow eyes. As I stroked their smooth fur, they rubbed their bodies against my legs. The howling had stopped and I pushed open the entrance of the shrine. The cats accompanied me as they had Pir when he made his rounds about the courtyard housing those tightropes.

The shrine's courtyard was strewn with broken glass and scorched debris, and resembled a ruin from antiquity. An eerie silence gripped the place, punctuated only by my footsteps.

A lone figure sat hunched beside a meagre fire near the staircase and looked up when he heard my footsteps. His haggard face and long braids caked with white dust made him look like a statue.

'Ya Mushkil Kusha!' he shrieked, shaking his head from side to side, throwing his hands in the air. A cloud of ash flew off his body as he turned to look at me with bloodshot eyes.

'Come sit here with me, brother,' he pleaded. I could see there was dried blood on his face, but I saw no visible wounds and wondered what horrors the man had witnessed, or participated in, during last night's activities.

I squatted by his side and stared into the flames which had begun to die out.

'I'm very sorry about what happened here,' I said to him, my feelings truly sincere.

He just sat there, staring into the fire and digging absently at the crumbling embers with a stick, but said nothing.

'I'm looking for Pir Pul Siraat and Tarzan. Do you know anything about what happened to them?' I asked.

'It's all over, Ismael,' he said with a hoarse voice.

It startled me to hear him say my name. I looked at him closely. His face was obscured by ash and grief, and tears streaked the wearied flesh. Then I knew who this man was. He was the dhol player whom Pir had invited into his quarters after I had swallowed the contents of the yellow vial.

'Please tell me, did Pir survive or was he killed? I must know. If he's alive, I need to see him, please!' I begged, gripping the man's arm. 'I'm sorry, but I don't know your name,' I added.

'My name is Pappu. Pappu Saien.'

'Help me, Saien.'

'I can't help you, Ismael. That bastard has taken down the best of our people.'

'Saien, do you know Tarzan? Is he alive?'

'Only Allah knows if he's alive or dead. Ahhhh! I live to see this day!' He sighed, rubbing the side of his head with his palms and dislodging more ash from his hair.

'Saien, please. If Pir is alive, take me to him,' I begged. 'You know where he lives.'

'No one can enter Pir's abode without an invitation,' he said solemnly.

'Not even in emergencies?'

'No.'

'Not even in catastrophic times like these?'

'Pir's abode can be found only by going into the intermediate world—the one between this world and the next. Unless you're escorted there, you cannot find it. Those who could have escorted you are all dead, Ismael,' he said softly, his voice choked with tears.

So Pir had survived. I was elated. The revelation only confirmed what I already suspected: Pir, like Chacha Khidr, was no ordinary earthly personage. He hadn't been speaking in metaphors or poetry when he told me he was a hybrid. He was neither jinn nor fully human, but I had no clue what kind of hybrid he was.

I touched the headband on my forehead, remembering the headphones in Pir's ears, his big military-style black boots, the pack of John Player's Gold Leaf cigarettes he had, his coppery skin that glowed in the light of flames, his fiery gaze and his not-so-secret dislike for the best of creation: humans.

I left the courtyard in complete emotional disarray as the cats accompanied me back to my car. Tarzan was likely dead as far as I knew, blown to pieces by his own bodyguard. If *that* was the case, the black book probably still needed to be retrieved from the water tank back at the hospital. After all, it was the thing on which Khalifa's powers rested, his ticket to Paradise, as Pir had put it. But how was that to be done?

Standing beneath their tree, the cats waved their tails in the air. Waving back at them, I sat behind the wheel and rolled down my window.

'I wish you guys could tell me how to find Pir,' I said, as I turned on the ignition. By the time I got the headlights on, the cats had vanished. It was then that I heard Pir's voice.

'Ismael, can your hear me?' his voice loud and clear inside my mind as before. It felt so strange I almost forgot to breathe.

'Hello Ismael, it's Pir Pul Siraat,' he said inside my head again. Stunned, I touched my headband. I almost pulled it off without thinking when he spoke again.

'Your headband is a telepathic headset. We're going to be using it to communicate,' he said.

'Pir! Hell! Can you hear me?' I said out loud, feeling ecstatic to hear his voice.

'You don't have to shout. In fact, you don't have to speak at all. Just keep calm and think.'

'Pir, how is this possible?'

'Everything is possible, Ismael. We have our own ways of communicating with one another, just like you have yours,' he said.

'I must say, this is pretty outrageous,' marvelling at something that would put any hi-tech corporation to shame. At that instant, the face of Don Miguel rose in my memory. I remembered how he had tapped his headband over his temple and told me: *The people of the spirit world have their own special methods of communication.* Had he been in touch with Pir and Chacha through his headband the whole time I was tripping on Ayahuasca under his supervision? He had to be, for why would he say: *A great task has been given to you, Ismael. Make yourself available to it, no matter how strange it may appear.*

'Pir, is Tarzan dead?' I asked and held my breath, afraid of the answer.

'Tarzan's here with me.'

'He's alive? Yes!' I yelled. A sense of relief coursed through my body and I smiled. 'Did he get you the book?'

'That's exactly what you're going to do for me right now. I want that book.'

'That's exactly where I was heading, after hearing about the blast and thinking Tarzan hadn't made it. I'm shocked at the loss of so many lives Pir, I'm deeply sorry.'

'We're living in a war zone, Ismael,' he said. 'If we lose this war, the world will be counting its dead for a very long time.'

'Where will I find you once I have the book in my hands?' I asked him, remembering the dhol player's shocking news that all the guides who could take me to Pir were dead.

'Once you get the book, send me your thoughts and tell me of your success—make sure you have the headband on. I'll let you know then what the next step will be,' he said, and then he was gone, just like that.

'Pir, Pir! Don't go!' I cried, but there was just an echo of my own thoughts.

I looked down at my watch. It was 10.40 p.m. Once I got the book I could probably make it back to my father's house by midnight.

17

PIR'S WORDS PLAYED OVER AND OVER again in my head during the twenty-minute drive from the shrine to the hospital. I only marvelled at the telepathic headband that enabled psychic telecommunication between distant parties. Was it purely technological with some chip embedded that was capable of things I had only read about, and which were rumoured to be used by the Green Berets?

Or could I be having some kind of auditory hallucination thanks to the multiple concoctions I was given to ingest, Hoor Afza included? Or was this something even stranger; something that sprang from a world only Pir and Chacha Khidr could understand?

Whatever the explanation may be, it was Pir's voice that had resounded within my head over my left temple with the best news of all: Tarzan was alive. The boy had a bright future under the tutelage of someone like Pir. His death at such a young age would have been a terrible loss. Besides, I just liked the kid. And what of Chacha Khidr? He had to be alive too. He was clearly even less a part of this world than Pir and had probably defied death a thousand times.

I drove through the gate of the hospital, looking for signs of any suspicious activity. All the lights were out and the place looked deserted. To make sure someone driving through the gate couldn't see my car, I left it at the far end of the empty parking lot.

As I walked across the tarmac to the hospital entrance, I tapped my headband. I also wondered if Laila was on duty tonight at the reception desk.

'Pir, hello! Are you there?' I thought but got no answer.

I climbed the steps to the emergency room entrance and paused. It would be damn near impossible to find my way around in the dark once I was inside the building. And I would never be able to navigate through that tunnel of junked furniture piled outside the bathroom door.

I thought about going to the drug store across the street for a flashlight, even a keychain mini-light maybe, when the door swung open. I was pleasantly startled to see Laila barreling through the darkened doorway.

Her huge kohl-lined eyes widened when she saw me. She had an unlit cigarette in one hand and a Styrofoam cup in the other. We just stared at each other in silence for several awkward seconds.

'I love the headband, Ismael,' she said, grasping for something to say.

'Good to see you again, Laila,' I replied, flashing her a broad smile. It was the truth. I couldn't remember one girl out of the many whom I had slept with, once upon a time in New York, who had made me want her with the kind of passion I was feeling at this minute. This shrouded beauty in black with her big, black gorgeous eyes said all that needed to be said. I was more than delighted to see her again, but there was a part of me that also knew this girl was trouble.

'I'm on my break. Come have a smoke with me.' She said it like a dare, sensing I probably wouldn't refuse her offer. Not waiting for a reply, she glided over to the service ramp and leaned back against the cement railing.

I knew I would never reach the bathroom unless I smoked with her. The task of getting the book had suddenly gotten a lot more complicated than it seemed a moment ago. 'Sure, I could definitely use one.' I followed her down the ramp.

Laila sighed, lifted the edge of her veil and took a sip from her cup, then set it on the ledge beside her. Pulling a white pack of Marlboro Lights out of the folds of her burqa, she tapped one halfway out and pointed it towards me.

I shivered with excitement; to be in such close proximity to that dazzling pair of eyes was sheer bliss. She flicked her lighter and lit my cigarette first.

The girl had style! With a smile on my face, my instincts triggered, I leaned back against the railing next to her, our bodies just inches apart. I took off my headband, stuffed it in my pocket, while brooding. I was expected to perform better this time around and I was already failing. Regardless, I didn't want Pir to intrude into moments of my personal life.

'I had a feeling you'd be back,' she said, as she slid her veil from over the corner of her mouth, and pressed the cigarette between her lips.

She slid her body closer to mine, but still not touching, and lit the cigarette which looked as if it was suspended in the darkness by magic. She looked toward the sky and took a long drag. I wished she would just take the damn veil off.

'I don't know—it feels like I've known you for a long time,' she said, exhaling into her veil. With an eerie effect, smoke rose through the thin black fabric of her burqa.

'It's uncanny. I actually feel the same way.' I slid towards her and stopped when our bodies touched.

'I liked your headband. The red looks good on your face. Why did you take it off?' She gently pressed herself against me.

'To cool my head.'

'I love the Nike slogan.'

'Me too!' Was our conversation going to stay so inane?

'Just do it!' She turned to face me. 'Life's too short.'

'Just do it?!' I squeaked, unsure of what she was up to. Even in New York City such careless sprints to the finish line were frowned upon.

'Yes,' she whispered, closing up whatever little distance there was between us and pressing her shoulder into mine.

I clasped my hands in front of me and stared at the glowing tip of my cigarette, watching it rise slowly away from my body. Damn, the girl didn't stand on formalities.

'Can I see your face?' I asked, swallowing hard. 'I'm not really into anonymous sex,' I added with a smile, unable to find anything else to say.

Laila flicked her cigarette away and watched it roll down the ramp into oblivion. Her lips brushed the rim of her cup as she slid in front me. Her veiled face was inches from mine now and her breath, through the black curtain over her face, was warm against my cheek. Her eyes were aflame with passion and bore into mine.

I lowered my head to give her a kiss where I thought her lips would be but she turned away. Then suddenly she turned back and embraced me with such hunger that I felt as if she was going to devour me, her body pulsating with raw energy. Her large, firm breasts pressed against my chest flared my own fire to a new high. I was burning with desire. Any sense of control I had was now gone. Feeling my hardness, Laila pressed her crotch against me and swayed her body with mine.

'Just do it,' she pleaded in my ear, biting my earlobe through the fabric of her burqa.

'You're a dangerous woman,' I panted, breathing hard into her ear as my arm encircled her waist and I pressed her body tightly against mine. I knew I had fallen headlong into the pit of my lust and only a miracle could keep me from fully indulging in it. Unlike fear, my lust was proving too hard to get a good handle on; it needed my active participation to die down. Where the hell was my willpower? It seemed to have gone to sleep somewhere. I had to put up a fight.

'Would you please take your goddamn burqa off?' I asked. Inside the voluminous black covering, her body felt like that of a girl in her mid-twenties. Slim, toned, hot. But I could be terribly wrong in this land of strange uncertainties.

'This is not New York City! We'd be crazy to do it right here,' she whispered with a deep sigh.

I wanted to tell her that wasn't quite what I had in mind when I asked her to remove her burqa. All I wanted was to see her face, but I didn't say anything. I relaxed my grip on her waist and she pulled away, her small hand dragging across my chest.

'Come with me,' she said, the voice of a confident tease returning. Grabbing her cup from the railing, she started walking up the ramp.

'I know a secret place,' she said over her shoulder.

'You're playing with fire, Miss Night.' But I was the one getting singed.

'Night has to seek fire to become illuminated,' she said.

'Uh-oh... They're selling a variety of stones for people like us in the market,' I said, struggling to slow things down.

'Yes, we're good for the economy,' she quipped. 'Come on, let's get out of here.'

Suddenly I was hit by strange kind of déjà vu. I felt like I had already lived a lifetime with this girl, as if I knew her all the way down to the root of her soul. I shook my head to dispel such fluffy notions.

'Not tonight. I've got things to do.'

'Ah! Men. Scared of getting stoned.'

Now she had challenged my manhood.

What if she turned out to be the agent of some secret society? What if her crowd didn't jibe with *my* secret society? Under the circumstances, anything was possible. I was afraid to touch my headband, which was still safely tucked in my pocket. I was afraid to put it on lest Pir started barking orders in my head. What if he called while we were making out? He would surely wonder why I didn't have it on. I assumed that it had to be on my head for the communication to take place. What if the headband was communicating right from my pocket? What if Pir could not only talk, but also see my activities through this telepathic headset of his? Was it just simply stupid and dangerous to assume anything at all about Pir? It definitely seemed like it.

'Hey listen…' I started, as she headed for the door, its glass reflecting flashing red lights. Damn! It was the Commaqaadis!

'Stay quiet and follow me,' she whispered.

'Yes, ma'am,' I dashed behind her, as the flashing red lights neared the hospital gate.

The power was still out as we walked past the glass-panelled entrance down the dark hall toward the rear of the building, skirting along the wall separating us from the emergency room waiting area. I knew exactly where we were headed.

A minute later we stood in front of the ten-foot wall of rusting hospital junk. Laila's lighter came in handy and I was able to see the twisted cabinet Tarzan and I had used the night before. The girl was taking me closer to the object of my mission. So far so good. My desire was in harmony with my mission, geographically speaking. I was on the right track. But could I resist her? I wasn't sure. *Be strong*, I told myself. *You can do it.*

We crept through the same tunnel he had led me down, and we exited through the same broken closet door. The bathroom still smelled of Tarzan's handiwork on the briefcase. The flame from the lighter began to splutter just as we reached our destination.

'I can't keep it on—it's burning my finger,' she said, extinguishing the flame and my hope of seeing her face.

We stood in pitch darkness, listening to our breathing, ready to devour each other. My desire for her was like a blaze that had all but consumed whatever was left of my sense of duty.

If this were going to happen, it would have to in a standing position, unless I could find myself a chair or a bench from the pile of junk.

Laila threw herself into my arms. Mustering the last of my willpower, I jerked away.

'Wait!'

'What's the matter? What's happening?' Laila asked, touching my face with her fingers.

'I'm going to look for a chair or something,' I said, heading toward the door. 'Just stay put. I'll be back.'

'What? Where are you going?' she asked, obviously confused and sounding annoyed. 'We don't need a chair.'

Without replying, I opened the door and dashed out of the bathroom, making sure to close it behind me.

I stood in the dark by the pile of junk, my mind racing. I had a feeling that Pir must be trying to get in touch with me, so I took the headband out of my pocket and put in on.

'Where have you been, Ismael?' Pir roared in my head.

'Sorry, Pir. Can't explain right now—but I'm right next to the book,' I thought, hoping Pir wouldn't pick up any of the savory details of the last few moment from my mind.

'Are you sure?'

'Yes.' I moved away from the door and stuck my head under what my probing fingers told me was a wooden desk balanced atop the steel beams of what felt like a bunch of IV stands and end tables.

'Waiting for further instructions, Pir,' I whispered into the underside of the desk.

'All right, now I'm not going to repeat myself, so listen very carefully.'

'Go ahead,' I said, taking the measure of the desk with my hands. It seemed perfect for the intended purpose.

'First, find a quiet place where no one will disturb you, somewhere you can lie down for ten to fifteen minutes.

Then open the book and examine its pages closely. You'll see scored indentations dividing each page into small squares of a centimeter in size.'

'Yeah, I know exactly what you're talking about,' I said, remembering the look of the pages.

'Good. With the book in your hand, carefully tear one square from one of the pages and then close the book. Next, remove the headband and tie it around the book as if it was your head. Make sure it fits snuggly. Did you get all that?'

'Yeah, got it. Go ahead,' I said, feeling a little annoyed and confused.

'Then lie down on a comfortable spot and put the torn piece of paper under your tongue.'

'Then?' I muttered apprehensively.

'There is no then, then.'

'Not another drug, Pir! Please. I'm still not over my jet lag or the other chemicals,' I said, feeling exhausted and dejected.

'Well, what can I say? Your desire to see Paradise was so heartfelt and sincere that it moved heaven and earth. See you soon,' he said and then closed off his thoughts. He was gone, just like that.

'Paradise!' I said out loud, moving the desk and banging it against the pile to let Laila know I was still out there. Did he mean he was going to see me in Paradise?

I slowly straightened up, using the top of my head to lift the desk off the broken poles. Steadying the bulky weight with my hands, I inched toward where I thought the door was. Thankfully, Laila was standing there to guide me through. She flicked her lighter on just in time and I managed to get the desk through the door by tilting it slightly. In the light of her flame, my weirdly distorted shadow jerked across the floor of the bathroom revealing exactly how precarious the maneuver was.

'We needed something really sturdy to support our weight,' I said, trying to catch my breath and thinking the only way to get rid of this girl would be to satisfy her *now*. I had no choice but to do it for the sake of my mission.

'Passion doesn't need any external support,' she told me, locking the door from the inside. 'Do you realize the desk only has three legs?'

'Would you please help me?' I asked, kneeling on the floor, feeling stupid as hell.

She scrambled to help me get the thing off my head, then stepped back. Once the desk was on the floor, it fell over the moment I let go. She turned on the flame, her gorgeous eyes staring at me quizzically.

Still kneeling on the floor in a humbled state of genuine despair, I felt torn between my duty and my desire. This burqa-clad temptress, whose face had remained elusive to my hungry eyes, had proven to be as formidable a force as Pir. I was pretty sure he wasn't listening at the moment.

Maybe it would work if the desk, which was about four feet high, was moved closer to the sink and we used the latter as a support for the missing leg. What if the height of the desk and the sink turned out to be uneven?

'What's wrong?' Laila asked. She came over and threw her arms around my neck and crushed her body into mine. Suddenly, I regained my wits. There was something really weird about her behaviour; even her movements seemed strange. She came off as too horny and over the top for my taste. At the very least, I had to see her face if I was going to allow her to take up any more of my time and energy. My desire began to wane.

'Sorry,' I said, disentangling myself from her arms. 'I just can't do it, not like this, not until I see your face,' I gently placed my hands on her slim waist to show her we were still in negotiations. Just then something beneath my hand began to vibrate.

Laila pulled away from me and dug a cell phone out of her burqa. She looked at the number.

'I'll be there in a minute,' she said into the phone. Hanging up, she touched my face with her fingertips.

'You stay here, love. I'll be back. They've brought in a head-injury case. I have to go.'

'I guess we're calling it off for the night.'

'It's not even midnight yet,' she said. 'Ismael, please don't go! It won't take me more than ten or fifteen minutes at the most,' she pleaded.

Ten or fifteen minutes. That's exactly what I was looking for.

'Okay fine—I'll wait.'

'See if you can find something sturdier than that desk. I have to run,' she said, heading toward the door. 'And keep the headband on your head. It looks so sexy on you.'

'Leave your lighter with me, if you don't mind. You can use the light on your phone to get out,' I said.

Without a word, she handed me the lighter and disappeared out the door and into the dark maze of junk.

I flipped the lighter on and climbed on top of the commode. Reaching into the tank and feeling around, I breathed a sigh of relief. The book was there, lying on the bottom of the tank, right where I had dropped it.

Going over Pir's instructions, I looked around the room for a place where I could sit and lean against the wall. The most suitable spot was a six-foot-wide area between the door and the sink.

Laila had left her styrofoam cup on the sink. I picked it up, smelled it and cautiously took a sip. As soon as the vile liquid touched my tongue, I spat it out into the sink and wiped my mouth in disgust with the back of my hand. Holy crap! Laila had been drinking the goddamn Hoor Afza. No wonder she had been acting so provocatively.

Making myself comfortable beside the sink, I opened the book and tore one of the little squares from the top corner of the first page. I then pulled my headband off and slid it over the book's leather-bound cover from top to bottom—the only way to fit it snugly. I looked at my watch. It was now 11.30 p.m. I extinguished the lighter, said my *bismillah,* and put the little square of paper under my tongue.

Immediately an effervescent sweetness bubbled across my tongue and flowed through the roof of my mouth into my brain. My forehead tingled as if a host of butterflies were fluttering behind my eyes. My heart pounded in my chest as a delicious vibration washed through my body from my head to my feet. Feeling a little apprehensive, I turned on the lighter and looked at my hands and arms. There was no sign of shaking; the flame in my hand was perfectly steady and surrounded by an intense multicoloured halo. Taking a deep breath, I flicked the lighter shut and the room sunk in darkness.

The inner shaking intensified and my head swelled with a roaring noise. I felt as if I was being suspended in space and immediately the noise surged into a shrieking wail. Then all sound and sensation melted into a brilliant white light that shattered like glass into a million diamond-tipped arrows, which plunged toward the core of my being. My body felt so heavy, like I was weighed down by a massive boulder.

Keeping my eyes shut, I allowed the arrows of light to pierce my body. Then something hot and fleshy shot into my mouth and started moving around. I heard Laila's voice from far away and tried opening my eyes but my eyelids refused to budge.

'You're all sweet like honey.'

I almost gagged when I realized Laila was on top of me, her tongue hungrily exploring the interior of my mouth. I tried twisting my torso to get her off me, but my body felt paralyzed. I had lost all power to resist and my limbs hung loosely at my sides like those of a dead man. I tried to speak, but my tongue refused to move. I panicked, realizing I wasn't even breathing.

'Come back!' Laila screamed.

That was the last thing I heard before I lost consciousness.

18

❦

THE THUNDEROUS ROAR OF WATER crashing over rocks jolted me awake. I opened my eyes to a clear blue sky and a waterfall to my left. The air was warm and humid, and the scent of cinnamon drifted through the air. Except for a faint sweetness from the magical potion that clung to my lips, the bizarre scene in the hospital bathroom seemed like nothing more than the lingering tendril of a bad dream.

I looked at my body and sat upright. I was completely naked, not even wearing my watch. A woman was lying beside me wearing nothing either, but her wheat-coloured skin was radiant and a veil of jet-black hair was thrown over her face. She was asleep; her arms were spread out and her breasts displayed like golden dunes rising from a desert ground.

Mesmerized, I let my gaze follow her luscious curves until it fell on the black book pressed between the grass and her right hip. My red headband had slid to the edge of the cover and was about to fall off.

Was this Laila? I wasn't sure because I had never actually seen her face. I remembered zoning out in the bathroom after dissolving that tiny piece of paper under my tongue as Pir had instructed. I had been completely immobilized as Laila pinned me to the ground and her hot tongue ravaged the inside of my mouth.

The woman stirred in her sleep, her beautiful face looking toward the sky. Her shaved pubic area was as smooth as a baby's belly and an insistent stirring in my loins made me look around for something to cover myself with.

We lay in a grassy sloped meadow. One side merged into a bay bordered by steep blue granite cliffs of an inlet that led to the sea. Near the shore, a hundred feet or so from us, the huge waterfall poured down the face of the cliff and crashed against the rocks, sending plumes of mist and spray into the air. On the other side of the meadow, rocky cliffs were crowned by a knoll covered with shrubs that shimmered as if lit by the sun.

Except that no sun hung in this strange monochromatic blue sky. Luminescence seemed to be radiating from the ground and everything glowed as if lit from within. I got to my feet and stood, marvelling at the stark alien beauty of this dreamlike terrain and the unknown woman who slept at my side, oblivious of her surroundings.

Could this beauty be a hoor; one who had drifted away from her flock? I glanced at the girl's ankles, looking for signs described in the traditional Islamic texts, but her ankles were not translucent. I walked over to a patch of vegetation, my feet relishing the exquisitely soft grass beneath, but my mind scattered like beads of mercury. Something had gone very wrong. There was no sign or word from Pir. Hopefully, he was on his way and would appear any moment. It was 11.30 p.m. when I had last looked at my watch but I had no idea what time it was here or if there even was a 'here'.

I broke off several leafy shoots from the shrubs and wrapped them around my waist, tying each of them in a knot. Satisfied that they had adequately covered my private parts, I thought of taking some for the woman but decided against it. I was in no hurry to give up the vision of such a beautiful naked woman.

By the time I got back, she was awake. She sat like a yogin, her back straight, her radiant black hair covering her breasts and her hands covering her face except her eyes. They were Laila's eyes; and in her lap lay the black book.

'Ismael! Is that you?' she asked, keeping her face covered and pretending not to see me. 'Where are we?'

'Laila! What the hell are you doing here?' I demanded, drawing closer to her. 'You were supposed to be attending to a head injury back in the emergency room.' As I said this, I realized how ridiculous I must have sounded.

'Is this a dream? Everything here is so—so beautiful.' She said, gazing at our surroundings with bewildered eyes.

'Yes, it is. In a dream, you know, you're permitted to unveil your face.'

'No!' she hissed. 'You won't like me if I let you see my face,' she cried, her head still buried in her hands and thrashing back and forth like a village mourner. Her reaction completely baffled me.

'Why would you say such a thing?' I knelt beside her.

'See this side of my face?' She pressed her right cheek with her fingers without lifting her palms. 'The first stone hit me here,' she said through her tears. 'It blew my cheekbone and knocked me out. That's the only reason I'm alive today. They thought I was dead and left me there to rot.' Her shoulders shook.

'Who are these people?'

'Men.'

'My God!' I placed my hands on her head and stroked her hair.

'It took a long time to heal, leaving this ugly scar under my eye. That's why I refused to take my veil off when you asked me to.' Her sobbing continued.

I held her wrists and gently moved them away, only to find an impeccably beautiful and unblemished face.

'But your face is perfect and lovely. I don't see any scar. What are you talking about?' As she touched her cheek and slid her trembling fingers over the soft flawless skin, her eyes widened and she gasped in happiness and covered her mouth. 'You're right! Oh my God! Ismael, how can this be?'

'May I have the book, please? Actually, just the headband.' I asked.

She slid it off the book and handed it to me without uncovering her lap.

Pulling it over my head and adjusting the logo, I collected my thoughts and beamed them to Pir, my brows furrowed with the effort. But there was no reply.

'Hello! Can you hear me? Pir, can you hear me?' I whispered, tapping my temple this time.

'Who are you talking to?' she asked, her voice filled with curiosity and amusement.

I stayed silent for if I mentioned Pir, I would have to explain a whole lot more. And the last thing I wanted to do was compromise Pir's mission. I struck my temple several more times in order to establish the connection but without success.

'Look, I'm really sorry about last night,' she said. Her cheeks flushed. 'I couldn't control myself and when I came back and saw you lying on the floor, I just couldn't help it.'

'I thought it was illegal for women to drink Hoor Afza.'

She turned her face away without saying anything.

'You see this,' I told her, taking the headband off and holding it in my hand. 'This is a special kind of phone. If we can't make it work, we're struck here forever.'

'The minute I saw you in the emergency room that night, I knew you were different. Special,' she said, her eyes searching mine, not having heard what I had just told her.

'Well, thank you,' I slid the headband back over my head, giving my temple yet another tap. 'Hello, hello.'

'Ismael, it's so strange. I feel it all happened such a long time ago.'

'What happened a long time ago?' I asked distractedly, listening for the sound of Pir's voice in my head.

'The stuff in the bathroom—the time when we met. It all feels as if it happened in another life. Do you feel that way too?'

'I need to make this thing work,' I said, ignoring her questions, speaking more to myself than her. I took the infuriating piece of red fabric off my head and lashed the air with it several times before putting it back on.

'So what's next, boss?' She was now composed and her lips curled in a smile.

Her beauty was mesmerizing; her supple skin radiated vitality and her eyes were suffused with a calm, steady desire.

'I'm going to take a walk up that hill and see what's on the other side.' I pointed towards the grassy knoll. 'It looks like a ten-to fifteen-minute walk.'

'Ismael, you are a true gentleman. How many men can keep their cool with a naked woman sitting right beside them?'

Had she known what was stirring beneath the canopy of leaves around my waist, she would have thought otherwise.

'You want to come along?' I asked, jumping to my feet and quickly turning away from her.

'No, I want to go look at that waterfall. It's so magnificent! You go on up. We'll meet back here. Sound good?' she asked. 'And please, don't forget to bring some leaves back for me,' she added, rising to her feet with effortless grace and making sure the book still concealed her.

I wondered what would happen if the book got wet. It could wash away whatever the pages were coated with. Then it struck me: why not tear out a couple of the tiny squares and put them under our tongues. That would probably beam us out of here. It was a wild thought, but certainly worth a try—but only if Pir and I failed to make contact, in the next twenty-four hours.

'Would you mind trading that book for my leaves?' I asked Laila, thinking that on my way up the hill I would harvest another eco-friendly organic loincloth.

Laila pursed her lips and stared at my canopy of leaves as if giving the trade a great deal of thought. I felt uncomfortable under her mischievous gaze as it wandered over my not-so-well-hidden private parts. I wished I had used a few more leaves to make my cover denser.

'Sure, that works. Here,' she said, thrusting the book toward me and locking her eyes on mine in case my gaze was to drop. 'Now, may I please have the leaves?' She demanded with a smile and an outstretched hand.

Keeping my eyes on hers, I smiled and untied the precarious foliage from my waist and extended the leafy strands to her. A few had fallen off during this maneuver. We made our exchange without allowing our eyes to take unfair advantage of the awkward trade-off. As soon as I got the book in my hand, I turned and sprinted in the direction of the hilltop, savouring her hot stare on my bare ass.

'Wait!' she yelled from behind. 'Would you be kind enough to loan me that headband of yours? I need something to tie my hair with.' Her request was innocent enough, but I knew better than to part with it. What if Pir tried to contact me?

'You can have it when I get back,' I said, turning to look at her. She had her hands on her waist and looked ablaze with an inner light but was modest as hell. She had certainly made better use of the leaves than I had. She nodded, then turned around and headed toward the waterfall.

I continued toward the top of the hill, the book held firmly in my hand. Had Laila been accidentally transported here because she was kissing me when I passed out? Or was she here as a trap? I remembered her soft, hot tongue probing the inside of my mouth and tried to block the memory as it rose to demand the renewed attention of my cock.

I stopped by the shrubs and took my time to make a new garment for myself. To my satisfaction, it turned out to be a significantly improved design over the earlier version.

What I thought would be a fifteen-minute hike to the top turned into what felt like an hour. The sound of the waterfall had faded and the light had dimmed. The once-blue sky changed to a pale mauve. I had trouble locating Laila near the water, but then spotted her running in my direction. I stopped and waited for her to catch up with me. When she reached, she was out of breath, her face beaming with joy. Quite a few leaves had fallen away thanks to her sprint.

'What's going on?' I asked, stealing a glance at her breasts, at the rosy orb of flesh around her nipples that showed through her hair.

'I was looking at my reflection in the water. My face really is fine, perfectly normal! Ismael, I want to stay here forever.'

'Are you crazy?' I asked her, resuming my walk up the hill and adjusting the leaves around my waist.

'Ismael, we can live a perfect, happy life here—just you and I,' she said, following me. 'We'll make love—day and night and have lots and lots of children.'

'And then what?' I asked, without looking back at her.

'Then we'll grow old, watching our children grow. We'll play with our grandchildren and then one day we'll move on to the next world,' she explained, as though I should be delighted by the proposition.

'I'm afraid we're already in the next world,' I told her, wondering where the hell these grandchildren of ours were going to come from, barring incest. It all seemed like a very creepy idea.

She remained quiet as we ascended the grassy slope, zigzagging our way toward the ridge. Just below the summit we stopped to catch our breath. Standing in front of me, she clasped her hands under her chin, closed her eyes and started moving her lips.

'What are you doing?'

'Praying,' she said, opening one eye.

'That may be the only way we get out of here. Maybe I should join you,' I said.

'I'm praying to Allah to keep us here forever.'

'Isn't that like meddling with his plans?' I did not like where this was heading.

'He's known to change his mind if you ask sincerely.' A model of piety, she touched her face with her palms and blew her breath over her chest.

'How do you know for sure what's right for you and what isn't?' I asked, trying not to show the irritation I felt at this line of talk.

'Allah has given us the ability to know right from wrong.'

'Oh. The moral sense!'

'Yes, that.'

'So you seriously believe that staying here is right for you?' I asked, thinking she be completely out of her mind.

'Yes.'

'And what about me?' I threw my hands in the air, growing more and more annoyed.

'Man doesn't know what's right for him. That's why Allah created women to help them out.' She stated this way too forcefully.

'I don't agree with you.'

As the words left my mouth, the sky darkened over the inlet and the air exploded with a crescendo of noise. A black undulating shape filled the chasm over the water and advanced toward us. The screeching was unbearable and we had to cover our ears.

Ababeels!

It was the exact same sound I had heard just before I zoned out from drinking tea at the Bihishti Tea Corner.

We stood and watching in awe as a vast flock of tiny black birds zoomed over our heads. And just as suddenly it became still, silent, and the sky returned to its previous shade of mauve.

'What was that?' Laila asked with had her hands over her temples, her eyes wide.

'Ababeels,' I replied.

'Ababeels? So frightful!'

At that instant, the text of the *surah Al-Fil*, the Elephant, shot across my upper visual field in blazing red-gold Arabic script: 'Have you not seen what your Lord did with the companions of the elephant? And send on them birds in flocks. To throw on them stones of baked clay. And He made them like eaten straw.' It was one of a handful of surah I knew the translation of.

I recited these lines silently, imagining the sea of bloody carnage in the wake of Abraha's army as it advanced upon the Kaaba with its legion of elephants 1,500 years ago.

We continued walking, watching as the treetops came into view over the crest of the ridge. One of the trees shook and something moved within the canopy of leaves.

'Did you see that?' I shouted, pointing toward the tree.

'What was it?' Laila asked, equally alarmed.

'I'm not sure. Maybe some animal.'

The rocky cliff on each side of the knoll formed a natural pass which separated the stark landscape of the inlet from a strangely contoured country on the other side. It was like standing on the rim of a bowl and looking into it. Brimming with an exotic array of plant life and dotted with waterfalls, a seemingly interminable slope directed our gaze toward something hazy green at the bottom of the valley before ascending again. There it was, forming the opposite rim, occupying the elevated horizon like a band of dark clouds. The Wall! The perimeter of the most coveted real estate in the universe, Paradise. Laila gasped at the sight of it and gripped my arm, her body lightly trembling against mine.

'All praise to Allah! This surely is Paradise.' Her face was illumined by a peaceful glow of love; not passion this time, but love.

'Not exactly, technically speaking.'

'But look at that massive wall! None other than jinns could have constructed one of this size. How far do you think it is from here?'

'Seventy years on the back of a horse,' I said, remembering my conversation with Ibrahim at the Bihishti Tea Corner.

'Seventy years! How do you know that?'

'I just do. I also know that the Paradise you're talking about exists behind that great wall.'

'Really?'

'That's all I can tell you.'

She then turned to look at me and said, 'Ismael, it's time for you to explain how we got here.'

'It's complicated.'

'Try me.' She stared at me with her eyes wide, unblinking and demanding.

I considered her request for a moment. She looked too innocent and clueless to be a trap. And the truth itself was so wild that it would only make her laugh. I decided to spill the beans and held the book up for her to see.

'See this? It contains the tickets to Paradise. Literally.'

'Tickets to Paradise?' she asked with a hint of amusement in her voice. 'You mean those little coupons?'

'Yeah, *coupons*. They're good for a free ride,' I said, shaking my head and starting down the slope and away from the cluster of trees where I had spotted suspicious animal activity. 'I'll explain everything, I promise. First let's find someplace comfortable to sit down.'

She followed me silently.

Hoping Laila wouldn't notice, I tapped my headband repeatedly, visualized an 'SOS' in big bold letters and beamed the image at Pir, but no luck.

After having walked a couple of hundred steps, absorbing the surreal vista of a bowl-shaped landscape of staggering dimensions, we came upon another cluster of gigantic trees, each a hundred or so metres tall. Their roots rose off the ground like ledges and provided us with a natural seating area. We sat face-to-face and drew a few deep breaths.

'Are you ready for my story?' I asked, leaning toward her, drawn by a strong magnetic current. She radiated some kind of intoxicating warmth and my loins rippled with desire.

She bit her glistening lip and brought her face closer to mine. Our lips met and hers parted for a hot intake of breath.

Putting the book down, I stood up with her wrist in my hand and pulled her up. In the next moment we fell over and were rolling on the ground, wresting like wild animals, the leaves tumbling away from our heaving bodies. Without a warning she pulled out of my arms and sat upright. She stared at me, her eyes huge and pensive, her knees drawn up to hide her breasts.

'Ismael, do you accept me as your wife?'

'What kind of question is that?' I was completely taken aback.

'You'll have to say yes if you want to have me. Let's not risk our chance to enter Paradise.'

'For heaven's sake, last night you were all over me in that goddamn bathroom! Now all of a sudden you need to marry me before we can make love?' Ravishing as she was, I was in no mood for tying the knot with a strange, possessive woman I didn't really know, especially under such bizarre circumstances. Deep down I knew I had failed Pir, thanks to my unbridled sexual urges. Lust, women. My greatest weakness. For such a refractory case as I, death would be the only cure for such an affliction.

'Circumstances alter cases.' She smiled mischievously. 'So, what's your answer?'

I looked at her in utter disbelief and then a thought occurred. Why should I care when I had an option that would be perfectly halal according to the precepts of Sharia? I saw no reason why it wouldn't be acceptable to this newly minted Muslimmah.

'Okay, fine. Let's do the Mut'ah, the temporary marriage.'

'Although I'm not a Shia, that'll do for now.' She smiled. 'We can always convert it to a permanent one later.'

'Our contract will hold until we get back to our previous lives, or as long as we're stuck here.'

'It's a deal.'

So she asked me three times: 'Do you accept me as your lawful wife?' And I answered her each time: 'I do.'

'We are now married. Promise you'll never cheat on me.'

'For God's sake, Laila!'

She climbed on top of me, her knees on either side of my body, resting on the ground. Her nipples touched my chest as she bent over and played with my hair. Her breath on my face was hot, a fevered and rhythmic chant of desire.

'Ismael, I don't ever want to wake up from this lovely dream. Do you really love me?'

I lay hypnotized, staring at her ecstatic face as she took all of me inside her. She winced, then swung her head and threw her hair back as she started to grind against me. I took my headband off and put it around her forehead. She licked her lips and my fingers, and I shut my eyes. Mid stride she screamed, then collapsed on top of me, her pelvis filled with my throbbing cock still moving.

I heard a rustle over my head. Looking up, I saw the huge ass of a monkey retreating nimbly into the branches of the tree. And in his hand, the creature tightly gripped the black book.

'Hey!' I yelled, writhing under Laila's body in the throes of my orgasm and hers. 'Come back! Hey, you little shit, come back here. Fuck!' I screamed. But the monkey just kept climbing hand over hand and soon disappeared into the dense green covering overhead.

Laila kissed my cheeks, her breath still hot with desire. Her body twitched as I lay spent beneath her. I lamented the loss of our tickets to get out of this place, not to mention the chance of entering Paradise. Most importantly, what would Pir say? He seemed pretty adamant about a lot of things, but chief among them was his desire for that book.

I finally disentangled myself from Laila and jumped to my feet. Berating myself, I climbed up the tree trunk through the heavy branches as far as I could, but there was no sign of the mischievous thief.

Later, as we lay side by side on the grass staring up at the vault of space overhead, dusk crept over the hillside and bathed everything in radiant light. The air felt exquisite against our skin. The heavens were dotted with tiny lights, as if dangling from the hand of some celestial being as he watched from above. We made love again, gently this time, and then fell asleep; each surrendering to our private dreams.

When we awoke, the sky was a pale golden and the trees were full of birds in song. And we were starving.

After making love so wildly that our bodies were covered in bruises, we set off down the interminable slope toward the valley. Along the way, we gathered more leaves and fashioned new garments for ourselves. There was fresh water for us to drink and the air was sweet, warm and fragrant.

The trees were heavy and drooping with varieties of un-familiar but delicious fruits and we eat our fill of many of them. Still there was no appearance of the sun, that is if there even was one in this peculiar land, and daylight lasted only a short while. Dusk returned rather quickly, and to our amazement it turned to dawn without any intervening night. It was disorienting initially, but after a few of these sunless cycles we got used to it.

If this was how the punishment for my cardinal sins was going to look, then I wasn't complaining. However, the realization that my chances of getting out of here alive was pretty slim made me increasingly anxious.

We slept whenever we pleased, ate whenever we felt hungry, made love at each rest spot and continued our descent toward the valley. Along the way, we spotted several black monkeys squatting among the branches of the trees but there was no sign of the book among this troop. Eyeing us curiously and emitting low-pitched screams, they stood their ground without abandoning their perches and made no attempt to approach us.

It didn't take us long to realize we had lost all sense of time. Our descent continued for what felt like a lifetime. Laila's hair began to show streaks of white as did my beard which now reached my navel. The soles of our feet, after repeated blistering, had become thickly callused and our knees were swollen and throbbing with pain from the exertion of our perpetual downward march. To ease our discomfort, we made walking sticks out of fallen tree branches.

When we finally reached the floor of the valley, we followed a winding creek and at dusk came to a broad trailhead. Too exhausted and in pain to go any further, we made our bed in the tall, soft grass and went to sleep.

We woke up to the excited chatter of a gang of twenty or so wild-haired, topless women with white skin, extraordinarily beautiful faces and long legs. They spoke in a monosyllabic tongue, which sounded surprisingly musical and pleasing. Before we knew it, they had us surrounded and each woman carried a wooden spear pointed to our throats. Each of them wore a palm-sized green leaf over her pubic area.

Rubbing our eyes, we bolted upright and stared at these newcomers. Laila looked distraught seeing so many strange women around us. They had radiant skin, translucent over their ankles, through which the marrow could be seen within the core of their bones. It was the strangest thing to see, but in no way did it diminish the otherwise beautifully shaped legs.

Hoor! That was the only logical thought that came to my mind for the women's ankles fit the description of a hoor, a woman of Paradise, as stated in Islamic theology. Had we in fact landed in some forlorn corner of Paradise that happened to exist just outside its boundary wall?

19

D RAGGING US TO OUR FEET, the women tied our hands behind our backs using coarse vines as strong as rope. They marched us with their spears pointed at our backs over a thick, moss-covered trail that snaked through a humid forest of gigantic trees with smooth red bark and trunks twice the size of sequoias.

We passed several thundering waterfalls and crystal-clear ponds teaming with fish whose bodies glowed from within. We even spotted a three-legged fox, a double-headed deer, antelopes with horns mangled together in an ungainly mess, and a pair of winged horses white as snow.

After what seemed like several hours, we entered a dark, narrow, rocky canyon that opened up to a clearing about the size of a soccer field. Ensconced within a circular ring of red and black volcanic rocks, which jutted from the earth like a massive ridge of broken teeth, the place resembled an ancient coliseum. Its rocky face was cut in broad uneven steps, both horizontal and vertical, and was dotted with dozens of caves. At the far end of this amphitheater, another huge waterfall emptied itself into a pool where several women were bathing, playing and splashing around. Their laughter could be heard over the sound of the water.

The women marching us chatted in their melodious voices as they tied Laila and I to the gigantic trunk of a solitary tree whose canopy could easily provide shade to a whole village. It stood at the centre of the clearing with a lone guard watching over the settlement.

A sudden hush fell over the women as a gust of wind hit my face. Everyone looked up. My eyes blinked uncontrollably as I followed their gaze.

A winged creature, the hideous unnatural blending of a man and bird, glided through the air fifty feet above us. Its wings flapped unevenly as if with great exhaustion as it began to descend, landing just a few feet from us. The bizarre personage wore a tattered off-white cloak and was about five feet tall with a bowed back and drooping shoulders. He seemed to be in the advanced stages of some wasting illness.

He looked almost three hundred years old. Folding his wings behind his back, the man-creature stared at Laila and me with beady black eyes which had hardly any white in them. His elongated forehead and large hooked nose that appeared hard and beak-like were remarkable features on his otherwise human face. The creature was bald except for a few patches of fine gray feathers which grew out of his temples against the side of his face.

Moving his shoulders from side to side and clearing his throat, he looked like he was about to say something when the crowd parted and a stunning long-legged, luminous beauty emerged and stood before us. All I could do was stare in horror and fascination.

The woman's chest was dominated by a mammoth single breast, both taut and supple, without a hint of sagging. Her demonic nipple pointed straight at us as she stood beside the winged old man. She licked her upper lip a few times, as her big black eyes stared unblinkingly at me.

The woman whispered something in the old man's ear. He nodded in response, then bowed as if in supplication and clasped his hands in front of his body. He resembled a statue, the classic image of humility. The woman stepped closer and stopped in front of me, her feet spread apart. I glanced down and saw that, unlike the other women who wore the green leaves, she wore a red heart-shaped leaf over her crotch.

'I am Queen Xenobia!' she declared in perfect English with just a trace of an accent I couldn't place. 'Language?'

'English, Urdu and Punjabi,' I said, turning to look at Laila. She nodded her head in agreement. 'Some Arabic, as well,' I quickly added.

'Ah! Excellent. I've always had a fondness for Arabic,' she said, tossing her head.

'Uh… Well, I can read and write in Arabic, but I can't understand it,' I hurried to correct her, lest she started chattering in Arabic.

'Oh? How is that possible?' she exclaimed, wrinkling her nostrils and narrowing her eyes.

'It's very possible,' Laila chimed in. 'That's how it's always been done in my country.'

'And which country would that be?' Xenobia demanded, silencing Laila with an icy glance. 'Never mind. I don't really care,' she continued, turning away from Laila and looking at me again. I could see she had made Laila simmer with rage at being dismissed like that.

'Here, we speak all languages known to man. However, we have no capacity to understand women. I am one of the few, very few, who does understand them.' Her glance swept over the hushed crowd that seemed to be growing as we spoke.

'We mean no harm,' I said.

'Where are we?' piped in Laila.

'You were caught trespassing in the Dump,' Xenobia replied.

The winged creature shook his head as if in disagreement, but didn't lift his eyes from the ground.

'Dump?' I asked. She had just negated my suspicion that we were in Paradise. 'We never intended to trespass onto your settlement. We were just lost while hiking down the big green slope—we're from the other side of the ridge, you see,' I explained, thinking the Dump she was referring to meant this particular settlement of hers, or perhaps its adjoining jungle.

'This side or that, it doesn't matter. It's all part of the Dump we hate,' she said with a stern look.

'I wouldn't call it *that*,' the old man with the wings protested, speaking for the first time.

'You've never been dumped, Fukraeel,' the queen barked, looking over her shoulder at him. 'There's a difference between retiring here by choice and being discarded like trash just because we didn't come out perfect.'

'Who are we to question our fates?' the old man said meekly.

'What are you talking about? Where are we?' I couldn't help interfering.

'You,' the queen said, looking at me with an appraising eye. 'You may consider you're in Paradise.' She then glanced at Laila and smiled, but her eyes remained cold and distant. 'I'm not too sure if I can say that about you, my dear. Paradise is for men only.'

Laila straightened up, the rope around her torso tightening. She fixed Xenobia with an angry glare, her enraged face indistinguishable from the colour of my red headband she wore. Xenobia stepped closer to me and raised her hand.

'He's my husband,' she growled. 'Don't you dare put your dirty hands on him.'

'Laila, please! Stay calm,' I whispered in her ear.

'I don't like this place, Ismael. You'd better not do anything stupid here.' She started to sob.

'It was you who prayed to Allah to keep us here forever. I warned you not to ask for something you've no frickin' clue about. That's why I don't pray.' I said. 'Now be quiet and let me do what I can.'

Queen Xenobia turned and began addressing the assembled women in a language I had never heard before. The group had grown considerably since we arrived and now they crowded around their queen.

Most of them had conspicuously uneven breasts and a few had no breasts at all. Some women had very large ones with no nipples. I spotted one woman whose buttocks had no cleft in the middle; some had six fingers and some had missing toes. All of them had some bodily defect, but for their faces and legs, which were ravishingly beautiful with creamy, unblemished skin.

When Queen Xenobia finished her address, four women stepped forward from the crowd, followed by four more. They put their spears down, untied Laila and dragged her towards the forest. Entangled in the eight pairs of hands, she convulsed like a fish out of water. Her screams, piercing my heart and ears, faded as she was hauled from the canyon and swallowed by a dark crevice within the rocky massif. Horrified, I slumped against the tree and accepted my fate, still under the curious stares of these hauntingly beautiful women.

Soon, they untied me and marched me behind Queen Xenobia under the shadow of their spears. She led the procession up rocky steps into a large and luxurious cave that was decorated with a king's ransom of beautiful things.

Her three-room dwelling opened up to the waterfall and was pervaded by the atmosphere of the rain forest: misty, green and dark, and well stocked with a profusion of exotic fruits, nuts and fragrant flowers. Situated on a ledge next to the mouth of the waterfall, the queen's perch enjoyed a commanding view of the entire settlement. It was truly an aerie worthy of a great chief.

I was told by her in no uncertain terms that I was to be her sex slave from now on and if I refused or ever attempted to escape, I would meet a grievous end.

'You will get one hundred lashes a day for each day you don't perform. And without food or water you won't last long. Your choice couldn't be clearer.'

'Yes ma'am,' I muttered, suddenly overcoming by performance anxiety. For the next couple of days, despite her best efforts, she couldn't turn me on.

'I can't perform under stress.' I told her, still feeling frightened and heartbroken by the loss of Laila. Besides, it was that hideous breast of hers that independently turned me off.

'No worries. We've arrangements for all sorts of stress.' Xenobia smiled and poured me a tablespoon of some thick white liquid.

'What the hell is that?' I took the spoon from her and stared at the creamy liquid with disgust.

'Sex nectar, courtesy Fukraeel.'

'Do I have to drink this?'

'You've no choice, my dear Ismael.'

I emptied the spoon into my mouth without further argument and I realized the potion tasted like honey-sweetened kefir.

As I would soon discover, this sex nectar which she made me swallow three times a day was a remarkably potent aphrodisiac with addictive properties. It had been smuggled out of Paradise by Fukraeel.

He lived in a one-room nest made of twigs on top the encampment's only tree. The mouth of the queen's cave afforded a clear view of the old angel's comings and goings.

Xenobia told me that before his retirement, Fukraeel had served as a minor functionary in the lowest rung of Paradise. He possessed no sex organs, but he wasn't without a fine aesthetic sense and libido. To exercise that sense, he had become adventurous and resorted to illegal means to compensate for his congenital impotency. He dosed himself with this illicit amorous nectar on a daily basis, something many angels did during the golden years of their retirement.

Since he had no competition and these women of the Dump had never encountered a real man, Fukraeel had been enjoying every moment of his time. 'Until I showed up,' said Xenobia. 'He was devastated by my arrival, especially after discovering that his stash of illicit sex nectar had been stolen by me. He had stored it in the airtight bowling-pin-sized clay gourds in his nest.

'From then on he despised me. But he was too fearful of me and my gang of Amazons to harm me in any physical way. In a state of learnt helplessness, Fukraeel's spite towards me only intensified with each passing day. I pitied the old man, and of course that only made things worse.'

One day, as she sucked my toes, her breast tucked between my calves, Xenobia said, 'He's utterly useless—doesn't even deserve your pity. He's just a dirty old angel who should be spending his remaining days worshipping.'

Xenobia kept me in her cave for what seemed like a month. Her wild company helped cure some of the gloom and despair that had overtaken me after witnessing the cruel ejection of Laila from the settlement. But I missed her terribly and I felt so alone.

During these strange times of surreal sex and otherworldly orgasms, I noticed a gradual but conspicuous weakening of my memory, something I suspected was the side-effect of the nectar I had been ingesting religiously three times a day. Alarmed by this peculiar loss of my precious faculty, I made a habit of starting each day by reminding myself who I was, where I came from, how I landed in this place, my meeting with Pir Pul Siraat at Shah Jamal, Tarzan's smiling face and my trip to Hell on Chacha's bike over the tightrope. I remembered the first time I made love to Laila, the red-assed monkey that ran away with the black book, my obscure mission, the success of which depended upon my gaining trust of Abba whom I had yet to meet. And then there was my own quest—to know whether Paradise and Hell were real, and the refractory nature of my weaknesses, indiscretions and stupidities. These few minutes of daily recollection were my only hope of keeping my sanity, my identity, my purpose and my quest alive. It was the rope that connected me to my past life and I needed to hold on to it for as long as I could. But the loss of my headband was a constant reminder that I could remain here forever.

Who knows how long I would have remained in Xenobia's cave had she not detected an impending mutiny brewing in the settlement over her exclusive rights to my concubinage. Her subjects, having been deprived of their share of me for so long, were on the verge of revolt when she reluctantly released me.

Including Xenobia, there were seventy-one women in the colony. They had divided themselves into ten groups of seven and they had a plan. With the guarded blessing of Xenobia, I was to spend one day with each of the ten groups and then move to the next at dawn. I was allowed to sleep for a few hours before facing the next cohort of ravenous, albeit defective, hooris.

On the eleventh day of the cycle I would return to Xenobia to complete the cycle. Only with her was I allowed the luxury of an orgasm. The girls protested against this injustice, but Xenobia stood her ground. This naturally shifted the onus onto my ingenuity to violate the queen's command as I saw fit.

'Time is a curious thing, Ismael,' Xenobia said to me one day after I asked her how long they planned to feast on my immutably hardened manhood. 'Before you know it, we'll all be old and withered. Enjoy it while it lasts.'

'The way things are going, the supply of nectar isn't going to last much longer,' I replied. I had no idea what would happen once it did run out and I sure as hell didn't want to grow old here. It was not my desire to die in the Dump; especially without seeing the real Paradise.

Time raced dizzyingly at a frenzied pace thanks to the shortened days and the absence of a real night. In order to keep track of the passing days, I began carving lines into the bark of the tree that housed Fukraeel's nest.

It seemed the weeks had flowed into months and the months into years as I got used to living in a state of perpetual orgasm which was impossible to describe, but it took a toll on my daily practice of recollection. Memories I had been holding on to so dearly began to fizzle out at an alarming rate. For example: all I remembered of Pir and Chacha Khidr was their hypnotic eyes; Tarzan, his perfect white teeth; Laila, her embrace; and Abba, his temper. My quest, engulfed by my heightened lust, had been reduced to a state of jello, an amorphous mass of incomprehensible propositions and conjectures.

Xenobia marveled at my prowess and rolled back her earlier strict limitations. She learnt to share me with her subjects unreservedly. But in some strange way it only increased her power and control over them. So nourishing and potent was the milky white nectar I consumed daily that I would often go for long periods of time without eating anything else. My body even stopped expelling waste altogether, including semen.

Before my arrival, the women, whose congenital bodily defects had rendered them unsuitable for inhabiting Paradise, had been unable to perform their only function, the sole reason they had been created—to provide carnal pleasure to men. This had resulted in them suffering from various mental illnesses since they were devastated at being condemned to an utterly useless existence in this godforsaken place with an equally useless creature, Fukraeel, for company. My arrival had changed *all* of that.

By the end of the first year, I had become so proficient in the art of satisfying multiple partners simultaneously that I was pleasuring all seventy-one including Xenobia in the span of a single day.

Despite possessing superhuman sexual stamina, reserved only for the men dwelling in the real Paradise, I was aging alarming fast. By the third year my hair was snow white and thinning, and my muscles had become soft and my skin flabby. By the fourth, my back stooped, my fingers became knotty and arthritic, and my skin wrinkled and sagged from my starved frame.

By the end of the fifth year—by when I had given up my desire to get out of here alive—most of my teeth had rotted and fallen out. Like an old man, I was hobbling around with a cane. Thanks to the nectar, whose end though looked inevitable now, I remained very much functional, discharging my duties of a sex slave. In order to reach Xenobia's cave, I now had to be hauled up in a litter constructed for that purpose.

The women aged as well, but at a slower and less distressing rate. Their skin, once translucent, became dull and opaque, their breasts sagged, their legs and buttocks became flabby and developed ugly stretch marks, their vaginas turned lax and stopped lubricating. Xenobia even began carrying her breast in a sling that hung around her neck.

The supply of the heavenly nectar ran out at the start of the sixth year, plunging the entire community into a downward spiral from which it never recovered. Deprived of the potion, I began to regain the memories of my childhood, but it was too late. I was already an old man heading toward the grave. Xenobia tried a host of different herbs to treat my erectile dysfunction, but with no success. I had lost all interest in sex forever.

Once I was officially 'out of service', the settlement lost its immune system and quickly lapsed into decay and disease. Xenobia developed a festering sore on her breast that enlarged and eventually spread over her entire chest. It oozed yellow pus and smelled like a rotten corpse. Soon she completely stopped venturing out of her cave. All the women were afflicted with disfiguring ailments, the most common being leprosy and gangrene of the arms and legs. Soon the ground was littered with their blackened, rotting-off body parts. Their once charming little caves became graves from which the afflicted women never emerged.

Feeling like a shrivelled, empty husk, I spent my time beneath Fukraeel's tree, valiantly fighting off his mocking, amused gaze and waiting for death. The bastard had not aged a bit; perhaps he had already aged as much as he ever would by the time of his retirement.

Every day around dusk, he would flutter down from his nest, his wings quivering behind his drooping shoulders, to honour me with his sweet company. He briefed me extensively and in lavish detail on all the various tortures I would soon be experiencing in my grave for all the debauchery he had been a witness to and that I so willingly indulged in.

Sensing the imminent approach of my last breath, Fukraeel began digging my grave, the one he took such delight in telling me about. The old angel informed me that he had known both Munkar and Nakir—a pair of terrifying angels whose sole job it was to inflict torture on the damned within the grave. In him I saw a reflection of my father, remembering the bedtime stories Abba used to tell me. His favourite characters indeed were Munkar and Nakir; his favourite plot, torture in the grave.

Within a matter of days, Fukraeel had excavated a hole large enough to accommodate me without the undignified squashing of my sad corpse.

Finally, the day Fukraeel had been waiting for all these years arrived.

'I'm very concerned about you Ismael,' he said morosely. He stood tall beside me, using the wooden shovel as a cane, sweat pouring out of his forehead. I lay on the ground, flaccid and bathed in a cold sweat and gasping for air. It took supreme effort to sputter even a few words.

'I've done nothing wrong,' I said, with as much conviction as I could muster while wiping the spittle from my lips. My chest started rattling and wheezing with the effort.

'It is I, Fukraeel!' he suddenly roared, straightening his back and glaring down at me with contempt, his wings now flaring behind him. 'It is I who bears witness to all sins, great and small, that you, Ismael, son of Ibrahim, have committed before my eyes!' He stood before me, vengeful and defiant, and I saw a shadow of the angel he must have once been. Then he sighed, just a tired old man again.

I wanted to tell him that he was a nobody, that no one had ever heard his name where I lived. He wasn't documented in any of the theology books I had read. But I remained quiet. I didn't want to waste my last breath on him.

He squatted down beside me and looked into my eyes.

'The hedonism, the debauchery and the mistreatment of women. Each act of yours has been recorded by every one of your organs. In the grave, each part of your body will declare its sins and Munkar and Nakir will be standing nearby, taking notes. Even I shudder thinking of what they will do to you.'

'My witnesses,' I said, pausing to catch my breath, 'are going to be these seventy-one lovely hooris…'

'They're not allowed to be witnesses,' he screamed angrily, putting his palm over my closing eyelids. 'So long Ismael! Remember, no one knows torture better than Munkar and Nakir. Say hello to them from me when you meet.'

I wanted to reply, but my tongue just lay in my mouth and I stopped breathing as my head slumped to one side. The last thing I saw before darkness closed around me like a cold shroud was that grave, dark and wet like the mouth of the earth waiting to swallow me.

20

$\oint$

AN EXCRUCIATING PAIN SHOT through my chest. When I opened my eyes I saw two owl-faced beings staring down at me. Standing on either side of my head, they folded their trembling black wings against their shoulders. The dank grave that had held me was now a four-walled cell. My decrepit body lay on an inclined bench a few feet off the ground. The slope put my head a foot or two lower than my feet.

The angel standing to my right jabbed his knuckles into my ribs, causing a fresh round of unbearable pain. Devoid of any white, their eyes looked like black marble and their bodies were covered with fine shiny black feathers like a crow's, but their limbs were of a human.

'Hey, man! That hurts,' I said. 'I'm up! I'm up!' As I tried to sit up, an elbow slammed against my chest and forced me back down, knocking the wind out of me.

'Not so fast,' One of them said.

'Look,' throwing my right hand in the air, forcing a smile I said, 'My name is—'

'American?' Removing his arm from my chest, the angel shook my hand, giving it a squeeze that nearly snapped the bones in my fingers. I let out an inarticulate wail.

'I'm Munkar.' His voice had a fluttering quality, as if he spoke through an electric fan. He grabbed my balls and squeezed them tightly. I let out another scream. 'Welcome!' he said.

It took me a while before I was able to speak.

'Easy, easy!' I said, moaning and raising my hands in the air. 'Let me get oriented to this damn place first. Okay?'

Without warning, Munkar put his hand around my throat and squeezed until my eyes bulged and I started coughing violently.

'First question: who is your Lord?' The other angel, Nakir, demanded as flames flew out of his tongue and singed my cheek. His thundering voice was so loud that dirt and a few pebbles dropped from the ceiling and landed on Munkar's wings.

'My Lord is the same as yours,' I sputtered through my teeth.

'No! You are lying. Tell us the truth!' Munkar bellowed.

The two angels looked at each other, their brows raised and their eyes roving within their sockets. Before I could protest, they had my wrists and ankles manacled to heavy iron rings built into the bench I was lying on. Nakir stood behind my head and laid a damp cloth over my face. Then Munkar poured water over my covered nose and mouth. I choked and gagged as water trickled into my bruised windpipe. Just before I passed out, they stopped and uncovered my face.

'What is your religion? Say it!' Munkar roared.

I coughed and spit out the last of the water. 'I want to talk to your superior!' I gasped, then coughed some more and struggled to catch my breath.

'Superior?' Nakir said, giving me a puzzled look.

'The head angel who makes the policy around here,' I demanded.

'Policy?' Munkar asked, furrowing his brows and rubbing his forehead. He then looked at Nakir. 'Do you know what he's talking about?'

'I think I do,' Nakir answered, staring at me, his hand absent-mindedly stroking the feathers where his waist would have been were he a man. 'Policy! Hmm. Would you like that hot, cold, orally or rectally? It's your pick.'

Before I could answer, my body began to shiver, filling the cell with a low hum that soon became a tremulous twittering. Panicking, I lifted my head and looked around. The sound originated from my fingers, toes, lips, nose, even my eyes and earlobes. The loudest of the noise poured out from the area below my navel and above my genitals.

Oh shit! I thought, figuring I was really done for now as Fukraeel's explicit warnings reverberated in my head.

Both angels now held quills and notebooks in their hands; black leather-bound volumes in which they furiously scribbled all the details of my past deeds, concentrating on different parts of my body. They began with my upper torso, rapidly moving to the lower and more offending regions. When they reached my groin, their pens became a blur and their eyes bulged with excitement.

Standing on either side of my hips, they scribbled at a dizzying pace until they ran out of pages. For a brief moment they looked at each other, their eyes darting back and forth, before they extracted a fresh set of notebooks from under the bench. These also proved woefully inadequate to fully contain the breadth and depravity of my escapades in the Dump. Throwing their quills and notebooks away, they stared at my penis that still buzzed loudly. The two just shook their heads in disbelief.

'Have you ever seen anything like it before?' Munkar asked Nakir.

Nakir rubbed his chin, gritted his teeth and shot me a fiery glance.

Realizing that I was in serious trouble, I shouted in desperation. 'I'm a friend of Fukraeel! He asked me to say hello to you. He told me all about you.'

'How the fuck do you know Fukraeel?' Nakir shouted at me.

'What's your name, brother?' Munkar asked, a sudden hint of gentleness creeping into his trembling voice.

'Ismael.'

'Profession?'

'It's complicated,' I replied, my eyes following his movements behind my head, noticing he opened a scroll before his face. The light in the room brightened and Munkar came and stood next to Nakir.

Putting their heads together they stared at the parchment, Nakir's fingertip sliding over the text from top to bottom.

'His name isn't on our exit control list,' Nakir announced to his partner. 'And he knows Fukraeel. That's very strange!'

'Yes, very strange indeed.' Munkar agreed, nodding.

'I told you. I'm not your ordinary, run-of-the-mill, dead guy. Now can I talk to your supervisor, please?'

Instead of replying, they disappeared from the room with a whoosh, leaving a trail of smoke that smelled of something long dead. They weren't gone long when my cell started filling up with rats. These rats materialized by the hundreds out of the dirt walls and dropped from the ceiling, some landing on my chest and skittering away. Soon the ground was a black undulating carpet of screeching rats, their numbers swelling by the minute.

Still shackled to the bench, I watched in horror as their mass surged like a wave. Soon their jagged yellow teeth and razor-sharp claws would be ripping into my flesh. I closed my eyes and prepared for the most hideous death imaginable. I doubted this would be the last amusement Munkar and Nakir would draw from their legendary storehouse of horror. I wondered how many deaths of unspeakable agony and torment I would have to endure before I be deemed fit to proceed to the next stage of purification.

With another swoosh of feathers and flap of ebony wings, Munkar and Nakir reappeared and surveyed the room that was now bursting at the seams with the deafening squeal of the rats. Hovering over my head, their wings a blur, the feathered duo removed the manacles and pulled me to my feet.

'Congratulations, my friend! It seems you're on your way to Paradise after all,' Munkar said warmly, his eyes surprisingly tearing up with emotion.

'I'm extremely sorry for any pain or discomfort we may have caused you, sir,' Nakir said crisply. 'You know how it is; we must do what is part of our job.'

'Paradise?' I asked, looking at Munkar in utter shock.

'We've been told that you've passed all the necessary steps to gain entry into Paradise,' Munkar said, now sporting a kind and affectionate look. 'And that included a little taste of torture in the grave.'

I was speechless and couldn't trust what I heard. It had to be a mistake or something, I thought, while having trouble processing this information.

'Lucky bastard, I'd say!' Munkar said, wiping his tears.

'Now close your eyes—we're leaving,' added Nakir.

Before I even had the chance to react, I exploded into a million tiny particles of dust.

I awoke to the sound of a pleasing female voice—speaking in English—over a telecom system.

'Welcome to the VIP salon of the Intiqaal Lounge,' the voice was saying. 'Your orientation will begin shortly. We'll make every effort to ensure that your stay with us is as enjoyable as possible. Please feel free to ask any questions you may have.'

Covered in dirt, my decrepit, worn out body lay on a white marble floor beside a rectangular pool of clear blue water under the compassionate gaze of seven ravishing, black-eyed beauties. They kneeled over me, their skin shining through their gauzy diaphanous robes as if lit from within.

A number of white-winged angels flew about overhead. They carried all sorts of things: chairs, chaises, bedposts, mattresses, pillows and cushions, trays with food and drink, towels and robes, shoes and many strange looking objects.

'My lord, welcome,' one of the women said, massaging my hand and smiling, showing a beautiful set of white teeth. She had very long jet-black hair, eyes that glittered like polished onyx and moist red lips which curled in a charming coquettish smile.

'I'm Veena,' she said, and introduced me to the rest of the pack. They bowed their heads and smiled when their names were mentioned. Veena continued, 'We're here to help you turn back into a young man again.'

'How is that possible?' I asked, feebly raising myself up onto my elbows and looking down at my horrid self.

'My lord, you leave that to us,' a woman chimed in; it was a voice that sounded like the tinkle of a tiny crystal bell.

'You must be a very special man—a saint perhaps. We've never seen Munkar and Nakir fast track someone in here with such urgency,' Another woman added. 'Special men deserve special treatment,' she whispered in my ear.

'The procedure we employ to make you young again is completely lust-free,' Veena pronounced in her sweet voice, softly rubbing my chest with her fingertips. 'Just relax, sir. Let us do our scared duty.'

They carried my tired old body to a pool. The water was warm and oily and smelled of sweet herbs. The girls took turns scrubbing my dirt-clogged skin using an abrasive sponge made of some plant material. After the bath, they dried me with perfumed towels and rubbed fragrant oil into my hair.

I was made to lie down on a divan draped with crimson silk and piled with colourful pillows. Forming a circle, the women kneeled on the floor beside me and told me to close my eyes. They then applied a blindfold over my eyes. I felt their hands, and later tips of their tongues, lapping gently at my withered flesh. Soon my entire body was vibrating with vitality and I was drenched with their saliva.

My blindfold was removed and I was taken into the pool a second time. But instead of water it was now filled with cardamom-scented milk. My skin glowed with youthful radiance and as the girls washed the saliva off of me, I could feel my bones growing stronger, more substantial.

I was brought back to the same divan, blindfolded once more, and guided, without any effort on my part, through seven orgasms without once losing my erection, the pleasure only heightening with each successive act. The last one, by far the longest and most stunning, didn't produce any semen from my body.

'In Al-Jannah one doesn't produce any waste,' Veena spoke quietly in my ear, as if telling me a secret.

'But what happens to the food one eats?'

'It changes into musk,' she replied. 'Your body will ooze it in place of sweat—it drives the virgins crazy.'

I emerged from the pool feeling buoyant. A pair of handsome young male angels landed beside me. They carried fresh garments folded over their arms: a blue silk robe, its neck and cuffs studded with diamonds and rubies, a gold turban speckled with thousands of tiny iridescent five pointed stars, a pair of leather sandals and a finger-sized glass vial of perfume that smelled of moist earth.

I was then served a thick green beverage in a white china cup. It tasted like cough syrup and made me groggy. I lay down once again on the divan and closed my eyes and immediately memories of my past flooded in. They were vivid but fragmented, like the pieces of a moving three-dimensional jigsaw puzzle. Slowly these fragments started to coalesce.

'What the hell did you put in my drink?' I asked one of the angels as my speech began to slur, but pleased at the same time.

'My lord, it's restoring your memory,' Veena said. 'You may feel a little tipsy during this phase of your restoration. Take a nap if you like.'

Then it all came rushing back to me. So intense was the complete and sudden recall that I bolted upright, my palms on my temple and my eyes blinking uncontrollably. A gentle fragrant musk exuded from my forehead.

It had all happened only a moment ago; the ruined bathroom in the hospital, the book bound in black leather, the red Nike headband, Pir's instructions for my journey. I was supposed to meet with him in Paradise, to hand over the book. But where was the book now? I panicked until I remembered the monkey. What if he had chewed it up and ripped it apart? How was I going to face Pir after all that had transpired? Laila! Whatever happened to her? She had my headband. Abba! He must be returning home from Islamabad today.

Had I died for real? Suddenly, the last seven years spent in that celestial dump—the place never visited by night, the retirement outpost of Fuqraeel whose dream of attaining manhood with the help of the smuggled nectar was shattered by my arrival—felt like a fleeting moment in that vast span of my now eternal life.

My brooding came to an end with the arrival of my escort, a middle-aged dark-skinned angel with a graying beard and stiff smile who wore a green turban and a plain yellow robe. His wings were dull gray and his name was Braqeel. The women bade me farewell while he took my hand.

'First stop, Hauz-e-Kauser,' he said, his powerful wings bristling with a nervous energy.

21

❦

'HUAZ-E-KAUSER! I'VE BEEN LONGING to drink that sweet-tasting water ever since—'

Before I could finish my sentence, I disintegrated into a cloud of light. The next moment I materialized beside a heart-shaped pond filled with sparkling water. Not much bigger than a twelve-person hot tub, the pond was set in a grassy mound a couple of feet off the ground. It was bordered by a dazzling array of exquisite tiles depicting intricate Arabian geometric patterns in blue, white and gold. Water flowed from a golden faucet and collected in a round bowl of white marble. Several rough clay cups lay scattered on the overgrown grass beside the marble bowl. The pond was cordoned off by Day-Glo orange hazard tape that was stuck to wooden posts with flashing lights.

'Alas! Hauz-e-Kauser is no more,' Braqeel said in his morose voice. 'It's been off limits for quite some time now.'

'Why? What happened?' I asked, stunned by the revelation.

'It's the water.' Braqeel said sadly, shaking his head side to side. 'It is not fit to drink anymore.'

'But it looks so clear!'

'Clear but not clean—it's contaminated.'

'With what?'

He refused to divulge anything more except that it had been under investigation for quite some time. He then successfully derailed the discussion by diverting my attention to the famous virgins who awaited me.

'Don't think that seventy-two is all you're going to get,' he told me, as if trying to allay my greatest and most natural fear. 'If you desire more, all you've got to do is tell your ladies to introduce you to their slave girls.' He flashed me a mischievous smile. 'They may not be as beautiful, but you'd be surprised by what they can do to heighten a man's enjoyment of the heavenly sphere.'

'How many slave girls are we talking about?' I asked, scratching my head.

'Each of your seventy-two virgins has been granted seventy-two slave girls,' he said, his wings quivering with excitement.

'That's an awful lot of women!' I started to feel a bit overwhelmed.

'Never say that again!' he hissed, arching his thick brows and piercing me with his black eyes. 'I've never heard that complaint before. You've got a problem with women?'

'No, that's not what I meant,' I added quickly so as not to offend him.

I wanted to tell him about my insanely vibrant sex life serving a horde of wild women in the Dump. I had been there, done that. I wanted to tell him that I wasn't his ordinary pious Joe from earth who was going to start drooling at the promise of unlimited sex with countless women because he hadn't gotten much in his earthly existence.

Thinking carefully, I decided not to say anything. It would be more interesting to check the place out. For me, this place had always been a mere metaphor, a work of the human imagination. I just stared at the sad, limpid pond before me that was in dire need of the immediate attentions of a Hazmat team. It crossed my mind that if I ever made it back to New York, I would ditch my thesis in favour of something more fruitful. Though what that was, I didn't know. The sight of the ugly orange hazard tape around this glorious pond that was supposed to be filled with the sweetest tasting water in the whole universe made me feel inexplicably sad and defeated.

Our next stop was a vast green parkland at the centre of which stood a palace of gleaming white marble. The magnificent edifice was topped with a number of steeples and towers of various sizes and was so monumental in scale that it would probably take a lifetime on the back of a swift horse to circle its perimeter.

The delicate crowns of the lofty turrets disappeared into a radiant purple sky with gigantic orbs emitting soft soothing vibrations which circled around each of the towers. Overhead, angels drifted in a formation like migrating swans carrying packages and bundles. The air smelled of jasmine and my skin tingled.

'My job was to bring you to the Guest House of Al-Jannah,' Braqeel said to me, pointing toward the colossal mansion. 'I'm not allowed to go any farther than this.'

'Guest House?'

'It's for people traveling back and forth between Al-Jannah and other worlds,' he said. 'You're on your own from here.'

'What am I supposed to do now?' I asked him, feeling alarmed at the prospect of being left to my own devices in such an incredibly vast space where it would take me years just to reach the entrance of the Guest House.

'To move from one point to another, all you have to do is will it,' Braqeel said, as if reading my mind. 'See that entrance?' He pointed towards the centre of the building where a gate like a glittering reflective mirror stood open and waiting. 'You are expected in the welcome tent just to the right side of the main gate. Now it's time for me to get back and pick up my next passenger.' He stretched his wings and flapped them a few times like a runner warming up for a sprint. He then rose into the air, becoming a brilliant white streak across the sky.

Keeping my eyes to the right of the gate where the tent was supposed to be, I willed myself to be there. Nothing happened with the first two attempts, but the third time I burst into a flash of light. When I opened my eyes, I was standing at the doorway of the marble estate.

Hundreds of women draped in diaphanous multicoloured silks stood around the lush grounds like exquisite statues. About two hundred feet ahead, against the horizon, I saw a large red awning supported by poles: the welcome tent. Lounging under this canopy on divans were a number of people wearing colourful robes.

So this was the Guest House of Al-Jannah, the Muslim Paradise. It made me wonder just how many other kinds of Paradises were there and if this one was exclusively for Muslims.

A coterie of dark-skinned beardless youths clad in red loincloths milled around outside the red canopy as if waiting for orders. Dazzled, I wandered through the dreamy gardens, lulled into a peaceful reverie. The air was heavy with the smell of night-blooming jasmine. On my right a delicate pink marble fountain gushed a stream of milk and on my left a stone-lined trough filled with fragrant honey meandered through flowerbeds of white lilies and red tulips. A multitude of trees dotted the lawns as far as my eye could see. Their branches drooped under the weight of ripe fruit, their blossoms dripping nectar. Even the grass was manicured to perfection.

I was about a hundred feet from the awning, pleasurably immersed in this otherworldly serenity of my surroundings, when a swell of agitated voices rose up in the air. The severed head of a bearded man landed about twenty feet from me and rolled across the ground like a bowling ball, stopping beneath a wall of stones supporting the stream of flowing honey. I froze where I stood.

A moment later, a human leg sailed through the air and landed just a couple of feet from where I was standing. I dropped to my knees, retching, when I heard a woman's voice shouting my name. Standing up, I saw a woman wrapped in a flowing black burqa racing towards me. She halted just a few inches from me and lifted her veil. I gasped when I saw her face.

'Laila!' I whispered. She looked ravishingly young and beautiful.

'Ismael! Where have you been?' she said, throwing herself in my arms, sobbing and burying her face in my chest.

I stroked her hair and surveyed the area that was teeming with women laughing and talking in small groups. They seemed unfazed by the flying dismembered appendages, as if it was just business as usual around here. Laila pulled herself away from me and repositioned her veil over her face.

'You'd better stop looking around. They won't dare lay a finger on you here, not as long as I, your lawful wife, am with you.'

'Looking around?' I yelled, as if she was an idiot. 'Didn't you see what just landed here? Look at that!' Baffled by her indifference, I pointed to the carnage at my feet.

'It's a big problem here in Jannah,' she said.

I wasn't sure what to make of this information. To be honest, her burqa bothered me more than anything else at the moment. Last time I saw her she was practically naked.

'Why in the hell are you wearing that burqa?'

'Married women must wear full hijab here, Ismael,' she replied quite seriously. As I started to speak, I was shocked to see Chacha Khidr over her shoulder. He was sprinting toward us with a burlap sack in his hand.

'I'm just so happy to see you, Ismael,' Laila said. 'I know it'll be a little confusing for you at first, but soon you'll—'

'I'm happy to see you too, but I'm still not so sure about that burqa. How did you get here?'

'It was your headband. It worked! Pir Pul Siraat tracked me down, but we couldn't find you. Xenobia and her bitches had that dump of theirs camouflaged by methods known only to them.'

Upon hearing the name of Pir, I was filled with a mixture of excitement and terror. I had a lot of explaining to do, having arrived in Paradise without the book and the headband.

'Where is my headband?' I asked her.

'Pir has it.'

I remained quiet. The meeting with Pir wasn't about to go well, that much I knew.

'How did you do there in my absence?' She narrowed her big black eyes in an interrogative stare.

The last thing I needed right now was to be reminded of my days as Xenobia's sex slave.

'I survived by dying.' I avoided her gaze and looked over her shoulder at Chacha. 'Look what he is doing.' Laila turned around, and we both watched as he gathered the human remains and put them in his sack. Once all the pieces were stowed and the sack tied up, he walked over to a stream of fresh water and washed his hands. His appearance hadn't changed a bit, and nor had his job!

'Now you see the scope of the problem, Babu?' Chacha asked, looking at me with the sparkling eyes I remembered.

'Wait a minute, Chacha.' I walked over to him. 'Are you telling me that all those knuckle-heads blowing themselves up on earth are actually landing here, in Paradise, in bits and pieces?!' I was shocked and acutely aware of the fact that Abba's Mujahid Vest probably had been used in about two-third of the cases.

'Not all, but only those whose desire for Jannah has become a greed. Desire, if not coupled with need, becomes destructive,' he said, standing up and hoisting the sack over his shoulder. 'The world is not some place which is located over *there*, far away from *here*. It exists within the world, but behind an invisible curtain.' He turned and began walking toward the awning, then stopped and turned around. 'Now you've seen with your own eyes the kind of mess we must deal with over here. And you're going to help us clean it up,' he continued, patting his sack, and walking away. 'Follow me. Pir is waiting for you.'

I recalled his words when I met with him for the first time on my Ayahuasca journey back in New York. *Babu, you're going to help us clean up a big mess.* I remembered him emptying his sack on the floor of Pir's quarter in Shah Jamal. *Delicate and subtle! I am fed up with being delicate and subtle. It's time for action. A military action.*

What felt so gratifying was that despite all my spectacular failures on the Path to High Knowledge, I was still in play and still relevant to the mission, whose details had just begun to emerge from the thick fog of my adventures.

Next I remembered the words of Pir. *Khalifa has something very special planned, a real spectacle. If he's not stopped very soon, this world and the Next will need a major cleanup that will stretch into the not-so-foreseeable future. Without that book, he won't be able to bring his plans to completion. Your job, Ismael, is to help us stop the man in his tracks.*

I began to sense the scope of my mission. It was a big deal for sure, though how big I had no clue. What was I going to tell Pir about the book? Considering the number of waffled pages in that thing, it was sure to be packed with enough power to help transport a whole village to Paradise. Had I not bumped into Laila the other night, I would have landed straight here in Jannah after having ingested just one tiny stamp off its page. And then there was this *backup copy* still on the loose somewhere in that hellhole of a place scarier than the real Hell. Was Khalifa planning a mass exodus to Jannah? If that was the case, how could I, single-handedly, stop it from happening?

As Laila and I strolled behind Chacha, I wondered if his human carrion could be put back together in the form of a living, breathing human. But there were more important things to think about so I took a deep breath and braced myself for Pir.

As we neared the red awning, the dark-skinned boys arranged themselves in a single line, their hands clasped over their navels and their heads bowed. We walked past them and stepped into the shade of the canopy. Inside I saw Tarzan and Pir Pul Siraat sitting on a richly draped divan that looked like the throne of a legendary emperor. Like Ottoman sultans, they lounged among cushions of red velvet, their backs resting against bolsters of rich golden brocade.

A couple of legless marble slabs floated in the air around the lounge, laden with baskets filled with all kinds of fruits: pineapples, apples, guavas, mangoes, bananas and pears. There was even cut watermelon, red and white grapes, cherries and multicoloured berries. There were platters of dates, figs and olives, cheeses of countless varieties; jars of jams, honey, juices and wines; breads of all shapes and sizes. It looked exactly like the gourmet section of a high-end kosher grocery store in Manhattan.

Tarzan had grown; he was now taller and more filled out. Dressed in a purple robe with intricate gold embroidery around the collar and cuffs, he looked like the prince from a fairytale. Only a couple of days ago, he was a handsome teenager with a bright smile, selling bhang papads out of his carry-on stall in Fortress Stadium as he repeatedly pulled on the loop of his fake martyr vest. I also remembered his expertise with explosives and his ability to control as stubborn a mind as Wali's.

Tarzan's face broke into a broad smile when our eyes met. For some odd reason I felt sad looking at him.

Draped in a voluminous, shimmering green robe, Pir smoked a cigarette and looked us over. But unlike Tarzan, he wasn't smiling. He wore a black headband without any insignia and looked quite worried.

'Welcome to Paradise, sir,' Tarzan said to me, standing up and throwing his arms in the air. His face was radiant with joy.

As I hugged Tarzan, my eyes caught sight of a metal cage

sitting on the grass beyond the far end of the awning. It was surrounded by a dozen heavenly beauties who giggled and stared at whatever was inside the cage.

'Thank you, Tarzan. I'm so very glad to see you.' Cautiously, I moved over to Pir who didn't get up to greet me. After shaking my hand, he gestured for me to sit on one of the divans across from him. Laila sat beside me while Chacha bounded over the lawn toward the cage.

'Ismael, do you know why you are here?' Pir asked in a low angry voice as he nailed me with a look more than furious.

'I am here because of you.'

'Correct!'

'Do you have any idea what it took to get you here?'

I remained silent.

'I was forced to lie to get you out of the hands of Munkar and Nakir.' I was pretty sure I knew what he meant. I recalled my grave, my water-boarding session at the hands of those two deadly angels, the ceaseless buzzing of my penis and the squealing mass of rats ready to devour me. And then how things changed. I remembered the teary-eyed Munkar's words: *We've been told that you've passed all the necessary steps to gain entry into Paradise.*

'I'm sorry.' I was well aware he knew what I was thinking.

'You've screwed up. Seriously. Not once but twice.'

'I am the one who screwed up,' Laila spoke, her voice cold and flat. 'Ismael can't be blamed for something he had no control over.'

'Lady, I am not addressing you. Please be quiet. This is between him and me,' said Pir, picking up a tattered book from the divan beside him and holding it toward me. The book's black leather binding had been chewed up very badly. 'Thanks to your brilliant work, Jannah is now populated with monkeys.'

'But—'

'There's no *but*!' Pir roared, skewering me with his glance. He then looked at Laila and his expression began to soften. 'Not that I have anything against this lovely lady, but Ismael,' he continued, pausing for a moment as if considering what to say, 'You were supposed to come here alone, by yourself, not with a companion. Your only task was to deliver this book to me, safely and in one piece.' He flicked the ash off his cigarette into a white porcelain ashtray. 'I want to know exactly what happened. Don't leave out even the smallest detail,'

I glanced at Laila. Her face was composed but there was terror in her eyes.

'Go on. Tell them the truth. It's okay. He can't do anything for we're a married couple now,' she whispered to me. 'Just don't mention Hoor Afza.'

Recalling the events of the night in that ruined bathroom was like viewing the past through a stereoscope, for they seemed to have transpired simultaneously both a lifetime ago and just last night. I told him how I ran into Laila—whom I had known from my earlier visit to the hospital—outside the emergency room and how I was about to get myself a flashlight from the drug store across the street when the red lights appeared on Jail Road. I was left with no choice but to run inside in the dark, hoping to find the book before it ended up in the wrong hands and how Laila helped me with her lighter. Without that I would never have found my way in the dark.

I paused and scratched my head, trying to conjure some plausible scenario that would explain Laila's presence in the Dump. But everything just sounded lame and unconvincing. I knew Pir wasn't buying my explanation.

'And then you started moving furniture,' Pir said. 'Right?'

Lowering my gaze, I bit my lips. Thankfully, Laila came to my rescue, breaking the painful silence that was accentuated by Pir's searing gaze. 'Please. I'll tell you exactly what happened.'

Laila stood up and faced the divan where my two benefactors sat. 'Leaving Ismael in the bathroom, I was called to the emergency room to register a head-injury case which had just arrived. When I got there they told me the patient had died. I don't know where it came from, but a strong feeling occurred to me that Ismael's life was in danger. So I ran back to the bathroom and it turns out I was right,' she said, nodding with satisfaction.

'I found him lying on the floor. He wasn't breathing so I'd no choice but to start giving him mouth-to-mouth resuscitation. He was dying right before my eyes! What choice did I have? The next thing I knew, we were lying completely naked beside a waterfall in some wilderness.'

Laila's answer startled me. She seemed to be telling the truth; and if she was, it was more than likely we both had died in that accursed bathroom. But if she was lying, wow, she was really good at it.

'Interesting,' Pir muttered, glancing at Tarzan, not certain if he believed her. 'What do you have to say about all this, lieutenant?'

'I think they crash-landed in the Dump because the power of a single ticket meant for only one person, which Ismael sir put under his tongue, got split between two people during the mouth-to-mouth resuscitation. One ticket wasn't strong enough to propel two bodies all the way to Paradise,' Tarzan proclaimed.

'You make an excellent point,' Pir replied. Then he glanced at Chacha Khidr who was involved in an animated conversation with a knot of hooris beside the cage. 'But that's only a partial reason,' he added slowly, looking at me and shaking his head. He looked disappointed. 'You create the kind of world you've been intending, secretly or otherwise. Sometimes an intention lurks in one's mind like a snake in a thicket,' Pir continued without taking his eyes off me.

I knew what he was trying to say. I wanted to tell him it wasn't my fault that I harboured the kind of intention he was referring to: of having an unlimited supply of virgins in the afterlife. First, I wasn't conscious of it. Second, it was Abba who had embedded his indelible footprints on my mind ever since I was a child.

'Perhaps the intention you're talking about is part of my genetic makeup, my upbringing, maybe even my fate. But I can't do anything about that,' I offered, in a bid to absolve myself of the guilt he was trying to impose on me.

Pir seemed ready to reply but he looked at Laila and then settled back into his cushion. I figured he didn't want to say anything classified in front of her.

Why was sex so jealously regulated on earth and so utterly unregulated in Jannah? The memory of my seven lust-free orgasms in the Intiqaal Lounge was still fresh in my mind. Clearly, having sex was not the issue here. It was all about where one should preferably be having it. I knew Pir was reading my thoughts and would enlighten me at some point. And where were the male equivalents of the hooris?

'Those monkeys in that cage have probably taken a few squares each from the book. That's probably how they ended up here,' Pir explained, his anger now gone. 'Tarzan, any idea what we should do with them?' Pir narrowed his eyes as his face broke into a mischievous smile.

I breathed a sigh of relief at the change in direction this conversation was taking. If Pir grilled me on how the damn book got into the hands of the monkeys, I would have to concoct another elaborate lie, something I clearly wasn't very good at and, of course, I feared Pir was reading my mind. Thinking this, he stood up and walked over to me.

'Ismael, now we've got the book, and we've got you out of the hands of Munkar and Nakir. We wasted time so we must get back to work immediately.'

'Yes, sir,' I was relieved to be safe with Pir and back on track.

'And don't forget, you still haven't been reunited with

your father,' he said, attempting to orient my short-circuited existential GPS.

'Yes, sir,' I said again.

An angel in a white robe appeared overhead, circled once, then landed beside Pir. He was a good six feet tall, fair, young, with a trimmed red beard and was very handsome. The red tips of his otherwise white wings matched the colour of his cowboy boots.

'Apollo!' Pir said, turning toward the angel. 'What are you doing here in Jannah on a fine day like this?'

The angel whispered something to Pir, then took a couple of steps away to stand erect like a guard with his hands clasped behind his back while he stared unblinking past us.

'Ismael, someone from the Greek quarters would like to meet with you,' Pir said.

'Greek quarters?' I asked, feeling Laila's fingernails biting into my arm.

'That's where the pagans live,' she whispered in my ear.

'Pagans? In Paradise?' I asked.

'There're all kinds of paradises in Paradise,' Pir said. 'There's a Christian Paradise, that's where most angels receive their education. Then there's one for the Jews, and an Islamic Paradise you already know about. There's one for the Hindus, one for the Buddhists, another for the Zoroastrians and so on. And there's one called the Greek Quarter.'

'Who wants to see you there?' Laila whispered to me.

'I have no idea.' I squeezed her hand and stood up. I was excited, but at the same time a little anxious at this new development. If I made any wrong moves, chances were better than ever that I would spend another lifetime wandering about a world crazier than the Dump. God help me, I muttered to myself. God, please help me.

'Your ride is here,' Pir said, as he pointed at the angel and grinned through closed lips. Finally, he had cracked a smile. 'I want you back here soon. You've got work to do,' he added.

'I'll be back—soon,' I said, wondering what that meant. For my current location was clearly outside time.

Apollo did look like an honest and hardworking being—as opposed to Fukrael who radiated contempt for all things human and oozed a fondness for anything shady and unwholesome. As soon as Apollo took my hand we became streaks of light across the horizon.

22

WE REAPPEARED BESIDE A thundering waterfall, surrounded by a growth of old pine which covered a steep mountain slope. Before I could orient myself, Apollo rose into the air and waved goodbye. He thrust his arms forward, then vanished.

The place looked strangely familiar. Like déjà vu times twenty familiar. My heart raced in anticipation. There, beside the waterfall, I spotted her: my Sophie. She stood in the exact same spot I had kissed her that first time on earth. There was even the same rainbow that had formed behind her in the curtain of mist over her shoulder.

The water crashed against the same boulders and roared down toward the valley. The mauve flowers which covered the green slopes were the very same, as was the deafening sound of splashing water and the electrified air filled with passion. The only thing missing was the rest-house where I had stayed with Abba more than a lifetime ago.

Sophie seemed to have matured by only half a decade; she was curvaceous and more ravishing than ever. However, she wore the same black skirt and had the same golden hair. In her hands was the same bouquet of violets she had held that day, so long ago.

This stunning replay of time had completely blown me away. I pinched my arm to make sure I wasn't dreaming. Sophie broke into a radiant smile as she walked toward me, slowly. For several seconds I forgot to breathe.

Transfixed by her beauty, I was entrapped within a timeless web of love. And then, in a flash, I saw within me, lurking like an anaconda in the misty thicket of a dark forest, the truth that had been guarded jealously by my subconscious ever since she had become my father's bride.

I knew beyond the shadow of a doubt that she had died. I remembered my willed vision of her, after having drunk two bottles of Hoor Afza in the backseat of the car. I had seen her strolling through the violet hue in a green meadow, unaware of her stalker, the dark-skinned, bearded man who took her into the underworld.

She stood just inches away, her breath warm against my neck and her eyes twinkling like the brightest star in the northern sky. In a daze, I kissed her. She tasted the same, just like fresh apricots.

I wrapped my arms around her and drew her closer to me. For a brief second Abba's face floated in my mind. The realization that his face and that of the dark-skinned, bearded man carrying Sophie away were the same tortured me and enraged me. But that face dissipated like a foul mist as soon as I willed it away, and I kissed her deeply and without guilt. *If I could just take her back with me to earth, the world would be such a great place to live.*

I thought of Laila, my temporary wife. She was certainly beautiful, caring, and in all, I liked her a lot. She was great in the sack, but I could never connect instantly, on the deepest level, with her as I had done with Sophie.

And then I remembered my misstep with Laila and how it had landed me in that horrid Dump. What exactly had I learnt from my trials? How was I better than that moth, the one which set itself ablaze each time it saw a flame? Whatever happened to my will?

I pulled back from Sophie. 'No, we can't do this.'

'Why?' Surprised, she looked into my eyes.

'I can't explain it.' I averted her gaze.

'You know, you aren't required to behave like a saint in Paradise.' She wrapped her arms around my neck and gave me a long passionate kiss.

'Are you sure?' My momentary resolve melted against her moist lips like an ice cube in hot water.

'Yes,' she answered, and I had no choice but to take her at her word. I was indeed incurable—a man chained to his nature.

We exchanged not a single word from then on, allowing only our tongues and fingers to communicate all that was necessary in the language of passion. In the next minute we were rolling on the ground, our clothes discarded in the tall grasses that hid our bodies from all eyes but our own.

Later, exhausted and at peace, entangled in each other's arms, we lay naked. The experience of making love to her had been a completely earthly one, in sharp contrast to the mechanical, utilitarian coupling with the women of the Dump. I shuddered when I remembered the red rock compound of Xenobia and her cohorts, the conveyor belt of perpetual sex, fueled by the nectar from Al-Jannah, as they ravaged me with their insatiable appetites. Sophie rolled over and rested her head on my shoulder.

'This has to be a dream,' I said. 'I love these pagan quarters of yours.'

'It is rather unbelievable that you're here,' she agreed, nuzzling my neck with her face.

'How come we're in Kafiristan?' I asked, combing her hair with my fingers.

'I willed it that way,' she admitted, nibbling my earlobe with her teeth.

'Willed it?' I asked, wondering what the implication of her words were.

'Yes—the same way people will things on earth and they happen. Except there they happen over a period of time and here, they happen instantly.'

'Mind creating matter,' I said.

'Without the help of time,' she explained. 'You need a little practice to create things exactly the way you want them.'

'Like creating Kafiristan in Paradise.'

'Yes, you can say that,' she smiled mischievously. 'All you need is a good memory to create whatever you want from your past.'

'But seriously, aren't you guys the kafirs, the infidels, who are supposed to be in Hell?'

She propped herself up on one elbow, and looked into my eyes. 'Who says?'

'The books.'

She laughed softly. 'Well, now you know that isn't true,' she said. 'Paradise is for all who do good in life, regardless of their faith.'

'That's what I've always thought.' I hoped that someday I would be able to convince Abba of that. 'How did you discover I was in Paradise?' I asked.

'I've got my connections,' she said.

'Really?'

'Really,' she whispered, and kissed my cheek.

'You died then? After you left Abba?'

She nodded without a hint of sadness in her eyes.

'What happened?'

'I don't want to talk about it. Why don't you tell me how you died?'

'I'm not exactly sure I'm dead or not at the moment, but I do know I'm being sent back to the Earth.'

'I always felt you were special, Ismael.' Her eyes sparkled like the water of a clear mountain lake. 'I'll wait for you,' she continued. 'When you return, we'll build a little hut for ourselves down there in the meadow.'

'But only if I can make it back here. I'm not too thrilled about living in the Muslim Quarter for all eternity.'

'Oh yes! I heard there's an epidemic going on over there,' she said.

'What epidemic?'

'It's just a rumour. But they say it's polio. I've heard all kinds of weird things are happening there.'

'Oh!' I said, remembering that Hauz-e-Kauser had been shut down due to some undisclosed contamination. Was the source of contamination an infected body-part that might have landed in the sacred pond?

She climbed on top of me and kissed my forehead, her braids brushing against my face.

'Why doesn't everybody just live in one big Paradise?' I asked, putting my hands on her thighs. 'Like one nation under God, one big happy family?'

'People have different tastes. You create your own Paradise according to your nature, or your own vision of things,' she said, bringing her face to closer mine and staring into my eyes. 'As a man you should be very happy. In your quarters there are a million naked women who want nothing but sex.'

'Oh please! Don't talk about them.' I cringed at the thought of the Dump. 'Why? What happened?'

'I just want you,' I said, ignoring her question. 'I love the natural look of a woman's body and I can't stand burqas.'

'Where did the burqa thought come from?' She rubbed her breasts against my chest.

'Accident.'

'Must be a serious one.' Her tone was playful and light.

'It is—kind of,' I said, strangely enough, feeling a sudden irresistible tenderness for Laila.

'I wish you a quick recovery.'

'Thank you, but I can handle it,' I said, feeling rising apprehension and guilt.

I could easily, or legally, say goodbye to Laila whenever I wanted, since ours was a temporary contract to fulfill a specific purpose that was limited to the physical confines of the Dump. That purpose had been served and it was time to move on now.

'Promise me something,' she said, caressing my neck. 'You'll stay with me when you return.'

'I promise.'

After we had dressed, Apollo appeared and landed beside us on the soft grass.

When Apollo dropped me back at Pir's lounge, everyone was sitting quietly and the place was enveloped in a heavy and serious atmosphere. Tarzan looked at me quizzically and Pir's expression was unreadable as I took my seat on the divan next to Laila. Her eyes shined with a nervous curiosity.

'Who did you see, Ismael?' she whispered in my ear. 'And why are your clothes dirty?' She was looking at the green smudges on my blue silk robe.

Before I embarrassed myself by trying to concoct some transparent lie, Pir, who had been watching closely, stood up and motioned for me to join him. 'I need to have a word with you.'

I looked at Tarzan for a clue, but he simply shrugged and raised his brows.

Laila shrank away from me as I stood up. And I followed Pir to the edge of the canopy. I couldn't help but think how hopelessly incorrigible I was.

'Mankind is incapable of change. There is no reason to take things personally. But more importantly, this isn't the time for you to sort out your love life,' he said in a flat tone that would tolerate no opposition or doubts.

I, too, had understood my father's limitations like Pir had mine. And if the mankind as whole was so deficient, then Abba's lifestyle shouldn't be regarded as unbecoming after all. There had never been anything personal in his actions and thoughts. He was merely acting out like a child who had no control on his impulses. This was especially true now given the added toxicity of Paradise Water he had been consuming for years. I felt depressed realizing the depth of man's depravity, the distance between Pir and mortals like Abba and myself.

'Yes, Pir.' I had no doubt that he could read me like a book.

'Good.' I was almost certain that he was appreciating not what I had said, but what I had just realized.

He smiled and put his hand on my shoulder as if I were an old friend, or a son, who had been gently, but sternly, corrected in his ways.

'Your quest to know whether Paradise and Hell exist may be over, but our mission is not. While you were gone, another book has been shipped to the Khalifa, just as we predicted. This backup copy is identical in its potency and power to the original book, the one you were sent to retrieve.'

'That doesn't sound good,' I said, avoiding his intense gaze.

'We have to prevent Khalifa from exploiting the power of the book,' he continued, his hand still resting on my shoulder.

'Pir, if you don't mind,' I cut in, sensing he was in an unusually receptive and friendly mood, 'if I were you, I'd go after the person who's making all these books.'

'You can't go after the Master Chemist,' he stated, shaking his head. 'You can only try thwarting his tricks. It's like playing a game of chess with the grandmaster. But don't worry. There are no more books to come after this.'

'The Master Chemist?' I asked.

'Instead of knowing who he is, you'll serve yourself better by knowing that if you play your cards right, the world may be saved from a catastrophe,' Pir said, as he moved toward the cage. His face was creased with worry and something else I couldn't quite place. Was it fear?

'What catastrophe?' I asked, walking by his side.

'You can't be told more than what you already know, and that's enough for now. We've spoken about this before,' he said sternly. 'You must realize no matter how crazy it sounds that the Khalifa's security forces include the mind-reading cats, and if you knew the whole breadth of your mission before the time of executing it, you'd be a huge security risk for us. And we can't take that risk just to satisfy your curiosity. The information would be hacked out of your brain as if from a computer hard drive. Then you won't be present when you need to be in order to pull the plug.'

'Pull the plug?'

He ignored me. 'You'd be arrested the minute they got wind of any such information floating around in your brain.' He pulled out a black headband from his pocket and handed it to me. 'Here's your new tele-band. The red one you gave to Laila is no longer effective. And by the way, where is the Quran I gave you?'

'In the pocket of the robe I was wearing back on earth. Wherever *that* was before I came to wherever *this* is,' I said, realizing I was about to leave Paradise, probably for good. I took the headband and stretched it over my head.

'I'd like to stay here a bit longer,' I said. 'If that's possible, of course.'

'Good to know you've been following my instructions, Ismael,' Pir said, ignoring my request completely. 'Tarzan will take you back now.'

'What about Laila?' I asked, sensing something ominous must have happened to her back in that bathroom in the hospital.

'You can ask her yourself,' Pir said, as we headed back to the lounging area.

Tarzan and Laila sat deep in conversation and I heard Tarzan saying, 'I know, I miss Lahore too, a lot.'

Pir dropped down onto the divan beside Tarzan and I beside Laila. She touched my arm, her eyes glistening with tears. The air was heavy with the scent of fresh-ground cinnamon.

'I'll be right here waiting for you, Ismael,' she said.

'But you should come with me,' I said, as I held her hand.

'I can't go back, Ismael. But I know you'll come for me one day so we can be together forever,' she replied and squeezed my hand.

Her words stung deeply and filled me with sadness. She had been good to me, possessive definitely, but she was one hot woman under that awful black burqa. I felt sad and guilty that I had cheated on her with the love of my life. But hey, this was Al-Jannah, the Islamic Paradise with its liberal sexual mores, the last place in the universe where one was expected to behave like a saint. And no matter how much I wanted to change, I still wasn't one to pass up a good time.

Tarzan came over.

'Time to go, sir.'

Then Chacha shouted from afar.

'Stop, don't leave yet!' Dropping his bulging burlap sack on the ground by the cage, he ran toward us. 'Be safe, Babu Ismael,' he said, giving my shoulder a friendly shake. 'Make sure to empty your mind when you are around cats.'

'Wait!' I barked. 'Not so fast! I've got questions—a whole lot of them.'

Without any warning, Tarzan grabbed my hand. The air was filled with the crackling sound of static electricity and then we were swallowed by an empty space.

We landed just outside the entrance of a familiar green tent. It was the Bihishti Tea Corner, by the same picnic table where I had drunk tea with Chacha Khidr in what seemed like many lifetimes ago. I still wore the clothes given to me in the Intiqaal Lounge.

It seemed as if Ibrahim had been anticipating our arrival. He emerged from the tent, all smiles, the moment we touched down. He carried a tray with two steaming cups of tea and a plate of biscuits, the taste of which had remained as clear in my memory as if I had them only yesterday.

A red bicycle was parked a few feet away from the table, leaning on its kickstand. Far on the horizon stood the immutable walls of Paradise. Behind those walls lurked the unfinished business I had with Sophie and Laila, one that would have to be sorted out some day. It was between the black burqa and red shawl; between the heavily regulated world where beauty was kept hidden, and the world in harmony with natural laws and expressive beauty. Laila was my companion during a time of need which had now served its purpose, but Sophie was my inspiration, the anchor to the bottom of my being. I realized now that I had loved Sophie all my life.

'Welcome back, Babu,' Ibrahim said, as he set the tray on the table.

'I missed your tea, Ibrahim,' I said, sitting across Tarzan, warming my hands on the cup and breathing in the fragrant steam.

'Once you are done with your tea, you may go into the tent and change,' said Ibrahim, looking at us with a warm smile. 'Tarzan, please tell Chacha that I could use a helper-boy.'

'I'll certainly let him know.'

As soon as Ibrahim left, I bombarded Tarzan with questions.

'Did you survive the blast at the compound?' I asked pointedly. I had been dying to ask him that particular question.

He shook his head from side to side and then up and down, all the while with a broad, toothy grin on his face.

'I wish I'd get a straight answer on occasion,' I said, feeling frustrated and fighting my rising irritation.

'Sir, there's no such thing as death—you move on to the next world when you die in the one you're born in,' he said, sipping his tea.

'Tell me what Khalifa is up to and who this Master Chemist providing him with all these books is.'

'Sir, one day you will get the answers to all your questions. But remember, the success of this mission doesn't hinge on you knowing very much about it.'

'But I know nothing!'

'Less is more. You've got the headband and you've got the Quran. That's pretty much all you need. Remember, the headband is for telepathic use. Whenever you can't talk, just think; but think clearly and you'll be able to communicate.' Tarzan pushed the plate of biscuits towards me. 'Have some.'

'Who is Pir Pul Siraat, really? And Chacha Khidr? Where do they come from?' I asked, taking a bite.

'Smuggled goods,' Tarzan said sheepishly, holding the cookie in front of his face and examining it.

'Tarzan, please. I'm asking you an important question here.'

'I'll explain what I can. Chacha—he's been around a long time and has seen it all. As for Pir, well, there are different theories about him.'

'What kind of theories? What do you mean?' I asked, thinking that Chacha had to be the real Al-Khidr, the Green One. The one who taught Moses—his appearance adapted to the milieu he was carrying out his working in.

'Chacha told me—not that I necessarily believe everything he says—that Pir is the IGP,' said Tarzan.

'IGP?'

'Inspector General of Paradise.' Tarzan, amused by my confusion, cackled.

'Give me another theory.'

'That he's a former prophet who left the comfort and luxury of the highest level of Paradise to take matters into his own hands,' Tarzan said. 'Some say he's the Messiah everyone down there has been waiting for, the one cleaning the place up before he declares himself in the Middle East.'

'Interesting! Which theory do you believe in?' I probed, sipping my tea and wondering which Messiah he could possibly be— the Jewish one or the Islamic one.

'Neither,' Tarzan replied with a toothy grin on his face.

'So you don't know?'

'Sir, I'm more interested in eating mangoes than counting them,' he said. 'I've got a good life here—though I'm not too excited about it—but still, I don't ask questions, the answers for which I have no use.'

As we finished our tea, the sky grew dark. A shrill noise rose up in the air, intensifying as it drowned our conversation. A gigantic, dark cloud of ababeels appeared overhead that took several minutes to pass out of sight.

My gaze followed this vanishing cloud.

'It's best if the mission is accomplished without having to turn everything to husk,' Tarzan said, leaving me more confused than ever. 'Time to change clothes, sir. My cycle is ready; it should be a short ride.'

'How come we can't beam ourselves to earth like we'd been doing in Paradise?'

'We can't. Because Hell lies in between, and only Chacha and Pir know how to move about between the spheres directly.'

'Oh, I see,' I said, nodding. But of course, I really didn't.

After having changed into a single length of unstitched white cloth, large enough to be worn as a toga, we hopped onto the bike. Waving goodbye to Ibrahim, Tarzan put the tires on the cable and stench of sulfur hit my nose as Tarzan began peddling.

'Ibrahim, I'm going to talk to Chacha about the tea-boy for you,' he looked back and shouted.

Although the novelty of seeing Pul Siraat over a river of magma wasn't as strong this time, the ride was as horrific and terrifying as before. Thankfully it was short, and we crossed over quickly without an incident. We rode over a flat surface in complete darkness and then Tarzan braked.

We got off the bike and walked for a minute or two in the faint glow of his eyes until we stood by the door of the hospital's bathroom. Compared to where I had been, this world seemed completely real. I touched my forehead to check if Pir's headband was still there. Happily, I noted, it was. Tarzan passed like a ghost through the solid door into the bathroom and I followed, gliding through the wall and feeling only a slight resistance against my body.

Once inside, I saw the hazy outline of two bodies lying on the ground. One of them was mine, clothed in my unmistakable patched robe. The other, draped in a burqa and lying beside me, was Laila's. The sight made me sick to my stomach and I shook uncontrollably, feeling like I was going to pass out.

'Now what?' I asked, my voice shaking and my teeth chattering audibly.

'Sir, be calm. All you have to do is lie down on top of your material body and you'll sink right into it. It's better if you keep your eyes closed.' The strange glow of Tarzan's eyes was enough to dispel the darkness around us, but it had an unsettling effect on me. 'Sir, good night, and best of luck. Make sure you keep the Quran on your person at all times.'

'Tarzan, don't leave yet. One last question, I promise,' I begged.

'Yes?'

'Who is this Master Chemist?'

'I've never gotten a straight answer out of anybody on that question myself,' Tarzan said. 'My guess: Iblees, the Devil. Someone whom the Almighty likes to play chess with. No further questions now, sir. Good night!'

He broke into a million particles of light before disappearing from view. I was left standing in my toga in the darkness, feeling more unsure of things than ever.

Had I not seen Hell and Paradise with my own eyes, I had have taken his answers to be mere metaphors at best and a big joke at worst.

Still shaking a bit, I sat down on the dirty cold floor beside my body and stopped myself from analysing what was happening. I lay my hand on the forehead of my inert form. It felt warm, but my hand passed through the skull as if I was made of smoke. Without daring to indulge in any further experimentation, I laid down on top of my corporeal body as instructed, closed my eyes and surrendered to whatever was going to happen.

A sound like the whine of a chainsaw filled my head, growing louder by the second. It felt really strange to be back in my earthly body, but the noise subsided and I opened my eyes.

It took some serious effort to raise myself up from the floor. My body shambled as if it were filled with lead. Laila was still lying beside me, her skin warm, but she wasn't breathing and had no pulse. I looked at my watch. It was 11.35 p.m. I had made this whole celestial journey in just under five minutes.

Before I left the scene of the crime, I pulled the burqa away from Laila's face and let my fingertips feel the asymmetry of her cheekbones. She had been telling me the truth. This was, in fact, reality. My eyes welled up with tears when I realized this woman had given her life for me. I kissed her lips, then gently put her head on the floor and covered it with her veil.

I got back to my father's house at 1.10 a.m., feeling like burnt celluloid. Had it not been for the potholes which kept bouncing me around the car and rattling my teeth, I would have fallen asleep at the wheel.

Faisal Town was steeped in darkness due to a power outage when I arrived. Ghulam Rasool, with a gas lamp dangling from his hand, opened the gate and I parked the car near the porch. As I climbed out, the old man eyed me suspiciously.

'Salaam Saab. Are you feeling all right?'

'Please get me some water. I need to go to bed.' Thankfully he didn't ask more questions, but just quietly followed me into the house.

Wali was asleep in the servant's quarters so I didn't have to deal with him giving me the third degree. I stumbled into the living room and tripped over the curled-up edge of the carpet. Ghulam Rasool raised the lamp above his head and white light splashed across the painting over the fireplace where it loomed larger than life. It writhed with a hideous energy and I stared at its hypnotic beauty, marvelling at its size, its impeccable brush strokes and its ominous foreboding mood. It was indeed a masterpiece worthy of any museum on the planet.

Ghulam Rasool led me into my bedroom, lit a candle on the bedside table and pointed to a jug of water and a glass.

'Saab, if you need anything, just call out to me,' he said. 'There's water in the jug and just so you know, the lights may or may not come back on tonight.'

'Thank you. Please don't wake me for breakfast. I'll call you when I'm up.'

As soon he left, I pulled out the Quran and the headband from my pocket, and tucked them under my pillow. I put on my pyjamas, and the second my worn and exhausted body hit the mattress I was out like a light.

23

❧

I AWOKE UP AROUND NOON from the dreamless slumber of the dead. My head felt like it did after an all-night party. I dragged myself to the bathroom, emptied my bladder, then stole a quick glance at myself in the mirror. I looked like I had been in a fight; dark circles under both my eyes made them look bruised and swollen. My cheeks were sunken and hollow beneath a stubble that was on the verge of downright pious and fully legal. I was starving.

Ghulam Rasool delivered a tray with a hearty breakfast to me, consisting of French toast, a glass of milk and tea. I ate in bed as he hovered over me. With his hands around his waist, the old man watched with obvious approval as I feasted on this manna from heaven. My praise of his cooking skills brought smiles of delight to his care-worn face and I had to plead with him not to bring me another stack of the dessert-like confections.

'Hajji sahib is expected sometime this evening, saab,' he informed me, dusting the crumbs off my bed and into the tray with a small whisk.

As soon as he was gone I went back to sleep. This time, however, my sleep was cluttered with dreams which were chaotic, vivid and populated with the usual suspects. From time to time Laila entered my dreams wearing various dresses, masks and makeup. And Sophie was always strolling in a meadow, always being stalked by some unknown man. I was awakened at dusk by the sound of my father's voice.

'It's just the jet lag. Get him some more tea.'

Startled, my eyes shot open and I instantly recognized his six-foot frame outlined dimly in the doorway. He stepped into my room and his loose white robe flared as if on some unseen currents of power he carried about his person. He had gained some weight but not much, and his fist-length beard, once jet-black, had become a wizened gray.

Though obviously older, my father's face was almost completely devoid of wrinkles and his eyes possessed the same penetrating glare that had always made my heart sink. Suddenly, it seemed as if I had never left home. I was once again the same eighteen-year-old kid. I jumped out of bed the same way I used to—terrified when he would walk into my room unannounced.

He stopped at the foot of my bed, his eyes scanning me from head to toe like a laser beam.

'Salaam, Abba,' I muttered, scratching my chest and feeling a churning in my stomach. 'It's been such a long time.'

'Ismael! How did the miracle happen?'

'What miracle, Abba?'

'Wali told me about what happened the other night but he is given to exaggeration. Tell me, did it really happen?'

'I know my Quran, Abba,' I said, feeling a prickle on the back of my neck.

'You've always been full of surprises—you haven't really changed, Ismael.' There was a faint smile on his face and I detected just a hint of warmth in his otherwise cold stare.

A rustle behind my back made me turn around and I was startled to see a large, brown long-haired cat standing on my bed, sniffing my pillow. My heartbeat quickened and sweat beads poured down my forehead. Pir had said that the Khalifa was using his specially bred cats to extract the deepest inner thoughts from anyone he was suspicious of. I held my breath and tried to keep my mind as blank as possible.

'Don't be scared,' Abba said, looking at the cat affectionately. 'Nofel is a good cat.'

Nofel growled and pushed my pillow onto the floor, revealing my Quran and headband. Abba stared at these items, his eyes narrowing. 'So what are you reading these days?' Abba asked, picking up the Quran and flipping through its pages. He parted his lips and I heard a sharp intake of breath.

'What a magnificent copy you have in your possession, my son!'

'It's great to see you, Abba,' I said, thrusting my hand toward him.

'Where did you get this?' he asked, ignoring my hand, his eyes locked on the book.

'Oh, you know, I got it from this antique store down in the East Village in Manhattan. It's owned by a Moroccan friend of mine.' I stammered. My arm had started to shake.

'Never seen anything quite this beautiful,' he whispered seemingly to himself. His eyes glittered with undisguised greed as they darted, almost snake-like, over the book's surface.

'It's my constant companion in this transient world of ours, Abba. By the way, I've got something really nice for you.' I was about to withdraw my hand when he reached out and gave it a hurried squeeze.

Damn! I shouldn't have said anything about his gift. Since Wali had no recollection of our visit to Fortress Stadium, this could complicate things.

'I've got everything I need,' he said, smiling. 'I still can't believe you've really come back—to faith.' Thankfully, he didn't seem too interested in his gift.

'I missed being with you, Abba,' I said, feeling the cat's furry torso against my legs.

'Ismael, please say something believable,' he said, staring at the cat.

'Abba, would you please ask Nofel to leave the room?' I asked, holding my breath.

'So you missed being with me?' He let out a laugh and shooed the cat away.

'I swear by Allah...'

'Do not try to fool me, Ismael. You are known to swear falsely.'

'Abba, people change—and twelve years is a really long time,' I said, feeling a sudden cramp in my stomach. 'How's the family? Where is everyone?'

'Alhamdolillah. Everyone is well.' He handed back my Quran. 'For the most part, I'm in Islamabad these days. I have two houses there now; one for Farzana and one for Rukhsana.'

He had always been unapologetic about his love for women, especially really young ones. It made me wonder just how many times my father had married and divorced in my absence.

'Any more kids, Abba?'

'It hasn't been the will of Allah—so far. Man can only try,' he said with a shrug and then added, 'I've never once thought you'd see the light of faith.'

'Who can question Allah's will?'

He opened his mouth to reply but before he could utter a word the *maghrib azaan* filled the air. These were the loudspeakers of a dozen neighborhood mosques which were soon joined by even more mosques that had turned the call to prayer into a senseless wall of meaningless noise.

The power came back on just as the azaan stopped. Abba walked over to the light switch by the door and flipped it on, making me feel exposed in the bright light hanging over my head. My stomach churned once again and I desperately wanted to run to the bathroom.

'Where did you go last night, Ismael?' Abba demanded, his eyebrows raised. 'I was told you didn't return until one in the morning.'

'I just wanted to drive around and see Lahore. Get some fresh air, you know. But the roads are pretty bad.'

He looked directly at me. Nofel, rubbing its body against his legs, stared at me with its large, unblinking yellow eyes.

'Hmm. But why didn't you take Wali with you?' I felt like I was undergoing some kind of interrogation. Though I couldn't tell if I really was or if this was just the old man's way.

I shrugged and kept my mouth shut while forcing my mind to be completely blank.

'It's time for maghrib,' he snapped. 'Why don't you take a quick wash and join me in the drawing room for the namaaz? Don't be late.' He opened the door and walked out, Nofel at his heels.

'Sure thing,' I muttered under my breath, as I dashed to the bathroom.

I took a hurried bath and put on my freshly laundered robe that Ghulam Rasool had hung next to my bed. Unfortunately, there wasn't time for the leisurely bathroom time I was longing for.

Putting my headband on, I went to the drawing room. There, by the fireplace Abba, Wali and Ghulam Rasool sat on their respective prayer mats waiting for my arrival, their heads covered with white skullcaps. They stood up as I entered the room, their curious eyes staring at my headband. Thankfully Nofel wasn't around.

'It's a substitute for the cap,' I said, touching my forehead to soothe their obvious anxiety over my headband.

'Sirji, faith requires complete covering of the head while praying, otherwise it can easily leak out. Especially through such a big hole as that American style cap you're wearing,' Wali declared through pursed lips.

He turned without waiting for my reply and started intoning the *niyyath*, the pre-namaaz prayer in Arabic. My father nudged me towards the prayer mat placed in front of the other three.

'Ismael will lead the prayer tonight,' Abba announced.

'Subhan-Allah!' Ghulam Rasool cried. 'I am a happy man who has lived to see the day when our Ismael saab will lead the prayer.'

Reluctantly I stood on the leading prayer mat and assumed the role of the imam. They all stood behind me in a line, their shoulders touching. The mushroom cloud in the painting loomed imposingly over my *qiblah*, the direction of Kaaba. My stomach cramped violently a couple of more times as I waited for Wali to complete his recitation. Just then I deeply regretted having postponed my private gastrointestinal ministrations when I had the chance.

I took a deep breath and mustered all of my willpower to bear the burgeoning agony in my belly. I touched my earlobes and as soon as I said *Allah Hu Akbar*, the text of the Quran streamed across my eyes like a fiery ticker tape. Since I could shuffle the text with the force of my will alone, I chose some obscure verses to impress my father.

My pronunciation was flawless. Feeling happy that my stomach had eased up, I was doing the second of the three *rakaat* of maghrib when the lights went out again. On the third and final rakaat, I was struck violently by a renewed urge to run to the restroom. It happened when I was kneeling, my hands resting on my knees: a small amount of gas escaped me, despite my superhuman effort to stop it. It wasn't loud, but it was clearly audible.

A commotion erupted behind me but I continued the namaaz as if nothing had happened. Out of the corner of my eye, I saw Wali standing beside me. Clearly, he had broken his namaaz.

'Sirji, what are you doing?' he snapped. 'You have to stop praying! Once the *wudu*, the ablution, is broken, the namaaz becomes invalid.'

Startled, I turned around and saw my father staring at me angrily, his fists knotted and resting on his thighs. Ghulam Rasool had stuffed his skullcap into his mouth and his eyes bulged like he was in mortal anguish.

'I'm so terribly sorry,' I apologized. 'My stomach hasn't been right since I landed.'

'Go do your wudu again,' my father commanded like I was his servant. 'We still have a few minutes before the time for maghrib runs out.' Then he turned to Ghulam Rasool and growled, 'Get your cap out of your mouth and light some candles.'

'We've got to do the whole namaaz again, sirji,' Wali said.

'Who says we have to do the whole namaaz?' Ghulam Rasool asked, as he lit a large candle on the fireplace mantel. 'We have to do only one rakaat and we're done.'

'You don't know what you're talking about, Ghulam Rasool,' Wali said, his voice trembling with rage.

'Be quiet, both of you!' my father's voice boomed. 'I'm not taking sides here. It's best if we consult the book of *Fiqah*, and not go by mere opinions.'

As he walked over to the bookshelf in the far corner of the room I darted out and headed for the bathroom. After relieving myself, I was doing my wudu while squatting on the floor beside the water bucket when I heard someone clearing his throat in my head. I reflexively touched my headband.

'Pir, is that you?' I whispered.

'Hope everything is moving along smoothly, Ismael,' he said.

'Kind of,' I whispered, as I continued my ablution in the dark.

'You can't afford to be on your father's wrong side, ever. Tell me what happened.'

'A minor mishap but I think I can handle it.'

'Good! Remember though, you really don't have to speak out loud when we're talking—just use your thoughts. It'll feel awkward at first, like learning to ride a bike,' he said with a chuckle. 'But you'll get the hang of it. And it's safer too.'

'Got it!' I told him by projecting my thought.

'Your father leaves for Islamabad tomorrow morning. Go with him and stick to him closely at all times. Do you read me?' Pir asked.

'I read you clear!'

'We want you to be in Islamabad with him and your Quran should be with you at all times. Did you get that?'

'Yes.'

'The last time you went off course, you crashed in the Dump. There's no margin for error this time,' Pir said. 'Do not try to contact me, instead you wait for my call.'

'Yes, Pir,' I replied, while washing my feet.

'Ismael, think of this mission as traversing the Pul Siraat.' And with that, Pir went offline.

I dashed back to the candlelit drawing room where Wali and Ghulam Rasool were engrossed in a heated argument and about to come to blows. They lowered their voices as soon as they saw me. My father sat on the carpet pouring over a large, thick book that lay in his lap. At his knee was a lit candle.

'So what's the verdict?' I asked, taking my position on the imam's mat once again.

'*Fiqah* is silent on the matter,' Abba said, with a look of resignation on his face. 'It's an unusual case since it involves the imam himself.'

'Why don't we do *ijtihaad*—decision-making through personal effort,' I asked.

'Ijtihad for a fart!' Abba looked at me incredulously, shaking his head from side to side.

Ghulam Rasool had stepped on his mat behind me. 'Go ahead, saab. Let's do one rakaat and get it over with,' he said. 'I'm not saying an additional one if it's not needed.'

'Sirji, ijtihad is not applicable in this situation,' Wali replied. 'The rules are already as clear as daylight on this.'

'Why not look in the *Fiqah* to see if it's okay to do ijtihad in a situation like this?' I glanced at my father.

'Time has passed for the namaaz-e-maghrib,' Ghulam Rasool declared. 'Look outside. It's already night.'

They continued arguing over the cutoff point of when it is considered too late to say maghrib.

'It's not night as long as you can see a plucked hair held to the sky,' Wali added.

I had the longest hair in the room so I plucked one and handed it to him. 'Why don't you go out and check for yourself,' I asked.

'Everyone, stop!' my father stood up, his eyes flashing. 'I say, there's still time.'

Both Wali and Ghulam Rasool abruptly walked out of the room, heading in opposite directions. Wali went outside and Ghulam Rasool disappeared into the kitchen.

'Islam is the simplest religion there is,' Abba said to me. 'Alas! Only if we know how to follow it properly.'

'Exactly, Abba,' I said.

'Since we've got very little time left, maybe it is best if you do your own namaaz and I do mine; separately so we can finish it quickly.'

'It's all my mistake, Abba,' I added sincerely. 'If given another chance, I'll make up for it.'

'What happened was not a good omen,' he said, pulling his mat away from mine. 'You haven't changed, Ismael.'

'Abba, please!'

He said nothing but just started his namaaz five feet away from me so I followed his cue and began mine.

I was indeed walking on the Pul Siraat, where even a light gust of wind could initiate a hurricane and blow everything to hell. Having finished our respective namaaz, Abba and I remained seated on our mats, our hands raised in prayer, our lips moving without uttering a sound. Shadows danced about the room and the painting, making the canvas seem like a living, breathing tableau and no simple work of art.

Abba blew on his chest and rubbed his palms over his face as I copied his gestures.

'That's a great painting, Abba. It must have cost a fortune,' I said. 'A bit frightening, though. Where did you get it?'

He stared at the painting, rubbing his temple, as if considering what to say. 'It was a gift,' he finally replied. 'A gift from Khalifaji to me.'

'Wow! From Khalifaji! Really?'

He nodded his head in affirmation, his eyes shining with pride.

'Who made it, Abba?'

'A certain retired General—this was his last masterpiece before he died. I'm forgetting his name at the moment.' I could tell he had deliberately censored that information.

'Well, it's clearly a museum-quality piece,' I said.

He grinned and scratched his neck. He was about to say something when Ghulam Rasool entered the room rolling a cart of food topped with tea, samosas and shami kebabs. He must have been eavesdropping on our conversation.

'Saab, your Abbaji is very, very close to Khalifaji—not many people are aware of that,' he said, smiling with satisfaction, as though bathing in the glory afforded him by his master. Then he composed himself and began to pour tea into our cups.

'You must be a very important person, Abba. You always were a leader.'

'Tomorrow I'm meeting with Khalifaji in Islamabad' he said, straightening his back.

'Abba, didn't you just come back from Islamabad? That's a lot of travel.'

'If you have a good car, the distance doesn't matter,' he said, his face tightening in a smug, self-satisfied smile.

'Oh? What kind of car are you driving these days?'

'Mercedes Benz SE505X, custom made.' Lifting his eyebrows he stared at me, as if trying to read my reaction.

'Abba, wow! That's an expensive car.'

'Bought and paid for by the state. I'm certainly not wealthy enough to afford it otherwise.'

'Well, Khalifaji is very kind to you, it seems.'

'Anyway, one day I'm in Islamabad, one day in Lahore. Khalifaji has entrusted me to communicate his messages in person with certain important people.'

'I see.'

'The Day of Judgment is upon us, saab,' Ghulam Rasool interjected with excitement as he handed me a cup of tea. He then looked at my father. 'Am I right, Hajji sahib?'

'Ghulam Rasool, your eyes and ears are too sharp for your own good.'

'Saab, I've been with you for the last thirty years. I don't need my eyes and ears to know what is happening,' he said, handing my father his cup.

'What's going on, Abba?' I felt as if my 'mission' was about to be revealed at long last through this innocuous master-servant conversation and my heart started to thump against my ribcage.

Before my father answered, Nofel appeared in the room and curled up on the carpet beside him. The cat's yellow eyes were radiant in the light of the candles and his tail swayed back and forth like a cobra. I immediately emptied my mind of all thoughts.

'Help yourself to the shami kebab, saab. I've made them especially for you.' Ghulam Rasool held a plate of warm round patties in front of my face, his eyes seeming to float above the plate in the steam. I could sense their mushiness and taste their meaty flavour in my watering mouth.

It was time to change the conversation lest Nofel tagged onto my stream of thought.

'How's your business these days, Abba?'

'By the grace of Allah, business is very good,' Abba replied, sipping his tea.

'What kind of business are you in, exactly?' I asked casually, as I poured green chutney over the kebab. I wanted to see if he would tell me the truth.

'Transportation,' Ghulam Rasool chirped, but my father threw him a cold stare.

'A couple of years after you left,' Abba began, as though launching into one of the great desert tales, 'I bought a new chemical plant in Kala Shah-Kaku. A few years later, I added a garment factory to my holdings. And by the grace of the Almighty, we now manufacture and export quality products to China, Russia and to the far end of the Maghrib,' my father continued, taking a bite of the samosa Ghulam Rasool placed in his hand.

'Saab, orders have started to come from Europe and even America,' Ghulam Rasool chimed in. 'Why don't Wali and I give you a tour of the factory, if that's okay with Hajji sahib?'

The prospect of visiting a plant manufacturing suicide vests with Wali and Ghulam Rasool gave me the shivers. 'Abba, I'd rather go to Islamabad. I came here to spend time with you and don't want to be here in Lahore by myself.'

'For that, I'll have to get approval from Khalifaji,' my father said, as he ran his fingers gently over Nofel's spine.

'Please, Abba. Otherwise I'll be wasting my time in Lahore doing nothing,' I said, biting into the succulent kebab.

He quietly sipped his tea, smoothing his eyebrows from time to time. He was thinking.

'Please, Abba,' I said again.

'Ismael, I just heard you reciting the Quran with my own ears. Wali saw you doing the same thing the other night. Your turn-around is all the more mysterious and remarkable considering you've been living and breathing in the same air as the *kuffaar*, the infidels, for so long. And now you somehow defy all logic for having resisted becoming an infidel yourself. Not only have you apparently rekindled with something I was certain you never had to begin with, but you are able to do it so very, very well. This whole thing has to be a miracle; some kind of sign.'

As my father spoke, his eyes became teary, glistening in the dancing flames of the candlelight. He fell silent, looking up and staring at the painting, contemplating. He seemed to be trying to collect his thoughts and regain his composure.

Turning to Ghulam Rasool he said, 'Go and see what Wali is doing outside. Tell him to prepare my car. We'll be leaving for Islamabad early in the morning. And make sure you feed Nofel—he hasn't eaten anything all day.'

Nofel trotted behind Ghulam Rasool as he left the drawing room. The front door of the house creaked open and slammed shut behind him. Once Nofel was out of the picture, I relaxed and let my thoughts wander beyond their self-imposed dark prison.

If the Khalifa was planning a spectacle, as Pir had called it, then Abba was part of it for sure. Whatever *it* was. My curiosity gnawed at me and I wondered what role I was supposed to play.

In all this darkness, there was one small, bright spot: a leisurely drive in my father's custom-made Mercedes Benz through the 200 miles that snaked through the lush plains of Punjab and merged with the foothills of the Himalayas, the Margalla Hills. These low-lying hills, hardly reaching more than a thousand feet in elevation, provided a picturesque backdrop to the otherwise flat capital city.

'I'll be calling Khalifaji shortly, asking if I can bring you along,' Abba said as he stood up. 'I'll be very busy tonight.'

'Thank you, Abba.'

'Perhaps he will let you join the Friday Prayer too,' he added, without looking at me as he stood and walked over to get his shoes from the edge of the carpet.

I had no clue what day this was. I looked at my watch and noted it was Thursday.

'What's happening on Friday, Abba?'

'Allah, out of His infinite mercy, has brought you here to be with me, Ismael, to witness history in the making.'

Something big was going to happen tomorrow, the very something Pir said would have serious consequences for this world and the Next. I also knew that without his mysterious book, Khalifa couldn't move forward with his plans.

If tomorrow was to be his D-Day, then Khalifa must have got his hands on the second book that Pir mentioned had already been shipped. Was he planning a mass exodus to Paradise by having himself and his associates ingest the stamps, the so-called tickets to Paradise?

Or did he have something else in mind; something that sent dismembered body parts flying through the air and landing near Chacha Khidr's ominous burlap sack? If that was the case, how was I supposed to stop him from carrying out his plans?

'I'll see you tomorrow at the morning prayer, at *fajr namaaz*,' Abba said, slipping his feet into his sandals. 'Let Ghulam Rasool know if you need anything. I'm not going to eat dinner tonight; I've got a lot of work to do and many phone calls to make.'

'I'm not hungry either, Abba. I'll see you at the fajr prayer, Inshallah.'

When he left, I stared at the painting where it loomed darkly from the mantle. Was Abba in on Khalifa's schemes? It seemed pretty obvious that the answer was a resounding *yes*.

The mystery surrounding my mission was now driving me insane. Sitting in my room I was wide-awake; my mind was afloat with inescapable thoughts, fears and misgivings. I needed a distraction to occupy my mind and soothe my jangled nerves. I decided to dive into the namaaz of *ishaa*—the longest of the five daily obligatory prayers.

I chose some of the longest passages of the Quran because I wanted Abba to peek in and catch me in my act of flagrant piety. It was well past midnight when I heard his footsteps and felt his presence at the door but I continued to pray without letting on that I knew he was watching.

He left without saying anything, returned an hour later and found me still praying. And I wasn't even halfway done yet. He stood at the door for at least five minutes before wandering back down the hall. When he showed up again around two in the morning, I knew he had been moved by my reverence for Allah, though only slightly. Sitting with my legs folded under myself, I blew on my shoulders. I still had two final rakaat of *nafil*, considered optional but spiritually beneficial, to go before concluding my prayers. I looked at his dark figure standing in the doorway and felt thankful for not having eye contact with him.

Once I was done, he said, 'In all my sixty-plus years of life, I've never seen anyone who'd spend so much time on one rakaat. Are you taking any medications, Ismael?' Abba had always been good at sniffing out trouble.

'Of course not, Abba,' I said. This was a huge lie, though, considering the assortment of novel chemicals that must have been flowing through my bloodstream and bathing my brain at the moment.

'Khalifaji would like to meet with you in person.' His voice betrayed his excitement.

The news struck me like a projectile piercing through my forehead. For the next few seconds I couldn't breathe. 'Khalifaji wants to see me? Are you serious, Abba?' I gasped.

'Yes. He believes you're one of the signs he has been awaiting; first shown to him in a dream.'

'Me? A sign?'

'Who taught you your faith, Ismael, in America?'

'I'm my own teacher, Abba.' I was feeling a surge of confidence. I would be going to Islamabad with him! One of the critical tasks of my mission had been accomplished, though I was far from winning Abba's heart and mind.

I looked at him in a daze. He stepped forward and sat on the bed, staring at me with great interest. 'No man can learn his faith with such perfection as you have without divine guidance,' he said, studying me. 'You have to tell me, Ismael, who brought you back to your faith? I must meet this man and kiss his hands.'

24

MY FATHER PRESIDED OVER the fajr prayer amidst a sea of flickering yellow candles. When it concluded, Ghulam Rasool was sent to fetch tea, Wali to find Nofel and I was instructed to remain seated on my prayer mat for a chat. Having served us, Ghulam Rasool scurried back to the kitchen to prepare breakfast for five people since my father was expecting guests.

These guests were Abba's business partners and also happened to be high-ranking VIPs within the Caliphate. After breakfast, the five of us would be travelling to Islamabad in my father's car; a vehicle that also seemed to be a high-ranking notable within the regime. The three guests had been wanting to experience for themselves, for some time now, the otherworldly luxuries of my father's car.

The distinguished guests were the Chief Qadi of the Sharia Court of Punjab, the Imam of the Badshahi Mosque and the Grand Mufti of the Fatwa Council. The thought of being trapped in a car with these three strangers on such a long road trip put a serious damper on my already precarious spirits.

The plan was to head straight to the Faisal Mosque in Islamabad to attend a historic Jumma congregation with various hand-picked luminaries of the Caliphate. Khalifa himself would be there to honour the ceremony and admission to this auspicious occasion was by invitation only. I had been to this mosque once before, on a school trip when I was just a boy.

I remembered being completely blown away by the size and scale of the place. To my boyish imagination it had looked like a huge space station when it was actually intended to resemble a Bedouin tent. The design was the brainchild of Turkish architect Vedat Dalokay. Four minarets shaped like sharpened pencils towered hundreds of feet above a triangular Prayer Hall that looked a lot like a massive tent pitched at the green foothills of the Margalla Hills.

From what Abba said, or rather hadn't said, it didn't sound like even he knew the exact purpose of this mysterious gathering. It could also be that he just didn't want to divulge any of the secrets he had been privy to. The conversation then turned to his infamous car, which of course I was dying to see for myself.

Abba told me how much he loved racing along the motorway because there was no speed limit. He loved driving this car so much that he had refused the official driver who had come as part of the deal. The Benz could make the trip to Islamabad in two and a half hours—a distance of about 230 miles. Abba's record, however, was just under two hours.

My father's eyes widened when he described the 100-mile-an-hour warm-up, how the car hugged the road at 120, and how you never felt out of control even at speeds over 150. Describing the cruise along the motorway, my father had used words like 'freed from time and space', and 'the cares and worries which belong to the world'.

'This is the closest one can get to experiencing Jannah while still on earth,' he said in a serious tone. He remained silent for a good ten seconds then, as if gathering his thoughts. 'Owning the best possible ride, one can get in life is *Sunnah*. In my case basically this means that every mile I drive, the closer I get to Jannah.'

I lowered my head, thinking of Sophie living in the Pagan quarters of Paradise. What would he do if he ever found out that I made love to his seventh wife in Paradise? He was the epitome of greed—greed for Paradise.

'I never thought earning swaab could be as easy as slamming the gas pedal,' I said. I felt happy with my decision to leave this bizarre world of his when I was eighteen, and I couldn't wait to get the hell out of it once my mission was accomplished.

'Yes, it is so, son. Allah's ways are indeed mysterious.'

This was the first time he had called me 'son'. I must have been doing something right since he was definitely beginning to soften.

By the time he went to change for breakfast, the candles had fluttered in the morning light that spilled through the open windows. I wandered outside to take a look at the magical car, and there she was—a gleaming black Mercedes-Benz. Parked alongside was the ravaged-looking Corolla with its fake camel top. Compared to the black beauty, the Corolla could easily have passed for a pile of scrap. A palm-sized green flag bearing the Caliphate logo was tethered to the circular coat of arms of the Benz at the end of its hood.

I stared at the smooth sleek lines, marvelling at the unapologetic disparities life was capable of displaying, the incongruous nature of reality, the lopsided nature of cause and effect and the deceptive linearity of time. Before I was finished contemplating, Wali, carrying Nofel in his arms, appeared next to me.

'The moment this bastard sees a female cat, he loses his mind,' he said, looking angry. 'Sirji, I've asked Hajji sahib many times to get him neutered.'

'And what did he say?' I asked.

'It's against the Sharia.'

'I think he's right.'

'Sirji, I can prove that he's wrong,' he said, putting down Nofel who dashed back into the house. I kept my mouth shut so he wouldn't launch off into some new tirade on religion.

Before Wali could say another word, a car blasted its horn outside the front gate. He raced toward it and threw both sides wide open, then stepped aside and bowed deeply.

A black top-of-the-line Toyota Land Cruiser with tinted windows rolled ominously into the driveway and braked six inches away from my shins. Three men wearing identical starched white robes and headdresses emerged from the plush interior of a vehicle that seemed suited to Darth Vader. Or someone who admired him greatly.

As soon as the car had discharged its passengers, it retreated silently and disappeared from the compound. Wali then closed the gate and ran back inside the house. Ignoring my presence, the guests started fingering their mobile phones.

A moment later, rubbing his palms together, Abba came rushing out of the house, his face radiant with happiness. Once he finished hugging his guests, he turned to me and I could tell from his face he didn't like what he was seeing. Maybe because this was the first time he was seeing me in the daylight, but I must have looked like a wreck. In the hooded glare of my father's disapproving gaze, I somehow felt unclean, impure. Of course! I was wearing the same patchwork denim jellaba he had hated when I bought it twelve years ago.

'Meet my son, Ismael. He's just returned from America,' Abba said, sounding awkward and looking slightly embarrassed. The three wizened grey-beards stared at me with narrowed eyes. None of them smiled.

'It's a pleasure to meet you all,' I said, standing still.

'My son lived in the belly of the Great Satan for a decade, so pardon his appearance. What's important is that his faith is stronger than all of us put together,' Abba said, as he tried to regain his bearings. 'Ismael, come. Let me introduce you to my friends.'

As I shook their warm, flaccid hands one by one, Abba introduced them by their names and titles, all of which were long and complicated. In my mind, I assigned each of them a nickname according to their job description. Qadi, or the Judge, was six feet tall with broad shoulders and a head too small for his body. Imam, fair skinned, looked impossibly round and reminded me of a grenade that was about to pop. And Mufti, the issuer of fatwa or rulings according to Islamic law, was a little guy, barely five feet tall and thin as a blade of grass, wearing a black patch over his right eye. I had no doubt the patch was well earned and worn to strike respect and awe.

Once the guests were seated in the drawing room, Abba asked that I follow him to his bedroom.

'Didn't you bring anything else to wear besides what you have on right now?' he snarled at me as he closed the door of his bedroom behind us. He made no attempt to hide his anger.

'No.'

'Is this how the believer dresses in the land of the pure, and out of all the days, on a Friday?' he demanded.

Without waiting for a reply, he flung open the double doors of a huge walk-in closet. Inside was a vast collection of robes, headdresses and pre-wrapped turbans neatly hanging from hangers and hooks and laid out on countless shelves. They were all arranged by seasonal wear, colour, fabric and importance of occasion.

'No one, absolutely no one, wears denim jellabas here anymore,' he growled. 'Only liberal extremists used to wear robes like yours,' he said, as he carefully extracted a light-brown robe of high-quality cotton from one of the covered hangers. 'This one is tight on me now but should fit you fine.'

'I'm sorry, Abba, I honestly didn't have the time to shop.' I took the robe from him along with a white keffiyeh and a coil of black tasseled rope to keep it in place. 'Abba, if you get tired from driving, I could take the wheel,' I offered, trying to distract him and lighten the mood. 'Just let me know.'

He gave me another of his long hard looks. 'Maybe on our way back.'

His answer made me wonder again just how much he actually knew about Khalifa's plan. If he was in on it, he probably wanted to enjoy the last ride of his life by driving his own beloved car. And why not? If I were him, I suppose I would want to break my previous record too.

Wearing the authentic Arab dress, the thawb, I joined everyone in the dining room. It was a little loose on me, but didn't look too bad. My face was washed, my beard combed and I wore Pir's psychic headband under my headdress, ready to transmit whenever required.

God knows what Abba was saying about me because when I took my seat next to him, his buddies were all smiles, their faces radiating warmth.

I sat across from Imam, who pushed a plate of sticky halva toward me. Qadi, seated next to him, held out a basket of steaming pooris, and Mufti, sitting at the far end of the table, shut his solitary eye for a little while longer than a blink would take as he sipped his tea. It could have been a wink, but I wasn't too sure.

'So, Ismael,' Imam said, clearing his throat. 'If what your father has told us about you is true, I'm truly impressed. I would very much like to see a demonstration of your ability.'

'It's unbelievable that after living for all these years in a place like America, created for the sole purpose of keeping Satan busy, you're able to hold on to your faith,' Qadi said. 'Quite remarkable, indeed!'

Abba's face glowed with pride as he listened to their comments. He was in for a huge surprise—provided, of course, my mission was a success. I tried to feel sympathy for him, but I just couldn't find any.

'In honour of this auspicious repast, I propose that Ismael describe for us the kind of foods we'll be eating in Al-Jannah,' Mufti suggested, looking me in the eyes as his face broke into a mischievous smile. 'Hint: it's in the Quran.'

The pointedness of his request startled me at first. Surely, I could recite any part of the Quran in Arabic. But that did not mean I understood the meaning of what I was reciting. Pir's download hadn't come with a translation. Feeling at a loss for the answer and panicking a little, I tried recalling the food I had seen lying on the floating slabs of marble under the red canopy in the Guest House of Al-Jannah.

Overwhelmed by the sheer variety I had seen, I lowered my head and thought of where to begin. Then I saw Nofel sitting beside my chair, staring at me with his piercing yellow eyes. I immediately shielded my thoughts, straightened up and looked around the room.

'Abba, would you please send Nofel away?' I asked, shaking my head and feigning confusion. 'I just can't concentrate with him staring at me like that.'

'Where's Wali? He should be feeding him. We've got a long journey ahead,' Abba said. 'Ismael, go ask Wali to take Nofel into the kitchen.'

'Excuse me, sir,' I said to Mufti, as I stood up from my chair. 'I'll be right back.'

As I came out of the dining room, formulating my answer to Mufti, Nofel followed me. In the hall I bumped into Ghulam Rasool as he was rushing out of the kitchen carrying a basket of fresh pooris.

'Abba asked to keep Nofel out of the dining room. Please tell Wali to feed him,' I said. 'The cat is coming with us to Islamabad.'

'I'll never understand what your Abbaji likes about this cat.' He said as he headed toward the front door, coaxing Nofel to follow him. I was about to return to the dining room when Pir Pul Siraat's voice sounded inside my head.

'Hello. Can you hear me?'

'Yes,' I whispered. 'Loud and clear.'

'Make sure you satisfy Mufti. He isn't too comfortable with your presence and just so you know, he knows how to read information off the cats. Your father doesn't.'

It was comforting to know that Pir was listening.

'Nofel was planted in your father's house by Khalifa's men. He's trained to keep an eye on your father. But be careful of him; he's also trained to smell trouble.'

'Thanks for the heads-up,' I thought toward him. I could feel the connection and his silent nod.

'That's what friends are for,' he added, and then broke our connection.

When I returned to the dining room, Abba was talking animatedly and enjoying the unwavering attention of his guests. He was speaking about Khalifa's dream so I sat and helped myself to some more halva, savouring the delicious sweetness as it dissolved on my tongue. When Abba finished describing the dream, they all looked at me as if I was some kind of holy relic. All but Mufti. He just sat dabbing his lips several times with his napkin as his solitary eye roamed around in its socket. Unlike Imam and Qadi, Mufti seemed wholly unconvinced of my lofty status.

It was time to deliver the fatal blow. I cleared my throat, poured myself a cup of tea and looked Mufti in the eye. I was now ready for the knockout punch.

'Mufti sahib, first of all, no human can ever hope to grasp the sheer variety of foods which are available to the believers in Jannah,' I said. 'Gently flowing streams of milk, honey, pure water and other nectars criss-cross the lush rolling grounds which stretch to eternity. The celestial palaces there are so large that one needs a lifetime to circle their grounds.

'Trees grow there in abundance which are so large that a fleet of horses must gallop for seventy years and beyond to escape the shadows of even their saplings. A magnificent purple sky lies overhead like a priceless carpet spun of the purest silk while the air drips with a heady intoxicating fragrance.

'There, under a red canopy, the truly faithful will be lounging on costly divans and leaning against soft cushions. The pious will be served pure, sparkling wines without alcohol by beautiful youths wearing red loincloths, their skin glistening as if massaged with priceless oils. As for the beautiful women? They are scattered about like butterflies by the scores; all with big round eyes, voluptuous breasts and translucent ankles through which the marrow may be clearly seen. Their skin is radiant, as if lit by a heavenly fire from within. Some of these beauties play the harp, all for the pleasure of the purest among the faithful.

'Around you will be placed lovely baskets overflowing with ripe fruits of all kinds; numerous varieties of cheeses, olives, dates and figs, as well as nuts in great and varied abundance. For your ease and convenience, everything will be at hand on floating slabs of marble.' I stopped here, realizing they had gone into trance-like states, their eyes out of focus as if gazing upon some far distant scene. No one said anything for a long time. Finally, Imam cleared his throat.

'Subhanallah! Mashallah! What a recitation.' he said, swaying his massive ball-like torso and smiling at my father. 'Hajji sahib, here is the kind of son every father dreams of having. I congratulate you for having already attained the highest level of Jannah—thanks to Ismael.'

'Very impressive!' Qadi nodded his little head. 'A bit improvised though, if I may add.'

I eyed Mufti out of the corner of my eyes. He was squirming in his chair, waiting for his turn to comment.

'Not merely *a bit*, but rather profusely improvised,' he announced, leaning forward, his hands gripping the table in front of him. 'Some of the things you've mentioned, like the purple sky, the red canopy, the cheeses, the floating tables of marble, the red loincloths on the youths, the women playing the harp—none of these are mentioned anywhere in the Quran. I would be very happy if you can give us some references which specifically mention these things. I must humbly submit that some of the information is quite new to me.'

Suddenly Pir's voice thundered in my head, making my skull vibrate like a tuning fork.

'Tell him to fuck off!' he roared.

'It may not be possible,' I said, addressing Pir but not realizing I had said it aloud.

'Indeed!' Mufti said, sitting up stiffly in his chair, his eyes shining victoriously. 'One must be very careful when speaking of such important matters without proper reference to back up one's claims of special knowledge.'

My father came to my rescue.

'Ismael, show them your Quran.'

'Abba, some other time, please,' I said, feeling uneasy about his suggestion. I tried changing the subject. 'I can assure Mufti sahib that the things I have mentioned do indeed exist in Jannah and Inshallah, all references will be provided to him in due time.'

'Enough discussion, son,' Abba said, turning towards his guests. 'I bet none of you have seen anything like this.' He nudged me with his elbow. 'Come, you may show us your Quran now.'

Reluctantly, I pulled the book out of my pocket and held it up in the air. I cringed when Imam reached for it, his glistening fingers still smeared with the oil from the pooris. He held the book in his hand and kissed its leather cover with his glossy lips before examining its pages.

'Where did you get this, Ismael?' Imam hissed, a look of astonishment lighting up his round face.

'From an antique store in Manhattan,' I answered.

'Subhanallah! My Allah can make a flower sprout from a rock,' he said.

He swayed his head several times and then passed the Quran to Qadi, who turned out to be a gentleman. He wiped his fingers on his napkin before taking the book into his hands.

'Truly unique!' He said. 'Amazing calligraphy. I have never seen a Quran with burgundy pages and golden, handwritten text.'

The book then went to Mufti who sniffed it first before putting it on the table in front of him.

'Quite unusual, really! An antique book retaining the smell of fresh leather,' he said, staring at the pages.

My heartbeat quickened as he took out a magnifying glass from his pocket and held it to his eye and began examining the text.

'This ink looks fresh, as if it was put on the page only a few days ago. May I check it a little more closely?' he asked, steadily looking at me.

'Please go ahead, Muftiji. Go ahead.' Abba's face quivered with excitement.

It was when he dipped his fingertip in his glass of water that I threw my hands up in alarm.

'Mufti sahib, I'm not sure what you're trying to do. But this book you're holding is a living, breathing being. No tampering, please.'

I knew I was on solid ground with this one. Tampering with the holy text, even the intention of doing so in any shape or form, was punishable by death—provided the intention could be proved.

Mufti recoiled at my abruptness as if shoved from his chair by a physical force.

Qadi gave me an approving look.

'I'm afraid Ismael's statements carry weight,' he said. The comment made Mufti cross his arms over his chest and avoid looking Qadi in the eye.

Before the situation could get any worse, Ghulam Rasool came into the room carrying a tray of five tall glasses of sweet creamy lassi, another treat from his arsenal of specialties. He served my father's guests first, beginning with Imam who gulped down more than half of his glass in the first swallow. He paused for a breath and then emptied his glass, throwing his head all the way back. Slamming the empty glass down on the table, he wiped the white foam from his mustache with the palm of his right hand.

'This young man speaks the truth, Muftiji,' Imam said, glancing at me and nodding with approval.

'My intention has never been to tamper,' Mufti said curtly, passing the book to Abba who handed it back to me.

'Khalifaji's dream has come true, as far as I'm concerned. Don't you think, gentlemen?' Qadi asked, taking a sip of his lassi.

'Without a doubt, *that* young man is Ismael; and the light in his hand is this most glorious Quran he just showed us,' Imam said.

'Exactly! It's a divine green light. The Almighty is letting Khalifaji know that all is well. He's telling him to go ahead with his plans,' Abba said, looking his guests in the eye one by one.

I wanted to know more about Khalifa's dream but wisely refrained from asking about it. This just wasn't the right time or place.

Abba's comment made Mufti restless and he shifted in his chair. Qadi lowered his head and massaged his temple but Imam, however, remained unperturbed. He gave Abba a sharp nod, not saying anything.

For several minutes, a long and uncomfortable silence hung over the table that was broken only by a rather loud and prolonged belch from Imam. A rancid odour filled the air and clung to my nose for a painfully long time.

It seemed Abba, unwittingly or deliberately, had tried to let me in on the secret they all shared. He could have been testing the waters to see how his guests would respond to these casually uttered remarks about Khalifa's plan while in my presence. After all, I had come from America, the enemy and a country known for planting spies within the Caliphate; though so far there had been no success.

'Seems like we're going to be attending a very special Jumma Prayer,' I said, smiling into the friendly face of Imam. 'Would you please hand me that bottle of mango pickle, Imam sahib?'

'I think we should hurry,' Mufti said. 'We have a long journey ahead of us.'

'You may relax, Muftiji. We have plenty of time,' Abba said. 'You leave that to me.'

Once Abba and his friends finished eating, I excused myself from their esteemed company and retired to my room in the hopes that Pir might contact me. I was dying to know more about Khalifa's plan. I was pacing back and forth when Ghulam Rasool walked in. 'Anything I can do for you, saab?'

'Do you by any chance know what's happening in Islamabad today?' I asked, trying to sound as casual as possible.

'Something that's to change everything, saab,' he said, shutting the door behind him lest our conversation be overheard. 'Something that will make Khalifa very, very powerful.'

'How do you know that?'

'I heard your Abbaji talking to someone over the phone a few days ago.'

'Come on, Ghulam Rasool,' I said. 'Please tell me what you know.'

As he opened his mouth to speak, there was a knock at the door. He opened it and Abba walked in.

'I was looking for you in the kitchen, Ghulam Rasool,' Abba said. 'Go and load the trunk with food. We won't be stopping to eat along the way.'

Ghulam Rasool hurried off.

'Ismael, we're leaving in ten minutes,' Abba said. He turned around to leave when he paused. 'Why do you look so distracted?'

'Still jet-lagged Abba. Would you please tell me what's going on in Islamabad?'

'What time is it?' he asked.

'It's quarter to eight,' I said, looking at my watch.

'By two o'clock this afternoon, all will become clear.' He said nothing more, just gracing me with a quick smile before he left. I couldn't tell if the smile was sincere or merely long-practiced affectation for throwing his prey into confusion.

I went into the bathroom, which was filled with sunlight pouring in through a small window fitted with a wrought iron grill. I was standing at the sink looking at myself, admiringly in my new clothes, when Pir spoke in my head.

'We won't be in touch until you get inside the Faisal Mosque. Until then, under no circumstances are you to attempt to contact me,' he said.

'Yes, sir.'

'Chacha Khidr sends his blessings and Tarzan is giving you a thumbs up.'

'And Laila?'

'She says she's praying for you.'

'Wait! Don't go!' I began to panic.

'It's not safe to talk now,' he said.

'But I'm alone in the bathroom.'

'Are you sure?'

I looked around and froze. Nofel was sitting outside the windowsill staring at me through the grill.

'Holy shit!' I grabbed a towel and smacked it against the grill, hoping the damned thing would run off. 'Get lost, motherfucker!' Nofel growled as he jumped off the ledge and disappeared. 'It was Nofel, sorry. He's gone now.'

'Nofel? This is what I mean. You cannot, and I repeat, you cannot under any circumstances disregard my instructions. I've told you before; you're on a tightrope—one slip and you're gone.'

'But I didn't do anything,' I protested.

'We have to do something about Nofel. He probably already knows too much,' Pir said and then closed the connection.

I headed to the porch with a growing sense of unease. Ghulam Rasool was loading a crate containing a couple of thermoses and cups into the trunk of the car. Wali, orange cloth in hand, circled the car in search of wayward blemishes to eradicate.

'One thermos has tea and the other lassi,' Ghulam Rasool said. 'The drinks can be reached from inside the car.' Opening the rear door he showed me a passage between the middle of the seat through which the cups and thermos could be retrieved without having to stop the car.

'Where is Nofel going to sit?' I asked.

'He usually sits in the backseat, but also likes the trunk. He goes back and forth though the opening in the middle.'

'You have to put him in the trunk,' I said firmly. 'That's where he's going to sit.'

At that moment, Abba and his guests came out of the house. As they stood beside the sparkling black Mercedes as it lounged near the porch like a panther, there was palpable tension in the air. Each man naturally felt it was his right to command the front passenger seat next to Abba. But they all knew there was no way Imam would fit in the backseat with two other passengers and they looked at each other without saying anything. Wali broke the tension by opening the rear door and gesturing me in first. I slid into the middle seat, feeling content with the wide-angle view I had through the windshield.

Imam opened the front passenger door and sank into his seat, filling all the available space between his corpulent form and the dashboard. His massive back blocked half of my visual field as Mufti sat on my left and Qadi on my right. Nofel was put in the trunk and thankfully due to Mufti's diminutive size there was ample space for all of us in the back.

We were zooming down the motorway by 8.30 a.m. It looked like a deserted runway that stretched to infinity just for us. Imam had dozed off and begun snoring with an incremental crescendo of noise—his chin bobbing up and down on his chest. With a frown on his face, Abba pushed the gas pedal a little more. A sudden powerful acceleration slammed me back against my seat. This deliberate maneuver failed because Imam's ample girth was able to absorb the sudden impact quite well. It did, however, transform the character of the snores which now overwhelmed the cabin like a buzzing saw, much to the dismay of everyone.

Qadi spoke. 'He drank a whole jug of lassi.' He and Mufti were clearly annoyed by this breach of propriety. 'Hajji sahib, please do something,' he pleaded.

Abba was doing 90-miles-an-hour but it felt like we were going no more than 40. He jacked up the volume on the stereo system and flooded the cabin with a Quran recitation in the attempt to drown out the snoring. He kept increasing the volume while slowly pressing the accelerator further. By the time he reached the maximum sound tolerable by the human eardrum, the speedometer read 149-miles-per-hour.

Things outside flew past us, probably more from the sheer physical impact of the sound than from the speed itself. Imam did not wake up and his snores became even more annoying. During the necessary pauses in the holy text a reciter of the Quran must observe, the noise was downright unbearable.

Lowering my head, I pressed my temples and gave Imam's shoulder, which had started to block my view, a forceful nudge with my forehead. He awoke and looked around in a daze. Abba lowered the volume without slowing the car down. By then he was doing 155-miles-an-hour and overtook an eighteen-wheeler that at first I had thought was coming at us from the opposite direction.

'Ismael, would you please get Imamji a cup of hot tea?' Abba asked, looking at me through the rearview mirror.

I was in no mood to put my hand in the compartment currently occupied by Nofel.

'Yes, I need a cup of tea. That lassi was a bit too heavy for me,' Imam said, leaving me with no choice but to access the trunk through the back of my seat. *Damned cat.*

'Anyone else want tea?' I asked.

Both Qadi and Mufti politely declined.

Reluctantly, I folded my seat down a bit. All I saw was Nofel's snarling face as he tried to squeeze past the opening and get into the main cabin of the car.

'No, no! Stay there!' I tried to shoo him back into the trunk.

'Why don't we just let the poor animal ride up here? It must be suffocating in the trunk,' Mufti said. 'It can sit on the floor next to my feet. There's plenty of space for him here,' he added, allowing the cat to enter the cabin. Of course Nofel took advantage of the opportunity and squeezing through the opening, the animal curled up beside Mufti's feet.

I grabbed one of the thermoses from the basket—luckily it turned out be the one filled with tea—and handed Imam his cup. Putting the thermos back in the trunk, I closed the opening and leaned back in my seat, emptying my mind of all thoughts. Mufti petted the cat's lush fur and stared into his eyes. After several moments he leaned back in his seat, scratched his neck and glanced sideways at me. At that moment, I knew Nofel had communicated something damning about me to this man.

No one spoke for a long time while Imam noisily slurped his tea. This was only slightly less obnoxious than his incessant snoring. Abba set the cruise control at 130-miles-an-hour and then started swaying his head as he listened to the sacred recitation.

Keeping my mind empty for such a long time proved to be a strenuous exercise. Soon I started to doze off, but I felt too lethargic to get myself a cup of tea. They were all talking about the intrinsic qualities of the water of Hauz-e-Kauser when sleep overpowered me.

I woke up when the car stopped abruptly at a security check post on the exit ramp of the motorway. Under an azure sky, the green peaks of the Margalla Hills topped the horizon. I glanced at my watch to see it was 11.00 a.m. Abba had made it to Islamabad in about two and a half hours.

Six gunmen draped in black robes ran up and surrounded the car as Abba put down his window.

'What can I do for you?' he asked politely, looking at the man standing beside his door.

Slamming his heel against the asphalt, the gunman gave Abba a stiff salute.

'Sir, just making sure, sir!' he cried, looking straight over the car, his hand glued to his temple.

'Good job,' Abba said with a smile.

'Let them pass!' the man shouted, turning on his heels.

As the barrier rose, the soldiers snapped their salutes in our direction. Whether it was to Abba and his august companions, or to the flagged black Benz gleaming in the sun, I couldn't tell. Abba floored the accelerator once again. In a matter of seconds, we were cruising along the Kashmir Highway, heading toward the heart of the capital city.

25

WE WERE STOPPED THREE more times at heavily armed checkpoints along the Kashmir Highway. It seemed like more of a formality than a necessity, but it was a stark reminder of the charged atmosphere. At each stop I also got the distinct impression that Abba and his companions really enjoyed watching those kids squirm when they recognized the car.

Once we turned north on Faisal Avenue toward the Margalla Hills, the place began to look more like a military garrison. Army vehicles with olive drab and green camouflage lined the avenue. Pickup trucks were mounted with machine guns and manned by robed men with black bushy beards as they tore up and down the roads leaving dusty trails.

There wasn't a single civilian vehicle in sight. At the far end of the avenue, partially hidden by dense foliage, stood the massive edifice of Faisal Mosque that was highlighted against the rolling green hills.

'Mashallah!' Imam exclaimed, waving excitedly at a knot of men clinging to the top of a camouflaged Toyota pickup truck. He was still waving long after they had disappeared in the rear view mirror.

'Khalifaji has better security than the president of America,' I observed, eyeing the brown armoured vehicles parked at the side of the road, their guns raised at a 45-degree angle as if saluting the morning sky.

'Of course!' Mufti said proudly. 'He's more important than your president in the eyes of Allah.'

'My president? Mufti sahib, I've left America far behind and I do not care about its president.'

'The young man knows how to speak his mind,' Imam replied with a smile.

'It's called the American style,' Qadi added, as he winked at me.

'You know, I had almost given up on my son,' Abba said, his face bristling with pride. 'Deep indeed are Allah's mysteries!'

'Hajji sahib, those who are guided by the Almighty Himself can't go astray,' Qadi said.

'The chosen ones are directly plucked out by the sanctified hand no matter where they are,' Imam added, clucking with approval and nodding to himself in agreement. 'Mere mortals like us can never hope to understand the divine secrets.'

I could tell Mufti wanted to say something, but he kept quiet and simply put down his window and stared at the distant hills. The air hitting my face smelled of petrol.

A few seconds later, he rolled the window back up and squirmed in his seat. His solitary eye stared at Nofel who was lying at his feet, pretending to be sleeping with his head on his paws.

The closer we got to the mosque, the heavier the military presence became. We were stopped at the intersection of Khayaban-e-Iqbal, which was thickly barricaded by tanks and desert camouflage Hummers. The mood of the men manning this checkpoint was very different than at previous stops where the guards were noticeably younger. These men were seasoned and aloof, tense and thoroughly unimpressed with anything or anyone.

They were robed in desert camouflage fashioned into Saudi-style thawbs strapped with black leather belts and brass buckles in the shape of a crescent; the official symbol of the Caliphate. They didn't care about the kind of car we were driving, about the Caliphate's flag stuck on its hood, or the rank and identity of its occupants. The invitation to step out of the car was in the form of a barked and authoritative command.

Having thoroughly searched the cabin and the trunk of our vehicle twice, they swiped its underside with long-handled mirrors and bug-detecting devices. Finished with the car, they began to pat us down roughly and a little too intimately for my liking. Then they requested Abba present his papers and ID.

At the end of the intersection, I spotted a line of anti-aircraft guns, partially camouflaged by shrubs, flanking grassy strips that ran along the avenue. Nofel had sprung from the car and raced off to do his business. He emerged growling from a clump of bushes and stood at a distance as if waiting for us to pass. He then dashed toward us the moment we were cleared by the guards and leapt back onto the floor of the car where he curled up and pretended to go back to sleep. Everyone was quiet and Abba drove on with a grim face.

I closed my eyes and remembered the words of Pir Pul Siraat: *Khalifa has something very special planned, a real spectacle. If he is not stopped very soon, this world and the Next will need a major cleanup that will stretch into the not-so-foreseeable future.*

Bloody hell! The 'real spectacle' couldn't be just a few hundred Caliphate diehards storming the gates of Heaven. It had to be much more than that, considering this huge military presence. What the hell was Khalifa really planning? And what exactly did my handlers, who surely weren't from this world, have in mind about how to stop him? Was I part of some mysterious divine intervention coming into play?

Clearly, I was in the midst of a military-grade mayhem of cosmic proportion. And I was the one chosen to put a stop to all this madness. But how could I achieve it all alone unless I was like a guided missile carrying a mysterious payload which ought to be delivered at the right time and at the right place? I had no doubt in my mind the place was the Faisal Mosque.

Something soft touched my knees, something warm. I opened my eyes and gasped when I saw Nofel's curious eyes peeking over my knees and boring into mine. Mufti had a mischievous smile on his face, his eyes focused on the cat. All thoughts came to a screeching halt and my eyes blinked in rapid succession from the shock.

'It looks like we're preparing for war,' I said, laying my hand on Nofel's head and trying to pet him. He growled and jerked away but continued to stare at me. I tried to keep my thoughts to myself and not convey my mounting apprehension.

'Today the promise of the Caliphate of Al-Bakistan is going to see its fulfillment,' Abba said. 'What do you say Imamji?' He gave Imam's enormous thigh a slap.

'Jazaak-allah, Hajji sahib! You've indeed spoken the truth,' Imam said, grabbing the door handle and shifting himself about in his seat. 'Mashallah!' He rolled the window down but immediately rolled it back up while I held my breath.

'Abba, I don't understand,' I said, smelling a pungent odour that filled the cabin. Qadi lowered his window and frowned and Mufti and Abba did the same.

'Mufti sahib, why don't you give Ismael the details?' Abba said.

'Hajji sahib, we've sworn by our lives not to talk about this matter in front of anyone, regardless of his or her relationship to us,' Mufti said. 'Unless, of course, the person is authorized by Khalifaji himself.'

'Mufti is correct,' Qadi said.

Abba scratched his temple but kept quiet. We were trailing a black Bentley by fifty metres or so and seemed to be in the midst of a motorcade of vehicles fit for a gaggle of Saudi princelings.

At the end of the Faisal Highway, separated by a series of manicured lawns, rose a gigantic, white tent-shaped structure of modern design that was the main Prayer Hall of the mosque, plus its four towering minarets. The unadorned tapered caps glittered in the midday sun and the central complex was fronted by a broad courtyard large enough to accommodate 40,000 worshippers.

We turned onto a side road that was streaming with even more fabulously expensive cars than ours. The whole structure and its grounds were lined with armed military personnel standing at attention, their ubiquitous Kalashnikovs held tight across their chests. Abba drove his car around the rectangular courtyard of the mosque and slowed at the main entrance. He parked about ten feet behind the Bentley that was already swarming with armed guards.

The guards pulled the Bentley's doors open, guns trained and ready. Four men stepped out wearing black robes, red headdresses and sunglasses. They were followed by a huge Siamese cat with thick lavish fur and an elegantly pointed face. The youngest among them pointed in our direction and said something to his companions. They all turned to stare at us as if trying to determine our identity.

'You know who they are?' Abba elbowed Imam.

'The Chairman of the CPVPV and his three sons,' Imam answered.

'CPVPV?'

'Committee for the Promotion of Virtues and Prevention of Vice,' Qadi answered firmly.

'Oh!'

Once the men and their cat were escorted to the entrance to the mosque and their Bentley valeted, the guards approached our car and pulled open the doors.

'Abba, are cats allowed in the mosque?' I asked.

'Of course! They have been for centuries,' Abba said, climbing out of the car and handing his keys to one of the guards.

As we waited to be escorted into the mosque, the roar of a monstrous engine ripped through the air. Heads snapped around as a black Ferrari with red stripes approached the reception area. It shuddered to a halt behind our car and the driver gunned the engine once more before killing it. A hush fell over the crowd as its gull-wing door rose toward the sky.

A tall, dark-skinned man clad in a tight black leather robe, orange headdress and a pair of reflective wraparound sunglasses climbed out. He must have been in his fifties since his tight pointed goatee was snow white. Leaning his tall frame against the hood of the Ferrari he gave us a wave and we all waved back.

I whispered. 'Who is this?'

'He heads the Ministry of Women's Affairs,' Abba said, without taking his eyes off the man.

Standing beside Abba, Mufti swayed his head from side to side as if reciting scripture. His solitary eye glanced at me from time to time and made my skin crawl. Nofel, as if in love with him, rubbed his torso against the man's legs. They seemed to have bonded all too well during the trip and their proximity was making me increasingly nervous.

Suddenly a gust of wind swept through the area. Robes and headdresses fluttered in the air and in the next minute all was calm again and the wind died down as quickly as it had come. Nofel parted with Mufti and started to meow while staring at a cat with silky white fur. It seemed to have materialized out of nowhere, wearing a red collar and standing its ground about twenty feet from us; it was the most beautiful cat I had ever seen.

Waving his tail, Nofel approached the newcomer, taking measured steps. The cats stood nose to nose looking into each other's eyes, then turned and sniffed each other's butts. Mufti looked restless.

'Nofel! Come back,' he shouted.

Startled by Mufti's yell, the white cat dashed off and disappeared into a waist-high green hedge that bordered the roundabout. Nofel threw a defiant glance at Mufti, then took off after his newfound girlfriend and vanished into the hedge.

'Muftiji, let it go—that's Nofel,' Abba said. 'He's not returning until he's had his way with her.'

I overheard Qadi whispering into Imam's ear: 'A pet's behaviour is a reflection of its owner's.'

Imam said nothing but gave a quick nod at Qadi as he tried to hide a sneer.

Mufti rubbed his palms, looking remorseful. He had lost his telepathic buddy, his only witness to the inner workings of my mind. But I was relieved to be able to think without somebody, or something, sifting through my deepest thoughts.

A couple of armed guards escorted us through the main entrance into a colonnade beneath the courtyard. This was the ablution area fitted with dozens of faucets and on the wall above the faucets was a sign: No Mobile Phones Beyond This Point.

We took off our shoes and handed them over to a lad who was too young to grow a beard, but who wore a 9-mm Uzi over his shoulder. He reminded me of Tarzan as he handed each of us a numbered token in exchange for our shoes and cell phones. He tucked each phone into the shoe of its respective owner and then looked at me expectantly.

'I left mine at home,' I stated firmly.

He stepped forward and patted me down to make sure I was telling the truth.

After doing our wudu and drying ourselves off with towels brought on a silver tray by another armed beardless lad, we were taken upstairs to the courtyard. At the far end of it stood the triangular Prayer Hall guarded by the four imposing vertical shafts, each 90 metres tall.

And then it came to me in a horrifying flash. What stood before me was the same structure which, in my dream—the one I had when I dozed off after calling Abba back in my apartment in New York—I had taken to be a huge tent. I had seen myself standing in this very courtyard at dusk, light in my hand, facing a veiled, black-robed man whose overwhelming shadow concealed the light in a large dark band. Even though the place was spooking me out, I knew my mission was about to be revealed at long last.

In the porticoes bordering the courtyard stood hundreds of clone-like armed and bearded men who looked like toy soldiers from this distance. The party of the chairman of the CPVPV, including their cat, was more than halfway across the courtyard when we were told to proceed.

A gentle breeze blew from time to time making the midday sun pleasant against my face. As we walked on the cool tiles, escorted by a cortege of armed guards, I marvelled once again at the sheer size of the minarets which remained just as impressive as they had in my boyhood memory.

The minarets looked different somehow today, though they still were very modern. A silvery metal covered their tapered heads, something I didn't remember seeing earlier. I was about to ask Abba about this innovation when a crescendo of noise rose in the air. Stopping in our tracks we looked up, but the sky was clear as far as I could see. Suddenly, a dark cloud appeared over Margalla Hills and swiftly descended across the plain. In the next moment, the hills disappeared behind an undulating black sheath and I was swallowed by a wave of déjà vu.

'Ababeels!' I shouted.

Mesmerized, everyone watched the opaque black mass plunge toward the mosque, spiralling, swelling and contracting. The noise became deafening as the sky continued to darken and the minarets disappeared from sight.

'Whoa! Will you look at that!' I yelled, glancing at my companions for confirmation that this was indeed an astounding sight.

Mufti uttered a shriek as he covered his head with his hands and his lips moved rapidly. The ababeels flew past the mosque and toward the city. It turned back around, spiralling toward the mosque with incredible speed and dexterity. This time, the swarm passed overhead at a higher altitude, retreating back toward the hills and leaving behind a multitude of terrified faces and a loud recitation of the surah Al-Fil from the quivering lips of Imam.

Abba stared at me, opened his mouth to say something, but was too stunned to speak. Qadi had his eyes closed, as he muttered a prayer.

'It's a sign,' Abba finally managed to say.

As the party began moving again, all clearly shaken, I recalled my previous sightings of this mythic flock of ababeels: once in the company of Chacha Khidr, another in the Dump and then with Tarzan. All three were undeniably auspicious occasions well outside the confines of anything approaching normal reality.

The wide columned entrance to the Prayer Hall was flanked by more gunmen. They stood at attention, shoulder-to-shoulder, and stared straight ahead. An opening in the middle of this formidable wall of security was manned by a different breed of guards. The monster cats, around twenty of them, were restrained on leashes by handlers robed in hooded cloaks.

Our escorts brought us to a sudden halt about fifty feet from this final checkpoint. The chairman of CVPVP and his three sons—their cat now nowhere to be seen—walked into the group of the monster cats. They made it through this living, breathing, mind-reading scanner without any incident. Once they had disappeared into the hall, we were motioned forward. I emptied my mind as we began walking toward the phalanx of cats and their disquieting handlers.

Mufti led the party while I was the last one following just a few feet behind Abba. I avoided making direct eye contact with any of these peculiar creatures. They all had dark coats and fierce golden eyes, and seemed restless in my presence with a few pulling on their leashes. Some hissed as I passed. By the time I was three-quarters of the way through the passage, every single cat had stood up snarling at me.

I held my breath and continued to move ahead purposefully. One large gray cat with bloodshot eyes broke rank from his comrades and approached me from the side. One of the guards raised his hand.

'Stop right there!' he commanded.

I froze in my tracks. The cat stood on its hind legs, rested its forepaws on my chest and began sniffing me all over. The guard holding his leash stepped forward and gestured for me to empty my pockets. As soon as I took out the Quran he grabbed the book and began flipping through its pages, his face twitching with a nervous energy.

'What's your name?' he demanded with a piercing look.

'Ismael.'

'ID?'

I extracted my US passport from inside my robe and handed it over.

'American?' he asked, scratching his chin. 'The mosque is off-limits to anyone not a citizen of the Caliphate.'

Mufti gave the guard a knowing look and nodded his head approvingly. 'Correct. That has been the decree of Khalifa for many years,' he said.

Imam and Qadi exchanged glances but kept quiet.

Abba cleared his throat and glared at the man. He took out a folded slip of paper from his pocket and held it between his fingertips in front of the guard's face.

'I'm Hajji Ibrahim, a close friend of Khalifaji,' Abba said. 'Ismael is my son and is here by the personal invitation of Khalifaji.'

The commotion caused a stir among the other cat-handling guards. They drifted over and eyed me suspiciously. The cats growled and strained at their leashes. Sweat broke out on my forehead but luckily was absorbed by my headband. Clearly, draining my mind of all thought seemed to have failed. Even Chacha had warned me that this technique wasn't foolproof.

The guard returned my Quran, swiped the paper from Abba's hand and disappeared into the Prayer Hall.

Feeling like a mouse in a trap before these angry cats—which still growled and strained their leashes as if longing to pounce—I began to recite the *surah Al-Nas*, Mankind, under my breath. This surah was believed to be the most effective way to repel bad spirits.

At that moment something remarkable happened. The cats settled down and turned away from me. Out of the corner of my eye, I saw two enormous black cats standing unattended a short distance away. As soon as I made eye contact with them, they let out a howl. It took me only a moment to recognize them as the ones which had accompanied me to the shrine of Shah Jamal after the blast that killed Tarzan. They were the cats of Pir Pul Siraat. Pir had left nothing to chance.

All eyes were on these two newcomers when the guard with Abba's piece of paper emerged from the hall.

'Let him go,' he shouted over the howling match that had ensued between Pir's cats and Khalifa's. Restraining their animals, the guards stood down and moved away from me.

Taking my hand, Abba led our party into the Prayer Hall. The sweeping interior was devoid of a single column and could easily accommodate around 10,000 worshippers at a time. A profusion of geometrical cutouts dotting its multifaceted walls let in plenty of light and ensured the place was well illuminated. The hall looked strangely empty, except for a cluster of about 200 men gathered before the famous book sculpture. The *mihrab*, carved in the image of the Holy Book, indicated the direction of the Kaaba and was set against the *qibla* wall at the far end.

Except for the massive chandelier with its golden wheel of twinkling lights that hung over the centre of the hall, the structure was amazingly bereft of curved lines—a sharp departure from the tradition.

'Abba, what was that piece of paper?' I asked, walking over a vast blue carpet that was divided by parallel golden lines indicating rows.

'I knew it would be useful,' Abba said, winking at me. He then looked at Mufti. 'Don't you agree, Muftiji?'

Mufti remained quiet while Abba put his hand on my shoulder.

'I had Khalifaji fax me a letter of invitation for you—with your name on it,' he said aloud for the edification of everyone in the party. Abba was known to always play his cards right.

'Excellent thinking, Abba,' I said.

He knew a good many people in the crowd, as did his three companions. Mufti, Qadi and Imam drifted away and mingled with their many acquaintances and Abba took me around and introduced me to his friends, mostly in their fifties and sixties. The Emir of Punjab was a solemn-faced, short, stocky man with a squarish black beard that framed his large, round face. General Hajjaj Hijazi of the Caliphate Army was tall and lanky with big bushy eyebrows, a right eye that never blinked and a blow-dried beard dyed unnaturally black. There was also a minister with a paralysed arm and dim eyes, a group of four pompous-looking industrialists and a handful of other assorted self-important luminaries with long meaningless titles.

Invariably, their welcoming smiles fizzled out and turned into uncomfortable stares as soon as Abba informed them that I had just returned from America. The General stared at me fixedly, biting his lower lip as Abba described my miraculous skills as a hafiz, despite my prolonged and unsupervised immersion in the Great Satan. He merely nodded without comment, which made Abba look awkward and uncomfortable.

Later, as Abba was introducing me to a famous retired cricketer with a long conical beard and no mustache, I caught sight of Mufti standing beside the General, whispering in his ear and glancing at me.

Just then, the sound of the azaan pierced the air and the crowd fell silent, though there were many stragglers still wandering in. Abba gestured for me to follow as he walked along the qibla wall away from the gathering. Once the azaan had been said, Abba halted and began saying his four rakaat of Sunnah: the non-obligatory portion of the Friday Jumma Prayer. Standing ten feet from Abba, I began saying my namaaz too. Thoughts of Pir, who hadn't contacted me since we left my house, filled my head.

'I'm right here.' His calm, reassuring voice was like a sweet, healing breeze. I was able to relax and take a deep breath.

'So good to hear your voice,' I replied silently, bowing in *rukoo* with my hands on my knees and the cloth of my keffiyeh like a curtain over my cheeks.

'I've been worrying about you,' Pir said.

'What were those ababeels for?' I raised myself briefly before going into prostration, my forehead touching the ground.

'On a day like this one, all options are on the table,' he said. 'Extraordinary times call for extraordinary measures.'

'What the hell is happening that's so extraordinary?' I straightened up on my folded knees, and then went into prostration again.

'I'll let you hear it directly from the horse's mouth,' Pir said. 'How is Mufti, by the way?'

'He thinks I'm a mole,' my lips touched the carpet. 'He's let a friend of his in on it too,' I said.

'Which friend?'

'General Hajjaj.'

Pir remained quiet for a good five seconds before he continued.

'The mission has remained fluid,' he said. 'As they say in America, it's not over until the fat lady sings.'

26

REALIZING THAT I HAD BEEN in sajdah for an unusually long time, I stood up. Abba had already finished his prayer and had left his spot. I was curious to know if that beautiful white cat was in any way connected to Pir.

'It took me quite an effort to find a willing candidate for Nofel,' Pir said, responding to my unformed thought. 'Now, no more questions.'

'Thanks for sending your jinn cats,' I whispered, but I could tell that Pir had gone offline.

As he broke the connection, I heard faint voices behind me. Hearing my name, I turned and saw Mufti, General Hajjaj and Abba deep in conversation about twenty feet away. Sensing that I was looking at them, they stopped speaking. Then Abba said something to Mufti, pointed at his chest with his finger and took off in my direction. My heart sank seeing the angry look on Abba's face. Mufti must have said something compromising about me. Whether Abba believed it or not was something yet to be determined. Mufti and General Hajjaj had become a threat faster than I had anticipated.

As Abba and I made our way back to the assembly, which had swelled considerably since we had left, he touched my arm.

'Mufti thinks you're a spy,' Abba said grimly. 'And General Hajjaj seems to agree.'

I shook my head and didn't say anything.

'I'm serious,' he said tersely.

'He just doesn't like me for some reason.'

'Just say it's not true,' he halted in his tracks and gave my arm a squeeze, all the while staring into my eyes.

'Abba, please! Do you really think I'm a spy? Why would I be?'

'I don't know what to think anymore, Ismael. Just don't embarrass me in this place. That's all I ask.'

'Abba, I'm sorry I asked you to bring me along. I was better off in Lahore.'

He opened his mouth to say something but became distracted by a sound rippling through the congregation that was sitting shoulder to shoulder in seven perfect rows in front of the sculpture of the Holy Book. Abba seated himself next to the last man in the front row and gestured for me to sit next to him. To my dismay, both Mufti and General Hajjaj, who had been walking parallel to us all this time, hurried to join the end of the second row, positioning themselves right behind me.

Suddenly, a hush fell over the assembly. The chandelier dimmed, softening the room with a golden glow. Everyone stood up and looked expectantly toward the entrance of the hall.

Leading the procession that appeared at the entrance were a dozen or so masked gunmen who marched crisply, machine guns angled across their bodies and pointing toward the ground. Then a lone figure walked in carrying a black briefcase in his right hand. He was of medium height with a plump body, wearing voluminous black robes and a huge black turban.

'Long live al-Amir ul Momineen,' the crowd chanted in unison, punching the air above their heads.

'That's Khalifaji,' Abba whispered sharply in my ear.

Khalifa had a brown shawl draped over his shoulders and glided over the carpet with such fluid motion that he appeared to be floating a few inches above the ground. He was trailed by a dozen men in plain khaki robes and stiff, green peaked caps, their chests medalled and their collars decked out with bronze stars. They were pushing six flatbed trolleys piled with large black suitcases and boxes of various shapes and sizes.

The next wave in the procession consisted of another team of masked gunmen. As the procession drew closer, the crowd parted and the welcoming chant was replaced with the shouts of 'Allah Hu Akbar'. Following Abba's lead, I threw my arms in the air and roared the battle cry.

Standing this far from the centre, it was hard to see Khalifa's face. All I could see of him was his big black turban bobbing among the curtain of arms. He took his position in the centre of the first row of the assembly, flanked by his masked bodyguards.

I had to move several steps to my right to accommodate these new entrants. The men in the khaki robes pushed their trolleys around the crowd, parking them beside the exquisite marble mihrab. The chant died away as Khalifa seated himself on the carpet, folded his legs under him and laid his hands on his thighs.

'What's in those boxes?' I whispered to Abba, as the men unloaded the carts.

'Only Khalifaji knows,' Abba whispered back.

When the whole assembly was seated, Imam, who had been missing in action along with Qadi ever since we arrived in the hall, stood up at the far end of the front row and made his way to the *minbar* just to the right of the book sculpture.

'Masha-Allah!' Abba said, beaming with pride. 'Our own Imamji.'

Imam stood on the first step of the minbar and began reciting the Friday *khutbah* into the microphone in Arabic. This was the most boring part of the otherwise colourful Friday Congregation I remembered from childhood. Everyone enjoyed it when the imam entertained us with miraculous stories about saints and prophets, jinns and angels. Then he launched into the khutba and those who could get away with it caught a nap.

Meanwhile, the men handling the trolleys had taken out a couple of large-frame computers from the suitcases, along with rolls of cables, wires and motherboards. Another suitcase contained half a dozen laptops, which were turned on and booted up by a team of four men. The unpacking and setting up of the equipment continued through the drab khutbah. By the time it was over, two spotless white screens had been unrolled and applied to the two marble pages of the book sculpture. I marvelled at the incongruity of the display in here.

The screens matched the exact dimensions of the diagonally held panels, and hiding behind their opaque whiteness was the Kufic script of the *surah Ar-Rahman*, The Beneficent, engraved in gold. The rectangular column in the middle, separated from the screens by just a few inches and engraved with the name *Allah*, remained uncovered. The set-up reminded me of a giant white bird with its wings folded, preparing for flight.

'Abba, any idea what's going on?' I whispered, sensing a rising anxiety coursing through the crowd.

'Patience!' he hissed, jabbing my knee with a bony finger.

Imam finished his khutba, stepped down from the minbar and waddled back to his place in line. Then Khalifa, raising his hand, gestured for Imam to halt.

'I, the Amir ul Momineen, command you to lead the Friday Prayer,' Khalifa said in a thundering voice.

With his hands clasped in front of his belly, Imam turned around and stood on the leading prayer mat, placed five feet in front of Khalifa's spot, which was in line with the central column of the mihrab. An eerie silence gripped the room which was broken only by a loud beautiful voice uttering the *niyyath*, the intention, which came from somewhere in the back row.

Then everybody rose to their feet. The technicians stopped working and took their places among the worshippers. Imam said the *takbir*, touched his earlobes and began the two rakaat of *farz*, the obligatory portion of the Friday Jumma Prayer. I went through the motion of the namaaz without thought or feeling. All the apprehension was driving me crazy.

The namaaz turned out to be a brief affair, followed by a boiler-plate *dua* when everyone just sat with their palms up. Everything was business as usual up until this point.

As soon as Imam stood up and vacated the leading prayer rug, the techno-wizards resumed their work and the assembly erupted into hushed chatter. A wooden divan with a Persian rug and a pair of black cushions resting on one side was placed a few feet in front of the book sculpture while a wooden table holding a laptop was placed at the right side of the divan.

'Abba, seems like we're going to be given a presentation,' I said, looking at the pen-sized laser projectors being affixed atop a pair of tripods placed in front of the screens.

'It took us more than a decade to reacquire the capability,' he whispered.

'What capability?' Finally, he was opening up.

'To make bombs.'.

'Really?' I asked, feeling terrified of the prospect of Khalifa in possession of nukes again. And what did this have to do with the presentation? Though it seemed clear that at last the pieces of the mystery were coming together and my questions were being answered.

Many years ago, the nuclear stockpile of the country, along with its nuclear reactor, had been disabled by spyware launched from a foreign government. It had been all over the news at the time. No government had taken responsibility, but everyone suspected either the US or Israel—or both—of being the culprit.

'None can defy the will of Allah,' Abba said.

'But how did we manage to escape detection, considering all these satellites spying over us day and night?' I leaned into him and glanced over my shoulder. Mufti and General Hajjaj locked their eyes with mine, their jaws clenched with anger. They were watching my every move. Thanks to the background noise, they could not eavesdrop on my conversation with Abba.

'Khalifaji always thinks beyond the obvious,' Abba said with a broad smile on his face. 'He is the man who possesses special knowledge and strange powers.'

The chatter died as Khalifa rose to his feet, the briefcase still clutched in his hand. Flanked by his bodyguards, the man glided toward his throne and placed the briefcase on his lap. One of the khaki-robed technicians adjusted the microphone height for him.

Despite appearing a bit stooped, Khalifa was an imposing figure. His lush black beard reached the middle of his broad chest and was dramatically marked by a four-inch wide stripe of white running from his lower lip to the beard's pointed tip. He craned his neck forward, throwing a sweeping glance over the crowd.

Without the customary prayer: *In the name of Allah, the Most Gracious, the Most Merciful*, Khalifa began to recite the holy scripture. And as soon as he did, the same text started running across the upper portion of my visual field. I saw he was reciting from the last third of the surah number 9.

I wished that Pir could add on a translation feature to this clever programme.

Khalifa paused, closed his eyes and murmured something under his breath. Glancing at the audience, he resumed speaking in his native tongue in a clear and measured voice.

'All praise be to Allah, the Lord of the universe, without Whose command not a leaf would move. I, al-Amir ul Momineen, the commander of the faithful, Khalifa of the Caliphate of Al-Bakistan, hereby declare that those who are present under this magnificent roof at the grandest of the houses of Allah outside Hijaz, the blessed land of Saudi Arabia, have been chosen to witness and be part of the miracle allocated to me by the Most High for the purpose of bringing an end to an era.

'I, al-Amir ul Momineen, Khalifa of the Caliphate of Al-Bakistan, have been given the task of ushering the faithful into a new epoch to be marked by a worldwide jihad against the followers of the Great Deceiver, ad-Dajjal. On this blessed Friday, in this holy mosque, by the grace and will of the Most High, we intend to set forth a chain of events whose impact will continue until the world enters into yet another era—the time of peace— when the faithful will have conquered the world and declared Allah its sovereign ruler.' He paused, his eyes sweeping the hushed crowd like a beacon. Then he threw his right hand into the air. 'Begin!' he cried, tossing a glance over his right shoulder.

Suddenly the screens sprang to life with multiple images of the Faisal Mosque. The screen on the right displayed an aerial view of the mosque and seemed to originate somewhere in the adjacent Margalla Hills. The screen on the left was divided into four equal squares, each showing a close-up of the gleaming point of one of the four minarets. It was only when a helicopter flew across the right screen that I realized the images were live.

As I leaned into Abba to ask about the metal coverings of the minarets' tops, Khalifa began speaking again. 'How many of you know what is going to happen today?'

Everyone raised his hand, except me. Khalifa's head moved side to side as he surveyed the crowd. It stopped when his chin touched his left shoulder and his eyes fixed on me. My pulse quickened and my breath caught in my throat as he slowly raised his finger and pointed directly at me. My back stiffened when our eyes met. I was a rat caught in the gaze of a cobra.

'Wonder of wonders! Hajji Ibrahim's own son, Ismael, the carrier of light,' he cried out, like it was an auspicious declaration. 'This young man seems to be the only one who knows that he does not know. The rest of you know nothing.' His voice thundered.

A nervous murmur rose then and fell as hands were retrieved from the air, heads turned in my direction and glances directed at me like arrows from all sides. Holding his head high, Abba put his hand on my thigh. The warmth from his palm felt pleasant and comforting through my robe. Mufti and General Hajjaj whispered behind my back, but I couldn't make out what they were saying.

Khalifa looked over his shoulder again to where the men were still busy working on the computers and other devices. I exhaled and thought about Pir. I needed help. Where was he?

'Are we ready?' Khalifa addressed the men at his back. They nodded and Khalifa turned around and brought his lips to the microphone.

'This auspicious occasion requires me to offer my deepest regard for those who are not with us anymore. May Allah grant them the highest Jannah!

'It took seven years, seven long, arduous years, and more than five thousand dedicated souls, to accomplish what you're going to witness today. They were the brightest and the best that the Caliphate had to offer. This is a true miracle.' Khalifa looked back and extended his arm toward the men setting up the equipment. 'These are the few who have been left behind to complete the miracle.'

Khalifa looked at his bodyguard on the right. As if on cue, one of the men handed him a bottle of Paradise Water. A hushed whisper broke out behind me and Abba's face was unreadable except for a blank incredulous stare. I leaned toward him.

'Abba, do you know what he's talking about?' I whispered.

'Five thousand men have been transported to Al-Jannah, and the very man who runs the transportation business for the Caliphate doesn't know a thing about it,' he said, sounding absolutely mortified, confused and even angry. His answer left me shocked. I swallowed several times and cleared my throat as I tried to digest what he had just said.

'Abba, I thought you knew everything that was going on here.'

'We were told it would be an underground atomic test somewhere in the desert of Sindh, to be broadcast live for a select few.' Abba now sounded quite disturbed.

After taking several swigs from the bottle, Khalifa wiped his mouth with the back of his hand and continued. 'Before we move on, it's my duty to remind you: the higher one's station is in the eyes of Allah, the harder it becomes to stay on course. If you find yourself thinking too much about the task at hand, remember this verse of our great poet, Hazrat Qibla Llama: *Mad love jumped into the blaze without fear, while the Intellect stood by watching the spectacle from afar.*'

Khalifa opened his briefcase and pulled out a black leather-bound book.

'Have I ever told you a lie?' he asked, bringing his lips close to the microphone.

'No!' the crowd roared in unison.

Khalifa nodded several times, then raised the book over his head.

'I swear by the One in whose hands lies my life that this book contains the keys to al-Jannah. One key for each of you.' He opened the book, and waved it in an arc over his head. 'Oh you people, would you believe me if I were to tell you that the book which I hold in my hand is soaked with a powerful invisible energy?'

'Yes! Yes! Yes!' the crowd chanted.

'Do you have faith in me that I will never lead you astray?'

'Yes!' This time the affirmation was even louder.

'Would you all like to live an eternal life in al-Jannah and enjoy its delights?' Khalifa asked.

'Yes!' Again the words were deafening.

'Then know that each page of this book is laced with enough power to transport fifty of you straight to Paradise—no questions asked along the way, no meeting with Munkar and Nakir, no accounting of your sins, no walk on Pul Siraat, no fiery pits and no raging fire of Hell's inferno. Just an immediate route to Paradise.'

He paused, took a swig of Paradise Water and glared at the stunned congregation. Abba's jaw had dropped almost to his chest, his brows nearly touched his hairline and his eyes bulged. A combination of déjà vu and a flood of real memories overpowered me.

My mind raced over the image of Tarzan and his exploding briefcase in that bathroom in the hospital. Next to him, I had been holding a book just like the one Khalifa now raised in his hand. Shit! It was all making sense now.

'Yes! Shit,' Pir's voice slid through my cranium. Before I could respond, Khalifa began speaking again.

'Such is the reward for those who follow their Khalifa, those who believe in him. Why? Because they know that Khalifa represents the will of Allah. Now I'm going to ask the last row to stand up and come to me one by one to receive their ticket to Paradise. They're to recite verse number one-one-one of the surah 9, which says: *Indeed, Allah has purchased from the believers their lives and their belongings in exchange for what they will have in Paradise. They fight in the cause of Allah, so they kill and get killed.*

'After each one of you has received a ticket, let it rest on the palm of your right hand and wait for further instructions.' Khalifa stood before the congregation.

I counted forty or so men who got up from the back row. With their hands clasped below their navels and their lips moving without a sound, they walked in a single file along the edge of the assembly toward Khalifa who received each man with a handshake. Then he tore little pieces of paper from the pages of the black book and placed one in each waiting palm.

'This is serious, Abba.'

'I have no idea what Khalifaji is doing today,' Abba said, his voice now filled with anxiety. 'But I can tell you that this new technology often concerns an old-fashioned businessman like me.'

'Abba, are we all going to die?'

'Death comes at the appointed time—not a second late, not a second early.'

'What happened to the minarets? What's that metal on each of their tops?'

'Khalifaji had them modified a couple of years ago. Don't you think the sheen of the metal highlights them nicely?'

'Yeah, sure. Nice work,' I mumbled, wishing more than anything that Pir would just beam me the hell out of here.

It didn't take long for the entire congregation to stand one at a time before Khalifa and receive his psychedelic benediction. From time to time, a chopper or two flew across the screen on the right, the one with the aerial view of the mosque. The screens showing the minarets against the clear blue sky were devoid of any movement. Staring at these four odd-looking metal-tipped spires on the screen, I pushed my thoughts to Pir.

'Pir, what's going on?'

'You're in a better position to see what's happening. I'm just listening.'

'We're all getting ready to take off. I not ready to die another death.'

'Once you're a part of Chacha's team, you'll survive a hundred deaths.'

'That's good to know, but small comfort,' I said, brooding over the meaning of his answer.

The front row now rose to its feet; I was the last one in line. Abba, having already received his portion, walked backwards towards his seat, lest he accidentally turn his back on Khalifa. Now it was my turn to stand face-to-face with al-Amir ul Momineen. His eyes had a hooded, dreamy quality, yet were flecked with a fierceness that made him look crazed and otherworldly. He looked at me without blinking, his lips stretching ever so slightly in a smile. He then extended his hand for a handshake. 'So it was you,' he whispered, giving my hand a painful squeeze.

'It's a great honour to be invited by Khalifa, al-Amir ul Momineen, on such an auspicious occasion,' I said, to acknowledge his position.

He turned around and took his seat on the divan, then picked up the microphone to speak. I was left standing in front of the not-so-friendly crowd. I had not been dismissed, nor had I been given the key to Paradise.

'Today, I've received two clear and righteous indications from the Most High. The first: the ababeels, which some of you might have seen on your way here today. Never before have they been seen in such large numbers. Remember, these birds once turned the mighty army of Abrah into pulp. Today, their presence in the vicinity of this mosque is the clear and precious sign we have been waiting for.'

Keeping his eyes on the crowd, Khalifa raised his hand and pointed toward me.

'The second auspicious sign is this young man standing in front of you. He was shown to me in a dream; one in which he carried the *noor* in his hand, the light of Allah. By his presence here today, my dream has become a reality. Those who have eyes to discern the divine signs need no further reassurance that Allah has graciously accepted our hard work.'

He put the book down on the divan and struck the keyboard of a laptop in front of him.

Standing in front of so many people, all of whom stared at me, was an unsettling and terrifying experience to say the least. My legs felt like they were filled with lead and my mind was a chaotic frenzy of energy. It was almost impossible to think clearly. Everyone held their right hand in front of their navel, the stamp-sized ticket to Paradise resting in their palm. They looked to be in a trance.

Khalifa nodded twice at the men in khaki uniforms who were seated at the outer edge of the screens. The men, waiting for this signal, began to furiously type into their laptops; a hum filled the air. I felt a deep rumbling vibration under my feet as if the earth was being moved about by heavy machinery, far below us.

Vertical cracks appeared in the metal shields over three of the minarets. The fourth remained unchanged. These cracks widened and the metal plates moved away from the minarets like the petals of a flower. My heart began to pound as Khalifa's voice boomed across the hall.

'Today is the Day of Judgment for our enemies and our enemies' friends. By the grace and decree of the Almighty, I, Khalifa of Darul Islam, declare Jihad against Darul Harb—the land of the infidels.'

27

HOLY SHIT!

'Stay strong, Ismael,' Pir's cool and even voice purred through my head.

'I'm trying,' I replied silently, turning to look at Abba. My father, like every other man in the room, had his eyes fixed on the screen with his hand in a fist pressed to his side.

Stunned, I stared at the screens as the surreal blooming continued atop three of the four minarets. The metallic panels continued to slowly fall away to reveal missile warheads rising toward the sky. It was all so simple and obvious. Damn!

Khalifa began to speak again. 'What you see on the screens are indeed as they appear, missiles, the fruit of the labour of those who are no longer with us in body, but who remain with us in spirit through their sanctified work. Each of the three missiles is loaded with a very powerful nuclear warhead.'

With a pointer he scribbled across his laptop screen and names appeared in red on top of the four images of the minarets: Abu Bakr, Omar, Uthman, Ali—the four Caliphs of Islam who succeeded Prophet Muhammad—the name Ali was on the image of the tower that had not opened.

'Abu Bakr will be heading to Israel to annihilate the eternal enemies of Islam. Omar is destined for Iran, the troubled land of the Shias, the apostates who, according to my intelligence sources, are preparing to fire their own atomic missile right now, the Mehdi, on us. Uthman is headed for India, the land of the polytheists and conspirators. We did not have enough raw materials for the tower of Ali at the moment, but if we had enough uranium, he would have been aimed at the Americans in the Strait of Hormuz.'

He paused for a breath. The ominous vibration under my feet had become louder and my whole body quivered. The missiles, affixed to their launching pads fitted within the hollow of three minarets, continued their rise into the sky and Khalifa glanced at the live video feed for a few seconds before turning back to his mesmerized audience.

'O you who believe! Know that the time has come for the Final Battle. O you who are faithful! Know that Allah has prepared a great reward for you in the Next World, and a grievous punishment for those who rebel. O you who desire none other than Allah! Know that I am commanding Ismael, son of Ibrahim, to recite to you the *surah Al-Qiyamah*, The Resurrection.'

My head snapped. He was addressing me! I ran through the holy text as it streamed across my eyes and I pulled up the desired surah in less than five seconds, gasping when I saw the English translation running beneath the Arabic text. Pir had indeed thrown in an upgrade for me.

'That's exactly what I need!' I thought, beaming my thanks to Pir.

'Since you've wished for it.'

'Do you think I can pull it off?'

'Shush!'

Khalifa's voice was booming over the crowd once again.

'All missiles will fire simultaneously, bringing our sacred jihad to the enemies of Allah. Once they disappear from sight, everyone here must recite their shahaada three times and then place the ticket to Jannah under their tongue. Am I clear?'

The crowd started chanting 'Allah Hu Akbar' over and over.

'After the recitation of *Al-Qiyamah*, I will push the button and seal the fate of all the evil-doers forever.' His voice sliced through the deafening battle cry. 'O Allah, accept our sacrifice as you have Hazrat Ibrahim's.'

Khalifa stood up, glided over the carpet toward me and tore off one of the tiny paper squares from the last page of the book. Lowering my eyes, I opened my right hand and prayed it wasn't shaking enough for him to notice. Without a word he pressed the little paper into my palm and then closed my fingers tightly around it.

'I can tell from your face that you're dying to wet your tongue with the sweet water of Hauz-e-Kauser,' he said.

'Surely, your eminence, surely,' I muttered, keeping my gaze fixed on the floor and remembering the orange Hazmat tape stretched around that most famous of ponds with its contaminated water spilling over.

Suddenly, a solid wall of noise consumed the place, growing louder by the second. The sunlight pouring in through a multitude of skylights and cutaways in the walls dimmed as if the sky were covered with clouds. The warm glow of indoor light was transformed into a sickly piss-yellow haze. Khalifa's head shot around as the whole congregation stared upward.

'Here they come again,' Khalifa hissed in a low voice.

One look at the screens showed that the missiles had disappeared behind a dense black wall. Ababeels!

'It's time, Ismael,' Pir's voice gave me jolt. 'Take your weapon out. Now!'

'What weapon?'

'The Quran! Take it out of your pocket and pretend you need it for inspiration. Even the best hafiz can forget a line or two.'

With a fluid motion, my hand disappeared into my robe and slid the Quran out of my pocket and pressed it to my navel.

'Done.'

'When you're half-way through the surah, open the Quran and rip out the opening surah *al-Fatiha*, then tear out the last page, surah *Al-Nas*. Drop the pages. Raise the book above your head and close one of your eyes. Use your hand to cover it if you have to. And that's all there is to it.'

Shit! I remembered his words from a long time ago: *One day this Quran may have to be ripped apart to have its power activated.*

I remembered how he and Chacha Khidr had laughed at me for having expressed my fear of dying young. At that time, I thought they were joking!

One thing was certain: I wasn't getting out of here alive, one way or the other. I stared at the little piece of magic paper in my hand. The option of getting beamed out of here and straight into Paradise was starting to look really good. The alternative, of course, was getting torn to shreds by the mob for blasphemy. I wasn't too keen on that either, particularly since it would probably involve Abba's enraged face leading the pack.

'Ismael, remember. You are on Pul Siraat—one slip and you're gone. Failure is not an option.'

'I know, I know.' Unfortunately, I knew quite well.

The noise of the birds died. As their mass sped away from the mosque, the full light of day returned. The missiles had risen a good fifty feet above their point of exit and stood fully unsheathed against the clear blue sky.

My heart began to pound inside my chest. Dying for a glass of water, I glanced over at Abba who sat at the far end of the first row staring at me. His face was twitching; never a good sign even at the best of times. He gave me a quick nod. The poor man genuinely seemed to have no clue about the elaborate proceedings Khalifa had underway. If we survived, Abba would banish me forever, maybe shoot me in the head, or better still, have me wear a Mujahid vest and detonate myself at the time and place of his choosing.

The pirate-faced Mufti, sitting behind Abba in the second row, looked restless. He elbowed General Hajjaj whose face was a mask of resignation. They whispered to each other while glancing back and forth at the screens. Did they know what was going on or were they just as clueless and out of the loop as my Abba?

'Khalifa is a master at keeping his real intentions to himself. No one in this hall knew the full scope of his mission,' Pir elaborated.

'But that's not possible.'

'It's possible when you've made a pact with the Master Chemist.'

'The Devil? But that can't be!' *But why not*? I thought to myself. If Hell and Paradise were real, the Devil had to be real as well.

'Concentrate!' Pir commanded.

Khalifa returned to his divan, sat down and stared into the screen of his laptop. I craned my neck forward and brought my dry quivering lips to the microphone. After clearing my throat a couple of times, I weakly uttered the *bismillah*: In the name of Allah, most Gracious, most Compassionate. Then I began reciting as the surah's text slid before my eyes from right to left. Underneath, the English translation ran from left to right. Pir's attention to detail was absolutely marvelous.

I swear by the Day of Resurrection.
And I swear by the reproaching soul.
Does man think that We shall not gather his bones.
Yes! We are able to make complete his very fingertip.
Nay! Man desires to give the lie to what is before him.
He asks: When is the Day of Resurrection?
So when the sight becomes dazed,

and the moon becomes dark,
and the sun and the moon are brought together,
Man shall say on the day: Whither to fly to?
No! There shall be no place of refuge!
With you Lord alone shall on that day be the place of rest.
Man shall on that day be informed of what he sent before
and what he put off.
Nay! Man is evidence against himself, though he puts forth
his excuses.
Do not move your tongue with it to make haste with it,
surely on Us is the collection...

'Surely on us is the task to deny this sorry lot Paradise,' Pir's voice echoed in my head. 'Now, let's see some action, Ismael.'

Continuing the recitation, I opened the Quran and tore its first and last page from its leather-bound spine. The torn pages fluttered to the ground along with my ticket to Paradise. A scream shattered the air.

'What are you doing?' somebody shouted from the front row.

'Unbelievable! Did you see what he just did?' Mufti bellowed in rage as he sprang to his feet. 'He has torn the pages of the Holy Book.'

General Hajjaj stood up and fixed me with a stare of rage that pierced my resolve.

'Did you all witness what he has done?' he roared. 'Blasphemy!'

The disordered chaos ignited and spread through the assembly like a wildfire. Everyone leapt to their feet, their faces writhing with red, hot anger and barely contained as they stood like the feral jinn cats. I just stood there, not even able to draw a breath or move a muscle. There was no way to escape.

Only Pir could come up with such a ridiculous scheme. My legs trembled and I looked around for something to hold on to.

'That's Hajji Ibrahim's son!' someone cried out. 'Where is Hajji Ibrahim?' somebody else demanded hoarsely.

'The blasphemer must be killed first. Now!' a voice screamed hysterically from the back row.

Every man in the room was on his feet and heaving with rage. The crowd was ready to spring on me, all except Abba. He just sat there with his head in his hands as he stared at the ground in front of him. He couldn't even bear to look at me.

Sweat poured out from every inch of my body. Panicking, I looked over my shoulder at Khalifa who sat on his divan a few feet behind me. He gritted his teeth and his lips moved over them like an animal. His face quivered and his brows arched as he stared at me. He then lunged at me while his bodyguards aimed their guns at my head. The ominous click of a dozen *safeties* being switched off was the only sound in the place. Every heartbeat in the room waited for al-Amir ul Momineen to give the sign as to what to do next.

'Shit!'

'Shut one of your eyes, Ismael! Do it now!' Pir screamed inside my skull.

As Pir's voice faded, the sound of static short-circuiting came from the Quran in my hand.

'Put the Quran in your palm and raise it over your head,' Pir said, as a luminous crack like a miniature lightning bolt appeared in the black binding of the book. With one eye shut, I raised the book over my head.

Khalifa grabbed my arm and screamed in my ear.

'What the fuck are you doing?'

'It's the light…'

The moment I uttered these words, the book burst into brilliant white effulgence. Millions of tiny laser-like bands of molten light shot out in every direction. The air shimmered with a palpable energy and crackled with what sounded like a bug zapper going to work on a hapless swarm of mosquitoes. The rage, which a moment ago had seized the crowd, was now replaced by a stunned nervous confusion. It was one step away from utter pandemonium.

Khalifa let go of my arm. Dazed, he looked around and then staggered for a moment before dropping to his knees. He had stopped blinking and just looked ahead with an empty gaze. Oblivious to my presence, he sank onto his folded legs, his hands placed on his thighs. He might have been praying. Two of his bodyguards lurched ahead and fell flat onto their guns, their noses smashed against the ground.

The men in the khaki robes, who had been hammering away at their laptops, slumped where they sat. In a matter of seconds, the stupor spread through the entire assembly. People staggered, their knees hitting the ground with a thud. They were oblivious to their tickets falling to the ground.

In less than a minute, everyone had slumped into the same posture as Khalifa with their palms resting on their thighs. Everyone except Mufti and General Hajjaj. Strangely, they had remained standing and seemed unaffected by the light. Mufti raised his arm and pointed his finger at me.

'Sorcerer!' he screamed, and then ran toward the entrance, followed by General Hajjaj close on his heels.

'Pir, what the hell is going on?'

'Phototherapy—designed to give the mind a hard reset,' Pir said.

'Hard reset?'

'It's the light of the higher spheres concentrated in the book form. It'll purify their minds so their brains can resume working like those of normal human beings,' Pir said.

I kept my hand over my shut eye and grappled with the meaning of what he had just said as I watched Mufti and General Hajjaj cutting through the radiant beams which were illuminating the Prayer Hall.

'Well, apparently it didn't work on Mufti and General Hajjaj—just so you know.'

'Because they both are one-eyed,' Pir said. 'For the light to work, it has to enter both eyes.'

I remembered how General Hajjaj's right eye didn't blink when Abba introduced me to him. Now I knew why.

There was a long pause before he continued. 'We'll worry about them later. Let's get our job done. You must abort the launch. Now!'

'Yes,' I said, returning to where Khalifa kneeled like a statue, his body prickled by hundreds of tiny points of light. He didn't respond even when I waved my hand in front of his face a few times.

Holding the book over my head, I went over to the divan, sat down and examined the screen on Khalifa's laptop. It displayed the same shots as were projected on the bigger screens behind me. At the bottom of the display were two thumb-sized buttons: a red one on the right labelled 'Allah Hu Akbar' in black letters. The green one on the left had the word 'Inshallah' on it. Sliding my finger over the track pad, I moved the pointer to the green button. Inshallah, God willing, could very well mean the same as Allah Hu Akbar, God is great, under the present situation. I moved the pointer to the red button and scratched my head.

'It has to be the green button,' Pir said.

'What do you mean has to be?' I said aloud, my right eye still shut.

'Do what you think is right,' he said. For a fleeting moment I saw myself tight-roping over Pul Siraat: one wrong move and all would be blown to hell.

I moved the pointer to the green button, said a prayer, and clicked on it. A dialog box appeared: Are you sure you want to quit? I clicked yes. A faint humming vibration shook the room and the missiles started to slowly retract into the modified silos of the minarets. I exhaled in relief, though shaking uncontrollably.

'Done!' I cried, noticing the glow of the book dimming.

'Congratulations! You've saved the Caliphate from becoming a mountain of radioactive ash,' he said.

'Caliphate? I thought we've just saved India, Iran and Israel?'

'I'm not sure if Khalifa's nukes would have even worked, to tell you the truth, but the retaliatory strikes would have killed a hundred million people in the Caliphate alone,' Pir explained.

'Would you please guarantee that I have a place in Paradise now? I mean for real.'

'We're not done yet,' Pir replied. 'Now you must help Khalifa get to Paradise.'

'What?'

'Put one of the little squares in his mouth.'

'But he should be in Hell!'

'Just do it.'

Feeling confused, I walked over to Khalifa with the Quran glowing faintly in my left hand. I picked up the book of tickets lying beside his knees. There was still half a page of little squares left in it. I tore one out and shoved it in his mouth. He showed no signs of consciousness and shivered for a second or two; then his eyes rolled up and he turned white.

Khalifa fell backward and began convulsing like a fish in a skillet. Saliva poured out of his mouth and his face was a mask of agony as his laboured breath rattled in his chest. The Master Chemist's Paradise Potion was certainly not for the fainthearted. As I watched the poor wretch flailing around, I remembered my own experience in the bathroom of the hospital. Had I suffered like this? There was no way to tell. The mighty had surely fallen now.

The missiles had fully descended back into the silos and the huge panels were slowly closing. A few seconds later the minarets were harmless once again. Then the book stopped emitting light and went out like an extinguished candle. In my hand was a weightless mound of black ash. Letting my long-shut eye open, I blew on it and watched a few tiny flecks swirl into the air.

Khalifa was completely still, his eyes were closed and his chest ceased heaving. I put my thumb on his jugular. He was dead.

'Done.' I said, turning my palm and pouring the remainder of the ash over Khalifa's face. It was impossible to fathom that it was all coming to a successful end.

'Mission accomplished,' Pir said.

'What's going to happen to the rest of them?' I asked, glancing at Abba who, like everyone else, looked like he was under some kind of spell.

'They'll be detoxed from all those years of drinking Paradise Water; but not without losing some of their memory and a few of their healthy brain cells. It's collateral damage, if you will. You've been drinking it too, by the way. We'll need to get you into rehab too,' he chuckled.

His words made me realize that never before had I felt such an urge for Paradise. It wasn't exactly a burning desire, but it was definitely there—an unmistakable, insinuating presence, like an itch you don't really want to scratch. I could only imagine how intensely these men must have longed for Paradise for so many years.

'How am I supposed to get out of here, Pir?' I asked, picking up my own tiny slice of Paradise from the blue carpet where it had fallen during my Quran-shredding session. If push came to shove—and in my experience it usually did—and I was captured by Khalifa's men, this could be my only way out.

'No! No!' Pir said. 'You're not to do that.'

'I deserve it,' I said defensively, staring at the corpse of Khalifa where it lay in an inglorious heap on the floor. How on earth was this man, who had planned to destroy half of the world, being given a free pass to Paradise was an affront to my already boggled imagination.

'First of all, no human has ever been tested for using the ticket twice, and you surely don't want to be a lab rat on this one. Secondly, you can't be leaving your body at the scene of

the crime for reasons too complicated to explain right now,'
Pir said.

'So what is going to happen to me?' I asked, as I heard
a familiar noise growing louder. The ababeels were back,
darkening the sky over the mosque once again.

Suddenly the air was filled with the sound of howling cats.
They poured into the Prayer Hall in waves, hundreds, perhaps
thousands of them. They were gigantic and reminded me of the
rats materializing off the walls of my grave. They were followed
by armed men in black uniforms.

'They're here! Pir!' I screamed in my mind. 'I'm willing to
take full responsibility for cashing in on my ticket. I want out!'

'Don't! I'm sending someone to pick you up. Meanwhile, take
refuge behind the Holy Book,' he ordered. 'The sculpture.'

Still clutching my ticket, I dashed towards the sculpture. Once
behind it, I looked through a vertical chink of its central column.
The cats and their handlers had advanced halfway through
the hall.

'Pir, I don't think I'm going to make it.' I stared at the ticket
pinched in my fingers.

'Patience.'

Suddenly, it looked as if night had fallen and the cats' cries
were drowned by a deafening screech. Like an arrow, a long
dark band shot through the wide entrance of the Prayer Hall.
The stripe widened into a flying carpet of black feathers. I tried
to see if they carried the traditional stones in their talons and
beaks and remembered how the ababeels had rained them down
upon the elephants of Abrah's army, turning them into pulp.
But these birds were far too swift for me to catch sight of the
mythic stones.

A flash of light momentarily illumined the marble of the
sculpture. Startled, I looked back. Chacha Khidr was standing
three feet away from me, his eyes shining as bright as ever, his

solitary tooth sticking out of his gummy smile. He wore his usual clothes: the white dhoti and kurta with a long white cloth around his neck like a shawl.

'Babu Ismael, your ride has arrived,' he said, greeting me with a big smile.

Speechless, I stared at his bright, happy face. He then stepped forward and peeked through the opening. 'Pir likes to play rough,' he said.

The birds, now obscuring the ceiling, formed a huge black spiral overhead which began to circle the interior of the hall at a dizzying speed. Under the golden glow of the chandelier hanging from the centre of the place, Mufti appeared with his hands over his temples as he stared above.

The cats halted in their tracks. Overhead the feathered mass broke off into many spirals like coiled springs ready to crush the mighty cats.

'It's going to take a lot of cleaning to dispose all that cat pulp,' Chacha said in a matter-of-fact tone. He put his hand on my shoulder. 'The place will need a new carpet.'

Stunned, I watched this incredible remake of the original epic as encoded in the surah *Al-Fil*, The Elephant, of the Quran. In this version, the birds didn't carry any payload as they had 1,500 years ago, when each bird would carry three pellets made of baked clay, one clutched in each talon, one held in the beak.

Had Pir and Chacha been active then? More than likely. For they were clearly operating outside time. Had the ababeel event, as documented in the Quran, been their idea too?

The birds now hurled themselves down on the cats, burying each under a convulsing mound of feathers. I realized that I was witnessing the operation of a highly efficient live meat shredder. The job of turning the entire army of these specially bred creatures into husk took less than two minutes.

Having discharged its function, the cloud of ababeels took on the form of a giant stingray and began to exit the Prayer Hall. A crimson hue, having splattered off the pulped feline flesh, floated above the heads of the still dazed men; their Paradise tickets scattered on the blue carpet. The *sorry lot* had remained oblivious to the action that took place.

'Come. Let's go!' Chacha gave my shoulder a squeeze and we burst into light.

28

WE LANDED ON A PATCH OF SOFT GRASS, enveloped in a cloud of haze. Chacha Khidr was standing next to me, his hand still on my shoulder. My ears continued to ring from the screeching of the ababeels and my head felt like it was caught in a high-speed blender. I rubbed my eyes and tried to focus on where I was.

A hundred images raced over my brain; nose-diving black birds taking out an army of snarling cats and leaving a sea of red pulp in their wake; nuclear-tipped rocket minarets armed with a deadly payload rising into the sky and readying for lift-off; Pir's genius in thwarting a global nuclear holocaust without shedding so much as a drop of human blood and countless more visions, all surreal and unfathomable to the rational mind.

My vision cleared and I continued to feel overwhelmed. I was standing beneath the arched entrance to the Guest House of Paradise. As I looked around, I realized that, except for the headband around my forehead, I was once again stark naked. I darted away from Chacha, who was fully dressed of course, in search of some leafy vegetation to cover myself.

'Ahem!' Chacha uttered behind me, clearing his throat. 'You may use this for the time being.' He took the white cloth from around his neck and waved it like a flag.

Taking the fabric, I recognized the two unhemmed sheets of white cotton, like the sacred garb of the Hajj pilgrim, the *ihram*. I wrapped one sheet around my lower body and the other around my upper, leaving my right shoulder and arm bare.

'Much appreciated, Chacha,' I said, tightening the knot around my waist so it wouldn't swing open as I walked.

'We haven't used ababeels in a long time so it is good you were able to witness them in action.'

'I've got to give you people a lot of credit for destroying Khalifa's planned event.' I could not stop wondering about the aftermath of such a brilliantly executed operation. My head was still whirling.

But it was with mixed feelings that I realized I would never see my father again. It was a small price to pay, I suppose, considering the scope of the mission which was essentially to save a good chunk of humanity from mindless annihilation.

A smile appeared on Chacha's face, once more exposing his solitary shark tooth.

'Take a few deep breaths before we move on,' he said slowly.

I did as I was instructed, taking in more of my surroundings with each breath as I calmed down bit by bit. A breeze carried the delicate strains of a harp being played nearby and the air was infused with the night blooming queen. My body was warm, light and expansive. I flowed into the space and filled it around me, merging with a connectedness I had never experienced before.

'At last the ordeal is over,' I said. Part of me still wondered if any of it was real. A wave of pleasure coursed through my body like a gentle orgasm. I thought of Sophie, of the time I would be spending with her in the Greek Quarters by that waterfall of Kafiristan. Then I thought of Laila, the woman of unreal passion, with or without Hoor Afza, who had died while kissing me in that dark dilapidated bathroom.

'The end is just the beginning, Babu,' Chacha said, waking me from my reverie. He wasn't smiling now. This was the first serious expression I had seen on the kind, old face since our descent on the Pul Siraat over the fiery abyss. I didn't quite get what he meant and, once more, I began to feel uneasy.

'Let's go and see Pir,' he added, motioning me toward the red canopy.

We followed a stone path that meandered through the grass and I watched a huge orb slowly rising from the horizon into the radiant purple sky like a gigantic balloon. A tumbling brook of fragrant milk flowed nearby and a lazy stream of scented honey glinted in the morning light. The melody of the unseen harpist became clearer as we made our way over the soft grass toward the canopy. Butterflies fluttered on the delicate petals of iridescent flowers, bird-song filled every fruit-laden tree with pleasing melodies and angels darted about or hovered in delightful formations.

My pleasure intensified when I beheld a host of gorgeous women running about playing hide-and-seek amidst a large patch of gardenias. Their skin glowed with ethereal light, their ankles translucent and their laughter like tinkling petals which echoed the cosmic music of the spheres. Beauty of unlimited variety rose to greet my eyes like mist from the lake of eternal spring.

Passing by the dark-skinned lads in their red loincloths, we stepped onto the marble floor of the Guest House. They were all there, seated on their divans: Pir, Tarzan and Laila, still in her burqa. They all stood as I approached.

'Good job, Ismael. I'm very proud of you' Pir said, shaking my hand warmly.

'Thanks.' I looked into his jubilant eyes, hoping there would be no sign of rebuke about any of my usual peccadilloes. My journey had indeed been marked by my own stumbles and indiscretions. 'I know I could have done better.'

'Enough. You can't argue with success,' Pir said.

Without saying anything more, I walked over to Tarzan who seemed eager to speak to me.

'Sir, the world can never thank you enough,' he said, while he gave me a big bear hug.

'Tarzan, you're the real hero. In that jungle down there, you did justice to your name.'

'Thank you for saying that, sir,' he chuckled.

I left him and made my way over to Laila, who grabbed my arms, her big black eyes locking onto mine with great intensity. Tears moistened the veil over her gorgeous eyes, her chest rising and falling heavily as she looked at me.

'It feels like you've been gone for an eternity,' she cried. 'I'm still not used to how time passes here.'

'I know. It feels so strange.' Glancing over her shoulder, I saw the crowd of women gathered around the cage that sat a hundred metres away. The last time I was here, the cage had been filled with big black baboons from the Dump; those bothersome creatures which had chewed the book and somehow landed in Jannah. I wondered if they were still here or if Pir had managed to do away with them.

I joined Pir and the others on the divans, while Chacha took off toward the cage. Halfway there, he turned and waved at us.

'Babu, when you're finished, you should come take a look,' he shouted, pointing at the cage.

I waved back. My mind bubbled like a pot on the boil. I was overpowered by the need to understand all that had happened and the first thing I wanted to know was: 'Dead, or alive? Which am I?'

One of the boys handed me a chilled goblet made of gold that dripped with condensation and overflowed with an effervescent pale liquid that tasted just like champagne. Pir lit a cigarette and held the pack to me. 'Smoke?'

'No, thanks,' I said, thinking that a person of his stature should be above the earthly addictions.

'When you involve yourself with the affairs of the earth, you become addicted to combustion.' His voice rose inside my head, reading my thoughts again. I pulled off the headband with a snort of laughter.

'I see there's excellent reception here! I believe this is yours.'

'You can keep it,' he said with a smile. 'Think of it as a souvenir.'

'With pleasure.' I wrapped the headband around my left wrist.

Suddenly serious, Pir asked, 'Is something bothering you, Ismael?'

'Just wondering if the mission was entirely successful.'

'Of course! Most definitely.'

'But the rockets are still there,' I said, still not convinced my part of the mission was over.

'Not to worry. They'll be eliminated in phase two, which will all be divulged in good time.'

'Ah!'

'Anything else?'

'Well, I was just wondering what my "living arrangements" are going to be.'

Pir let out a deep roar of laughter that rippled across the serene air of the Guest House. 'Well, what exactly did you have in mind?' he asked, flashing a barely contained grin.

'I don't mind staying here,' I said, glancing at Laila, though feeling tense and awkward since I had to tell her about Sophie— the sooner, the better.

Pir shook his head, giving me another closed-mouth grin.

'Why would you want to live a meaningless existence?' he asked in a gentle voice. 'A life without a worthy goal is all but wasted. You'd be bored to death here.'

Shocked by his answer, I glanced at Tarzan who was smiling and nodding.

'Life on earth is so much more interesting, sir,' he said. 'It's much more fun. You don't know from one minute to the next if you'll even be alive or dead. What better place to live than on the edge? And here, boredom alone would drive you crazy! Here we live without a calling. Everything you want is just handed to you. Anything imaginable is created for you instantly by simply willing it. After a while, everyone starts missing earth. Trust me, sir, I'm telling you from personal experience. Believe me, I'd go back there if I was allowed to,' he said, scratching his sideburn.

'There's a lot going on down there that you're an integral part of, Ismael,' Pir said, ignoring Tarzan's not-so-subtle hint. His voice was calm but firm.

'I'm not sure if I'm ready to see my father,' I admitted to him and myself. I had no desire to return and face Abba after everything we had been through, even if the so-called 'phototherapy' had given his brain a hard reset.

'You're going back to your work,' Pir said.

'My work?'

'Ismael, it's time for you to understand something; something that is a critical. Right now you are in a world that exists parallel to the one you started your journey from,' he said.

'Parallel world?'

'Yes. There are countless possible outcomes to each and every moment that passes in the material world, and each outcome is creating a unique world of its own,' he said. 'And every now and then, these worlds intersect, making it possible to have the outcome in one altered by affecting the other. Do you understand?'

'I'm not sure,' I said, as I tried to work the meaning out of what he had just said.

'Okay, let me make it simpler,' he said, rubbing the side of his neck and thinking. 'We wanted to follow some of the logical outcomes along a linear time if over at the Caliphate certain things or events were to proceed uninterrupted or without the higher intervention.'

I had finally begun to understand, feeling somewhat uneasy. Parallel worlds of all possible outcomes. How was that possible? The sheer number of such worlds could be staggering. Was he talking about infinity?

'No!' he said, having read my thoughts. 'These countless possible outcomes obey certain economy and form only a handful of tangible worlds, each with its own time.'

'And it's possible to jump from one to another?'

'Precisely. You were sent in order to preempt the catastrophe the Caliphate was rushing headlong into—the illogical, disastrous and inevitable outcome when people confuse the letter with the spirit of faith.'

'So you're telling me that I'd been sent into a world that didn't exist in the normal sense, except in the domain of possibility?'

'All kinds of things are employed to ensure the smooth running of even the worst place in the universe: Earth. It's been a challenge.'

'I just can't wrap my mind around—'

'You can. By remembering that there's nothing out there except luminous dark emptiness. It's all within, the whole Cosmos.'

We were interrupted by Chacha's shout. Standing next to the cage, surrounded by a coterie of women, he was waving his arm in the air.

'Babu Ismael! Come!'

'Let's go take a look,' Pir said, standing up. 'Walking will do you good.'

Like a zombie running out of juice, I walked alongside Pir and Tarzan. Laila remained seated but I could feel her gaze on my back like a warm presence.

'How did you make Khalifa and me share the same dream?' I had been wondering about that for some time.

'Admittedly, that was Chacha's big idea in order to make the mission foolproof. Thanks to that little trick, Khalifa, already a highly superstitious man, took you as a genuine sign from the Almighty.'

'But Pir, how's that done?' I was overwhelmed with curiosity.

'Oh, come on now! You can't expect a magician to give away his tricks.' Nearby, Chacha giggled and nodded enthusiastically.

The girls surrounding the cage had on translucent garments with a warm pinkish hue that made their skin look deliciously creamy. They were beautiful with their big eyes and sleek voluptuous curves. Giggling mischievously, they parted to let me stand next to the iron bars between Chacha and Pir who seemed oblivious to their presence.

In the far corner of the cage sat a gloomy-looking young man in his twenties, stark naked and covered in black hair. His chin rested on his knees and his black beard flowed over his shins. His arms were clasped around his calves and his face was a mask of haunted bewilderment.

'Khalifa!' I gasped, staring at the unmistakable but a good three-decades-younger self of Khalifa. When I had seen him last, back in Faisal Mosque, he looked to be in his sixties.

'Yes, Khalifa,' Pir said in my ear. 'Chacha wanted him here.'

'But—but why?' I stammered.

'He can work at the Bihishti Tea Corner. You know our Ibrahim? He needs a boy to order around,' Chacha responded. 'I promised I'd get him one.

'I'd rather have him turned into a monkey and tossed into the Dump with his own kind, his only chance at rehabilitation,' Pir stated definitively with more than a hint of anger in his voice.

Chacha and Pir looked into each other's eyes without blinking, and I had no desire to get in the middle of it. There was no way to tell who was boss here. Maybe Pir was being truthful when he told me a lifetime ago that he was the deputy of Chacha.

'Give him a chance,' Chacha said softly, without breaking the fierce gaze he held with Pir.

But Pir shook his head and exhaled exasperatedly. 'Humans are beyond rehabilitation, as far as I'm concerned.' He then skewered me with his eyes.

'You'll pick yourself up wherever you find yourself to be—that's the golden rule of life,' he continued. 'You're ready for the journey, Ismael. You've been initiated into the mysteries of the universe and are now part of Khidr's hand-picked elite guard.'

Feeling dizzy, I grabbed the bars of the cage and rested my head against the cold steel. Khalifa stared at me, his eyes twitching in confusion. He looked like he was trying to remember me. Chacha Khidr put his arm around my shoulders and pulled me closer. His body was warm and radiated vitality.

'Babu, stop writing your silly paper about Paradise and Hell,' he said, and then gently gave my arm a squeeze. 'But write!'

'Write what?' I was confused.

'Your story—the story of your journey,' he said. 'You start writing as soon as you get back because memory is transient and the world impermanent. Only stories have permanence.'

'Your polio vaccine is tucked inside one of the cold packs on your kitchen counter,' Pir said. 'Don't forget to take it before you start your journey.'

'What kind of a hybrid are you?' I asked, beholding the glowing face of Pir.

'Will and matter.' He smiled, his gaze remaining fierce without any anger now.

'Whose will?'

'You should know the answer.'

'Almighty's?'

'Ismael, do you know why are you here?'

'Because of you.'

'Likewise.'

My mind ground to a sudden halt. Then I understood. It was vast, staggeringly complicated and yet so very simple. I almost laughed out loud as the gnawing confusion that had weighed so heavily on me dissipated and lifted from my heart like a flock of vultures. There was no ending and there was no beginning. It was there, all along, simultaneously. I looked at Pir who nodded his head, his smile broadening. Even without the headband, he knew exactly what was going through my mind.

'I'm going to reverse him just to see what he will look like,' Pir said, fixing his cold stare on Khalifa.

'No harm in giving it a try,' Chacha chimed. 'But I need him for Ibrahim.'

Suddenly it was dark all around, except the spot occupied by Khalifa, which was lit with a beam of light that made him look like he was on stage. Startled, I looked around and saw that the Guest House and its residents had vanished. Then the bars of Khalifa's cage melted away, right in my hands. My body shuddered and I had to take a deep breath to steady myself.

With a look of sheer horror on his face, Khalifa jumped to his feet. He shot me a fiery glance, lifted his hands in the air and then dropped them back on his head. I stared in pity and fascination as his forehead shortened and bulged outward, his nose flattened, and his eyes became smaller, deeper and beadier under bushy brows that now overhung his face.

In shock and disgust I realized I was staring at a Neanderthal. Continuing his regressive biological collapse, Khalifa's head became even smaller and I was unable to tear my eyes away from the spectacle. The whites of his eyes were gone and he stooped as his arms lengthened. Within minutes, his entire body was covered in dense black hair and his apish hands hung to his knees. He had turned into a big black baboon! I held my breath, absorbed this mesmerizing reverse evolution of what was once a good-looking homo sapien.

The ape let out an agonized scream and started beating his

chest. Then he charged, shrieking my name in a vile mockery of a human voice resonated over a monkey's primitive vocal cords. I froze with terror as he rammed into me with his shoulder, lifting me off my feet. I fell backward into a smothering emptiness.

I had no idea how long I had been in free-fall, but I slowly realized I was floating. I was nothing more than an awareness, a weightless presence in a void. I stayed suspended for what felt like a million years. Countless worlds were ripped out of the immense black sea of nothingness that I had floated in, in a seemingly great cosmic womb. Galaxies came into existence with the blink of an eye, only to be sucked back into this luminous dark void. Innumerable species crawled from the primeval mud, blossomed to unfathomable greatness and then succumbed to complete extinction.

Then a thunderous crack sounded across the vast black sheath of eternity, shattering all visible things into countless shards as if all of reality were nothing more than a sheet of glass. Once again I became aware of my weight, my posture, my surroundings and my body. I was sitting down somewhere, my ears abuzz with the sirens of an ambulance speeding down the block. I opened my eyes.

I was staring at a spider web on the ceiling of my studio apartment back in New York. A moth, trapped in its filaments, was fluttering its wings trying to break free. I was in a daze, drenched in sweat, my mouth parched. A bottle of Heineken was on the coffee table where I had left it. I reached out to grab it and stopped. Wrapped around my wrist was the headband of Pir Pul Siraat. The Heineken was still icy cold. I took a swig and looked at my watch. It was quarter to midnight and Sunday. I got up and stumbled toward the kitchen counter, my head spinning like a centrifuge overloaded with vials filled with God knows what.

The note was there on the counter. The empty vial of polio vaccine was there, so was the styrofoam cooler. I took both cold packs out of the cooler and extracted a sealed single dose of polio vaccine. I stared at the pink-coloured liquid within the chilled plastic vial, and then at Pir's headband, still wrapped around my wrist, my mind scrambling for a toehold.

I stretched the headband on my forehead and opened the window. The air was balmy and there was no sign of snow. An exquisite sense of well-being began to wash over me and I now understood that the snow I had witnessed right after taking my so-called polio vaccine had fallen in another dimension, in one of the parallel worlds with its own time. Vaccine, it was not. It was the distilment created to checkmate the Master Chemist on his own turf.

I was done with my thesis, with being an atheist, like I had been done with being a believer ever since I was a child. I had ended up being a Knower. One who no longer needed the crutch of faith. I wasn't sure if the potion left me permanently transformed—like the pawn that had managed to reach the other end of the cosmic chessboard—into a man with new powers.

I put the vial on the counter, pulled the stylus out of my phone and began writing, my hand trembling: *I met Petra on a Friday night late in October 2050. I met her in Grasshopper, a candlelit cannabis cafe in the West Village. The cafe was one of a handful of businesses which had managed to thrive in the aftermath of Isis, a Category 4 hurricane...*

I paused as I beheld Petra's face in my mind. It was then that realization hit me and blew me away. And suddenly everything fell into place.

The encounter with that bohemian beauty had been anything but random. She had been part of the Chacha's elite guard. That Friday night, in the candlelit cavern of Grasshopper, she had been lying in wait for me like a spider for a moth; her sleek red headband transmitting our conversation to Pir. The note was proof; its contents culled from my spontaneous psychotherapy session held over multiple lattes.

How effortlessly had she then handed me over to Don Miguel, the shaman recruit of Chacha from South America.

I wondered how many of us were out there carrying out the work of aiding the Higher Intervention to operate, to ensure the smooth running of the worst place in the universe, the earth.

I had toiled twelve years of my life to understand religion. That toil was nothing but a ruse that enabled me to avoid my inner struggle with my father, a fight between my world and his. The cover was finally blown. I felt light and totally free and was at ease when I picked up the phone to call him, to let him know of my imminent arrival in Lahore.

As the phone rang at my father's end, the text of surah *Al-Asr*, Time, started running across the upper part of my vision with the handy translation underneath: *By the flight of Time; Verily, Man is in loss.* The brush with eternity had surely left its fingerprints.

I smiled remembering the words of Pir Pul Siraat: *It's all within. The whole Cosmos.* I whispered his name and thanked him for his guidance; for helping me attain the necessary experience by Direct Perception on the Path to High Knowledge. It felt great to be a member of the elite guard of Chacha Khidr.

The phone stopped ringing and a recorded voice said: *All international circuits are busy at the moment. Please try your call later.* I was about to redial when I heard three distinct knocks. I touched my headband, for I wasn't sure if the sound came from the door or originated within my head.

I snapped the vial with the joyous certainty that the Pawn had been promoted. It was time for action. I emptied the distillate in my mouth and wondered what my next mission would be.